Would she trust me or would we die?

Blue flashes of lightning and the sickening orange glow of fire heralded Richmond's demise. Faintly, distant screaming reached me.

The Persian's hair drifted up, as did mine. Tiny blue sparks appeared in the air from the rear of our conveyance all the way back to Richmond.

"The atmosphere is supercharged by the airships." Elsie spoke matter-of-factly. She raised a hand and sparks arced between her fingers. Her straight brown hair blossomed into an enormous flower. "It's probably happening for miles around."

Ahead of us, the moon shone brightly on the sparkling surface of the Rappahannock River. I recognised the bridge destroyed in my dream.

We raced towards the exact spot I had seen for the Lady's demise!

"The flicker ball!" I pushed through the onlookers again and forced my way to Lady Kennedy's side with one desperate hope. "Give it to me, now."

"What?"

"You've trusted me thus far." I thrust my hand out to her expectantly. "You have to trust me one more time."

"I think I've trusted you about as far as I can." She drew the device from her pocket and held it in a tight, unyielding grip.

"You'd be dead if not for me, and you'll *be* dead if you don't take this one step further." Exasperated, I made a snatch for the device, but she kept it away from me.

"It's the only proof we have," she exclaimed. "No one will believe us without it."

The sound of the road changed as we reached the bridge.

I shivered at the memory of her and her Persian vanishing in a flash of light. "Which is precisely how the monsters know you wouldn't go anywhere without it." The air actually tasted like copper. "Give me the damn thing right damn now!"

She hesitated. . .

More Zen Bastard Adventures coming soon!

A Consequence of Hubris
A Consequence of Valour

Also available on **Amazon** by **John Robert Mack**

The Tango Triptych

Tango with a Twist
Stretches
Whiskey Tango Foxtrot

Coming soon

Spoilers
No Tengo Tango

Other upcoming titles

Third Testament: The Gospel of John
Danny Decker and the Horribly Unlikely Space Adventure
Zen Monsters
Tales of Mystery and Woe: a comedy

A Zen Bastard Adventure

A Consequence of FOLLY

John Robert Mack

A Consequence of Folly
This book is an original publication of Zen Monster Press.

Visit the author at
www.johnrobertmack.com
email: john@johnrobertmack.com
www.facebook.com/johnrobertmack

Contact the author for information regarding volume discounts for classes, studios and other organizations. Bring the author to your live event, in person or online.

This book is a work of fiction. Whilst names and places have been borrowed from history, rest assured it is a history from a parallel timeline and a product of the author's somewhat deranged imagination. Any resemblance to actual events, locales, or persons, living or dead from *this* dimension is therefore purely coincidental.

Cover by JRM
Zen Bastard portrayed by C.R.T.
http://rmodels.agency/modelpages/chris.html

For Dan. Because.

Part I

If the only tool you have is a hammer, you tend to treat everything as if it were a nail.

~~Lawrence M. Krauss

Chapter One

The captain of the HMS *Pirate's Folly* stood idly at the wheel just waiting for me to sneak up and break his neck. I lay prone on the roof of a warehouse some distance from where the ship docked, but my binocular goggles allowed me to number the feathers on the captain's bicorn hat. He had three.

His vessel was one of those hideous conversion contraptions: a former clipper ship with a massive steam engine crammed between her empty masts. Twin smoke stacks belched exhaust in the stern. The paddle wheel on her ass end was the crowning touch of indignity.

But sails were out, steam was in, and the United Confederacy of America was too bloody poor and backward in the Year of our Lord 1961 for King Edward to decommission a perfectly viable vessel of the Virginia Beach Coast Guard.

All to the better for me. The constant rumbling of the paddle would hide any sounds my compatriots might make. I loved the both of them and would willingly kill or die for either, but, bless their hearts, they didn't take to murder as effectively as I. Of course, the name Zen Bastard was known up and down the coast as someone who'd slit his father's throat when he was eight years old.

Shifting position, I adjusted my goggles and spotted Scopes where he hid in the darkness on the deck of the *Folly*. My Oriental friend fidgeted with one of his infernal clockwork contraptions: a brass and steel spider. His attention to the toy meant he'd already sabotaged the ship's telecom. I watched him a moment and couldn't suppress a smile. As much as I'd teased him about his obsession over the past twenty years, I'd always envied his single-minded devotion to puttering.

Another adjustment revealed Eddie as he ferreted his way from the ship's galley, pulling his long, black braids out of a net. Not for the first time, I wondered if the boy was too young for his first kill. Scopes would be quick to remind me that I'd already racked up more than one lethal adventure by the time I was ten, but my conscience queried whether *my* experiences were, in fact, the best arbiter. An inconspicuous stretch and yawn from the lad assured me the crew below-decks slept the deepest sleep pharmaceuticals could provide.

The three of us needed to time our final actions with those of our allies on the water, which would've been much easier had Tesla, Inc. hurried up and perfected their portable radio technology for me to steal.

High above in one of two crow's nests, a guard smoked.

A second guard leafed through a pornographic magazine in the other nest. My goggles clearly showed a glimpse of ankle and bosom which proved the man had tastes far tamer than mine.

So far so good. Our job was to keep the *Folly* docked so she couldn't aid the approaching slave ship, the *HMS Elizabeth*, when our pirate friends boarded her. Eager to see how our compatriots on the water fared, I flicked the goggles' night vision lenses, so recently upgraded by my puttering friend. Although it was an hour to sunrise, the waters off the coast twitched into view clear as day.

Mental note: compliment Scopes on the improvements.

The *Elizabeth* sailed towards the Fort Story docks. Our instructions from the Hammer told us the ship carried over three hundred innocent souls arriving from Brazil, destined for slavery. I'd never met the mysterious leader of the Abolitionists. No one had done. Our instructions for this job had been routed through a series of agents and left for me and my comrades at Salome's Garden, our favourite *rendezvous* in Richmond.

The Hammer, whoever he was, kept us busy and paid us handsomely to do his dirty work while he hid safely and anonymously in the shadows. Who better than pirates to steal slaves from Imperial ships?

Spotting our allies on the *Aquatic Railroad* proved more difficult. She ran dark to avoid detection and had been painted black from stem to stern. Since we spent our time stealing slaves from the Empire and hauling them to safety, it didn't pay to advertise.

I found her, already bearing down on the hapless *Elizabeth*.

Time to move.

I abandoned the roof and crept to the dock, tiptoeing agilely up the ropes and sliding onto the bridge without so much as a whisper or a fart. I scuttled my way along the bridge and crouched in shadow directly behind the captain—dressed from shoulders to toes in an exact duplicate of his uniform.

Scopes skulked at the base of one mast. Eddie lurked at the other.

The only difference between the captain's ensemble and mine was his enormous hat, the style of which had recently regained popularity throughout the British Empire. The resurgence of all things Victorian proved that recycling the last century was cheaper and easier than creating a new one.

The canons of the *Railroad* sounded their first volley.

That was our signal.

Whilst the captain stood riveted by the fireworks off the coast, I snatched his hat and plopped it on my own head. Before he could turn to admire how much better it looked on me, I grabbed his head by the chin and crown and snapped his neck neatly. It was harder than it looked, but I'd had lots of practise over the years.

His corpse dropped to my feet, and I stepped over it to take my place at the wheel before the men in the crow's nests turned their attention from the cannon fire to their captain. The hat hid my rakish black waves and Sicilian good looks from the men above, whose captain was white-haired, pale, and dead.

Scopes and Eddie began their rapid ascents to provide similar assassinations on the lookouts high above.

Which is when it all went to shit.

Scopes' call of warning was little more than a hiss and far too late anyway.

An enormous Negro appeared out of bloody nowhere and grabbed Eddie by the scruff of his neck. The shirtless mountain of flesh with a tiny black head perched on top had skin even darker than Eddie's. He hauled the boy off the mast and threw him to the deck.

Eddie jumped back to his feet in a flash, muttering curses, his short sword in one hand.

Scopes dove for a handy horizontal beam and swung to the deck whilst I leapt from the bridge and pounded across the boards as fast as humanly possible. No fucking turncoat slave would hurt my boy.

Eddie's choice of weapon demonstrated he had enough of his wits about him to keep things quiet. He held his own against the slave, who'd pulled out a monstrous blade of his own.

"We work for the *Hammer*, ya big lumbering bastard," Eddie pointed out.

The big lumbering bastard kept hacking away.

A shout from the crow's nest atop Scope's former post forced me to act with less discretion than my young companion. I had to keep the guards from sounding an alarm, and couldn't waste time being nice. Precious seconds might mean the difference between life and death for Eddie.

"We need you down here, mate," I shouted, hoping my costume would fool the guards. "It's a bloodbath!"

Still moving in Eddie's direction, I turned and took two steps backwards for a better angle on the crow's nests. I clicked the lens of my goggles for a tighter view and waited for one of the men above to start his climb over the railing.

When one did, I reached towards him with my right hand, flipped my wrist and caught the lethal work of art that slid into my hand with precision. A single pull of one finger fired the gun with more power than most folks expected from such a tiny, shiny package.

Not waiting to see if my target fell, I strode purposefully towards Eddie's opponent with the pistol held directly in front of me.

The gunshot had drawn the slave's attention. He glanced at me, then at Scopes who now matched my stride. The big man dropped his knife to the deck and raised both hands in surrender which made him much easier to shoot—point blank in the face.

Collaborators pissed me off *and* he'd tried to kill Eddie.

As the dead man fell to his knees, I utilised his broad shoulders to leap to the mast and initiate my climb to what was hopefully the final conscious crew member.

A hearty, "What's going on down there, captain?" drew my attention upwards. The second guard had begun his decent.

"Argle bargle rumplestein!" I returned, dropping from the mast and stepping away.

"What was that?" The seaman leaned out as if that would help him hear better. It wouldn't, but his stupidity did provide me with an easier target. A tiny lead bullet propelled his way with great force tore through his throat, silencing him forever.

The body toppled and I stepped farther away from the mast. "The sky is falling!"

A moment later, the corpse bounced off a protruding post and splashed in a messy heap at my feet, spraying me with blood and gore.

"Ugh. This is a brand new coat." I jumped over the body and reached for a rope, catching myself at the last second as my boot slipped in the mess. "Damn it, the boots are new too."

"That's what you get when you shoot'em in the neck, Zen." Scopes grabbed a rope and scurried towards the crow's nest. "Effective, but messy."

Unfortunately, the profound rolling of my eyes lost its effect because of the goggles. I quickly and easily overtook my studious friend, moving at speed to see how fared our compatriots out at sea.

"Are there likely to be any other surprises, Eddie?" I shouted over one shoulder as I reached the crow's nest and scrambled over the railing.

"Not bloody likely. I did a head count, and that's the only nipper I hadn't accounted for."

I prayed he was right. "Nipper? You just said *nipper?*"

No telltale movement betrayed enemies on the deck below.

"It's the latest with the kids these days." Scopes crawled in beside me and swatted my back.

"You're getting old, massah." Eddie grinned as he wrapped his legs around the rail of the nest, which wouldn't hold all three of us.

"Old?" I lifted my goggles long enough to raise an eyebrow at the boy, swatted his braids and gave him a fake scowl.

Eddie's nickname of "master" for me was ironic, by the by. He and his older sister Victoria had been part of a group Scopes and I led safely into Canada two years earlier. We'd snuck them across the Confederate border between Virginia and the Canadian province of Pennsylvania. When we reached Harrisburg, brother and sister asked to come back with us to help lead other slaves to freedom. We maintained the ruse that I was their master so no one asked uncomfortable questions. Fortunately for us all, my Sicilian blood won out over my great-grandmother's African heritage so I could pass as someone entitled to freedom.

I dropped a hand on Eddie's shoulder. "Good work trying to keep things quiet with the big guy."

His teeth flashed white.

"But why'd you give the infernal all clear when all was not—in fact—clear?"

The bright twinkle of white disappeared. "I figured the big bastard was passed out in the head." He dropped his chin to his chest. "I'm sorry."

"Why didn't you check? Afraid of seeing the brute with his pants down?" With a smile, I lifted his chin and brushed the braids out of his face. If he didn't always demand so much of himself, I'd be significantly stricter with the lad. "Don't worry, Eddie. Your Nebuchadnezzar'll drop in a couple of years."

"Zen!" He smacked my hand away, but he smiled again.

Scopes laughed as well.

Lovely.

We'd all lived through another adventure. The rest was up to the *Railroad*. I'd watch her safely out to sea, then we'd head back to our rooms to celebrate with Victoria who'd not been included because the *Folly* maintained an all-male crew. At fourteen, the lass could no longer pass as a boy.

"Good job, lads." I leaned against the rail, finally allowing myself to relax.

"Lads?" Scopes adjusted his spider with a tiny screwdriver. "I'm only two years younger than you."

"Ah, but what a difference those two years can make."

Scopes harrumphed.

Eddie hung over his shoulder and scrutinised his puttering with rapt attention.

I could have watched them together all night but had work to do.

I turned my attention to the ocean and adjusted the goggles to enlarge the scene as much as possible. Two tiny ships leapt towards me. Our men were transferring the slaves to the *Railroad*, where they could be shuttled back to South America. The scene was fogged only by the perpetual haze of smoke from the blackened and smouldering jungles of Brazil. Only God knew how long before the jungles burned out and the atmosphere cleared. Nothing Scopes could do about the haze.

I tapped the lenses of my goggles. "Excellent work on these things."

Scopes smiled. I knew how much he appreciated the praise. The scoundrel was like a brother to me.

"I think I've worked out the remote control on the spiders," he said.

I flipped the telescopic lenses so I could see the brass toy crawling along Scopes outstretched arm.

"See?" He set the controller on the rail and worked it with one hand.

"If your pet touches me, Scopes, I swear I'll give it a bath in the ocean."

As if it had a life of its own, the spider crouched briefly on Scopes' hand and jumped to my shoulder. I closed my eyes and braced for the freakish sensation of eight sharp feet plucking at my stolen jacket as the thing scuttled from one shoulder to the other.

"They've upped the power broadcast on the Richmond Tesla Tower. We can use our electrical equipment all the way to the coast now."

Rigidly suffering the attentions of his pet, I scowled at my friend. "Lovely. Now you can annoy me on the high seas as well as on dry land."

"Well, that too, but the important thing is that we can try out the new equipment I've designed."

I think perhaps my sarcasm was lost on him. Scopes and his toys. The man felt more comfortable tinkering with clockworks than interacting with flesh and blood people. With dread I anticipated the day he simply created clockwork friends and lovers.

Thunder rumbled in the distance and, as if startled, the little spider shuddered. Its brass legs folded neatly into a ball and it rolled off my shoulder towards the briny deep with which I had so recently threatened it.

Deftly, I swept the hat from my head and saved the creature from a watery grave. Presenting the thing to Scopes with a flourish, I chuckled. "Apparently, there are still a few bugs to work out."

Eddie groaned.

Scopes grabbed his pet and pulled some sort of tool from its place in the dreadlocks that fell past his shoulders. The tools fanned out above him and held his hair back out of his face. It reminded me of Indians I'd seen in Carolina, which was funny since Scopes hailed from Korea.

"*Bugs*, I said. There are *bugs* to work out."

"Spiders are arachnids, not insects," Scopes muttered. He grabbed another tool from his headdress and a monocle from a pocket. "Bugs isn't accurate." His smooth face wrinkled as he examined the darkening sky. "I think the Tower's down."

"He's not going to laugh at the joke, Zen," Eddie offered. "Give it up."

With a shrug, I flipped my lenses into place and gazed across the harbour. A tremendous fire blazed on the *Elizabeth*, which hadn't been planned, but things sometimes happened beyond our control.

As if to mock my casual appraisal of the situation, the slave ship exploded in a massive ball of flames.

"Bloody Hell!" I ignored Scopes' hand patting my shoulder for attention. "Look out there." I pointed, snapping a filter into place to keep from going blind. "The damn slave ship exploded."

Smoke obscured my view, and Scopes patted me with more insistence.

"Are you looking out there, man? The damn ship—"

Lightning struck the *Railroad*.

She exploded too.

Blue and white flames. Massive timbers blown to splinters.

"Fuck me senseless." My blood ran cold and I couldn't breathe.

Bodies charred to ash and pulp rocketed across the dark, bitter water.

The thirty men on board had been my family. I'd never laugh with them again.

Scopes knocked the hat from my head. He grabbed my face in both hands and forced my gaze upwards. After the swirl and confusion caused by the intense magnification of the lenses, my eyes settled on a plain piece of brushed metal very close to me.

I swept the lenses from my face. "Why the hell didn't you tell me a dirigible was—" The colossal metal monstrosity above us froze me where I stood. "What the hell's *that?*"

It *wasn't* a dirigible.

It wasn't all that close either, but it was indescribably huge—an enormous metal manta ray hovering in the air over the water and creeping south, seeking its next meal. Its skin was sleek like steel and lightning scattered from the black swirling clouds around it to play along the edges of its triangular wings. A brightly lit mouth opened at the thing's. . . head was the only word that came to mind. Bright blue lightning filled the space between its cephalic fins, for all the world like demonic horns made of Tesla coil.

A second metal monster glided over the spot where the remains of our ship still burned. Spotlights flickered over the wreckage, as if the thing hunted survivors.

Something exploded north of me. A third unholy monster moved through flames at the farthest end of the docks. Screams filled the air from the sailors, drunks, and whores on the shore pointing up into the nightmare sky.

That's when I actually saw one of the beasts at work. At the north end of the docks, its maw burned with white hot intensity and spat blue lightning at the clipper directly below it.

The worthy vessel exploded.

The metal fiend moved to the next ship in line.

The first demon I'd seen reached the southern end of the docks and began its own deadly assault.

A hand touched my wrist. Eddie's. He stared across the water and winced at every explosion. One arm held Scopes. The other hand took mine. In the distance behind Eddie and Scopes, fire reached into the night sky. An impossible metal behemoth crawled towards us through the air, destroying every ship in its path.

Scopes' eyes filled with wonder, his infernally curious mind trying to figure the things out. "Magnetic levitation?"

Eddie turned to me, his face asking how I could possibly get us out of this one.

Back to work.

After giving Eddie's hand a tight squeeze, I slapped my goggles into place, reduced the magnification and gazed across the shore. People ran screaming from the docks like rats in a fire, but no metal monsters flew over the land. They were only interested in the Navy, it seemed.

We had to get to shore.

These things were not men who could be fought and defeated. They were monsters or demons and the only logical course of action was to try our damnedest to escape them. Calculating distances, I realised we'd never swing all the way to the beach. The clipper beside us had stripped her sails, and if we hit the yards with our ziplines, we could swing out over the water, dive to safety, and swim up to the beach.

I adjusted the goggles and turned to my friends. "Eddie."

He didn't respond.

After tucking my pistol into my belt, I grabbed the boy and shook him. "We need to get off the damn ship. We need to find your sister."

He didn't move. Damn it.

Scopes stood immobilised as well. Was I the only man with a clear head?

The ship two over went up like a firecracker. We had seconds left.

"Scopes!" I slapped him hard.

He blinked, released from the spell.

"We need to go. *Now*. And don't waste time with your bloody questions!"

Grabbing him by the waistband of his trousers, I hauled him onto the railing of the nest and then scrambled up beside him, holding my right hand to Eddie. I yanked the lad up to my side and held him fast.

"Zipline, Scopes." I extended my left arm towards the ship next door. "Go!"

With a quick movement, I flipped the mechanism into my hand and fired it, trusting that Scopes followed my lead. I waited a brief moment for the hook to unfold and catch. After a quick tug to ensure the line had caught, I yanked on the handle to engage the spring and held Eddie as tightly as I could. I threw myself forcefully into the air, avoiding any sort of check on how close the monsters had drawn. Either we would make it or we wouldn't.

Gravity took us and we dropped quickly until the rope pulled taut. I swung my legs to maximise our momentum. Eddie's heart pounded like the thundering hooves of a race horse against my side. His arms held me fast and he buried his face in my chest as if he were a little boy again.

Damn it to Hell, in any other world, he *was* a little boy.

"We're the Pirate King and his plucky sidekick." I hoped the old game would calm the lad. "Not even gravity can hold us down!"

His face lifted from my chest to watch our flight. "I call Pirate King," he muttered out of habit. "You're the plucky sidekick."

"Plucky sidekick it is, son."

We soared between the masts and skimmed the deck of the neighbouring ship through air filled with smoke and burning embers. We rose again after we passed under the yard, climbing higher all the time. We reached the apex of our swing and I released the rope, wrapping both my arms around Eddie.

Suspended in the air for a split second, I felt an exhilarating moment of weightlessness, an instant of stillness between heartbeats where I believed I could fly to the moon.

A deadly bolt of electricity struck the ship below us and the concussion struck us in the air, filling my world right up with fire and ash.

Instead of falling, we rocketed even higher.

The explosion ripped Eddie from my arms and tossed me about like a Raggedy Ann, screaming and flailing my arms and legs as if that could somehow break my flight. I don't know how high I soared, shouting Eddie's name all the time, but when gravity finally asserted its dominance, the fall lasted an eternity.

Survival instincts kicked in and I curled into a ball, wrapping the captain's spare leather coat around myself against the fire and debris.

When I calculated my battered form was about to strike the water's surface, I unclenched my eyes.

I still had a long way to fall.

I forced two deep breaths into my lungs despite the smoke and found a quiet place in the midst of the turmoil. Stretching full length at the very last moment to avoid crashing into the water and breaking my back, I struck the surface in a passable dive and the briny depths swallowed me.

My goggles kept me from blindness, but the water filled my ears and muffled all the sounds from above. Screams and explosions grew muted and far away. I reoriented myself and hoped I held enough air to reach the surface. I'd never dived from such a height before, so I wasn't sure how deep I'd plummeted.

With the enhancements in my lenses, I could detect scattered flotsam and jetsam, as well as puddles of underwater fire that perplexed and frightened me. What in the world could burn under water? In a very odd way, the scene was peaceful, like a snow globe with everything shaken and drifting.

Until a dismembered arm drifted past. After that, I couldn't get to the surface quickly enough. When I broke the surface—my lungs about to burst—sound crashed back into my world, and I bobbed like a cork, gasping.

Screams, explosions, sirens, bells, panicked horses. . .

"Eddie!" I screamed. "Scopes!"

"Zen?"

Thanking God and all His angels, I spotted Eddie a few feet away, slipping under the surface of the water. I dove again and pulled him into the air, wrapping his arm around my neck.

"Hold on," I shouted, searching the water for some sign of Scopes. "Grab on with your other arm, son." When he didn't immediately comply, I turned to scold him—but the words froze in my throat as I looked down at the boy's right side.

His other arm was gone. And his shoulder.

He didn't cry out or panic. "My arm's gone," was all he said. He turned his glassy eyes on me. "You called me 'son,' Zen." He managed a crooked smile. "You mean it?"

I wrapped my brain in the same cotton it had enjoyed under the water. Sounds pulled away into the distance. The cold leached from my limbs and a wretched peace filled me from head to toe.

"Zen?"

"I did, Eddie." I pulled his head to my shoulder, only able to keep us both above water because so much of the boy was missing.

His heartbeat against my chest slowed to almost nothing, since there wasn't much left to pump through his veins.

"I meant it, son." I kissed his temple. "With all my heart."

"Aww, Dad," he muttered thickly. "The guy's'll laugh."

"Let'em laugh, then."

He smiled. "Love. . . you. . ." His remaining arm fell limp.

I couldn't hold him above water anymore. I couldn't.

"Goodbye, son." I squeezed him tight and kissed him one last time. Water closed over my head.

I couldn't release him. Our weight dragged us down.

My lungs forced me to breathe, and I choked on salt water. My limbs released Eddie without my say-so and the sea took him from me. I flailed into the smoke-filled air.

He was gone.

And I'd been worried how he'd feel after his first kill.

"Zen!" Scopes terrified voice reached me from the shore. He jumped up and down, waving his arms like a madman.

For a moment, I couldn't respond. Shock almost took me right there, but the idiot would carry on making a target of himself unless I stopped him. He should already be on his way to Victoria. The two living members of my misbegotten family needed to be kept alive, and apparently I was the only person who could see them to safety.

I swam to shore.

Of course we argued when I crawled out alone. I told him Eddie was dead, but he hadn't seen the extent of Eddie's injuries. He hadn't felt the little heart stutter to a stop. He didn't know the way I knew. He tried, even, to wade back into the waves.

I grabbed him by his shirt, pulled him out of the water, and shoved him towards the boardwalk where we could steal horses. He tried to push past me again, and I punched him. I couldn't think of any other way to get his attention.

"We can't help Eddie," I shouted. I pulled him back to his feet and held his face in both hands, nose to nose. "Victoria is in danger and we need to save her. We can still do something for Victoria." That seemed to get through, so I repeated it. "We need to save our daughter."

Scopes sucked in a ragged breath.

Canons from the Fort exploded over the sound of chaos.

Someone finally fought back.

I didn't wait to see whether the mortars had any effect. "Move, damn it! It's only going to get worse." I'd hug him later if need be. Anything like that now and we'd both end up dead.

Chapter Two

While Scopes and I raced from the Virginia Beach coast, Lady Hope Kennedy strode with purpose across the marble floors of the Capital Palace in Richmond. The first rays of sunrise warmed the windows she passed and her fashionable boots struck loudly against the stone and reverberated with the tread of a sturdy man.

The sturdy man who walked beside her, in fact, made no sound at all. His boots were soft leather, as were his breeches and vest. His immaculate linen shirt fell open to the top of his vest revealing dark curls on a broad chest, as well as several chains and pendants of dubious origin. His black hair fell in waves past his chin and dark, chiselled features.

The fact that he was allowed to go in shirtsleeves at even the highest levels of royal society was a testament to his relationship with her ladyship. While most assumed he was some kind of slave because of his Persian ancestry, he was, in fact, her closest advisor and friend. He was her Persian and needed no other name.

The fact that I have described him in detail before her ladyship is testament to the fact that had I actually watched them promenade through

the Palace, he would have arrested my attention long before I noticed
Hope's appearance. Let's not forget that this is my story, after all, even if
I cheat a bit and tell her part in it.

Her ladyship was a beauty, no doubt, somewhere past her forties
and the daughter of London royalty with all the pedigrees and fair skin
that affiliation implies. Her unashamedly dirty blonde curls piled atop her
head without a thread of grey in the perfect semblance of organised chaos
so popular at the time. A tiny faux top hat perched on the curls at a jaunty
angle with ribbons and feathers, her dress a fashionable autumn copper in
that neo-Victorian style which meant the cuffs nipped at her wrists, the
skirts swept the floor, but her ample bosom was accented rather than
hidden. All the corsets and crinolines, that only restricted her movements
anyway, had been avoided.

The dress screamed money.

It dripped aristocracy.

It was utterly inappropriate for the confident stride and stone-
carved features.

Her ladyship came to a halt at a turn of the corridor, cream-coloured
gloves clutched in one hand, a prodigious valise in the other.

Voices carried to her from around the corner. She drew in a deep
breath and closed her eyes like an actress about to enter the spotlight of a
vaudeville. The loudest voice belonged, of course, to her husband, Lord
John Fitzroy Kennedy, president of the Confederate States.

"...final touches on her makeup or some blasted thing." He drawled
in a way that always set Hope's teeth on edge with its affectation. "Why it
takes women so long to dress is beyond me."

She inhaled another calming breath. What would John think if he'd
known the real reason for her tardiness?

Her Persian coughed politely beside her. He glanced meaningfully
at the valise in her hand. With a brief pursing of her lips she surrendered
the case into his care.

"Especially beautiful women," offered the baron of Georgia. "I
understand why it takes an *ugly* woman so long, layering on the plaster to
rise above, as it were."

"I spoke to her Persian on the telecom," said Stone, her husband's
body servant. "He said she'd be down momentarily."

"Well, if her Persian says so. . ." Disdain bled from Lord Kennedy's tone.

Everyone's voices dropped in volume, including that of Gatsby, who was keeper of the treasury and Kennedy's closest advisor. His voice rarely rose above a whisper anyway. "Still seems demmed unusual to me, lordship, her and that Persian of hers, what?"

He was a toady. Hope loathed the man.

"Oh, do shut up Gatsby." Her husband's tone spoke of long-suffered annoyance. "As long as she insists on these forays into the slums to help the poor, she needs protection."

"But must it *always* be the Persian?"

"Are you volunteering, old man?" Kennedy's voice had turned decidedly cold. "Do you desire to spend your day tottering around the slums handing out soup or whatever the hell it is my wife does with her time?"

"He *is* a great big hulk of a man," Georgia pointed out. "Her ladyship certainly is *safe* with him." The baron was a sycophant and no two ways about it, but his wife, Margie, was Hope's closest friend, and he understood her relationship with her Persian.

There was a pause in the conversation. Hope presumed it existed because none of the men was brave enough to state the obvious retort aloud: who protects her honour *from* the Persian and is that something she would even *want* protected?

"Demmed strange we haven't heard anything from Virginia Beach, what?" Gatsby was nothing if not diplomatic. The point had been made. It was time to move on. "Have we any idea why we can't get through? Could it be a power outage?"

They gabbled on and Hope tuned them out.

The idea of a power outage was ludicrous. The Richmond Tesla Tower transmitted electricity to the entire commonwealth wirelessly and it worked perfectly. While one or two areas might be disturbed, the entire coast couldn't possibly drop out without the Tower itself failing. When would people outgrow their outdated thinking in terms of wires and cables? No electrical lines existed to go down.

However, the strange silence from the coast perturbed her as much as it did the diplomats around the corner. Her "charity work" involved some important proceedings in Virginia Beach, and she hadn't been able to contact anyone to determine whether their efforts had met with success.

"Mum?" Her Persian stared pointedly at the gloves she gripped tightly in her hand. She sagged slightly under the burden of the character she portrayed. He merely resumed his usual composure, eyes front and as still as a statue, but the faintest of smiles played at the corners of his mouth.

Hope allowed herself the humour of staring at his face in sardonic annoyance while she yanked on the gloves and buttoned them aggressively at the wrist. She inhaled one more deep breath and strode around the corner.

If anyone had seen Lady Kennedy before she turned the corner, they would've assumed this was an entirely different woman. *This* woman suited the dress perfectly and her comportment was flawless.

"Good morning, gentlemen. I *do* apologise for my naughty, tardy behaviour." She swept into the waiting assemblage with the vivaciousness of her breeding. Her smile beamed and her eyes twinkled with enough intelligence to be considered "clever for a woman."

Arms extended, she hastened to her husband's side allowing him a brief embrace, necessary on so public an occasion, but when he moved in to kiss her she offered him only her cheek. As they separated, she caught the brief disappointment in his eyes, so she favoured him with a carefully guarded smile to remind him that he'd made his bed himself.

He released her politely. Clever man.

The relationship worked because they needed one another and because John knew better than to press his affections after his betrayal. No amount of time would heal those wounds. He had to know that.

She addressed the assembly in general. "Rising before dawn, I *do* have *such* a time ensuring that I am made up *appropriately* to be seen in the light of day." She tuned out their asinine compliments and took her husband's arm so they could get on with their work.

Lord Kennedy stopped her, however, and Stone moved forward with a gay package wrapped in paper quite familiar to her ladyship. The shop owner was someone she watched.

"A present?" she enthused. "But what's the occasion?"

Georgia stepped forward and coughed politely. "My Margie insisted

I bring you a token to thank you for all your assistance, your ladyship. Her own charitable efforts have been so. . . much. . . enhanced since your assistance and. . . hrm. . . support. . .”

She leapt forward to save the poor man, who obviously had no idea at all why his wife had sent Hope a gift. If he had known the real motivation, he'd likely have had an apoplectic fit. Dear Margie. Such a good friend.

Hope lifted the top off the box. Oh! A blur of brass and silver leapt out and attached itself to her arm. Her Persian already had long knives in both hands and pushed the president roughly to one side, but Hope held up her free arm to pacify her protector. "A clockwork monkey!"

The clever toy reached her shoulder and perched there, clicking and whirring as it glanced animatedly from face to face.

"How delightful!"

"It's got babbaging too," Georgia explained. "Watch this." He turned his attention to the little monkey and spoke as if he were addressing a three-year-old, which really wasn't necessary. "Speak, monkey."

The monkey reared up on its legs and stretched its long, thin arms over its head before lightly pummelling its skinny chest and emitting a Tarzan call so similar to the sound from the latest flicker that everyone laughed. After displaying his trick, the monkey sank back onto his haunches and returned to his fabricated interest in the faces around him.

"He's delightful," Hope proclaimed.

He had Tesla wiring with clockwork and babbaging designed by a young man named Scopes, if Hope were any judge. The young genius had gained renown in certain circles with his clockwork contraptions and artificial limbs. If he hadn't been an Oriental, he'd have been wealthier than most of the men standing there admiring his handiwork.

"She spotted it in a Jap store in Virginia Beach," Georgia announced. "Clever fella for a Jap," he added, emphasizing Hope's opinion of why the young man was less successful than he deserved. "Insisted you'd love the little devil." He beamed at the success of his wife's gift, likely hopeful that he'd be the benefactor of Hope's good will.

She wiggled her fingers in front of the monkey, who followed their movements and reached out to grab them. How could a jumble of numbers add up to such intricate behaviours?

"I do love him," Hope declared. "Tell Margie she is a dear." She knew her friend meant to help young Scopes with a visibly placed creation on the shoulder of the president's wife. Good for her. The young man was a valuable resource in their charity work.

Pleasantries and gift exchanges exhausted, the president and his entourage hurried through the halls of the Palace to the east drive where sleek, black limousines awaited them, the latest luxury models from Tesla, Inc., decorated with the gentle curves and whorls of silver so common among the Tesla designs.

Scopes and I stole three horses to escape the shore. We rode through mobs fleeing the coastline and the inexplicable hordes forcing their way towards the docks to see what had transpired. We reached our rooms over the clockworks store where Scopes made his legitimate money as a toymaker, and I shouted for Victoria before we were on the ground and securing our reins.

She called down from her window. "What the bloody hell is happening?"

"Get our packs!" I called. "We need to leave yesterday."

"Where's Eddie?"

"He rode ahead to secure our country estate," I lied without hesitation. "*Now* girl, God *damn* it!"

With a look shifting between hurt and pissed off, she pulled out of her window but paused and nodded at the room next door that I shared with Scopes.

"You have a guest," she informed me with petulance. "A drunken guest. . . a drunken, *naked* guest."

"The evening improves by leaps and bounds." As Scopes and I stormed up the staircase to our rooms, I cursed under my breath. When we hit the first landing, I grabbed Scopes and pushed him into the wall pressing against him to hold him there. "We will, under no circumstances, tell Victoria about Eddie until we are safely out of the city. *Comprenez-vous?*"

He nodded.

We held that pose a moment while I forced bile down my throat.

He saw my struggle and pointed up the stairway with his chin to get me moving.

I took a deep breath before racing up to our room. No time for sentiment.

Victoria had already pulled our pre-packed traveling bags from under the bed and laid out dry clothes for us. Leo lay sprawled across the top of the bed. As Victoria had forewarned me, he was both drunk and naked.

"Eddie's new vest!" Victoria dashed through the open door to the room she'd shared with her brother.

While Scopes and I gathered the few oddments not already packed, Leo rolled onto his back forcing me to add erect to the previous list of attributes. On another night, preferably a night devoid of horrific slaughter and destruction, I would have enjoyed Leo's visit, had done so on numerous occasions while Scopes passed the time with a financially negotiated romantic partner of his own.

Tonight, however, was a bad night for a visit from Leo.

"I thought you'd like a surprise when you finished your work." He stroked the sheets with one hand.

"Get changed, Scopes," I threw over my shoulder. "The salt will play hell on your skin."

I swept up Leo's clothes in one hand and yanked him roughly to his feet. I pressed his clothes to his chest. "Get dressed and go." I filled my words with as much invective as possible. "What have I ever done to make you think I like surprises?"

Leo was a decent enough man, but he was also a weasel and a rich snob who slummed it with me for thrills. He was *not* someone I wanted to baby-sit while trying to save what was left of my family.

He stood there swaying like an idiot as I stripped off my wet clothes, bundling them up for travel. I grabbed the dry drawers.

"What's going on?" Leo asked, halting me between wet drawers and dry.

I shot a glance to Victoria. "Get our things onto the horses."

She nodded and took the bags with her.

Scrambling into my drawers, I turned to Leo. "Every ship at the

Fort has been destroyed. We're all dead if we don't get the fuck out of here, *now*. Move damn you!" Without sparing him another glance, I pulled on my dry trousers, avoiding Scopes' gaze because I knew he appraised me with a critical eye since he was much nicer than I.

"What are you talking about?" Leo ran a hand through long, perfectly coiffed blond hair.

I didn't respond.

Apparently, Scopes thought he deserved at least a modicum of kindness. He laid a hand on Leo's shoulder. "There's an attack on the coast, Leo. We need to get out of the city."

"An attack?" Apparently, something had wormed its way through the alcohol-induced fog. He finally started to dress. "Take me with you, Zen. Where are you going?"

I glanced at Scopes while I pulled my belt tighter. My friend's expression remained studiously blank so I knew he would support any decision I made, even if he didn't approve.

I stopped with my shirt in one hand and squared up to Leo so he'd know my words were sincere. "You'd be dead weight, Leo, and I need all my faculties so I can save the people who actually matter to me."

Leo stared at me in silence. Please remember he only visited me when he wanted to anger his remarkably wealthy parents.

Scopes turned away, grabbed a bag and tossed it out the window.

None of us could afford any more time and making him hate me was the fastest way to get us all. on. the. ruddy. *road*. Besides which, with Eddie's mangled body in my mind's eye, rudeness to Leo didn't so much as register on my guilt-o-meter.

"Go," I insisted.

He didn't bother to finish dressing, just took his shirt and boots and made his way out the door without a single word, which gave me a scrap of respect for the man.

Scopes fixed me with a disappointed glare that stopped me in my tracks.

"What?"

He continued to stare.

"We don't. . ." I didn't give a hairy rodent's scrotum what Leo thought of me, but my brother's opinion mattered. I tried to wheedle my way into his good graces. "We don't have *time* to be *nice. . .*" That didn't work, so I wasted three valuable seconds contemplating the options for leaving this situation looking like anything other than the Devil's bastard stepchild.

Damn it.

I pulled a spare gun out of a hidden pocket and muttered obscenities as I crossed to the window and pushed my bare torso into the night. "Leo!" I tossed him the gun, which he managed to catch due to my superb aim.

When he realised the nature of my gift, he held it out at arm's length between two fingers and a thumb as if it were rancid. "What if the damn thing had gone off in my hands? Do I look like someone who knows how to use one of these things?"

By all that's holy, it's impossible to be nice to some people.

Prompted by a pronounced throat clearing behind me, I refrained from insulting him. "You have people, Leo." Before he could whine about his stupid family, I pre-empted. "Being pissed at them is not the same as not having them. If I'm right about what's happening, they aren't going to care about the past, anymore, and you'll need the gun."

"What *is* happening?"

For all I knew, it was the end of the world. "I don't have words for it. But it's bad. The worst we've ever seen." I gestured at one of the horses. "Take a horse, Leo. Go home. . . and if we both live through the month, I'll find you and apologise for being a heartless bastard in a naked and messy way, all right?"

He smiled briefly. When he did so he was stunning. He glanced up and down the street and seemed to notice the commotion that had reached our neighbourhood. He handed the gun to Victoria and took the reins of the horse she steadied for him.

As he rose into his seat, he looked up at me, sober but smiling. "I'll hold you to that, Bastard." With a flick of the reins, he sped off.

For everyone's sake, I prayed I'd be able to live up to my pledge.

Ducking back into the room, I slammed into Scopes who must've been tied to my flank while I spoke to Leo. We stared at one other in silence. After twenty years of friendship we could carry on an entire conversation without the need for words. We moved forward into each other's arms and latched on. I looked around at the most luxurious home we'd ever known. Two whole rooms.

I allowed us ten seconds to share our pain and fear, then tucked it all back down into the nether regions of my subconscious and did what needed to be done.

We fled.

Hope and her Persian rode with the president and Gatsby as the sun rose, each pair facing the other in the comfortable passenger seats. The quiet whirr of the electric motor was almost undetectable in this model.

Her ladyship gazed out the window at the lavish Palace grounds and tried to ignore the political babble of her husband and his toady, but the sight of so many slaves working the gardens depressed her. She returned her attention to the other occupants of the car as conversation switched to the latest political efforts by the Lady Jayne Fonda, a sometime actress creating a disturbance with her efforts on behalf of equal wages for women.

"Giving 'em the vote is all well and good, what?" declared the toady. "With a quarter of our men killed in the Wars between the States, it only made sense to let 'em try their best to make up for the losses, but really? Equal wages? That's what slaves are for, aren't they?" Gatsby acknowledged Hope with a manly nod of the head. "Begging your pardon, ma'am, but if women demand the same wages as a man, we might as well replace 'em with darkies, what?"

And the man had no idea how offensive he was. Hope really wanted to kill him.

"Since the Crown burned out the Brazilian jungles with Tesla's peacekeeper ray," the president said, wisely raising a hand to stifle his companion, "the natives are practically leaping aboard the Imperial ships. Labour's extremely cheap again. Even the Canadians are hesitating to consider anything like equal pay." He folded his hands in his lap. "I fear the Suffragette movement has a long road ahead."

Hope barely managed to suppress a wince as she turned back to the window.

"I know more than anyone that women are an equal, if not indeed the superior, sex," the president admitted, "but when it comes to legislation, my hands are tied."

What? Hope drilled her most acidic stare directly into her husband's eyes.

"I apologise," he spouted quickly. "Horrible choice of words." His eyes opened wide and his back stiffened in embarrassment.

The Persian made a soft noise in his throat and gently touched the knife at his waist.

Gatsby, remarkably, held his tongue.

Hope shook her hair and stared out the window with unseeing eyes and a vapid pout. "I hate the word Suffragette. It sounds like a poor man's version of the Rockettes." She turned her gaze quickly to the men opposite and favoured her husband with the falsest smile of the week. "Dear John, *do* tell me we can get the Rockettes to perform for the Gala next month. You just *must*."

Something in his eyes died a little at the cart and pony show meant for Gatsby. Did he honestly believe she would ever forgive him? Even a little?

"Of course, love. I'll see what I can do."

She turned her gaze to the window and tuned him out so she wouldn't be forced to slit his throat with one of three knives secreted on her person. Or perhaps she'd stab him with one of her hat pins. She adjusted the gloves that hid the scars on her wrists. They itched for a moment, as did the other scars, the ones that prevented her from enjoying the latest fad of revealing bathing suits.

The buildings outside the silent vehicle drew her attention. Hovels supplanted mansions with barely two blocks' transition. Millions of pounds had been poured into the aristocratic landholdings surrounding the Palace. The unirail train was a marvel of invention as it slid silently from one mansion to another and the latest steam trains for the common man were a respectable effort, but as they drove farther from the Palace the glittering "glass and brass" of the aristocracy became the "mass and ass" of the common man.

Garbage lined the streets. Families lived two or three generations in a single apartment if not a single room. Conditions were worse now than they'd been at the turn of the century. Too many wars, too much expansion and too many bloody Royals sucking at the coffer's tit caused the poverty.

Hope sighed. The silence from the coast worried her. Her people were supposed to have liberated a boatload of slaves from Brazil a few hours earlier. They should be well on their way back to South America, hopefully somewhere not choked with smoke and ash from the devastated rainforests. Negotiations with several African countries to take refugee natives from Brazil were not progressing well.

Nothing was going well. The Crown raped the Colonies, the aristocracy raped the lower classes, and men raped the women. A seventy-two percent majority and women had had to fight for the vote after rebuilding the nation.

Europe's fight to re-emancipate *their* slaves proved an insurmountable obstacle.

Russia rolled over central Europe. China and India reduced the Japanese colonies in Australia and the South Seas to charnel houses. The Japanese had initiated aggressions as far back as the thirties, but the current slaughter was akin to schoolyard children stoning a bully and then whining that he'd started it. The entire planet was a violent playground filled with petty fights and incessant squabbling. When would humanity learn?

The simian grooming of the clockwork monkey on her shoulder startled her out of her thoughts. He chattered and pulled loose a strand of her hair.

"Naughty," she muttered, flicking the toy's hands.

He chattered again.

She was tempted to whisper, "Speak," just to annoy her husband. Instead, she pulled the monkey into her lap and amused herself with his realistic babbaging.

The faintest clearing of a throat from her Persian drew her attention. She exchanged a look to let him know she would be fine. No one needed to die that day.

They both smiled at the old joke.

Fortunately, the ride to her "charity offices" was a short one. The car pulled over so Lady Kennedy and her Persian could disembark.

The men exited the car to say their goodbyes and then made ready to depart for whatever version of ruining the lives of the lower classes they'd scheduled for the day.

The sound of sirens interrupted them.

A military car screeched to a halt in the centre of the road beside the royal limousine. Two sharply dressed agents leapt from the car, one of them shouting as he approached. "Your lordship, we have a runner from the coast."

The other agent dragged an unkempt man from the back of the vehicle and half led, half carried him to the president. "Every ship at Fort Story has been put to the torch, your lordship," the agent proclaimed.

"It's the 'Ammer, your lordship," the runner blurted. "'E's blown the whole coast to ashes and dust."

Lady Kennedy took two steps away from the men and drew her Persian with her. *What could have happened?* her face asked.

A shake of his head told her he was uncertain.

She raised one perfectly manicured eyebrow to indicate that whatever *had* happened, the Hammer couldn't possibly have instigated the attack.

An inclination of the Persian's head acknowledged his agreement.

"That ruddy bastard has gone too far this time." Her husband's loud, angry voice broke through the silent conversation. "It's bad enough he and his damn bloody Railroad keep stealing our property. . . but this?" His face reddened and his fists turned white as they shook at his sides. "I want the head of that bastard on a silver platter with the rest of his body twitching on the ground so I can rape him with a baseball bat myself."

A silence fell over the group, and, fortunately, Hope had the presence of mind to appear shocked rather than amused as every male face turned to regard her, the poor delicate female whose constitution shouldn't be assaulted with such course language.

She covered her mouth with the fragile fingers of one hand. "My goodness, John," she said with every ounce of feigned shock she could muster. "I certainly wouldn't want to be this Hammer person when you get your hands on him." She favoured the men with a wry grin. "I'm not exactly certain *what* you just said, but from your tone, I doubt it was anything pleasant."

Kennedy offered his hand to Hope, gesturing her towards the car.

"Yes?" She lost her smile, settled back and raised her chin.

Her husband dropped his hand. "The coast *is* under attack, Hope. There *are* protocols."

"A fort on the coast, miles from here, is under attack," she amended. "Feel free to play toy soldiers with the other boys, and if someone actually moves inland, you know where to find me."

The president stared at his wife, and she held his gaze defiantly.

"I have work to do," Hope insisted.

One of the agents coughed politely.

"Fine." Kennedy turned to the car and directed the runner to join him.

Gatsby's whispered comment was impossible to hear, but John's shouted response was not. "She was born a bloody *Churchill*, Gatsby. *You* try to change her mind."

With the men-folk back in their cars, Hope gave her Persian a worried glance before heading up the street to her real offices around the corner from the charity front she used when her husband insisted on driving her.

With short, impatient tugs, she tore the gloves from her hands and handed them to the stoic man at her side. Next to go was the skirt she wore over trousers, designed specifically so she could get rid of it when she had real work to do. Whilst trousers hadn't been adopted by the upper classes, they'd been legalised during the Restoration when so many women worked side by side with men to rebuild the homes and factories. Skirts were impractical for such labour.

One hand rose to the faux top hat and the other touched her hat pins, then both hands paused. No. She liked the hat.

Her Persian bundled the skirt and stuffed it into the previously empty valise.

"I want to know what the hell happened out there," she proclaimed, "and I want to know right now, damn it."

They reached the offices and, in deference to his wishes, Hope allowed her Persian to open the door for her. She swept into the building with her man close behind. "If someone is blowing up ships in my name, I damn well want to know why."

Chapter Three

We rode hard for an hour to escape the coast as the sun slowly rose over the trees. I sneaked glances over my shoulder all the way and led what remained of my family into a barn to steal supplies. While Scopes attached the horses to a simple box cart, Victoria and I loaded it with hay, grain, corn, potatoes, dried meat, and a goat who put up a bit of a fuss until he realised we were herding him into a cart full of hay.

"Where are we going?" Victoria demanded. "What happened?"

"We're getting the hell away from the coast." I arranged the bags of potatoes. "Something blew up all the ships at Fort Story."

"All the ships?" she asked. "That isn't possible."

"Were you there?" I snapped.

Unaccustomed to angry outbursts from me, she stopped her work and raised an eyebrow before looking to Scopes for corroboration.

I pulled the goat out of the cart and attached it to the back. "I'm not sleeping in goat piss tonight."

"Airships of some kind destroyed every vessel, Victoria," Scopes told her. "We don't know what they were."

I hadn't thought of airships. They'd been demons or monsters to me.

The colour drained from Victoria's face and her normally plucky demeanour fell to silence.

Before she could ask the inevitable questions about her brother, an old man's gruff voice surprised us. "What the hell do y'all think yer doing?"

My gun arm rose of its own accord, aiming a pistol directly at the centre of his chest, cocked and ready for action. His hands grabbed for the sky and a dark, wet spot blossomed as he soiled his threadbare trousers.

I froze. Something out there had killed my friends and my enemies indiscriminately. Was I really any different?

The old farmer stood before me, shivering in his shame.

I released the pistol's hammer and lowered the weapon, unable to steal the old man from his family. With a sigh of resignation, I shoved the gun into the back of my pants, yanked a wad of cash from a pocket and strode forward.

He stumbled several steps away from me, panic in his face, but I attained his side, pulled down one upstretched hand and forced the cash into it. Closing his trembling fingers around the money, I told him, "This is more than we're taking, good sir. I apologise for the fright. It's been a long night."

His eyes shot from my face to the wad of cash and back again before he gave a brief nodding agreement, clutched the money to his chest, and raced from the barn.

"You've killed for less than this," Scopes reminded me.

I looked him in the eyes. "It's not a time for testing karma, my friend."

He nodded.

We rode side by side in silence while Victoria slept in the cart. My friend pulled out his spider and let it scrabble from hand to hand. He gave me a knowing glance as if its movement should mean something to me.

I returned the look with no idea at all what his spider's newfound activity might imply. My friend was the one who knew all about his clockwork contraptions and scientific thingamabobs. As thoroughly as Scopes understood machines, they mystified me. I was proficient with *people*: how to converse with them, how to manipulate them, how to get them to do my bidding and smile about it.

Eddie often joked that I knew the babbaging of people as well as Scopes knew the babbaging of clockwork gadgets.

Eddie was dead. I pushed aside all the pain of his loss while I had two family members left to keep alive. Scopes would help me deal with all that after we were safe. If that ever happened.

Our "country estate" lay a short ride from the site of our theft. It was nothing more than an abandoned storehouse we'd found one day near a stream, hidden in a small stand of trees surrounded by cornfields. I jumped from the driver's seat and pulled open one of the great, heavy doors.

Victoria sped past me into the empty space. "Eddie?" When he didn't immediately rush out to embrace her, she knew the truth. She turned her eyes on me briefly before backing out of the way so I could steer the cart into the dilapidated structure. She cast her eyes down and stared at the straw.

We didn't unload the cart in case we needed to depart in a hurry.

"What happened, Zen?" She was several years older than her brother. . . than her brother had been, but she stood in the middle of that big open space and looked, for all the world, like a toddler who wanted to dart behind her mother's skirts. "What happened?"

I took her by the hand, escorted her back into the cart, and the three of us lay down in the sweet smelling hay while I told her everything. I made certain she knew her brother hadn't been alone at the end. It was little consolation, I suppose, but it was all I had to give her.

Scopes added his own details while he adjusted the spider's babbaging so it would maintain a lookout, crawling the edge of the cart. "It'll shut down again if the airships pass nearby." The little thing wasn't much of an alarm system, but it, also, was all we had.

Victoria wept, of course, and I drew her into my arms and lay back with her in the hay. Scopes curled up with us, and we held her while she cried herself to sleep. That's what she needed. Every fibre of my being protested that we should be on the road to someplace in the middle of the commonwealth where those metal demons couldn't find us or wouldn't care about us. But my little girl needed to cry and to sleep while we held her. When had any of us last slept?

And then Scopes needed to talk, so I let him chat himself into slumber. I didn't understand most of what he babbled. He thought the demons were made things, airships of some kind that used the planet's magnetic field to fly the same way a unirail train hovered over the magnetic whatsit of the doodad's thingamagummy.

Utter nonsense to me, but the words would keep his inner demons at bay and the quiet muttering comforted me. The crazy inventor and I had shared quarters for two decades and his incessant gibberish and gentle snoring somehow convinced me that maybe, just maybe, all would be right with the world once again.

The spider whirred and clattered on its vigilant watch, and I stared up at the pigeons fluttering in the dusty beams of light above us, hoping none of them shit on my face.

Four hours later, we still lived.

Apparently, a small shed in the countryside hadn't drawn attention.

Leaving Victoria sound asleep and the clockwork spider on its endless patrol, Scopes and I stumbled together to the nearby stream to bathe and wash the damp, soiled, sooty clothes we'd bundled along with us. The sun warmed my face and belied everything we'd experienced the night before.

When I tugged my shirt over my head, Scopes tsked and nodded. "I thought as much from the look of it in our rooms." He held up a jar of disinfectant. Apparently, the captain's spare leather coat hadn't been as successful in protecting my back as I'd assumed.

"Bad?" I asked.

My friend shrugged. "You've had worse."

Oddly, I didn't much feel it. I didn't feel much of anything. There were times when shock was a kind and comforting mistress. I scrubbed myself clean in the river and soaped the smoke out of my hair, careful to avoid pulling out the beads and trinkets in my rakishly wavy black curls. In quieter times, I'd pilfered interesting bits of clockwork to weave with pieces of string while Scopes puttered and we chatted. Who knew when we might have those moments again?

Scopes' hands on my shoulders forced me to sit in the water. "What did we see?" He applied an ointment that burned my back worse than the original injury.

"At first I thought they had to be demons or devils of some kind," I admitted. "But what you said makes more sense. Airships or something."

"I'm done back here," he told me. We dragged our clothes into the stream and plopped them into the water between us so we could scrub them and share the soap.

"Mind you, I didn't understand a lot of what you said." I hunkered down on my haunches in the Oriental style I'd picked up from Scopes and scrubbed blood from my best shirt. The damn stain resisted my efforts. "Who has the science to build something like that?"

"I've seen all the necessary technologies, Zen, but there's nothing I've heard of that could float something that big." If Scopes hadn't heard of it, in all likelihood the technology didn't exist. He pulled the shirt from my hands and tossed me some trousers.

The stain, miraculously, faded under his ministrations. I refrained from a jest about his ancestors being proud of his ability to carry on a fine tradition.

"Remember *Edison's Conquest of Mars*?" I asked him at last. "By that bloke Serviss?"

He whistled. "You think men from Mars?"

I shrugged.

"But they stopped at the navy. Why not move inland and overpower the army if they're an invading force?"

We continued our work while I pondered the horrible possibilities. "What's the best way to isolate us? To keep the nations of the world from joining forces?"

"Destroy all the navies and sever the transatlantic cable."

I nodded. The armies wouldn't matter in that case.

"They'd have to find some way to block the telecoms too," he added. "Maybe destroy the Tesla towers."

"But the spider's still working."

"So they want to isolate us, but probably not just kill us all outright."

Our eyes met over the laundry.

"They want us alive," I deduced. "For what?"

For what, indeed? A cloud passed overhead and we both shivered, glancing up. Anything in the sky could spot us easily.

We hurried with the last of the laundry, dragged it to the bank to dry and pulled on our drawers.

I helped Scopes arrange his hair-knives. To the casual observer, they were simply chopsticks—which many Orientals had taken to wearing wound into their hair—but Scopes' chopsticks could be turned into deadly, delicate weapons with a flick of the wrist.

"Couldn't they be more like the Martians in *Two Planets* by that German fellow?" Scopes tried to look back at me, but I held his shoulders and forced him to face directly ahead so I could make short work of the various tools and weapons he kept in his hair. "*They* were friendly enough."

I remembered Scopes telling me about the book, though I hadn't read it since I didn't know German. "We can hope." Finished with my task, I gently cuffed the side of his head.

"What do we do?" He turned to me with an expression that wavered between determination and trepidation. He obviously wanted to journey to Richmond for information.

"Dress in your better clothes." I handed him a clean shirt to fold. "I really think we should head out to the wilderness to hide, but, for your sake, I'm willing to check civilization once to see what's happening."

He impulsively grabbed me in a rough embrace. Growing up together in a box in an alley, we'd always been rather affectionate. Until Victoria and Eddie had come along, we'd been all the family we had.

Eddie.

After a minute, I held Scopes at arms' length. "There's going to be a lot more of that than usual, isn't there, Avery?" I forced a smile to let him know I was only teasing.

"In all probability."

We relieved our bladders into the stream and walked to camp to dress and make our preparations for a return to civilization. I could scarcely conceive that the events at the coast had been scant hours before.

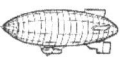

Scopes, Victoria, the goat, and I arrived in Richmond at sunset. The city overflowed with frightened and confused travellers. The outer circle, always home to the destitute and needy, was wall to wall with beggars and homeless refugees. Unwashed and broken vagrants lined the sidewalks, missing limbs or eyes or ears, castoffs from a series of wars that had killed more men than all the planet's previous conflicts combined. Streets that had only fifty years earlier been stripped of sewage with the advent of plumbing once again flowed with garbage that the Crown claimed it could not afford to remove.

A sense of dread filled the streets, as well. These people knew of the attacks on the coast, but most had no idea what had, in fact, occurred. Not even the people who'd fled from there. They only knew that if Richmond were struck, they'd be a human shield for the nobs living at its centre.

We'd been to the city often enough, but my blood boiled every time I drove through the Chattel Circle, as it was known amongst the aristocracy. England had thrown off the chains of slavery once upon a time, but reclaiming the New World after the Wars between the States and extending the Empire into South America had been expensive in both resources and lives. With all those Confederate slaves already accustomed to the work, it only made sense to reinstitute the practise throughout the Empire. So much free labour suddenly available after the destruction of the Brazilian jungles meant the common man had no means to earn a living.

Victoria distracted me from my musings with a quiet, firm voice. "We should give them the supplies, Poppa Zen."

"No." Not so quiet but equally firm.

"Fine." She turned and climbed over the seat into the cart.

I grabbed her skirts and pulled.

I'm certain she'd anticipated my grab since she stopped so quickly to glare at me over her shoulder. "The sky has, apparently, not fallen while we slept, Chicken Little." She swept my hand away. "We can purchase or steal more food. These good people cannot."

Her sincerity and intensity in one so young were, I am embarrassed to admit, comical to me, but I had to maintain my rough and tough reputation. I also knew that if I laughed at her she'd stick me with a knife.

"Fine," I shot back, pulling the cart to a stop.

"I thought so." She opened the back of the cart and reached into her vest, anticipating the rush of unwashed humanity. Before the first beggar could scramble up to overwhelm her, she fired three rounds into the air and brought the incipient hysteria to an abrupt halt.

"Now then," she called out, brushing her long curls back with one hand. "We are willing to provide y'all with supplies as long as you remember that you are civilised members of the human race." She waved the pistol across the crowd, creating a ripple of ducking and weaving. "Anyone who misbehaves, I will shoot dead, hear?"

Apparently, they heard.

"And anyone touches the goat, I will kill twice for fun. Understood?"

I groaned. "The goat?"

"I'm keepin' the goat." She turned to me with the gun upraised but ready for sport. Her face defied me to disagree.

"What are we going to do with a goat in a city?"

"I *like* the goat."

The animal took the opportunity to bleat its agreement.

Victoria smiled. "And she likes me." She glared at me again.

"Goats are good with mint jelly," Scopes muttered under his breath.

She cocked the gun. "I heard that, Uncle Scopes."

Neither of us responded.

"Mm-hm." Mollified, she focused on the task of handing out our legally purchased supplies.

What a constant source of wonder.

She looked up and saw me watching her. She cocked one hip with a fist on it. "You're just going to sit there and stare, are you?"

Scopes and I, needless to say, climbed into the back and assisted.

With our supplies gone, we didn't really need the cart anymore and, as crowded as the city had become, it more hindered than helped.

So did the goat. We sold the cart to a potter when we crossed into the middle districts where the artisans, scholars, and skilled tradespeople lived. After trying to carry the goat in her arms on horseback for a few miles while Scopes and I doubled up, Victoria admitted defeat. We sold it to a seamstress who promised not to eat it for dinner.

Victoria reclaimed her spot behind me. "Don't you dare say I told you so."

"I would do nothing of the kind."

The people of the middle districts kept cleaner and, to a surprising degree, maintained business as usual. The primary change was that we couldn't walk ten feet without hearing endless rumours about the attacks on the coast, each one more ridiculous than the last.

The Hammer had instigated the assault? Ludicrous since so many slaves had been killed. The Canadians had attacked? Always the knee jerk reaction: blame Canada. The Japanese had struck, finally bored with defending Australia from India and China? Ridiculous.

Demons. Martians. Ghosts. The speculators prattled endlessly. We ascertained for certain that the enormous metal mantas had devastated the ports all along the coast, destroying every oceangoing ship and dirigible. They'd also severed communication across the pond, as Scopes and I had predicted.

Then they'd stopped.

They skulked here and there, but always out to sea. They left the coastal cities themselves in peace and not one had ventured its way inland. The army had amassed on the coast, but the mantas just floated up and down the beach ignoring them. Why not attack?

We traversed the streets, observing and asking questions, greatly disturbed by the curiously festive tone. Apparently, in this part of the city at least, the end of the world generated as excellent an excuse for a party as any the city of Richmond had ever found.

As we rode into the city centre, the festive, nervous mood continued unabated. All forty meters of the Tesla Tower twinkled like a Christmas tree and the Palace gardens remained open well after dark.

Locals and refugees filled the grounds. Everyone seemed to feel a bit safer near what was, for all intents and purposes, a fortified military headquarters. It certainly was a pretty one, though, with Tesla torches in every tree and shrub.

We recognised a lamplighter as he walked the paths in red top hat and striped scarf, clicker in one hand absently performing his duty while chatting with the pretty girl on his arm.

"Clickety-clack, fill up your sack," Scopes quoted from the advert. As usual, he needed to gripe about the use of such elegant technology for such pedestrian labour. "I don't know why they don't simply wire the torches to one city-wide switch. Why have someone trudging around with a clicker turning them on wirelessly? Or they could use some kind of timer."

"Be kinder, Scopes," I teased. "Chances are that fellow couldn't get a date without the trademark hat and scarf."

He scowled at me.

"Well, just look at the nose on him."

He raised an eyebrow at my own rather Roman feature.

"I think it's romantic," Victoria said. "It reminds me of the old days you see in flickers when they had lamplighters for the gas lights."

"And if it was good enough for Queen Victoria, it's part and parcel for the twentieth century." Scopes shook his head. "I swear nothing has changed for seventy years."

Fortuitously, fate chose that moment to open a path into the water garden square and the hour chimed. Massive jets of water erupted into the dazzlingly bright air, sparkling like jewels.

We secured the horses to a post and joined the throng. The everpopular water gardens, nearly twenty meters across, remained Victoria's favourite spot in Richmond. After all she'd endured, I hoped to bring her at least a few moments of pleasure.

With her usual grace and decorum, she elbowed and shoved a path to the front of the crowd, apologising politely every time she poked an old lady in the ribs.

We settled into our spot as the clockwork dancers made their first turns. The delicate figures of brass and silver twirled and leapt like prima ballerinas and premier danseurs. Even Scopes had to admit he found the execution and babbaging impressive. The water cascaded and spouted dramatically, doubling as a means to obscure the wires and metal rods that supported the clockworks.

"It's like they're alive," Victoria whispered, and the light in her eyes erased all her pain.

When Scopes opened his mouth, I knocked the hat from his head to distract him, anticipating his need to ruin a perfectly lovely moment with logic. He bent to retrieve it, plopped it back on his head, and rose with a glare. At least he kept his opinion to himself.

After the show, we directed our horses to the one place in Richmond guaranteed to teach us anything worth knowing about the coastal attacks: Salome's Garden. Our various friends, confidants, and associates often spent numerous boisterous hours in her spacious confines.

The Garden remained an iniquitous haunt of the depraved and wicked, originally established by the infamous Oscar Wilde himself, shortly after his emigration to the Confederacy, which boisterously accepted his wild ways. The immense popularity of his plays and flickers enabled him to rise to levels of fame beyond anything he'd achieved in England. He opened the Garden near the theatre districts as a place to be seen with his notorious entourage. These many years later, the Garden flourished under the ownership of one of the wordsmith's young *"protégés."*

An apparent street orphan accosted us as we approached the ample stables attached to the Garden. "Oy there, good sirs. I'm afraid the stables is being utilised as a 'olding cell for the poor unfortunates as was going to be sold into. . ."

The boy noticed Victoria in her seat behind me and stammered. "For. . . the rightful property of the good business men as what lost their. . ." Unable to make sense of where our sensitivities might lie, he shrugged off his attempts at diplomacy. "There's a bunch of slaves in the stable since the slavers are all a bit leery of 'olding up on the coast. Lucky for you, you found a right honest street urchin who'll keep an eye on your animals for a pittance."

"What's your name, boy?" I picked him out immediately as an employee of the establishment designed to cater to the Garden's more colourful clientele.

"Oliver Twist, sir."

I laughed at his audacity. "You're mighty well read for an urchin."

"Me poor deceased mum was a lady of letters at 'Arvard University," he proclaimed with pride.

"Harvard?" Scopes repeated, glancing at me with a grin. "Didn't we bunk in an attic there for a while so I could sneak in a few classes? What, ten years ago?"

"Indeed we did. . . perhaps you're the lad's father."

Scopes regarded the boy and shrugged. "Hair's the right colour, but his eyes aren't graced with my almond shape."

The orphan grinned. "If you're 'Arvard men, you'll appreciate an educated bloke watching your 'orses." He wore a simple white shirt under a brown leather vest with aviator goggles perched on his forehead over a bright blue cap. A matching scarf around his neck pegged him as one of Chaplin's Kids, which proved my original assumption correct. The Kids acted as a sort of junior brigade aiding the Hammer.

I plied him with a catch phrase from the Railroad. "So you can teach them their letters?"

"Aye, equal education for all, I says." Which was the correct response. Without waiting for agreement, he purloined our reins and steadied the beasts so we could dismount, pulling sugar cubes out of a pocket for equine bribery.

While Scopes and Victoria removed our meagre luggage, I turned my attention to the orphan's scarf. I tugged it lightly. "Seen any good flickers, then? And you can drop the cockney. You've made the sale." For emphasis, I handed him a fiver.

He grinned wickedly. "Right you are, sir. Just saw *The Dictator* last week, sir, the coloured version." His voice dropped lower and his accent now placed him firmly as a former Canadian, most likely from *La Nouvelle* originally. The flicker reference was the last clue I needed to know I could trust the lad. He glanced around, then led us to a side lot where he had a few other horses tethered as well as two little Volts. The velocipedes looked like they'd barely transport a single man each.

"The nobs are all blaming the Hammer for the attacks on the coast. . ." Twist's statement was obviously meant as a leading question.

"But he wouldn't have allowed the slaves to be killed." After checking that we were alone and unobserved, I lifted the lapel of my vest to show him the tiny silver hammer hidden there.

He nodded, suspicions apparently confirmed. "There's been no word from the Hammer, sir. Were you there?"

"Indeed we were." I relieved Scopes of the burden of my satchel and banjo with a quiet word of gratitude. In public, I needed to allow my "slaves" to perform all the labour for me, but it galled me to no end. My friend acknowledged my thanks and we all turned our attention to the boy. "We're not certain what we saw."

He nodded. "That's exactly what everyone says."

"What's happened since?"

He shook his head. "Nothing."

I turned to Scopes. He'd have a better hold on this than I.

"Hard to say, Zen." My friend's face turned grave. "They might be waiting to see what we do. . . to see whether we're able to retaliate."

I scoffed at the suggestion. "How do we retaliate against *that*?"

Scopes shrugged.

The boy tugged on my sleeve. "Wait. . . Zen?" He appraised me critically. "Not Zen *Bastard*."

I smiled.

"Crikey! *You're* Zen Bastard?"

"My reputation precedes me." I tucked an elbow into Scopes' side.

Before I could preen my ego further, Victoria shoved her way between me and the lad, hand extended. "And I'm Victoria." She shook the boy's hand. "Thank you for watching the horses but please don't give Zen any more reason to play the pompous ass. His farts smell just as bad as yours. . ." She glanced over her shoulder at me. "Probably worse." She looked up to Scopes for corroboration.

Scopes nodded. "Worse, I'm sure."

Victoria aimed her petulance at me. "May we go inside to see if any of my friends are here tonight? I need a proper bath and a meal." She looked me up and down. "Bathing in a. . . a. . . *stream* like savages may be good enough for you boys, but a *lady* needs hot water and bubbles." She crossed her arms and waited.

I handed the boy another five quid before we took our leave.

"Anything else you need, guv'ner," he called after us, cockney accent firmly back in place. "Just ask for Oliver Twist!"

"Twist," I shouted without a backward glance. "Got it."

Ten seconds later, the main hall of Salome's Garden lay before us in all its opulent glory. A glut of revellers crowded the expansive floor, drinking and singing along with a piano-forte as twenty dancing girls performed on the stage. Working girls and boys crowded the balcony that circled the space, attempting to draw the attention of the customers below.

Chandeliers of Tesla torches blazed high above, but the air hung smokier than the world in general, and it assaulted my senses like a burning corpse. I almost walked directly out again.

"Victoria!!!" The exclamation warranted exactly that many points. A horde of shrieking girls surrounded our adopted daughter and carried her away, effectively preventing any hope of my escape.

Before they could melt into the crowd, I attached myself to one of Victoria's true friends—a working girl named Nancy—by grabbing her elbow. She glanced at my hand, then my face, and her grimace of annoyance melted.

I tucked cash into her revealing bodice. "Eddie didn't make it. Make sure she gets whatever she wants."

The girl drew the roll of bills from her premature cleavage and her eyes opened wide. She glanced at Victoria, met my gaze then nodded with certainty. At least Victoria would enjoy her bubbly bath. She had several friends amongst the daughters and younger working girls. As certain as I was that the girls would wax sympathetic to Victoria's sorrows, I knew a little grease on the axles always made the ride smoother. Our money would likely be worthless soon enough anyway. I might as well throw it around while we could.

Left to our own devices, Scopes and I descended into the cacophony of the Garden.

We took fewer than ten steps when a familiar Scottish brogue shouted. "Zen, ya Bast'd!" Scot pushed through the crowd and grabbed me. Thank God. I'd thought he and his ginger partner were both aboard the *Aquatic Railroad*.

"Ow," I said before his clockwork arm smacked me hard enough to bring out the pretty lights. That was his way of saying hello. I sucked in a deep breath, since I knew the giant's embrace would force the air from my lungs. Indeed, it did.

"Glad to see you're still pissin' and shittin'!" Scot towered almost seven feet tall and hulked nearly as wide across the shoulders. Scopes had replaced his right arm with clockwork. Similar brass and silver covered his left eye and most of his skull because of the explosion that had taken his arm. According to Scot, Scopes' eye worked better than the original. A wide-brimmed hat hid his shiny pate, but he wore his mechanical arm openly with pride.

For a single cold moment, I stared at his artificial limb, knowing that Eddie might have. . .

One of the few free Negroes in the Confederacy, Scot used his liberty as a pirate for the Hammer with the rest of our crew. Ironically, both he and his brogue actually hailed from Scotland. His grandparents had earned their freedom there, and he was the first to make his way back to the Confederacy. His accent ran as thick as the pride and joy swinging free to the wind under his family tartan.

Once the stars cleared from my sight, I spotted his partner in crime and piracy, Basil Rupert, ginger hair blazing. He dressed like a true Scottish gentleman from the top hat on his head to the spats on his shoes. The two friends made an amusing pair, since Basil Rupert appeared every inch a true Scotsman but was, in fact, Confederate born and bred in spite of the tartan he wore to match Scot's.

Scot was the more well known of the two because of his ferocity in battle but, whenever people approached them seeking the infamous Scotsman, they always walked up to Basil Rupert. Apparently, a darkie in a kilt wasn't Scottish enough for most folks.

He led us to his table, where another pair of survivors waved.

"Where's that little Negro stupid enough to put his life in your hands?" Scot asked.

"Eddie didn't make it," I told him.

Pointedly avoiding elaboration, I greeted the others: Nuke Johnson and his Mexican wife Stiletto Sal, who was proud of the nickname she'd earned from her creative use of footwear during the Mexican-Confederate war. Originally from the independent nation of Texas, they'd moved east where work requiring their particular talents seemed easier to find.

Did people out west actually wear cowboy hats and boots, or did husband and wife affect them as a sort of costume? I didn't know.

"Do you even own a shirt?" I asked Nuke, bare-chested as usual under his leather vest.

"Shirt? What's that?" He extended a hand for me to shake, which I did, touching the brim of my hat in Sal's direction at the same time.

She nodded a greeting.

Out of the corner of my eye, Scopes glared at Scot for mentioning Eddie, but the big man shrugged his innocence. Shaking his head as he pushed past to rejoin me, Scopes surreptitiously tapped a knob on Scot's arm, eliciting a muted bleat.

"Be glad I don't tell Zen where that button is," Scopes muttered before taking a seat beside me.

"Are we all what's left of the *Aquatic Railroad?*" Nuke asked.

"Plus Victoria." I nodded in the girl's direction. She and her friends threaded their way upstairs to the ladies' bathing room.

"Us and the Sneaky Pete brothers," Basil Rupert told us. "They have a room upstairs."

"What? All four?"

"Unbelievably so," Scot corroborated, "and they'd stayed on the damn boat until the moment it blew." He called a serving girl with a wave of his big, metal arm. "We dove into the water the moment we saw those damn giant things."

"Those boys have the luck of the devil himself." Basil Rupert drained his mug.

We lapsed into a contemplative silence. Well, silent other than the general hullabaloo of the room around us.

Since not one of us had drunk enough to broach the subject looming like an enormous elephant in the centre of our table, I raised my glass without a word.

As one, my compatriots raised their glasses as well.

"For now, we drink and make merry," Sal said. "Once drunk and made merry, we will mourn."

"For now, we drink," every last one of us agreed and swallowed his in one draught.

Scopes and I would likely find our own time when we managed to secure a private room for the night.

I scanned the crowd, seeking distraction.

Hello, yes? A burly Persian gentleman sat near the stage. Besides being a tall, dark drink of water in a vest that left his arms bare, he drew my attention because he sat alone at a table that could easily have accommodated four, and he watched the crowd rather than the stage.

My compatriots discussed the situation in the city. Apparently, no rooms were available anywhere, but Scot and Basil Rupert invited us to bunk with them.

Bother. Don't take me wrong, we'd bunked with our friends often, but sooner or later the spectre of Eddie's death needed settling. As much as I loved those men, I didn't see myself crying with them the way I could alone with my brother.

"As long as there's no whores tonight," Scopes pointed out. "We have Victoria to think of."

Our friends agreed without hesitation.

Double bother.

Something about the Persian drew my attention again, and I wanted to convince myself it wasn't just the ruggedly handsome face, muscular torso, and long, well kempt hair. I lost the thread of my friends' conversation until I heard a low whistle from Scot, which drew me back to the table.

Everyone stared at me with blatant mirth.

"Who's the Persian?" I asked.

When I turned to look again, the big Scotsman grabbed my face to prevent it. "He's just the Persian. No one knows his real name, and I'd recommend not drawing his attention to our table, my friend."

"Why not?"

Scopes laughed out loud, which ordinarily would've earned him a good smack, but under the circumstances, the sound delighted me. "You've never heard of Hope Kennedy's Persian?" he asked.

I gave him my silence as a response.

"He's her ladyship's personal bodyguard," Scopes told me. "Isn't there even some new song about him?"

"What do you suppose he's doing here?" My gaze wandered back to the gentleman in question.

Scot smacked me to stop my wandering eye. "Pro'ly the same thing we're doing here. Trying to see what folks are sayin' about the situation on the coast."

Doubtful. "You actually think the aristocracy cares what the peasantry has to say?" My eyes sidled back to the handsome man without assistance from my head in the hopes that Scot wouldn't notice.

"Well, we have a first lady who seems to care anyway," Scot said.

"God save the first lady," Scopes muttered.

A serving girl handed me a mug of beer timed perfectly to allow me to embarrass my friends with a loud-spoken, "God save the first lady," meant to carry throughout the room. It did, and I was saved from yet another swat from the Scotsman because the Persian himself, hearing my loud toast, focused his attention on our table.

Meeting my eyes evenly, the big man graced me with a smile before raising his glass and acknowledging my toast with a nod. He held my gaze for little more than a second before returning to his general perusal of the room, but that fleeting moment sent a telltale shiver down to the root of my dick.

Sharp kicks under the table from the friends who flanked me distracted me from my flirtation.

"None of that," Scot scolded. "If we can't bring entertainment back to the rooms, neither can you."

"I have no idea what you mean to imply." I looked from face to bemused face with my best innocent façade.

"You'd best cast your rod elsewhere anyway," Sal threw in, "if the rumours are true."

"Rumours?"

This time it was Basil Rupert's turn to scoff. "He really knows nothing of the affairs at court?"

Scopes shook his head and nudged me with an elbow. "Zen's too busy to waste his time with the peccadilloes of a bunch of useless nobs." He took a swig of beer and prepared himself for a smack on the back of his head. "Although he doesn't seem too aloof to drool over an aristocratic *knob*."

Never one to disappoint my best friend, I grabbed his hat and tossed it onto to the next table. "He could be the *King's* bodyguard, but it wouldn't make a slave a nob. What rumours?" Although I had to admit I wouldn't be adverse to a closer acquaintance with the aforementioned knob.

"Rumours that he guards the first lady's body so he can keep it for himself." Scopes retrieved his hat with an apology to the young toughs beside us. "Apparently her relations with the president have leaned decidedly formal in recent years."

Watching the Persian peruse the crowd over the rim of his beer, I had to admit he did seem the type to be more fascinated by the fairer sex. "Bother."

He exhibited none of the telltale signs I'd learned to identify over the years. Never one to set my fishing rod on an unstocked pond, I pushed the Persian and his bulging, bare biceps from my mind.

Turning back to my friends and cohorts, I raised my glass in honest salute. "Drink up, my friends. The world's about to end."

Chapter Four

Lady Kennedy stood quietly beside her good friend Margie, baroness of Georgia, at an enormous window on the *HMA Titania*. She contemplated the glorious view of the Virginia Beach coastline spread out below her. A bright noonday sun burned in an unblemished blue sky. The pearly grey water below held nothing larger than a local fisherman's scow. Normally a beehive of activity where massive ships that plied the Atlantic loaded and unloaded, the shoreline sported only a meagre trickle of unwashed seamen too poor to skip a day's fishing in the dark, haunted depths.

Margie sported a serious skirt suit of the darkest blue. Very modern, perhaps, but it enforced her rather severe resemblance to a public school matron. Her part in the "charity work" took place behind the scenes. Hope knew her friend hated drawing attention to herself.

Lady Kennedy's husband didn't keep nearly as quiet as the women, and he'd set his back firmly to the watery vista. "What I want are answers, general! How do those bloody airships fly? Why are none of the telecoms working? What the hell is happening on the rest of the bloody planet?"

His questions, along with his bluster, were pointless.

No one knew the answers.

They'd had word by wire from both Confederate continents. All the British harbours in the New World had experienced the same devastation as those in Virginia. Canadian and Texan officials had confirmed the same treatment. All ocean-worthy ships and transatlantic dirigibles had been wrecked while all land based troops had been ignored, which is why the president and his entourage floated over the Virginia Beach coast in the most luxurious airship in the Confederacy.

The *Titania* had been built as the most opulent and, indeed, one of the largest airships ever conceived, but, in deference to her aquatic sister's titanic misfortune, she'd been designed to fly no farther than coastal waters. Electricity powered her, which tied her to the Richmond Tesla Tower as if by tether.

With a sigh of resignation, Hope exchanged looks with Margie before turning away from the view. She glanced at her Persian—who wore full dress uniform at her request—and faced the diplomatic gathering.

"I realise that I am merely a woman," she began just loudly enough to interrupt her husband. Fortunately, even the most ignorant man knew that whenever a woman began a sentence with such words, he'd best fasten his lips and listen, which was exactly what the entire assemblage did.

Margie smiled and hid her mirth behind a fan.

Hope continued in a much more even tone. "But rehashing every detail we have already ascertained is simply too tedious for my poor, miniscule mind to contemplate when there are a few potentially significant factors I have yet to hear discussed, knowing full well that I may have merely neglected that discussion while distracted with my feminine obsessions with baking and needlepoint."

Several of the more intelligent and attentive gentlemen smiled at her sardonic tone. From their expressions, she surmised they might have long predicted a cunning strategist hidden behind her aristocratic and simple façade.

Poor Gatsby, though, toady that he was, must not have been able to see beyond his own witless ambition. His smirk indicated he thought all the smiles were at the lady's expense, not in her favour.

"My good woman—" he began, but the president held up a hand, abruptly cutting short the insipid man's words.

Hope acknowledged her husband's assistance with a curt nod

before continuing. "Whoever is behind this attack—and we have woefully little information to even speculate on their identity, despite the insistence of *some* that the aggressors must be Japanese."

She favoured Georgia with a scowl that his baroness accented with a soft "tut." The man had enough character to hold up under her ladyship's scrutiny and enough wisdom in the ways of women to let her continue.

"Whoever-it-is has scrambled our radio communications without interrupting our power supplies, apart from—" She held up one perfectly manicured hand to keep Gatsby from butting in. "Apart from a brief outage along the coast during the attacks. From what intelligence we've gathered, every time the airships appear, all power and telecom communications are interrupted, likely caused by some sort of electric or magnetic interference from the ships themselves." She clasped her hands in front of her breasts, for all the world like a schoolmarm with a roomful of boys. "But how are they maintaining a blackout on our telecom signals without interrupting the power? Both transmissions broadcast from the same towers, which appear, from all onsite inspections, perfectly operational. Also. . ."

She paused to step closer to one of the support posts that dotted the room. She placed her hand on it and gazed around the opulent airship. "How the hell did they know exactly which vessels cross the ocean? Just looking at her, this fine airship would appear, certainly, large enough for a transatlantic crossing. Yet here we stand, perfectly safe." She rapped her knuckles on the wooden beam. "Knock on wood."

The men around her chuckled.

"Further, the attacks were not simultaneous. Their force moved methodically—albeit rapidly—along the coasts and no reliable reports describe more than three or four vessels in the air at one time."

As she knew it would, this last bit of intelligence caused quite a stir in the crowd as the gathered military commanders demanded to know how she'd acquired it. Having predicted their questions, as well as knowing she couldn't admit that her information had been gleaned from her operatives on the Underground Railroad all up and down the eastern seaboard, Hope turned to indicate her Persian. "I assure you that my Persian has extensive sources in his efforts to infiltrate the Abolitionists."

Knowing they wouldn't take the words of a perceived slave, she waved a hand at a young man at the ship's consoles who worked the communication systems. His name was Monty, he had secret Abolitionist leanings, and he'd helped fit most of the pieces together.

"Your own expert can corroborate my findings, John," she said, knowing that appealing to her husband directly would silence at least a few of the more sceptical naysayers until the president had voiced his own opinion of her theory.

The boy needed a few moments to realise he'd been singled out, and, when he did, his pale face flushed.

"Well, boy? What have you found?" The president pushed through to tower over the young man.

Monty stammered a bit before finding his voice. "Her ladyship's right, your lordship." He ran a hand over his blond, buzz cut hair. "The attacks themselves lasted between fifteen to twenty minutes and occurred at intervals of two to three minutes. Apart from the common hyperbole of 'Good lord the sky was filled with the beasts,' all reports yield a number between three and five for the size of the attack fleet."

"Why the bloody hell didn't you report this?" A vein stood out on her husband's temple, and Hope knew she needed to intervene before he shot the poor man.

"He did, John." She placed a hand on the frightened man's shoulder. "Gatsby ashcanned the report as irrelevant." She allowed herself a satisfied glower in the toady's direction but chose to save him herself, mostly to avoid wasting time. "Corporal Sticks has another theory I'd like you all to hear." She knew full well it would gall Gatsby to no end that she had rescued him. She softened her voice to calm the young technician. "Tell us all your theory about Australia."

When he didn't speak up right away, she gave his shoulder a reassuring pat.

The young man ran his hand over his head again and took a deep breath. "Well, sirs. . . ladies. No one's heard a peep from Australia in over a week." He looked from face to face, apparently in a kind of awe that such prominent persons listened to him. "At first, I didn't think anything of it. They're at war, perhaps they just blacked out communication." He shrugged. "But after the attacks, I went back over the communications we'd received. . . and over the exchanges between the Japanese and their colonies. . . you know, things we'd decoded." He stopped there. Hope urged him on, and he continued. "I don't think the Japanese could get them to pick up the telecom either."

Gatsby had had enough, apparently. "So what," he blustered. "So the Japs couldn't get the prison colony to send them a case of that horrid beer they drink. What of it?"

The interruption seemed to spur the young man to greater strength. "I think Australia was attacked first. I think whoever attacked *us* tested out their assaults on the most easily isolated continent. When that worked out for them. . . they came here."

His words silenced the room.

Into that silence, Hope spoke quietly. "A handful of airships has systematically isolated all the major world powers. Ships with weapons strong enough to wipe out any military resistance and with a technology that precludes us from communicating—"

"Mr. President!" Monty had an ear once again attached to his headset. He quickly gave his attention to Hope. "Begging your pardon, your ladyship. . . But it's *London* on the line."

Once the ensuing havoc had been quelled, Monty put the telecom over a speaker so all could hear the news from London, which was much as expected. Coastal harbours across the globe from London to Kawasaki had been obliterated. Britain maintained cables that allowed them contact with most every nation on three continents and the story remained the same everywhere.

"Has anyone attempted retaliation?" President Kennedy demanded.

"The King tried, of course," the voice over the telecom told them. "As soon as the airwaves went silent, the Crown started conversations via cable everywhere he was able. The attacks began in Africa shortly after the last assault on Argentina. They travelled up the coast towards Europe, which gave the Royal Navy time to deploy the peacekeeper in Dover." It was the most logical first strike on the British homeland.

"Ah, well, that must have given them pause, what?" enthused Gatsby. "The bloody death ray ignited an entire rainforest. . . surely it put a righteous denting on that bloody, floating manta fish, eh?"

The silence on the other end of the line came as a cold shock. When the radio man finally spoke, his voice was soft and broken. "The peacekeeper beam didn't so much as scratch the metal airships and, in retaliation, the attackers destroyed the city. Dover's nothing but a crater on the edge of the channel. They couldn't even find bodies to collect for burial."

Silence filled the room.

"The airships moved inland for the only landward assault on record. Within moments of the destruction of Dover, they smoked the military compound that'd housed the peacekeeper technology sending a very clear signal that resistance would be met with the most brutal force imaginable. However, no actual communiqué has been received by anyone so far."

Hope watched everyone work their way towards the only explanation left to them: the attackers were not of this world.

A deep, rich voice broke the silent contemplation. "I think that's enough for now." The words drew all attention to the startling presence of the man in the centre of the room who had not been there mere moments before.

"I've lost the line, Mr. President," Monty called out before noticing the impressive figure.

The apparition stood seven feet tall and wore his black hair pulled into a pony tail. With a moustache and goatee, dark complexion and vaguely threatening smirk, the man's visage sent a chill down Lady Kennedy's spine. A clockwork monocle covered one eye under a tall, brown leather top hat. Gold and steel tubes and hoses enclosed his left arm.

A highly ornate, tight-fitting leather vest covered his torso, leaving his extremely large right arm bare. A rather prodigious leather codpiece protected and accented the man's giblets and black leather pants protected his legs down to enormous black boots with built-in steel clockwork. Brass and steel accents decorated everything.

Hope instantly knew in her heart that every least detail had been manufactured to inspire fear and, at the same time, his dark complexion would automatically cause consternation. She spent so many hours on fine-tuning her own façade that she recognised a man playing a carefully orchestrated part.

Please, John, she prayed, *let's not jump to conclusions.*

"Who the hell are you?" the president demanded.

Everyone took a single step away from him, but the stranger only smiled.

To Lady Kennedy's welcome surprise, Georgia made a point of stepping protectively between Margie and the stranger.

"I bring greetings from the great and powerful Kla'arkian Empire." He favoured the assemblage with a polite nod and rendered the strange word into four distinct syllables.

Lady Kennedy closed her eyes. If only John would realise that this man's skin colour did not define him.

"Kla'arkian Empire?" her husband bellowed, exaggerating the pronunciation for humorous effect. "Where the bloody hell's that?"

"A modicum of respect, John?" Hope laid a hand on his forearm to slow him down.

Once he had a head of steam, though, nothing short of a brick wall would faze John Fitzroy Kennedy. "Don't get ruffled, Hope. They send a darkie to negotiate? And they expect me to take them seriously?"

Hope forced a smile at the stranger, unwilling to even look at her husband though she spoke to him. "He just might *be* the actual leader, dear."

"Pah." The president turned his attention to the stranger. "So? Where's your empire? Where are you from?"

"We are from so far away it would damage your mind to conceive it." The man remained so smooth and calm, Hope knew exactly the conclusion towards which this audience progressed. She took a small step away from John but a subtle lifting of her hand prevented the Persian from assuming his accustomed place between his lady and the newcomer.

The stranger glanced at Hope's hand. He smiled at the Persian and then at the lady.

"Are you Martians?" John demanded.

Hope winced. Somewhere in a better world, John F. Kennedy knew how to negotiate. Why couldn't she have married *that* man?

The stranger leaned slightly to one side as if listening to someone.

The gesture confused Hope. He stood there alone. Did he have an unseen companion?

"The fourth planet?" The man burst into full-bellied laughter. "You actually imagine that lifeless rock might support a civilization? You are as ridiculously primitive as we feared."

"See here, boy!" Apparently President Kennedy's barely restrained composure had suffered enough abuse. "Just who d'you think you are? I am the president of the Confederate States of America, and I answer to no one short of the King himself. I will not be spoken to in such a manner by some lackey. Where is your master?"

Hope had already established the nearest exits and calculated her chances of survival should a leap of safety to the water below become necessary.

The nameless stranger remained unflappable. Was his indefatigable composure a good sign or an ill one? He took one step closer to the president.

"Who do I think I am?" He lost his smile as he spoke. "I *think* I am the commander of the fleet that is currently parked above your pathetic little world. I *think* I am in charge of the starships that have the capacity to eradicate all life on this miserable little rock." He smiled. "I *think* I am someone to whom you should like to be *very* polite."

Unable to contain herself a moment longer, Lady Kennedy stepped forward and executed a deep, respectful curtsy. "Pardon my impertinence, sir. In the interest of diplomacy and honour. . . what may we call you. . . yourself?" She kept her eyes on the floor, even when the armour-plated boots hove into view. She waited for some kind of touch from the stranger, but none came.

"This one understands diplomacy." The Kla'arkian commander spoke loudly enough to be certain the entire assemblage heard his words. "We will speak to. . . her from now on."

Lady Kennedy's heart nearly stopped at his words, but she caught the tiny pause while the commander determined her gender. It was an interesting fact to file away that no amount of shock would have caused her to miss. She arose from her curtsey while her husband blustered, apparently appalled that the commander of a military force would wish to parley with a woman.

Hope raised her head in time to see the Kla'arkian nod in the direction of the president.

The air around John Fitzroy Kennedy sparkled, and he cast about himself in astonishment as a bright translucent column surrounded him. He faded away with a terrible scream, and the column vanished with him.

Every soldier in the room shouted and pointed a weapon at the commander but they hesitated without any kind of direct order, allowing time for all ten of them to be simultaneously engulfed in columns of light and quickly disintegrated. In less than two seconds, the room fell still except for the quiet thrum of the dirigible's engines.

The commander turned his attention to Hope. "She is the spokesperson for your country, now. I will speak to *her*." He smiled and nodded in satisfaction. "What is your name, my good lady?"

For the first time in her life, the Lady Kennedy found herself speechless. She allowed herself two deep breaths before speaking. "Lady Hope Kennedy, good sir, at your service." She repeated her curtsy.

"Greetings, Lady Kennedy." He performed an elaborate bow. "I have chosen the name Lord Archeron while I am on your little world, with its titles and subtext. This man is your bondslave?" He pointed out the Persian whose hand sat poised on the hilt of his sword.

Lady Kennedy glanced from her man to Lord Archeron. "He is my Persian."

The commander nodded. "And the boisterous, disrespectful man. Your. . . husband?"

"He. . . is." Or was?

The commander reviewed the assemblage. "Then you are now president, no doubt. President Kennedy."

The men in the room muttered amongst themselves.

Hope could not prevent a gasp. "My Lord Archeron, please. Honouring me as your spokesperson. . . as *ambassador* between our peoples is honour enough. No one person could perform such duties adequately while attempting to run the Confederacy."

"You are a woman of great wisdom." He looked to one side, but what did he see? "Your former husband, sadly, doesn't seem to share such intelligence."

Hope exchanged a confused look with the Persian, who shook his head.

"Your words, my lord, perplex me," she admitted.

The commander's gaze swept the entire deck and he laughed. "I see.

You do not realise I am still aboard my own vessel, and your soon-to-be-late husband is enjoying my hospitality as we speak?"

What did he mean?

"My lord?"

"Persian." Archeron held his arms straight out to his sides. "Do me the honour of running me through with your sword."

The Persian twitched but did not move elsewise. Hope knew he would do nothing without her instruction.

"Go ahead. I assure you there will be no repercussions." The commander grinned at the dark-skinned fighter. "Go on," he said more quietly. "I can tell you want nothing better than to run me through."

The Persian held his ground, his eyes on Lady Kennedy's face.

Hope nodded one curt nod, holding her breath and praying she had not misjudged this strange commander.

In less than a second, the Persian's sword sliced through the air and buried itself in the commander's stomach. The dark warrior gave a cry of alarm as he overbalanced and shoved his sword arm into the amused commander's belly up to his shoulder. With a cry of disgust in his native tongue, the Persian withdrew and stumbled back.

A gasp rose up from the entire assembly.

A distinct absence of gore covered the Persian's arm.

Hope *refused* to react. "Your sword." She held her hand out.

He passed it to her, and she addressed the commander. "May I, your lordship?"

The commander nodded with a wry grin.

Slowly and carefully, Hope waved the sword through Archeron's figure. It met no resistance whatsoever as if she were striking a shadow.

"You're a flicker," she whispered, and the knowledge of it ran her blood to ice. A world that could create something so lifelike. . . that could destroy a city in a moment. . . was there anything that might be impossible for them?

She returned the Persian's sword. "You're not really here. You're up in your airship while you project this image to us."

Archeron nodded.

"And our men are there beside you on the deck of your vessel."

He nodded again.

"Why have you come to our world. . . and why have you destroyed our navies?"

"I see that you are a violent and warlike species, Lady Ambassador. I destroyed your navies that the transition to my rule might be easier and more peaceful. I want as few casualties as possible." He smiled cruelly and without warmth. "Bearing in mind that all casualties will be on your side. . . not ours."

Hope nodded. "So this is an invasion?"

"Oh, it is so much more than that, Lady Kennedy. It's also to be an enslavement. All members of your species will be privileged to labour for the rest of their days while I strip your planet of all its resources to the benefit of the Kla'arkian Empire. Those of you willing to help create a peaceful transition to the new paradigm will retain your stations of privilege. Those of you who don't will be put to work or turned into fertilizer like the. . ." Again, he glanced at a deck only he was able to see. ". . .late President Kennedy. The choice is yours."

"I. . ." She held her hands together to hide the shaking. "I'm not positive we will be able to convince our people to lay down arms so easily. As you said, we are a violent and brutish race."

He waved and a bright image appeared suddenly in the middle of the room.

The entire assemblage started.

One man fainted dead away.

Hope refused to take even a single step back from the image, which she ascertained was some kind of flicker suspended in space about three feet above the wooden deck. She recognised the Buddhist temple at Kawasaki in the former land of Australia, whose new name she could never pronounce. The sky loomed dark, riddled with lightning.

"This is an aerial image of Kawasaki taken three days ago, shortly after a similar meeting with their former government."

The word "former" struck Hope, and she shivered.

The commander chuckled and waved at the image as two airships slid into view. "Interesting sort. Very confident."

The drawings Hope had seen did no justice to the massive machines.

"They chose to puff up their chests and bluster and tell me. . . '*Anata no o shiri o sore o tsukidasu'* was the phrase they used, I believe." He chuckled again.

Blue lightning flashed from the ships and annihilated the city, turning it to smoking ash.

"For your species' sake, Lady Ambassador, I do hope you can be convincing."

Several moments passed before she could speak. The horror of the situation was one thing when all she knew came from a series of reports. Seeing such utter destruction for herself in horrible clarity shook her normally steely resolve. "Is there. . . is there a way for us to call up this flicker to show to our people? A projector of some kind we could use? The images. . . are very convincing."

"You see, gentlemen? I knew I made the right choice." The commander actually clapped his hands.

A small device materialised on the table beside Hope, a perfect sphere of brushed steel. Its appearance so shocked her she managed to hide her joy that she had persuaded him to offer something that might produce even a tiny jot of knowledge about the Kla'arkians.

"I would recommend against opening it, Lady Ambassador, to learn more about our technology." Was he psychic or just insidiously astute? "It will self-destruct if it is opened, levelling most of the city."

"I assure you I will take the utmost care with your gift."

"And now, gentlemen. . . ladies. . ." He looked around at the ashen, silent faces. "It is time to decide upon a new president." He gave Hope his attention again. "Who shall it be, Lady Ambassador?"

Hope spoke without hesitation. "Margie, come forward please and accept your new appointment."

A simple glance from the commander silenced the general uproar. As the baroness of Georgia took her place beside Lady Kennedy, Hope raised her voice and forced a measure of bravery. "England has been ruled by a Queen on more than one occasion, gentlemen. And I am certain that none of you would dare to insult the Imperial Rule of those esteemed ladies." Hope felt her momentum build. "What is good enough for the Empire is good enough for the Confederacy." She turned to face her stunned friend and took both of her hands. "Margaret, baroness of Georgia, do you accept the office of president of the Confederacy?"

The look that passed over Margaret's face was not fear or hesitation. To Hope, it said, *You damn well better know what you're getting me into.*

For the rest of the assemblage, she spoke aloud. "I do."

The commander barked out one brief laugh. "Then by the power invested in me by the fact that I possess a deadly fleet poised to destroy your entire planet, I pronounce you President Thatcher, leader of the Confederate States of America." He waved a hand at the Persian. "Isn't someone supposed to give her a whack with that pigsticker of his?"

Hope accepted the sword from her Persian and bade her friend kneel.

The commander was mocking them. He knew their rituals. He knew exactly what he was doing.

Hope went through the motions of a brief bastardization of a coronation. With the farce complete, the women turned to face the commander, waiting for him to make the next move.

He offered them a deep and formal bow. "And now, ladies. . . gentlemen, I give you until this time tomorrow to tell me how you wish to move forward. You can assist me or you can be destroyed. The same offer has been made to your contemporaries in all the world's governments. Those who comply with the most rapidity will be granted the most privilege."

He vanished.

The assemblage heaved a concerted sigh.

Before any outcry could be made, Ambassador Kennedy preempted it. "I assure you, gentlemen. My appointment was as much of a surprise to me as it was to you."

Any response was quashed by the appearance of what could only be the former president's body. It materialised in a column of light just as it had vanished, but naked and bloody on the floor. . . naked and unmanned. As everyone moved away from the broken, gory mess, the Persian grabbed Lady Kennedy and forced her eyes away from the gruesome sight.

He knows me well, she thought. *I'd have spit on the corpse or kicked it.*

A moment later, the bodies of the ten soldiers appeared as well, similarly disfigured and heaped in a pile like so much offal. The message seemed clear. For those men, Hope felt a tremendous loss. They'd given their lives in service to the Crown.

After a moment, Gatsby spoke. "I assure you, Madame Ambassador, not one of us resents your unprecedented rise to power."

The baron of Georgia was the next to speak. "Margie. . . d'you have any idea what you're doing?"

Turning to her consort and the rest of the men, President Thatcher squared her shoulders and took one deep breath. "I've been running Georgia for years, now, my dear, and everyone here knows it." She looked every man square in the face, then gestured at the piles of human flesh on the deck before them. "Do any of you *really* want this Godforsaken job?"

No one raised a hand.

"I thought as much." She turned to Hope and shook her head. "What have I done to make you hate me so?"

Lady Kennedy couldn't speak the truth out loud. Of the whole lot of them, Margie was the only politician in that room Hope trusted.

The former baroness of Georgia nodded with an ironic smile. "Well, gentlemen, we have some decisions to make."

The new president's consort said the words Hope dreaded. "What about this Hammer fellow? Mightn't he help us?"

And there it was. Inevitable. Hope would've suggested it to her husband if the bastard hadn't gotten himself killed. It was the next logical consideration.

"What about him?" Margie asked.

"Well, his people have been giving *us* a run for our money for several years." Her husband shrugged as if his thoughts should be self-evident. "He has his so-called Underground Railroad all over the country. If we want to try any kind of resistance, isn't it logical to obtain his input?"

"He is the most wanted criminal in the Empire." The newly appointed president studiously avoided so much as glancing Hope's way.

"I should think some sort of special dispensation could be arranged under the circumstances," her husband suggested.

Hope tap-danced on a high wire. "Are we certain we wish to attempt rebellion against such a force?"

After several minutes of increasingly heated debate, the president waved them all to silence. "All right, Lady Ambassador. I need a word with you in private." She gave the order for a return flight to Richmond and asked for the festering bodies to be moved respectfully. "I must speak with the ambassador. I will return before the *Titania* has docked in Richmond."

Hope kept her silence while they retired to the presidential suite. Alone in the fastidiously appointed state room, both women sat gratefully on the bed while the Persian stood watch at the door to be sure no one listened beyond.

"Have you completely lost your mind, woman?" the president demanded.

"I'm sorry, Margie. I didn't see a choice." Hope unbuttoned her vest and loosened her collar for more air. "I was shocked when he appointed me ambassador and when they took John, the only thought I had was, 'If I don't get Margie in on this, we're all doomed.'"

"Your first thought after, 'I hope they kill the son of a bitch,' you mean."

Hope didn't bother to suppress a smile. "Granted."

They stood in a companionable silence for a few minutes before Margaret broached the inevitable. "You realise we need to locate an ersatz Hammer. You've managed to give all the orders without showing your face so far. . . but *this*? These men will not take instructions by messenger pigeon, or whatever it is you do."

Hope dropped onto the bed. "I've been saying as much for months, now. I can't keep coming up with excuses for his reticence. Especially now. If I say so myself, he *is* the best man for the job if we have any hope of acting against these Kla'arkians." She stared at the lovely rococo paintings on the ceiling. "I need a stand-in to disseminate the intelligence we've spent years gathering. He needs to be a consummate actor: flamboyant, personable, and charismatic. . . and he also needs to be a true fighter and savvy enough to think on his feet when they cross-examine him on my plans." She raised her arms in frustration and let them flop onto the bed beside her. "Where are we going to find a *man* like that?"

The Persian startled both women when he spoke up. "I had a feeling you were going to ask that, milady."

Hope rose onto her elbows and regarded her Persian with interest.

"Strangely," he said, "I think I have just the fellow for you."

Chapter Five

I awoke to the sound of knocking on the door to our room. . . but what room were we in? It'd been that sort of night. Muttering incoherently, I rolled onto my back. The floral pattern in the paper on the ceiling offended my eyes, so I turned to ask Scopes where the hell we'd passed out.

Scopes did not lie beside me. Instead, the tousled auburn locks of his favourite woman of negotiable virtue spread like some sort of disgruntled Persian cat across the pillow beside mine. What was her name this week? Charity? Faith? Something like that.

Scopes himself was conspicuous in his absence.

The knocking repeated.

Ah. Scopes must have gone out for breakfast—or perhaps lunch? Maybe dinner?—and locked himself out of the room—

Aha! I lay in a room Scot and Basil Rupert had generously donated to us. . . so Scopes could spend the night with the woman named after this week's virtue, who now regained blurry consciousness beside me.

Wait. There was a reason I'd specifically thought about a *Persian* cat.

I sat bolt upright. I'd met Lady Kennedy's Persian!

Success! Quite certain of my location and with a vague recollection of the events that had transpired to bring me there, I pushed my feet out from under the blankets and tried to find the floor.

"Hold your giblets," I called out to Scopes, "while I figure out which end's my head and which end's my ass."

Reposing on the edge of the bed for a moment, I attended on the room to slow down and settle under my bare feet. Scopes could bloody well wait until I was certain I wouldn't fall down once I'd risen.

Trying to construct a timeline for the previous evening's debacle which ended with me waking up in bed with the woman whose name I simply could not remember, I pressed the back of my wrist to my mouth to keep down whatever was attempting to find its way up.

The prior evening hadn't begun as one that should've ended with a monstrous hangover. After our bountiful reunion with our mates from the *Railroad*, the Scotsman had told us of an assignment in the works.

As Twist had explained, several slavers had sequestered their "property" in the stables of Salome's Garden, totalling nearly two hundred lost souls. Scot wanted Scopes and me to provide a distraction while he, Basil Rupert, and the Texans snuck back to the stables and freed the slaves.

"Why don't you do the distracting?" I suggested. "All you have to do is climb up on the tables, dance a jig, and lift your skirt."

The Scotsman scoffed. "As if there's anyone here who hasn't seen what I have up my *kilt*." To emphasise his point, much the way he emphasised the name of his manly garment, Scot rose from his chair and lifted the skirt to his chest. Nobody seemed to notice, so he dropped the skirt and reclaimed his chair. "You were saying?"

I nodded defeat. "Point taken. . . and when did you get that thing pierced?"

"Last week."

"It didn't hurt?"

"Hell yeah, it hurt."

I observed the room with new eyes. Working an escape in our favourite haunt would be risky, maintaining anonymity nearly impossible. But I always had loved a challenge.

"Okay," I agreed at last. "Be patient, so we can all get out of here without anyone knowing we're connected to the escape."

My friend agreed with a grin and a nod.

One by one, my associates drifted off to a variety of entertainments while I caught Victoria's attention. I arranged for her to stay with her friends for the night, a bit surprised when she didn't insist on assisting in the assignment. Presumably, she understood that her brother's death lay too heavy on my conscience and too near in my memory. Smart girl.

When the table had emptied but for Scopes and myself, I leaned back in my chair with legs extended and my hands clasped behind my head. Scopes matched my pose. My brother and I had worked together long enough that setting our plans felt like sliding into an old, comfortable pair of drawers.

"Music, tarot, mesmerism, brawl?" I asked.

The man who was yang to my yin smiled. "Exactly what I would have suggested."

The dancing girls announced a break in their show.

Handshake, elbow, back of the hand, roll the wrist for a reverse finger clasp, slide away, and we set off for our respective jobs. I dropped five twenties into Billy's glass jar to get his attention.

The piano man smiled and nodded. We'd played with him before, and he knew the score.

I climbed on top of Billy's pride and joy, and Scopes handed me my banjo. I dangled my legs over the side of the pianoforte, folding my instrument seamlessly into Billy's tune.

Some of the folks who recognised me applauded lightly. A few who knew me better booed and called the cats in jest.

Scopes mounted the stage tuning his fiddle. He took up his usual post near the wings and played a counterpoint to my melody.

I glanced around the tables, sharing smiles with that evening's marks. . . er. . . audience. Scopes and I had played together on many a night and knew what the crowds enjoyed. We could make them dance to our tunes like obedient marionettes. Creating a distraction while the rest of our team released the slaves posed not even the slightest challenge.

Billy followed my lead on our first tune, a light and fanciful air that highlighted a lovely harmony Scopes and I had perfected years ago on long, winter nights in a cardboard box, a traditional drinking song that never failed to encourage the patrons to caterwaul along with us.

I stood on the pianoforte and divided the room with a single wave of my arm, changing the song into a simple round that would assure me the attention of the entire audience.

Next, I chose a somewhat more melancholy and mysterious tune. . . which is when I noticed Lady Kennedy's Persian had given me his undivided attention.

As accepting of the gorgeous man's unavailability as I had to be, a small part of me needed to try for at least an iota of his attention, so I hopped down from the piano and meandered my way through the audience towards the stage centre stairs. I moved among the tables singing a bawdy song, flirting with several of the women to the amusement and delight of the entire audience until I passed the table of drunken hooligans Scopes and I had already pegged as the beginning of the riot we planned to create.

They'd been noisy and rude, which was all well and good as far as that went, but they kept grabbing the waitresses and forcing unwanted and unpurchased attention. I flirted with them, keeping it light and joking: enough to render them uncomfortable and a bit dangerous but not adequate for them to cause any trouble. . . just yet.

A large blond hooligan lumbered to his feet, but the cat calls and jeers of those around him returned him to his chair.

Turning an about face at precisely the spot where the Persian sat behind me, I feigned surprise that he should happen to sit right there.

"I dropped into a chair that night," I sang, "and gave the girl a terrible fright. . ."

The verse of my song gave me the perfect excuse to drop into his lap and kiss his cheek, bringing a roar of laughter from the entire room. The Persian suffered my shenanigans with polite deference. Not wanting to push my luck, I offered a nod of thanks and went about my business as if the interlude had been a complete fluke.

When I joined Scopes on the stage, he stepped forward, pursed his lips and shook his head in a bit of staged reprisal for my naughty behaviour.

I waved him back to the edge of the stage and addressed the audience. "It's all in good fun, mates, am I right?"

They shouted hurrah.

"What was that?" I held a hand to my ear, passing the reins of music over to Scopes.

"Hurrah!" the crowd shouted.

I nodded and opened my arms to Scopes.

He performed an exaggerated shrug and smirked.

I set my guitar down and pulled a deck of tarot cards from my vest with a brief sideways nod to let Billy know he could use some of the money in his jar for a shot or two at the bar.

He winked and ended his phrase with a dramatic ornament, rose to his feet, and gave the audience a deep, respectful bow.

While the crowd cheered him off for his break, I pretended to shuffle the cards and searched the balcony for the lighting crew. The man at the spotlight waved a cap over his head. Wonderful. The house had been habituated to our antics and always played along because we provided free entertainment and a change from the usual dancing girls, so when I flourished the deck and asked whose fortune I should read, the lights in the room dimmed and a spotlight blazed upon me.

Scopes played programme music with an Egyptian flair.

Ignoring everything called out to me, I pretended to hear someone shout a name guaranteed to interest a certain attractive bodyguard.

"Lady Hope Kennedy?" I pointed into the crowd as if someone had said her name. As popular as she was, my falsehood immediately gained significant support.

Well, of course.

Fanning the cards dramatically, I spoke my patter and offered the deck for someone to scrutinise. As soon as the cards returned, I preset the card named the Empress, an indicator of maternal warmth, love and wisdom, and hokey enough to garner favour with this crowd. After a huge showy display, I pulled a card from the deck and thrust it directly into the face of the Persian with a dramatic, "And what is the card, my good sir?"

After the briefest of pauses, he called out, "Queen of Cups!"

What? That was certainly *not* the card I had manoeuvred into position. What was he doing?

I glanced into his face. Absolutely nothing. He had the stoniest, most intentionally blank expression I had ever seen in my life.

I turned the card: Death.

Oh, shit. It wasn't possible, not for Lady Kennedy.

And her very own Persian had seen it.

Bugger it!

What game are you playing? his dark eyes demanded.

I shook my head so slightly he'd be the only one to notice.

Scopes struck a discordant tremolo that shook me out of my torpor.

"The Queen of Cups it is!" I shouted, flashing the vile card quickly enough that no one would be able to examine it.

Mad applause.

"The Queen of cups is the loving mother to us all," I called out, shaken by my error and unable to avoid my rehearsed explanation of the Empress. "She signals the beginning of new projects. . ."

The audience stared up at me, wondering what the future held, hoping against all reason that we would not be swept away by whatever had destroyed the navy. Their fear tempered my distraction. Dear God, what had I been thinking when I suggested tarot?

"She is the great all-mother who will protect us in our hour of need," I called.

Scope's fiddle slowly transmogrified to something like a patriotic march.

"The Queen assures us that Lady Kennedy has us all in her thoughts and prayers." I carefully avoided the Persian's gaze. "With her behind us, the future can hold nothing but prosperity and glory." I shook a fist over my head, and the crowd shouted.

"God save the lady!" Scopes called from my side, startling me with his proximity. He normally held to the background.

"God save the lady," the crowd roared.

Scopes launched into a rousing version of God save the King reworded for Lady Kennedy. He passed in front of me, and a simple flash of his eyes told me to go find the Persian and fix things.

The man in question was already moving toward the exit.

I pressed my way to his side, giving my back to the bulk of the crowd, and grabbed his massive arm. "I am deeply sorry about that."

He glanced at my hand.

I released him and held the hand up in apology. "That, too." What the hell did he think? If the first lady's man suspected me of harbouring ill will towards the Crown on the same night as a slave break, I'd be hauled in for questioning before I had time to sleep off my hangover.

He stared at me with that damnable stony face.

"The card slipped," I said. "I am forever in your debt for rescuing me." I bowed my head. "I can only thank God you know the cards."

When I looked again, he held a hand towards me in an obvious request to see the deck.

"They're just cards, my good sir." And I hadn't shuffled them since they'd been tuned to Lady Kennedy. Allowing him to see the cards after I'd drawn Death in her name could prove disastrous.

His hand did not waver nor did he speak.

"They're just cards," I lied. "They don't really mean. . ."

What was he? A fucking statue?

Damn it all to hell and perdition.

I handed him the deck.

He headed back to his table, which a few meek bankers had been eager to appropriate since his apparent departure. He stopped and favoured them with that same blank expression.

They leaned away under his non-verbal assault and scurried away into the crowd that sang a fourth verse praising Lady Kennedy.

The Persian spread the cards in a single perfectly curved line.

Oh hell. He *knew* them. No one could casually slide the cards like that without years of experience. He likely read them as well as I.

"Draw." The tips of the fingers of one hand grazed the table an inch from the perfectly laid out curve. His eyes brooked no hesitation.

I slid a single card from the deck and turned it over: the Tower.

Damn.

"Draw."

The Wheel. Damn.

"Draw."

The Fool. God damn it all to hell!

I grabbed the cards I'd drawn and used them to slide the rest of the deck into one safe brick. "They're just cards, my good sir."

His dark expression stopped my tongue. "You know how to read them?" he asked. "Honestly."

Unable to lie, I nodded.

"And this is not how you set them?"

"Oh, dear God, no." My hand reached forward to touch him, but I pulled it back in a fist. "I don't know how they could have. . ."

"Don't lie to me." He grabbed my arm.

My heart pounded. I couldn't lie to him, but what the hell could I say?

Thank God Scopes kept the damn crowd singing.

"You must know what happened on the Coast, sir." I swallowed to buy a moment of time. "I was there. The Tower, the bolt of lightning. I saw it." A wave of pain hit my chest. "Many died and fell from a great height." I swallowed again. I had to fight the pain back.

The grip on my arm loosened but did not release. "You lost someone."

I could only nod.

His eye's softened. "I am sorry." His hand moved to my shoulder. He considered me for a long moment, then glanced to either side and drew closer. "And the Wheel?"

He meant to know whether I could read the details of the dire prediction. The sincerity in his eyes forced me to relax my thoughts and focus.

What did I see?

"A change," I said. "The Wheel always means change. A change in leadership? Will facing this new threat turn the wheel and bring someone from a great height to the lowest depth?" The images flowed in my mind. "I see bound hands freed and then held high with a sword."

I opened my eyes.

A tear slipped from the corner of his.

Damn!

My hand gripped the arm that held my shoulder. "I'm sorry. I didn't mean. . ."

He shook his head and quickly brushed the tear away. "You have no need to apologise." He released my shoulder. "I should. I'm sorry." He glanced at the cards in my hands. "And the Fool?"

Laughter bubbled up out of nowhere. "I'm the only damn fool in these parts, my good sir, for fucking up this whole act in the first place."

A cold chill rolled down my back.

Our eyes met. We both knew *exactly* what that card meant.

"I'm sorry," I muttered. "I didn't mean to imply. . ." I released my hold on his arm but couldn't look away.

"Do the cards ever lie?" he asked.

I forced a smile. "Only when they want to."

He smiled back.

Something in me twisted. Heat flooded my cheeks. I'd never felt that before, and I prided myself on having experienced. . .

No. Not even the joke. Not with him.

"Your friend seems to grow impatient." The Persian raised an eyebrow.

The roar of the Garden swept over me. The lilt of the crowd as they sang yet another chorus in praise of Lady Hope Kennedy told me they'd likely not endure one more repetition.

A glance at Scopes showed me the Persian's accuracy. I offered my friend the best smile I could manage under the circumstances.

I wanted to say more, to tell the Persian the cards had been wrong before. Maybe the future wasn't so dire after all. But all that would be a lie and, for some reason, this man was the second I'd ever met to whom I could not lie. I dashed to the stage.

At the last second, he grabbed my elbow. "You call a slave, 'sir.' Why?"

I allowed myself a deep cleansing sigh. "You're not really a slave, are you?"

After the briefest hesitation, he smiled. Without a word, he released my elbow and I bounded my way back to the stage, noticing he chose to stay and watch the show after all.

And what in the world should I make of that?

Huge questions filled Avery's face as I retrieved my banjo.

I met his stare with all the sincerity I could project and then graced him with the subtlest shake of my head ever performed. I had no idea what the Persian thought of me.

His brows knit for a moment, then smoothed over. He knew I'd answer all his questions after we'd saved the day.

The amazing and underrated performer that he was, Scopes launched us into our magical mesmerism act with a preset musical prelude, reminding me that we had a job to do. He usually kept to the shadows and edges, but when push came to shove, there was no man ever I trusted more to have my back.

We started with pulling dancer's undergarments from behind their ears and geared up for a final bit of fun. After the hideous fiasco with the tarot, I *really* needed a bit of fun.

A woman shrieked.

The aforementioned hooligans harassed yet another waitress. Billy had to physically remove her from their unwanted attention. Ah yes.

"You, sirs!" I shouted. They'd be the perfect dupes to start the barroom brawl in earnest. "Please good sirs, if you will, I can use your assistance on the stage."

The crowd encouraged them with shouts and whistles.

The ladies scowled as if wondering why I'd give such scoundrels special attention.

Well, they'd soon understand.

I mesmerised the young men.

Then I had them strip to their drawers.

The waitresses, as one, laughed their appreciation and pleasure.

Then I made the young toughs kiss each other.

The ladies catcalled with abandon and the men followed suit, likely hoping for a discount later if they supported the offended parties. What the hell. It was all in good clean fun. . .

Until one particular young tough rose to the occasion, as it were.

The crowd cooed.

Damn flimsy drawers.

I immediately released them from the spell.

The young toughs all laughed and cheered at the attention from the ladies, unaware of what had happened. . . until the blond bloke realised his indiscretion. As if to reassert his manhood, he slugged me.

Bam! But he projected the punch like such an amateur that he barely made contact with my chin. Oh, what the hell. I took advantage of the situation to melodramatically pretend the punch had landed, spinning twice on the spot before leaning out over the table on the floor below the stage.

 Scopes trilled a flourish on his fiddle.

For a split second, I hovered there while the audience held its collective breath. . .

Then I dropped like a stone onto the table, breaking it to the floor and spilling everyone's drinks.

Voila. Instant brawl.

The men whose drinks pooled into spots on the floor pulled the nearly naked ruffians off the stage, rightly blaming them for their losses.

Bear in mind most inns at that hour are fights just waiting to happen, so the way the brawl blossomed all the way to the room's perimeter should be considered no great feat of strategy on my part. However, having created a sense of festive camaraderie did ensure that this fight would escalate faster and more completely than the average. Everyone wanted to be part of the show.

For the moment, Scopes hovered at the edges of the stage, providing his trademark programme music for the fracas.

I prowled the walls of the room, tapping the more reserved gentlemen on the shoulder and slugging them when they turned to me, ensuring that no one would be left out.

At exactly the correct moment to escalate the simple bar fight, Scopes handed his fiddle to one of the dancers hovering in the wings watching the debacle. He bowed to her, straightened his coat, and ran at top speed for the edge of the stage, screaming his head off in his heathen, foreign tongue.

Reaching the edge, he hurled himself into the air, shouting and pinwheeling all four limbs to make sure everyone knew enough to get out of the way.

He landed on the wooden floor in a crouch, one knee and the knuckles of one hand pressed to the floor, his eyes staring down.

The room fell silent. They held their collective breath.

Scopes right hand reached slowly across his torso to his left hip as if he were reaching for a sword.

The circle around him reacted as one man, and the air suddenly rang with the scrape of metal from over a dozen swords, guns, and knives slid from a vast number of scabbards and holsters.

Scopes pulled his hand from his hip and opened it palm up to reveal a miniature version of his clockwork monkey.

"I got a monkey in my hand!" he exclaimed in singular non sequitur. He rose to his feet and displayed the toy for all to see. "Anyone have five quid for a clockwork monkey?"

Such a display from the normally quiescent Scopes had its usual effect. A bit embarrassed at having suddenly pulled their weapons for no good reason, the men in the circle looked about sheepishly.

Not wanting the fight to lose momentum, I sidled over to the big blond bloke who'd slugged me—still in only his drawers—and bumped him so his raised sword clattered into the blade of the gentleman beside him.

The clash of metal on metal was a starter's pistol reminding everyone that a weapon once pulled wants using.

Voila—instant sword fight!

A short time later, someone crashed through the plate glass window at the front of the inn. This brought the guards in from the outside, which had been the entire point.

Now the slaves in the stables could be freed.

A light brush against the back of my neck set me whirling one hundred and eighty degrees to find a meaty hand holding a kris dagger's point near my throat. It rested a millimetre from my Adam's apple, held by the Persian who also held my gaze for less than a second before pulling the blade away, spinning, and hurling it across the room where it sank into the chest of the man who must've originally thrown it. The man stared at the hilt protruding from his chest in the centre of a growing flower of red.

The Persian turned to me with no readable expression, blocking my view of the corpse who'd almost killed me.

Movement at his shoulder brought my pistol straight up, and I fired, my wrist sliding easily between his arm and his side because he was that tall.

The gunshot didn't startle him at all. He casually looked over his shoulder at the body collapsing behind him, its own pistol falling away from where it had pointed at the back of the Persian's head. He glanced down at the hand shoved between his arm and his side.

I withdrew the hand, and my pistol slid back into place up my sleeve.

He favoured me with the barest hint of a smile and nod to acknowledge the save then struck blindly to his right, his fist connecting solidly with a face hurtling in our direction. Coincidentally, the face belonged to the original blond hooligan who'd started it all. He dropped like a stone.

"I'm Zen," I said.

The Persian smelled of cloves. "I know." His eyes opened a fraction of a centimetre and he grasped me firmly by both shoulders. He spun me around to face the brawler running towards me who impaled himself on my suddenly upraised sword.

After kicking the body off my blade, I turned to find the Persian already gone.

He hung by one hand on a post of the balcony above. Pulling himself up the railing and over it, he then landed adroitly between a cluster of working girls and the ruffians who were pounding up the steps to menace them.

"It is not that kind of party, gentlemen," he assured them.

Knowing he could take care of himself, I scanned the crowd to find Scopes clambering his way back to the stage just as the alarms sounded. My brother waved at the side entrance, shouting, "The slaves are escaping. Quickly everyone, this way; we must aid this fine establishment."

Dozens of "helpful" drunks swarmed the guards, all of whom had rushed into the inn when the gunshots started.

I leapt to one of the few intact tables and waved my arms in an entirely different direction. "No, you idiot, the stables are *that* way!"

Utter mayhem ensued, and Scopes and I slipped backstage, where we quickly made certain Victoria was safely tucked away for the night.

Scopes bumped into a certain young woman named after one of the seven heavenly virtues. He took her by the hand, leading us into the heavens of the theatre and out a handy trap door, onto the building's roof.

From there the three of us escaped the mêlée to another inn several blocks away, where we'd agreed to meet our compatriots.

Basil Rupert and the Scotsman had been assigned the task of leading the escaped slaves away from the city, so Nuke and Sal told us we should take the boys' room for the night. We shared stories of the night's adventure and drank several bottles of scotch in Scot's honour. By the time we'd passed a fourth around, our Texan friends took their leave and Scopes, his friend, and I stumbled up to the room generously donated to us by our hardworking compatriots.

It was a well appointed room, with a porcelain tub in one corner furnished with hot and cold taps. While Scopes and his lady entertained one another in the bed, I ran myself a bubble bath and sank into it gratefully.

"To the well-hung Scotsman," I declared, waving the nearly empty bottle.

"Hear, hear," Scopes called back, his voice rather muffled.

At some point, Scopes took a break to wake me and prevent me snoring my way to hypothermia. While he tucked me into the bed, I informed him, "The Persian knew my name."

Scopes laughed. "Here we go." He patted my cheek. "Point that thing the other way, my friend." After pulling the blankets around my chin, he turned his attention back to Faith, Charity or Prudence. "We need to find you a willing lad."

An indeterminate number of hours later, I awakened to the sound of knocking, with the unnamed woman in bed beside me but a conspicuously absent Scopes.

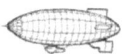

All caught up, I pushed to my feet and staggered across the floor. Scopes had been unusually patient in waiting for me while I ran through the events of the previous evening. Ordinarily, he'd pound incessantly until I opened the door.

Also, he hadn't responded to my advice about his giblets.

Glancing back at the woman, who now sat up and leaned heavily on one arm, I stopped with my hand on the door knob. "That *is* you, Scopes?"

"Indeed, it is not."

My hand tightened on brass as my eyebrows lifted in surprise. I didn't recognise the deep male voice. "Who is it?"

"I come in the name of the Lady Hope Kennedy on a matter of utmost urgency."

I backed away from the door. Holy Christ!

The woman in the bed clasped both hands over her mouth.

From what I could tell, we were both instantly awake and sober. . . and. . . naked.

Really, *really* naked.

I grabbed a pair of drawers. "The lady is here?" I squeaked.

Temperance or Faith scrambled from the bed and gathered her clothing.

"Indeed not," the man on the other side of the door said. "I am merely one of her humble servants."

I checked to make sure the woman was half decent, fully realizing it was probably a wasted point of chivalry. As if proving my point, she gestured at my drawers and whispered, "If you're going for modesty, those drawers don't help t'all. I can tell you ain't Jewish from here."

I opened the door.

"Zen Bastard?" The Persian? The man who'd traded lives with me in the tavern brawl the night before? He discerned my state and a gentle smirk played about his mouth. . . until he observed the woman. Finding her there in a state of general dishabille rendered him, unbelievably, unmistakably embarrassed.

"Madame. . ." He bowed his head politely.

"You. . ." I stammered.

"Indeed." He rose from his bow, and his whole posture shifted to something rather stiff and formal as he addressed me. "I apologise. . . I did not realise you had. . . company. . ."

It troubled me to have him think she was there for me. Bearing in mind I'd enjoyed my fair share of prostitutes and had been a whore myself more than once, but right then, right there, I just didn't. . . I just didn't.

"Oh. . . her. . ." Nothing came to mind that would not be rude to the poor woman.

"I'm here with his mate, Scopes," the woman interjected, coming to my rescue. "I'm *his* whore. . . not Zen's. Name's Prudence, by the way. . . well, this week anyways." She was still dressing. . . but in a strangely alluring way. I'm not sure how she managed that.

I hauled on random clothes as well: trousers, shirt. Something about the astonishingly striking man with rippling muscles rendered me self-conscious.

"The pleasure is mine, madame. I apologise if I have interrupted your sleep."

"No apologies, gov'ner. In fact. . . since I'm awake. . ." Her voice trailed off suggestively.

The epitome of professionalism, the Persian deflected her overtures. "Again I must apologise, ma'am, but I'm here on official business with Mr. Bastard and his associate. Do you know where your employer might be?"

She smirked and mouthed the word "employer" before answering the Persian. "Mr. Scopes went for scones. I expect him to return back d'rectly."

"Indeed." He pulled a mass of cash from his pocket. "I humbly beg apology, but I must talk to the gentlemen on a matter of the utmost urgency and hope this will recompense you for your time, your trouble and. . . your forgetfulness?"

She took the cash and examined it with an appreciative whistle. "Oy, this could buy a whole lifetime's worth of forgetfulness." She patted my arm in a friendly manner as she made her way past me. "Who are you? What's my name?"

She paused at the Persian's side to look him up and down, taking especial time to check out his bulging pectorals. "Mind you, a big strapping bloke like *you*. . . for this much I'd throw in an entire week of pleasure. . . before I forgot it all, o'course."

The Persian folded both hands over his chest in a gesture of respect and bowed to her once more. "I appreciate your generosity and promise to recommend your name and place of business to any friends of mine who require companionship."

She lingered in the doorway indicating the Persian with a practised wink. "This one is a gentleman right enough, even if he is a godless heathen. More Churchmen should be so polite." She looked him square in the eye. "And believe you me. . . I *knows* Churchmen. . ." She paused again before nodding in my direction. "This one's a gentleman too, you know. A 'gentleman's gentleman,' you might say." She gave me a final wink and departed.

"Interesting woman." The Persian closed the door behind her.

"One of many that she can be," I said.

He turned to face me. "Scopes is your. . .?"

Startled, I moved around the room picking up the leftover detritus from the evening's entertainments. "Scopes? Friend. . . partner. . . brother. . ."

"Are you a package deal?"

"I beg your pardon?" I stopped with a brassiere hanging from one hand.

The Persian glanced at the undergarment.

Flummoxed, I threw it into a corner with the rest of our clothes, gesturing to a vacant chair with the other hand.

He accepted the seat with a nod. "Sorry if I seem esoteric. . . I am here to offer you a job, and I'm trying to ascertain the parameters of your employ."

Esoteric? "A job?"

He examined the room from his seat, taking in the one bed, the tub still full of water, the single pile of clothes to which I had just added a woman's brassiere. It's astonishing how the decidedly mundane details of my life suddenly appeared sinister, or at least mildly titillating, when viewed through the eyes of an attractive stranger.

"Did you hear anyone last night?" he asked.

"Apart from Scopes and the woman? No. . ." Only then did I realise he was asking whether the room was soundproof. "No. . . we're safe as houses."

He cocked his head at me. "In all reality, how safe are houses?" When I didn't respond, he shrugged off the question. "Sorry. . . a lot is happening." He shook his head. "I seem to be engaging in a considerable amount of apology today. The cards you read. . ."

Which was the precise moment Scopes chose to make his entrance.

"Awake, my lovelies. . . I return with breakfast." He noticed the Persian and, of course, recognised him instantly, but he appeared uncertain whether he should acknowledge such knowledge. He also noticed Prudence's absence. He held out a pastry to the Persian. "Scone?"

The Persian, against all odds, took it and chomped down a large bite. As though this were the most ordinary afternoon in the world, he chewed with a face expressing delight at the pastry. He even made a yummy sound.

"Zen. . ." Scopes asked, sidling over to me and handing me a scone. "Who's your. . ." And the pause was really, quite long. ". . .friend?"

The Persian's countenance remained inscrutable.

Had our extracurricular activities of the prior evening attracted unwanted attention? Were we under arrest? But he'd mentioned engaging me. . . us. . .?

Around his scone, which he truly seemed to enjoy, the Persian made a dismissive sound. "Let's not play games, gentlemen. I know you work for the Hammer, and I know you have a most impressive record in the Underground Railroad."

"I don't. . ." I began. . . but faltered. We'd reached a certain honesty over the tarot reading. I couldn't lie to him now.

The Persian picked up the vest I'd worn the previous evening. With a final swallow of his pastry, he found and presented the silver hammer I wore hidden under the lapel.

"Okay. . . that. . ." Inhaling a deep breath, I closed my eyes for a moment to find my quiet centre. Scoff all you like, but it helps.

Scopes would recognise my centring technique and respect any decision I might make from that place.

The Persian allowed me the moment.

When I opened my eyes, I sat on the bed and gestured for Scopes to sit with me. "First of all, Scopes and I are indeed a package deal. Whatever job you have for one of us, you hire both of us or neither."

Considering his legendary loyalty to Lady Kennedy, the Persian was bound to appreciate our bond. He nodded.

"So. . . What could Lady Hope Kennedy possibly want with a couple of good-for-nothing pirates?"

"Your tarot reading last night," he said. "You have no idea how accurate you were."

To say we were shocked at his revelations would do a severe injustice to the utter panic, awe, and all-over astonishment that was stronger than any word in the English language could possibly convey. He detailed the scenario on the Titania for us, leaving out nothing of import. The complete explanation lasted over an hour, given the many questions my friend and I asked. When we'd exhausted our curiosity, a hush fell over the room while Scopes and I processed the information.

Scope spoke first and his question surprised even me: "How much?"

"Scopes!" I was far too shocked to strike him.

He smacked my arm instead. "He said a job, Zen. He didn't say charity work. Jobs pay." He turned his attention to the Persian, and I was impressed with my friend's carefully constructed blasé attitude, wondering how much of it was counterfeit, but impressed regardless. "How much does this job pay, Mr. Bodyguard?"

The Persian had relaxed as he told his story since we seemed to accept his word on the face of it. He actually smirked again. He had a very attractive smirk. "More money than you can spend in your lifetime."

Scopes shook his head at the vagary. "Oh, I imagine you'd be astonished by how much money I could spend in my lifetime."

"I paid Prudence a thousand pounds to bugger off so we could talk. Extrapolate."

"Oh." Avery extrapolated. "Oooh?"

The Persian personified the Sphinx.

Scopes and I faced one another and communicated through a series of facial expressions, nods and shrugs. After completing our personal negotiations, I turned to face the Persian again. "Let's pretend for the moment we are inclined to accept your offer. What happens next?"

The Persian held up a business card between two fingers. "You and your friend take turns in the bath. . ." He nodded at the tub. "And meet her ladyship at this address in one hour."

While I took the card, my fingers brushed his and distracted me. "One hour. . ." I traded glances with Scopes again.

"Horses. . ." we chorused. Our horses were across the circle at the Garden.

The Persian held up one hand. "Your horses are outside."

As though the heroes of a comedy, Scopes and I looked at him, at each other, and then hurried to the window to gaze outside. Our horses were, indeed, tethered below, guarded by the same urchin who'd taken them in the first place.

"Twist?" I called out, and the boy looked up, smiled and saluted. "How did you find us?"

Excited, he dug into a pocket and pulled out a cheap paper and bamboo fan, flipping it open with the finesse of an expert and waving it to reveal the familiar, smiling Buddha and ornate logo for Zen Bastard beer.

"Lady Kennedy's Persian had your secret emblem," he stage whispered, waving the fan again. "He told me where you were and gave me a fiver to bring the horses here." He made an elaborate wink and carefully slid the fan back into his shirt. "Said it was an Important Affair o' State."

Not certain how Twist had managed to enunciate the extra capital letters, I threw the Persian a puzzled look.

"Unusually large-busted women made up to look Asian handed them out at the inn as novelty souvenirs." He shrugged. "I passed it off as a sign that I bore a secret message from you." He quirked a smile. "I presume you were named for the beer and not the other way around."

More amused by the Persian's ingenuity than annoyed at Twist's mistaken trust, I pulled some bills out of a pocket, wadded them up and dropped them into the boy's eager hands. "Find copies of every daily paper in the stand on the corner, Twist, and bring them up to my room. Chop, chop."

The boy vanished with a flash of his blue scarf.

Scopes and I pressed shoulder to shoulder in the window. I held up the card so we could both read it. One side revealed the Lady Kennedy's name printed in bold, simple letters. The other side had an address printed by hand in blue ink.

"Classy," I observed quietly.

My friend nodded and our eyes met.

Were we really going to do this?

He shrugged.

Drawing back into the room, I noticed that the Persian had risen to his feet. Crossing the space to stand closer to him, I slipped the card into my pocket. I struggled to find the right words for my emotions. "You really think I can do this?"

The Persian raised an eyebrow.

"I've done a lot of unbelievable shite in my life and to a degree, I'm the most egotistical Bastard you'll find. . . but this is the *planet* we're discussing. This involves. . . *everyone*."

He appraised me silently for a moment before speaking, and I refused to squirm under his stare. He dropped a hand on my shoulder. "You are at the top of the lady's list at *my* recommendation." The moment might have seemed ridiculously histrionic if we hadn't been discussing a pact between myself and the Empire to effect the salvation of the entire human race from evil, invading aliens.

His hand was really quite large.

Really.

Scopes broke the potentially embarrassing moment by swatting the back of my head. "Tell her worshipfulness we'll be there on the hour. . . in an hour. . . after we no longer stink."

With nothing more than a nod, the Persian released my shoulder and departed.

When the door closed, Scopes elbowed me in the ribs. "I can *smell* how much you want him."

I chose not to deny the obviously true, and yet. . . "Last night. He knew the cards, Avery."

Scopes raised an eyebrow.

I nodded and shrugged. "I think they mean we're in this for real."

The eyebrow raised even higher.

"Really, Avery. I'm not just making it up. I saw it." I took a deep breath. "So did he."

"Saw what?" He held my arms.

Hell. What had I seen? "That I'm the Fool."

Anyone else would have laughed. Not Avery.

The moment passed.

He smiled and squeezed my arms. "So you're going to make a fool of yourself for this man? Not the first time I've seen that." He moved to the tub, stripping off his shirt and kicking off his shoes before reaching into the cold water and pulling the plug.

A few moments later, he threw the rest of his clothes to the floor and crawled into the warm, steamy waters. He looked up and made a face that asked why I wasn't already in the tub.

"I'm not sure I know what to do with the fact that our country needs us," I told him. "Our *country*. The whole damn thing."

He met my gaze evenly while he considered my words. "Do you even care about that? Really?"

Did I? I would lay down my life to save Avery or Victoria without a doubt. I'd take a bullet for any of the men and women of my larger family who'd survived the destruction of the *Aquatic Railroad*.

But the nation? Could I even conceive of that?

Scopes splashed the water in the tub. He lifted a bottle of expensive bubbly stuff. "Scot and Basil Rupert paid for this. We should take advantage."

And that was all he needed to say.

We shared the tub and Twist knocked loudly a short time later. He dropped off several papers while we scrubbed away. I offered him the last scone and told him to ready the horses.

Once Scopes and I felt fit to meet a personage of distinction we made our way across town to the address on the lady's card. I stared at the distinguished lettering, then up at the impressively ornate gate.

"She couldn't have just told us to come to the Palace?" I asked. "It's not like there's more than one hereabouts."

"I didn't even know it *had* an address." Scopes shoulder shrugged against mine. "Maybe she didn't want to seem pretentious."

I scoffed. "She lives in a palace. Pretentious conveys with the real estate."

Before we entered, Scopes dropped his hands on my neck. "They want *you*, Zen. I'm just so much baggage."

I drew him close and kissed his cheek, embracing him with all my strength. "We are a package deal, my friend. If I am going to face the gates of Hell, there is no one. . . *no one* I want at my side other than you."

When I released him, he wore a familiar grin. "There's going to be more of that than usual for a while, isn't there?"

"You bet your ass there will be."

Chapter Six

Lady Hope Kennedy gazed down at the bustle of activity on the drive below her. She turned the steel sphere in her hand absently as she watched the servants unload a cart.

"You seem more inclined to enjoy the view these days," her Persian remarked.

Lady Kennedy sighed without looking at him. "They have no idea what's about to happen to them."

"And what is?"

A snide comment faltering on her lips, she stopped turning the device and stared at it. "Are we really as bad as Lord Archeron undoubtedly will be?"

"Not you, milady."

She smiled. "But most people won't notice the change of masters, will they?" She watched the servants again. "They toil for aristocrats. . . they'll toil for monsters." Silence fell between them for a moment. "Maybe they already do."

Her Persian remained still. He stood near the cold fireplace, hands behind his back.

"Am I foolish for even trying?" she asked. When he didn't speak immediately, her eyes flicked to regard him. "With the Railroad, we just had to bring people to Canada. A thousand miles at the most. . . where can we go now?" She turned her attention to the steel sphere again. "Even the Moon would be insufficient." She sighed again, searching the sky for dark clouds, the original purpose for her position at the tall windows of the anteroom. "And this Bastard you found. . ." She closed her eyes and shook her head. "His name is ludicrous."

"I believe it's meant to be, milady."

"No doubt." She again regarded the message projector. "If we had more than thirty seconds, would we even consider him?"

"Pointless conjecture."

"I spent ten years building the Hammer's reputation. The name makes slaves' hearts beat faster and rich men's blood run cold. Hand someone a small silver hammer with an order and that order is followed without question. Will this pirate twenty years my junior have any hope of maintaining the legend?"

"No one can live up to the stories, milady. Not even you."

She arched an eyebrow at him.

He ducked his head in apology. "No flesh and blood person can meet the expectations of a legend."

Of course, he was correct. He was always correct.

Soft chittering drew her attention to the sideboard where her clockwork monkey puttered restlessly. He shifted from foot to foot as if bored, bringing a smile to Hope's lips. "At least the man with the ludicrous name keeps excellent company." She stepped closer and reached a hand towards the toy, who jumped from the sideboard to her arm, up her shoulder, and down the other arm. "His partner Scopes is a welcome addition to our inner circle."

The monkey perched on her forearm and reached tentatively for the shiny ball she held.

"It's as if he were drawn to it and afraid of it at the same time. I wonder whether his maker will be able to glean any information from the device."

The monkey looked at Hope's face, rejected the sphere and crawled up to his usual place on her shoulder.

Footsteps echoed against the marble outside the room.

Lady Kennedy drew herself to her full height and crossed to stand beside her Persian, facing the outside door as it opened. She folded her hands at her waist.

"Mr. Scopes and Mr. Bastard," the butler announced in a bored drawl, "mum."

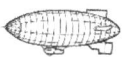

I swept my hat from my head and bowed deeply. "Lady Kennedy, your invitation does us great honour." The hats we'd picked up on the way. They were all the rage, shorter than top hats, with narrower, rakishly curved brims and creased tops. "And my sincere condolences on your husband's passing."

The butler left.

Scopes and I straightened.

"Your name is ridiculous," Lady Kennedy told me.

"It's meant to be." I replaced my fedora and gave the brim a brush with thumb and forefinger. "But you can call me Hammer anyway, I presume." I approached her and extended my hand, expecting to kiss hers. "It is indeed a pleasure."

She grabbed my hand in a strong grip and shook it as would a man. She was a striking woman, somewhere between beautiful and handsome. She wore a brown dress that leaned towards bronze and flattered her figure without compromising her position of authority.

Not allowing my eyes to leave her face, I scanned the room peripherally. Old but immaculate furniture filled the space: a desk, leather chairs, life-size portraits. Several floor-to-ceiling French doors dominated one wall and opened onto a balcony.

As soon as Scopes moved in to shake the lady's hand, the clockwork monkey on her shoulder sounded a shriek and leapt for my friend, clearing the space easily, chattering away and grooming the hair on the side of his head.

Scopes delighted beam fell to ash as he turned his attention to the astonished ambassador. "I'm sorry, ma'am. He must. . . he must have leftover babbaging. . ."

She approached Scopes as she would an old friend. He pulled his hat from his head and held it against his chest.

I kept mine where it was.

"He *knows* you. . ." she declared. "*You* as opposed to anyone else? How do you do that?"

Scopes blushed at the attention. He lifted the lapel of his jacket to reveal his own silver hammer pin. "He recognises this," Scopes admitted. To prove his point, the monkey shrieked and grabbed at the pin, then tried to gnaw on it. "It emits a signal. I programme them all to return to it in case someone tries to steal one from the store. I must have forgotten to remove the babbaging on yours. . . but didn't the baroness of Georgia buy this one?"

Lady Kennedy smiled. "Actually, she's the president now, but, yes, Margie bought him for me."

"Yes, yes, I forgot." He hit himself on the forehead in that nauseatingly endearing way of his. He tickled the monkey to distract it from the pin. "I can remove the babbaging for you, lady."

"Actually, he may prove useful as a messenger." She stroked the little toy's head. "Can you increase the range of the recall?"

I noticed that the Persian, at least, hadn't forgotten my existence. "Perhaps we should continue with the Hammer's interview, lady?" He regarded me with a friendly smirk, most likely reading my perturbation.

"Not that I'd want to interrupt such important affairs of state," I snarked, favouring Scopes with a dark look.

He blushed, startled at my tone.

Lady Kennedy didn't even bother to glance my way. She idled with the toy on Scopes' shoulder. "I haven't forgotten you, Mr. Bastard." She paused to roll her eyes before finally returning her gaze to me. "Why have you accepted this proposal?" Before I could more than open my mouth, she waved a hand at me. "Forget the first five reasons you rehearsed with Avery while you bathed." She folded her hands at her hip. "I don't have time or patience for bullshit. No sane man would say yes to this."

She'd meant to startle me. It didn't work. Of course her Persian had told her Scopes and I shared a room with a tub in it and, of course, she had complete records on both of us. Victoria and Edward as well, to be certain. Foul language on a woman certainly wasn't going to shock me.

"Fair enough," I returned.

She was correct in her assessment, though. No sane man would accept her offer and the speech she'd cut off would've been bullshit.

I watched Scopes putter with his toy. A faint smile played at the corners of my mouth, then faded as the line stretched tight. "I just lost a boy who was like a son to me. I'm not losing Scopes or Victoria."

My friend looked up at my sentiment.

"I don't give a damn about the Empire, milady," I admitted, "and the human race as a whole isn't worth a tinker's fart, but I will destroy anyone who tries to hurt my family. . . even if it's a bloodthirsty Martian with an entire fleet against me."

She regarded me with the most intelligent eyes I have ever seen. Finally, she said, "Bravely put."

I laughed raucously, surprising her. "Bravery? Bravery has nothing to do with it, milady. I'm just terrified of being alone." Silence steeled over us, and I think I shocked everyone—perhaps even Scopes—with my candour. "You said we don't have time for bullshit, milady, and you're right. We don't have weeks, months, or years to get acquainted. So. . . this is me." I held my arms out to my sides. "Can we skip the playful banter and tedious jockeying for position? You're in charge, and I will follow your orders to the letter unless I'm in the field and they no longer work, at which point I will pull my insanity out my ass and save the day for humanity if I am able." My hands stayed out at my sides while I awaited a response.

Lady Kennedy nodded and turned to her Persian. "His name is ridiculous."

The Persian nodded but apparently in good humour. "You can always call him Hammer, milady." He actually winked.

"I suppose I shall have no choice then, if only to save him from his own bad taste." She sighed and held her hands behind her back, her demeanour grave. "I believe our sense of humour is the only thing that will keep us sane in these times, but the gentlemen you need to convince have none, I am afraid. You needs must meet the president and her advisors, and they shall *not* be an easy audience."

The new president and ambassador found their friendship politically dangerous, now, so Margie needed to distance herself. She would speak out vehemently against my inclusion, creating an apparent rift between the two women.

"So when the men throw someone under the omnibus, it's only me," Lady Kennedy said.

"When? Not if?"

She smiled bitterly. "With these men in this situation, it's only a matter of time before someone sells us out."

"What happens to you? Recruiting the Hammer is your idea."

"What an excellent question," she remarked, "one of dozens whose answers won't present themselves until it's far too late to matter."

We passed the next few hours in training. I learned everything I could about the Hammer and quite a bit about the politicians I'd meet, a sorry sack of weasels in my humble estimation.

When my brain reached a point of saturation that could only be quelled by a really good scotch, I changed directions a bit. "So what do you have in the way of plans?"

Lady Kennedy held up the metal sphere she'd rolled in her hands the whole time we'd conversed. "This is what we need to overcome." She placed it on the table amongst the papers and books, depressing a small black circle that was the only ornament on the device. "It's also the only clue we possess to the Kla'arkian technology."

Scopes and I hadn't seen the flicker of the devastation at Kawasaki. Needless to say, it horrified and impressed us beyond measure. Once the images played out and the device powered down, Scopes snatched it up for examination.

"Milady," I muttered, using her title without the least hint of sarcasm for the first time.

She raised an eyebrow and gave me her full attention.

"What possible hope do we have against these machines?" I shook my head. "Really?"

She folded her hands on the table before her and glanced at the Persian before speaking, as she so often did. Her eyes seemed less guarded, her face more open. "Perhaps none, but I've fought against the Empire for ten years with little hope of winning that battle either." She fixed me with grim determination. "Would you have us surrender?" She raised the index finger of one hand. "Submitting to this invading force is still on the table and the public face of the Confederacy will do so, I am certain. Perhaps it is the most sensible way to ensure the continuation of the human race. What would *you* have us do?"

I scrutinised Scopes. Did we possess a chance—*any* chance—of defeating the invaders? I glanced at the device.

So did Scopes. He pressed the button and the images returned. We studied them in silence for a long minute.

My hand found his shoulder.

"All machines can be broken," he declared.

"If they had more than the four we've seen, they'd have used them," I supplied. "If they could commit an all-out assault, they'd have done it."

Scopes and I stared at one another. He raised one eyebrow to ask if I would take responsibility for the only option we had for winning this conflict.

I nodded.

His lips curled in the most miniscule smile ever seen.

I turned to Lady Kennedy.

"Millions might die but billions might live," I said. "Am I willing to sacrifice a measurable portion of the human race to save the handful of humans who mean anything to me?" Determination wrote volumes across my face. "Damn straight I think we can win." I watched the images. "It will cost us dear, but it's better than delivering all future generations into the hands of butchers." Scopes gripped my arm, and I smiled at the lady. "When the Hammer strikes, milady, let it be with my hand."

She nodded humourlessly, but with a measure of determination equal to my own.

The same servant who'd greeted us at our arrival led Scopes and me to the council chambers. President Thatcher and her consort, the baron of

Georgia, had the podium. The rest of the chamber lay in a rough circle facing them.

Our announcement and entrance created more of a stir than I'd expected. Apparently, the Hammer maintained as much of a reputation among these esteemed people as Lady Kennedy had intimated. As we moved down a central aisle to take our seats a bit to the president's left, I noticed that many of the politicians wore clockwork limbs and eyes. A further number wore performance enhancing prosthetic attachments to their limbs or covering an eye meant to let the rabble know they were wealthy enough to throw their money away.

The overall motif tended towards copper, steel, and silver, with a few of the more ostentatious and impractical models done up in gold. I spotted Scopes' work easily. More than a quarter of them wore either his designs or pieces obviously created in an attempt to mimic his style. He'd become a national trend without my ever realizing it.

In the middle of the room, a thought stuck me. I grabbed Scopes' left shoulder with my right hand, pressing close enough to speak into his ear without being overheard. "If there's a power outage, I know the actual replacement limbs are dead weight, but what happens to the gauntlets and such?"

The monkey climbed my hand and crawled up to my shoulder.

Scopes' raised an eyebrow. "Purely cosmetic pieces won't be affected, but anything with a physical enhancement will lock in position, I suspect."

"Yours too?" I asked.

He scoffed and drew back for a moment to display how badly I'd offended. Returning his lips to my ear, he muttered, "Of course not. Mine release the moment of a power loss."

A susurration of discomfort circled the room. Whether the consternation precipitated from our intimacy or at the interruption in the proceedings was immaterial. Both amused me. I took an extra moment to trade lapel pins with my dear friend so the monkey would remain on my shoulder. Let them make of it what they would.

A genteel cough drew our attention to the many eyes fixed upon us. "Hating to interrupt, old sweat, but perhaps we could commence the meeting, what?" Gatsby sounded every bit as loathsome as Lady Kennedy had indicated.

With a sweep of my hat, I bowed to the old goat. "My apologies Lord Gatsby, I realise you'll be needing your medication before too long." I rose and replaced my hat, which would insult them all a bit. Wearing hats indoors had become rather inoffensive as gentlemen's hairstyles had grown longer in the last few years, but men of a certain age and position still considered it impolite. Not enough to warrant comment, but impolite enough nonetheless.

"Not lord. . ." Gatsby corrected, as decorum dictated, which was why I'd said it in the first place.

"My deepest apologies, Mr. Gatsby."

Scopes and I took our seats, but I barely had a chance to test the cushion before needing to rise for the first questions. Lady Kennedy's coaching proved invaluable. Without it, the humourless, pedantic, and idiotic men and women who held the reins of one of the largest nations in the Empire would certainly have driven me to hysteria. How had the Colonies avoided devolving into chaos decades ago?

Within half an hour I hated each and every one of those disgusting weasels and would've felt similarly disposed against the president had the ambassador not warned me that she antagonised me, in fact, as a ruse. Clever yes, but annoying as Hell nonetheless.

"What do you possibly think you might do against a power such as this?" she demanded after yet another replay of the blasted flicker. She cut an imposing figure in a severe black dress, gazing down at us from the bench, a woman born to wield power if ever I'd met one. And I'd met more than one.

"The Railroad asked me the same question of an Empire with the power to defoliate most of Brazil in one fell swoop." I spoke calmly, arms at my sides and hands in my back pockets with a casual indifference I had been told infuriated old men. "I've freed over ten thousand slaves, and you only found me because I volunteered. . ." I paused and weighed just how self-serving I could be. . . oh, what the hell. "And I'd've never done *that* if the Persian wasn't so demmed persuasive, what?"

I met the handsome man's gaze and worked hard to add a sparkle to my eyes.

The Persian scowled, apparently unimpressed at my impersonation of Gatsby.

I addressed the assembly. "Concrete plans would be pointless at this juncture. We need to see what exactly these Kla'arkians intend to do. I offer my resources on the Railroad as a means of communication. Once Lord Archeron tips his hand, we'll need a system in place to respond as best we can."

The president pounded her fist on the podium with a better performance than I'd seen on any stage. "As best you can? What bloody help will you provide against *that*?" She pointed at the flickering images. "What will they do if they discover we plan to oppose them?"

"They already know." Lady Kennedy's voice broke out across the room like a trumpet.

Perplexed babbling filled the chamber.

As startled as the rest, I exchanged a glance with Scopes, who seemed equally nonplussed.

"What what?" Gatsby's voice carried over the chaos.

Lady Kennedy rose to her feet and spoke with a much smaller voice, immediately stilling the uproar her comment had caused. "Lord Archeron certainly knows I'll plan some kind of rebellion, which, I suspect, is why he chose me as ambassador."

Gatsby sputtered. "That was just a demmed coincidence, what?"

Lady Kennedy scoffed. "Nothing that man does is chance." She spread her arms wide to invite examination. "Look at me. I'm a daughter of the Empire. My father was Winston Churchill. My maternal grandfather was a LaFollette." She closed her arms and folded her hands at her hip in an already familiar gesture. "He'll be astonished if I *don't* lead a revolt." She raised her chin defiantly. "When he exposes the rebellion it shall be *my* head on the block." She turned to me with a wistful smile. "And the Hammer's, of course." She turned to the president. "We take full responsibility."

The president shook her head for several seconds. "I can't let you do that, Hope," she said, her voice sad and desperate.

The ambassador snorted a single, decidedly unfeminine laugh. "How long have you known me, Margie? How much luck did my father have forbidding me from marrying John? And he, my dear friend, was a Churchill."

The women stared at one another for several moments, and they might as well have stood in the room alone for all that the rest of the assembly mattered. We were merely witnesses to the most exceptional example of the art of political thespianism the world had ever seen.

At last, President Thatcher rose from her chair. "Then I wash my hands of the entire affair, Madame Ambassador."

The room filled with the scraping of chairs and the rustling of trousers as thirty gentlemen raced each other to be the first to rise. Margie swept from the room without another word.

Lady Hope Kennedy had lost her beloved husband the day before.

She'd acquired the least desired political appointment on the planet.

Now, she'd made an enemy of a childhood friend, a friend whose Presidency *she* had secured. She stood in the middle of a sudden hurricane of posturing old men, her chin raised an inch and her eyes closed while she regained her famous composure.

I wanted to applaud.

Lady Kennedy's servant hurried Scopes and me out of the room before politicians mobbed us with questions, the answers to which we'd quite likely not know. When we reached the original antechamber, we found an unexpected visitor. No sooner had the ever-present bored servant closed the door than my little Victoria strode across the room with her skirts aflutter, stopping inches from me and shouting directly into my face.

"Why the hell do you suppose it's all right for you to run off like that without telling me where you are?" Victoria's fists settled on her hips.

"How did you get in here?" I demanded without much hope of an answer.

"Don't you dare try to redirect me, Zen Bastard." She pointed a finger that had to be loaded. "What the hell is going on?"

"Perhaps I can best explain that, my dear." Lady Kennedy's voice from the doorway projected quiet dignity.

"Milady." Victoria's eyes widened and she dropped into the deepest curtsy imaginable.

Lady Kennedy brought Victoria to her feet with a single finger under the girl's chin. "Hello, Victoria. I've heard so many lovely things about you... allow me to apologise for your guardian's disappearance. I'm afraid I swept him from the brothel to the Palace myself." She favoured Victoria with a warm and generous smile. "I understand your loyalty so much better, Zen. She does render the world a place worth saving, doesn't she?" Returning her gaze to the stunned girl, Lady Kennedy placed an arm around her shoulders. "I'm afraid I need to borrow your guardian so I can try to save the world, my dear."

"Poppa Zen?"

The ambassador chuckled. "I completely understand your astonishment." But her gaze on me felt teasing. "How could such a ne'er-do-well ever save a penny, let alone a planet?" She moved towards the door with Victoria in tow. "Strangely, he managed a serviceable job with a load of grumpy old men." She looked at me over one shoulder as she reached the exit.

"More than serviceable," she admitted. "Please get some rest, gentlemen. The Confederacy's most self-important politicians will arrive during the night, and you'll need to be fresh to exasperate them as well as you did this lot today." She squeezed Victoria's shoulders. "I'm going to treat this darling young woman to a few things, but I promise to make sure she's back in her room before her curfew." She swept Victoria from the room with assurances of new gowns and a place of importance in her retinue.

When the Persian made to follow the women, Lady Kennedy simply waved him back with one hand, leaving him stranded in the room with us as the door shut in his face.

At a bit of a loss, he turned blankly to my friend and me. "It would appear that your daughter will be joining us."

"So it would appear." At a bar along one wall, I poured two scotches neat, then raised the bottle in the Persian's direction. "Would you join us?"

He nodded and crossed the room with Scopes.

I poured a third drink. As I handed him the glass, our hands touched with a tiny electrical discharge that startled us both. My heart perpetrated cliché by skipping a beat as did my breath by catching in my throat.

"Apologies, milord," I said.

He raised his glass to me. "May you keep surprising me."

"And so say we all," Scopes intoned and slammed back his drink.

"There is a saying in Ireland," the Persian informed us, glass still upraised. "When you make a toast between friends you must hold each other's eyes or find yourself doomed to twenty years of bad sex."

I froze. I scarcely breathed. Was he flirting with me?

He slowly brought the glass to his lips where the slightest intimation of a smile hovered.

I did the same.

He raised an eyebrow, and we both tipped the expensive liquor down our throats, not breaking eye contact even for a moment. We held the contact after the toast until he looked away and carefully placed his glass on the bar.

"Twenty years of good sex for us both." He nodded to me and to Scopes before gliding to the exit. "Thank you for living up to my expectations today, Hammer."

And he left.

"Was he *flirting* with me?"

"I. . ." Scopes grabbed the bottle, filled the glass with a double and tossed it back. "I have absolutely no idea."

I favoured him with my most acerbic glare and nudged him in the ribs with my elbow. "How could that *not* be flirting?"

He tipped a double or more into my glass and gestured for me to drink. "This is worth more than you or I made last year. Drink it." I complied and he poured. "He could be playing with you. He could be sucking up to the new boss."

"I'm only a pretend boss," I corrected. "Lady Kennedy calls the shots here."

"Pretend sucking?"

"Let's refrain from the sucking imagery."

"And so say we all."

We took the other bottle of scotch with us.

Chapter Seven

The city lay frozen, but moving.

Scattered amid the Palace gardens, elegant men and women smiled up at the Tesla Tower. Hair and skirts and great coats shifted in the breeze, but slowly as if underwater. The Tower's lights filled the haze with a wondrous luminosity, washing the pale faces nearly to white.

The colours bled too deep and rich, though, the contrast too sharp. The great glass coliseum from the world's fair a decade ago lit the night like a great aquarium filled with hundreds of unmoving pedestrians like mannequins behind glass.

Inside the Dome of the Confederacy, beams of light shifted and played over the statues like moonlight through the depths. I swear tiny streams of bubbles played over the scene at the edge of my vision.

Vision. . . that's what it had to be. A dream. Surreal. Only for the night. . .

Water Gardens, silver spray held in time as solidly as the sparkling, clockwork dancers.

A croquet field empty in the night, but a balcony on the third floor drew my attention, glass doors open and ghostly white curtains billowing slowly towards me, beckoning.

Rising from the field, passing through the glass doors, I found myself in a bedroom at the Palace: Oriental rugs, Victorian furniture, a four-poster bed with curtains drawn back to reveal a woman in repose, hair spread on the pillow, face peaceful.

The wind shifted and the curtains billowed into the room now.

Clouds boiled into existence over the city.

Rippling beams of light flickered across the room.

The lightning started.

The screams reached me next.

Lady Kennedy awakened and sat up. Lightning struck the balcony, arced from the shutters to the bed posts, and incinerated her. Her screams chilled my blood. Her hair crackled and burned. Her skin melted.

Her body convulsed and exploded.

Outside, the city devolved into chaos. I reeled at the sudden change in perspective as I looked up at the demon ship, the hideous steel manta ray vomiting electric fire from its mouth, ten times larger than I remembered and covering the city under its wings.

Lightning flashed. The world's fair coliseum detonated, then the Tower, and then the Palace itself, but everything moved so slowly. Like flies caught in amber, refugees ran at a snail's pace through the streets. Bolts of electricity caught them, screams cut short by fire and death.

The Tower toppled.

The unirail leapt from its track like a cracked whip and tumbled into the art museum, crumbling marble as if it were wet tissue.

Then the vision skipped and shook like a damaged flicker. It reset to Lady Kennedy's bedchamber. She sat up as if startled, her frightened gaze on the glass doors. Throwing the bedclothes to one side, she slid from bed.

She crossed the room.

She stopped on the balcony, longs waves of white cotton nightgown flowing behind her, pasted to her body like a second, naked skin, her delicate hands bleached white as they clasped the black iron railing.

Her gaze drew my attention to the croquet field below.

Lady Hope Kennedy stood frozen in the field in her travelling cloak, one arm upstretched and pointing at the demon vessel lurking above. Her Persian held his place at her side in his best suit, an arm protectively about her shoulders, one hand uselessly frozen on the pommel of his sword. As everywhere, their bodies were frozen in time but details like hair and clothing flowed about them like seaweed caught in the tide.

Lightning struck them, but the scene shifted and danced yet again.

A hillside outside the city. A steam driven vehicle of some sort hurtled down a country road away from a city in flames. Lady Kennedy and the Persian huddled together behind a railing on a rear platform of a. . . a caboose? While the vehicle sped away like hell-on-fire, the two of them stood motionless, long hair floating in the actinic air.

Their carriage reached a bridge and crossed a great river as jagged talons of electricity leapt from cloud to cloud, pursuing them.

The Persian pulled his ward closer as the lightning closed in.

The moment they cleared the far side of the river, a thousand fingers of blue-white light struck their conveyance and latched on.

It exploded in a brilliant white fireball.

The Persian and Lady Kennedy burst into particles.

The scene flickered once more and the lady lay quietly in her bed, the moonlight a pale blue through the closed French doors. Nothing moved. Nothing shifted. She held a pillow as a small girl would clutch a doll for comfort, and she wept silently into it, silent so no one would hear her sorrow.

"Zen!"

Pulled violently out of sleep, my disorientation frightened me.

Gasping for air and drenched in sweat, I clutched Scopes as tightly as Lady Kennedy had held her pillow. "They're dead! They're both dead!"

"It's okay, Zen. You're safe, now." He held me calmly while my eyes rattled around the room, recognizing the walls, the cheap paintings, the bundles of our belongings.

"A dream." I sucked in a calming breath, held it a moment. . . and released it slowly.

"Must've been a hell of a doozie. Was it a premonition?" He brushed the hair from my face with the hand not pressed against my chest. "Your heart's racing and you're burning up." When I didn't speak right away, he pulled me closer, murmuring words of comfort.

One thought burned through everything I'd seen. I didn't have time to tell Scopes the dream as I usually did. If I'd experienced one of my true visions I had no time at all. Staying still to get my breath back more quickly, I spoke quietly into my friend's shoulder.

"Why would an enemy with that kind of firepower levee an ultimatum with only one possible response then allow us twenty-four hours to reply?"

He sat silently for a moment. Then he snuffed in surprise. "To allow us to gather all our leaders in one place."

"I have to save the ambassador." With a final squeeze for the nape of his neck, I disentangled myself from my friend and the sheets. "She's the only one with a brain in the entire lot."

"You? Not we?" He stopped with one knee still on the bed.

I drew us nose to nose, throwing all my sincerity into my voice. I *needed* Scopes to understand. "You have to get Victoria out of the city. Once you have her safely away, and I save Lady Kennedy, you'll find me. I'm the Hammer, now. I'll be on the Railroad, and you can find me."

His eyes remained decidedly unhappy.

"I'm going into the centre of the danger, Scopes. We *can't* drag Victoria into that. Not after Eddie." I had yet to find the time to truly deal with the boy's loss, but life kept driving us forward. We had no time for tears.

His eyes softened.

"You *know* there is no one on this planet I would rather have at my side going into the fires of Hell," I told him, "but you need to get Victoria to safety. Please."

He gave me one sharp nod. He understood.

I released him and rushed to the wall, pounding it with a fist. "Victoria, darling! We're on the run again."

Pants. I needed pants.

Scopes held my drawers in one hand and trousers in the other.

I grabbed my trousers and struggled into them in a rush. "We'll deal with all this later, I promise. As soon as we save the world."

"You have to go before she sees you." He threw the drawers to the side and started pulling on his own clothes. "You don't have time to argue with her."

As I finished buttoning my trousers, he already held out my shoes, a shirt, and the coat that held the most weapons. Taking them, I hurried to the window, pulled out a hidden wad of cash, and passed it to him. "Take all the money. I'll be with one of the wealthiest women in the world. I won't need money if I save her, and if I don't save her I won't need money anyway."

"Don't." His eyes narrowed to slits.

My shirt went on inside out. "Sorry." I felt much the same.

Scopes face told me he feared we'd never see each other again. He moved closer to embrace me, but if he hugged me, I'd lose my conviction. I shoved my hand between us and clasped his wrist instead. He returned the hold in a soldier's grip. . . a warrior's. . .

"I will see you again *soon*," I said with conviction. "No need for all that." It had to be true. I'd make it true.

He gave me one sharp nod, and his grip tightened. "Make sure that big, fucking Persian looks after you for me."

His bravery nearly shamed me to weeping. But, no. . . no time for thinking, no time for sentiment, no time to do anything but get the job done. Bravery happens when you don't take the time to ascertain how well and truly fucked you are.

A knock at the door propelled me into motion.

"Soon," I insisted. "Tomorrow."

"Tomorrow."

I'd run halfway down the alley by the time Victoria leaned out the window shouting obscenities after me. I didn't respond, didn't turn for one last look. No pillar of salt for me.

The water engulfed me again, embraced me in its cold depths. The world pulled away as I hopped at the corner for one shoe and the other, then ran all the way to the stables before Scopes changed his mind or Victoria broke free of his grasp with one of the moves I'd taught her myself.

Just run.

Don't think.

Don't feel.

Run.

"You'd better think about stealing another horse, mister." Inside the stables, a familiar shape hovered in the shadows near our horses. "My master doesn't take kindly to horse thieves. Oh. . . master Zen."

I pulled the stall open. "Not master, boy. Never call me master. Call me boss if you have to, but never master."

"All right, boss." Now that he knew he didn't need to fight, he knuckled the sleep from his eyes. "What are you doing up in the ass end of the night? Some kind of secret mission? Can I help?"

I already stood on the mounting block and pulled myself up. No time for saddle or bridle.

I looked down at him. He might be a help. Nothing more.

A dark, blank face appeared briefly before me, but I forced all thought from my head and reached a hand down to the little bugger. "Hang on tight, Twist. We're riding fast."

With a grin, the boy used the block to leap up behind me. As I kicked our mount into motion, he wrapped his arms around my waist and did as told.

The city lay quiet.

Too quiet, like a cemetery.

The sound of our galloping hooves rang through the empty streets. I slowed for no one. The few pedestrians out so late or so early ran shouting out of my path, raising fist or finger as we passed like a storm.

But none of them stood frozen and nothing moved too slowly.

Especially not us. We reached the Palace in record time, and I reined in at the guard station, letting Twist slide down ahead of me.

"What business at the Palace?" one of two guards demanded before my feet hit the pavement.

"I need to see Lady Kennedy immediately." I passed him a small silver hammer she had given me just that day. She'd told me to use it in only the direst of circumstances and that she would respond to it immediately.

"That's not going to happen." The guard turned the hammer over in his hands with a blank expression. Apparently, the guards hadn't been apprised of its meaning, yet.

"Strangely, I'm fairly certain it is." I hurried to the gates impatiently and grabbed a fistful of iron in both hands.

Twist noticed the item in the guard's hand and jumped in excitement. "Crikey! I've been working for the bloody *Hammer* all this time?"

Pretending to gaze up at the Palace itself, I carefully attached one of Scopes gadgets on the unseen far side of the gate.

"Just get away from there now." The guard drew a sword.

Catching Twist's attention, I glanced at the ground near the horse's hooves and he immediately understood, dropping to all fours.

I hit the beast's back and touched a switch in one pocket, detonating the tiny bomb I'd attached to the gate. The explosion confused things enough for me to spur the horse through the swinging gates.

"Sorry, gentlemen," I quipped, "but I'll meet you at the Palace."

An alarm sounded. Lovely. That should get her attention.

Several shots rang out and struck the cobblestones on either side of the horse's hooves, but they stopped by the time I reached the centre of the parade grounds, shouting, "The Martians are coming! The Martians are coming!" Hopefully, someone had spoken to the ambassador, and they weren't about to fire a peacekeeper ray at me.

The immense palace doors—that I'd have had no chance of breaking down without another explosive charge—swung open slowly as I approached at speed. My steed clattered about the foyer, sliding on the smooth marble floor.

He snorted in fear, but I managed to calm him enough to leap from his back as Lady Kennedy and her retinue raced down one of the matching curved staircases that lead into the centre of the foyer.

A servant threw a rope around my steed's neck to control the beast as I hurried to meet the ambassador. Lady Kennedy tied her bathrobe over the same white, cotton nightgown I'd seen in my dream.

Several dark clad servicemen descended with her, as did the Persian—the sight of whom brought me to a halt at the foot of the stairs.

By all that was holy, what a sight.

He wore nothing but a pair of thin, white drawers that barely disguised the solid swing and bounce between his legs as he hurried down the steps, sword in one hand. Muscle covered his body and scars criss-crossed his bare skin, only highlighting his robust form without detracting in the slightest.

"Bastard?" The Lady's irate shout brought my attention away from the nearly naked man at her side.

She threw something at me: the hammer I'd passed to the guard out front. "What is the meaning of this? I've only known you for one day, and you need longer than that to earn my trust." She stood before me, three steps up and arms crossed.

"How did you even—" Utterly incapable of stopping myself, I glanced one last time at the Persian before giving her my full attention.

"Pneumatic tube, you idiot," she snapped. "Why are you here?"

Any mention of a prophetic dream might go amiss. "The Martians have no reason to give you a day to consider your response other than to gather all the leaders of the Confederacy in one city where they can deal with them easily." Twist slid to a halt beside me. "You and the president need to leave the city immediately."

She stared at me without moving for the length of one breath. "Are there clouds in the sky? I want to look for myself. . ."

I hurried to block her. "No, it'll be too late. I saw—"

"Saw what?"

Blast. I cast my gaze on the Persian. He'd seen me with the tarot. He'd understood. Maybe he'd trust this as well.

"I had a dream," I confessed directly to him. "I saw your lady die three times, and in one version you stood with her on croquet fields—you have croquet fields?" His face remained expressionless. "In the first she died in her bed wearing that exact nightgown." I indicated the gown with a wave. "I think I've averted that one." I gave his lady my attention. "Please God, ma'am, just get the hell out of here right now. If I'm wrong you can hang me in the morning but get. out. *now*."

She turned to confer with her Persian. Her eyes asked a question.

His nod answered her then he drilled me with an expression that held but one meaning: if I was wrong, I was on my own against her wrath.

I nodded.

"All right." Lady Kennedy waved instructions at the servicemen and women around her.

They ran off in different directions.

"Who's this?" She indicated Twist with a gesture before descending the last few steps and hurrying down the hall, forcing us to trot along to keep up. The Persian kept to her side and three new servicemen and one woman joined us as we walked.

"He's a runner," I explained.

"Fine." Without looking at him, she addressed the boy. "Take the horse."

The woman with Hope handed Twist a sealed envelope.

"Take this to the Drake Hotel," Hope continued without a pause. "The president is there with the visiting dignitaries." Her lips pressed together. "She never even had a chance to move into the Palace." She shook off the thought. "This will tell them where we go. Run!"

Twist, with a grin and a quick salute, dashed back to my horse.

We navigated the twists and turns of the Palace, burrowing deeper into the centre, which seemed wrong. "Shouldn't we be heading *out* of the building, milady?"

Lady Kennedy scoffed without breaking stride. "Do you think we haven't prepared for something like this? Perhaps we didn't know the invaders would be from quite so far away, but we're always ready for an invasion."

She brought us to a halt before a nondescript bookcase, pulled on a volume entitled *The Moral Basis of Individualism,* and stepped back as the bookcase slid straight up into the ceiling, revealing a tiny steel room that had to be an elevator.

"Bloody hell," I yelped as the others filed in, the retinue first then Lady Kennedy, and then the Persian, who grabbed my arm and drew me in beside him before the doors closed.

The car descended at such an unexpected velocity I stumbled into the Persian, who steadied me. My hand landed in the centre of his rippled abdomen, and the muscles twitched beneath my fingers. I pulled away in embarrassment. "Pardon me."

"Not at all," he returned politely.

Lady Kennedy spoke on a telecom attached to the car. "Get her *out* of her bloody bed, damn it. I've sent a runner with the location. I'm not trusting the telecoms with that information." She jabbed a button. "Get the unirails ready for immediate departure."

"A steam train would be better, milady." I spoke to her while facing front. "A unirail will lose power."

Ignoring my words, she continued with her preparations.

The Persian leaned closer. "The unirail is just to get away from the Palace. After that we will transfer to long distance transportation." Even awakened in the middle of the night, he smelled like cloves.

I nodded understanding and forced myself to focus.

Chapter Eight

The car slowed to a halt and the Persian grabbed my elbow, leading me forward as the doors slid open. At first confused by his hold, I stepped into the largest room I'd ever seen in my life. Without his gentle prompting, I'd have ground to a halt and everyone would have piled up behind me.

Busy people rushed to and fro like ants in a colony. We crossed the space with a purpose, and I took in the sights as best I could while the Persian led me.

Men and women in lab coats gathered a bizarre assemblage of equipment: clockwork limbs and animals, clockwork *horses* for God's sake like giant brass toys walking stiffly about on their own, oblivious to the pandemonium.

Unirails sped overhead in every direction and Tesla coils sparked and arced about us, so the invaders couldn't be too close yet.

Military men threw tarps over what could only be giant ray guns of some kind.

Tugging ineffectively against the Persian's hand, I pointed in their general direction. "Want big ray gun," I muttered in disappointment as he dragged me on.

We ground to a halt in the centre of a complex web of unirails that ran out in every direction and disappeared into tunnels all around the perimeter of the underground warehouse. The car before us had room only for two pairs facing one another.

Lady Kennedy pushed her Persian and me into one seat, pressed together side by side in a most distracting fashion. She gestured for her woman to sit across from us while the lady herself took a microphone from a nearby man in a lab coat.

Strangely, the microphone had no wire but her voice boomed out over the space nevertheless. "Please forget the equipment and proceed immediately to your designated escape vehicle, and God protect us all."

The car shot off without a sound and with a surprisingly gentle movement. The beehive of activity sped by below as we glided through the warehouse and aimed directly for one of the small tunnels that led out of the space. As we rocketed into the tunnel, illumination brightened in the car, casting a strange greenish glow.

The Persian's ribcage expanded and contracted, pressing his arm against mine. His bare leg shifted against my trousers. With a deep breath, I forced my more lascivious thoughts aside.

The Persian and I very likely held many lives in our hands.

I could not let my libido distract me.

"What else did you see, Hammer?" Lady Kennedy's voice remained calm and quiet. Even in her nightgown and housecoat, she retained a regal bearing. Perhaps breeding mattered after all.

"They're going to wipe Richmond from the map," I told her. "Most likely all the capitals and major cities. I saw you die in your bed. . . Then in the middle of the croquet field. . . at the back of a. . . caboose." I struggled to remember the details. "On a train, I think."

"How soon?"

I shook my head.

The Persian's hand touched mine. "Tell me one detail that didn't make sense."

I looked down at our hands and then up into his dark eyes.

"Everything floated as if underwater," I said without hesitation.

His eyebrows furrowed. "Sometimes the least significant details carry the most meaning."

"It was repetitive to the point of annoyance." I shrugged. "Does it mean anything to you?"

"Not yet." He pulled his hand back into his own lap.

Just then, the light in the car flickered and died, and the sense of motion, which had been faint but consistent, faded as well.

The ambassador's woman gasped.

Crawling to a halt in the midst of a close tunnel struck me as less than ideal. Could we even open the door without power?

Fortunately, the car coasted forward into a larger room.

"Thank God," the woman muttered.

As we drifted to a full stop, the Persian rose and pushed the glass door out of the way, answering my previous question. He also distracted me by climbing over me to exit the car with an unmistakable shifting in the fabric of his drawers.

I climbed out last with a hand from the perpetual gentleman and examined my new surroundings. We hurried across a much smaller space where a dozen people bustled. A pair of scientists waited beside an oddly familiar, large red omnibus.

"Your message was fortuitously timed," one of the scientists told Lady Kennedy. "We started the gas engine for the lights just a few moments ago and the steam on this behemoth is heated and ready to go." The heavy, dark-haired gentleman gave the omnibus an affectionate thump.

Lady Kennedy grabbed him unceremoniously by the shoulders and forced him up the steps to the little railed platform at one end of the vehicle.

"I say. . ."

"You're going with us, Nevil," she insisted. "You too, Elsie."

The woman, Elsie, started and followed us up the steps without a question.

The Persian grabbed my arm again and drew me to the far end of the platform so the others might pass.

Elsie pushed her eyeglasses farther up her nose and regarded me with an almost cross-eyed gaze. "Zen Bastard," she muttered. "The

Hammer. No point." She glanced at the Persian, gave him a very frank up-and-down appraisal. "Also no point. Different reasons." She disappeared into the omnibus leaving me perplexed for the hundredth time that night. . . or morning. . . whichever.

With a chuckle, the Persian moved to the top of the stairs and cupped his hands around his mouth. "Let's be off, people," he shouted with an impressive volume. "Drop whatever you are holding and climb aboard *now*."

They didn't need to be told twice. Together, he and I helped the dozen or so workers into the back of the omnibus as the floor shuddered, and I cried out in dismay.

A strong hand steadied me quickly. "It's just another elevator, Zen." The omnibus rose into the air towards the ceiling. "We're still underground."

"Of course we are."

We approached a ceiling which seemed extraordinarily immobile, but the sound of gears grinding brought a quick release of the breath I hadn't noticed I held. A panel in the ceiling slid quickly out of the way, and we rose into a dim, dusty barn. The moment the platform drew level with the ground, the vehicle shot forward through a cloud of straw dust, and the ancient doors opened onto a dark night.

The Persian gestured at himself. "I should probably dress."

I raised an eyebrow. "Don't bother on my account."

"What are you implying?" He lost his smile and raised an eyebrow at me.

Was that a joke or not?

He broke into a grin and stepped closer.

We stood in silence for a very pregnant moment.

He touched my shirt with one finger. "You've buttoned it wrong." He caught my eyes in his own and undid the bottom two buttons. A finger brushed against my stomach and the muscles twitched. Without dropping my gaze, he pulled the shirt a little away from me so he could fix the buttoning for me without brushing against the close of my trousers.

With his job complete, he ran a hand down my chest to straighten the fabric.

I couldn't breathe. "I really hope you're not still—"

An explosion shattered the night.

A dozen more shook the countryside, and the omnibus slid across the road.

Blue flashes of lightning and the sickening orange glow of fire heralded Richmond's demise. Faintly, distant screaming reached me.

Shoulder to shoulder, the Persian and I stared out into the night with the railing held tightly in our hands.

"I wish I'd been wrong," I murmured.

"Me, too."

Behind us, the door opened and Lady Kennedy suddenly stood between us at the railing. "My God, it's true."

Explosion after explosion detonated, preventing conversation. Others joined us. The skyline above the trees shone bright as more of the city caught fire.

"You saved my life twice tonight, Hammer." Her face grew pale and drawn in the faint glow from the death of Richmond. She didn't turn to look at me. "I guess I owe you my trust, now." Her hair, loose about her shoulders and protected from the wind by the body of the omnibus, lifted to float gently behind her. The fabric of her dressing gown rose, as well.

My heart leapt to my throat.

The Persian's hair drifted up, as did mine. Tiny blue sparks appeared in the air from the rear of our conveyance all the way back to Richmond.

"The atmosphere is supercharged by the airships." Elsie spoke matter-of-factly. She raised a hand and sparks arced between her fingers. Her straight brown hair blossomed into an enormous flower. "It's probably happening for miles around."

"It wasn't a train." I recalled the end of my nightmare. I patted the cold metal railing. "It just looked like a caboose because of the platform and the rail." I pushed past Elsie to the side and leaned over the railing as far as I could.

Ahead of us, the moon shone brightly on the sparkling surface of the Rappahannock River. I recognised the bridge destroyed in my dream. We raced towards the exact spot I had seen for the Lady's third and final demise.

"The flicker ball!" I pushed through the onlookers again and forced my way to Lady Kennedy's side with one desperate hope. "Give it to me, now."

"What?"

"You've trusted me thus far." I thrust my hand out to her expectantly. "You have to trust me one more time."

"I think I've trusted you about as far as I can." She drew the device from her pocket and held it in a tight, unyielding grip.

"You'd be dead if not for me, and you'll *be* dead if you don't take this one step further." Exasperated, I made a snatch for the device, but she kept it away from me.

"It's the only proof we have," she exclaimed. "No one will believe us without it."

The sound of the road changed as we reached the bridge.

I shivered at the memory of her and her Persian vanishing in a flash of light. "Which is precisely how the monsters know you wouldn't go anywhere without it." The air actually tasted like copper. "Give me the damn thing right damn now!"

She hesitated.

Unexpectedly, the Persian snatched the sphere from her hand. He cocked one massive arm and threw the device back the way we'd come. It sailed over the bridge, gathering blue sparks. They spun and whirled around the device in a growing maelstrom that sucked all the energy from the air at the back of the omnibus.

Hair and clothing fell still as electricity arced from the bridge to the metal sphere that finally dropped from the sky. It landed. . . and detonated in a fiery blast that lifted the end of our transportation and pushed us the last few feet to the riverbank.

The omnibus fishtailed twice amid shouts and screams before the driver regained control.

Lady Kennedy stumbled into my arms with a small cry.

The middle of the bridge, where the device exploded, fell to atoms before our eyes.

The entire bridge folded in on itself and tumbled into the river as electricity rippled and washed across the water's coruscating surface.

The echoes of destruction faded away, leaving only the sound of our engine and the distant rumblings of Richmond's demise.

Lady Kennedy didn't withdraw from my grasp. In her eyes. . . was that perhaps something more than gratitude?

"That's three times in one night," she said quietly. "Remarkable." In the midst of tragedy, her smile frightened me. If she should ever develop feelings I couldn't return. . .

"That's why you hired me, milady." I set her on her feet with a kind smile. Her own flickered and faded as she turned to watch the glow on the horizon.

"Who's that?" Nevil shouted, pointing at an approaching horseman. We all turned to follow his finger.

"Oh, what the Godforsaken *hell?*" exclaimed Lady Kennedy. "Can't we have one moment's rest?"

The rider approached from due south with unerring accuracy. The Persian reached for a gun that wasn't there, then seized one from a nearby serviceman.

But the moment some enterprising bloke on the omnibus trained a spotlight on the rider, I recognised him instantly.

"Twist!" I exclaimed with a shout of triumph, waving him towards us. I shoved my way to the side of the vehicle as he reached us and paced us unevenly. "Permission to come aboard, you damn scallywag!" I reached out to him, and he drove the unhappy beast ever closer until he could lift one leg over the animal's back to join the one closest to me.

"Grab me, Persian!" I shouted over a shoulder and trusted that the man would be there. Without waiting for the boy to slip off the animal, I leaned out much farther than was safe and simply grabbed a fistful of his shirt and yanked him from the horse's back. At the exact same moment, strong hands clamped down on the back of my trousers and pulled.

I ended up surrounded by a cheering crowd with the boy's arms around me so tightly I could scarce breathe. Twist's survival was perhaps a miniscule triumph, but it was the only one I had, and I determined to enjoy it.

When the sound died down a bit, the boy's strangled words reached me over the general hubbub. "I was on my way to the hotel, boss, but the clouds started overhead and all the lights went out. . . I knew I wouldn't even make it to the hotel, let alone get all them blokes out of the city." He gulped a desperate gasp of air between sobs.

"They wouldn't have waited, Twist," I reassured him. "I'm sure they got out."

"They can't have done." He shook his head frantically. "The entire city centre blew up." He trembled. "It blew up! I'm a horrible coward. . ."

"You did right, Twist." I dropped to one knee and forced the lad to look me square in the eye. "Avoiding suicide isn't cowardice. It's the right thing to do. We need you alive. *I* need you alive. You did exactly right." I pushed the boy's hair back away from his face.

He gasped a few straggled breaths.

"You did right, Twist. You did *right*."

A moment of peace seemed to flicker over his dirty face before a different and much deeper pain took its place. "It's gone, boss. It's all *gone!*" He threw himself forward into my arms with new sobs. "The city's *gone*."

His terror sobered us. We'd escaped a concerted attempt on our lives and had managed to snatch this boy from the clutches of death. . . but what had we lost?

I rose to my feet but allowed the boy to hold on with his face pressed into my side, my arm around him.

Lady Kennedy stared into the distance. Her lips moved, and I recognised her friend's name. Surely, she didn't blame herself for Margie's death?

The Persian surrounded Lady Kennedy with a massive arm, and she leaned into him for comfort, confusing me further. I considered the rumours that the two of them were lovers. Watching them together, staring out into the shattered darkness, I marvelled that I had ever entertained the notion that either of them might carry interest in me.

Turning my face to the dying embers of Richmond, I finally contemplated my true feelings. I'd done my job, accomplished my duty.

No, it was more than that.

I'd saved the one woman I truly believed had a chance of outthinking the bloody monsters who wanted to hurt the people I loved. If the president had been killed, Hope would take charge.

She would save the world. And thus my family.

But at what cost?

The horizon flickered and glowed with the death of a city.

Did Scopes and Victoria live? Had they escaped?

Twist made it out. So they could have too.

Yes, they must have done. They *must* have. Otherwise my entire mad race to save Lady Kennedy had been for naught.

The omnibus carried us across the dark Virginia landscape, over other rivers and other bridges.

"Don't be dead, Avery," I muttered too quietly for anyone but God to hear. "Please don't be dead."

Part II

The world needs heroes, and it's better they be harmless men like me than villains like Hitler.

~~Albert Einstein

Chapter Nine

Scopes rode hell-bent through the streets, leading Victoria away from the city centre. "Stay with me and don't slow down for anything!" he shouted. "If anyone gets in your way, you run them down!"

Fortunately, at that hour, the streets lay nearly deserted, but clouds covered the sky in a moment as they raced into the Chattel Circle. Electricity jumped from cloud to cloud, and all the lights extinguished at once.

Damn. Scopes navigated by the uneven light from the—

Boom! An explosion from the direction of the Palace!

Victoria screamed, but maintained enough of her wits to keep the horse galloping.

Scopes pushed mount his even harder. "Move, damn it!"

The streets would fill in moments as the residents of Richmond raced outside in curiosity, after which he and Victoria would be doomed.

If only Zen had been wrong.

The ground shook again, and Scopes chanced a brief upward glance.

The clouds glowed orange and red from the fires.

Damn. They were done for.

Lightning struck a building dead ahead, playing along the coppery tiles.

The roof exploded.

"Pull up," he shouted. "Pull up!"

He and Victoria crashed into one another as the horses reared and screamed. He snatched the girl from her horse. At least, they'd die together.

"I'm sorry, Zen," he whispered. "I tried."

A sudden twist of all his internal organs shocked him as much as the white, hot light and golden motes of glitter that filled his vision.

An instant later, he fell forward onto his hands and knees someplace else entirely.

Fighting a wave of nausea, he found Victoria beside him similarly prostrate but less successful at keeping her food down. The horrible reek of hundreds of emptied stomachs hit him then, and he did retch up his last meal.

He helped Victoria to her feet. They'd been instantaneously transported to dubious safety. Scopes recognised the method of conveyance from Lady Kennedy's description of her husband's death, which likely meant they were on the invaders' starship.

Hundreds of other surprised kidnapping victims surrounded them in a huge warehouse of a room. From the malodorous ambience, most of the other abductees had also lost their battles with nausea and, unless he was mistaken, many had also lost control of bladder and bowels. They huddled in groups in various stages of undress from full evening attire to complete nudity. They reminded him of his childhood: frightened, shivering prisoners with no idea of their fate.

How had he been pulled directly off his horse?

"What's happened, Uncle Avery?" Victoria crowded close to him, holding a hand over her mouth and nose.

"We're on a starship, Vickie." He threw an arm around her. "If they wanted us dead, they'd have just left us there for the ships to do the job. We're better off than most of Richmond."

Whilst he worked to gain his bearings, an occasional flash of golden light brought a new arrival who immediately fell to hands and knees retching. In a show of goodwill that impressed Scopes, folks with extra clothing lent jackets or cloaks to the naked.

A brilliant flickering lit the dim recesses above them.

As one, every face turned upwards.

Bloody stupid herd animals, Scopes thought, unable to stop himself from following suit. A blinding white flash was the last thing he saw.

When Scopes opened his eyes, he lay face down on a floor constructed of an unfamiliar material: grey, smooth, and cool under the hand he wiped slowly across its surface. It wasn't tile, though, as the entire floor spread out in one continuous piece. The slightest tremor vibrated it, as well, as though he travelled on a vehicle with the smoothest ride imaginable. Dim light proved him the room's only occupant.

I'd taught him, many years before, to process as much information about an unknown location as possible before allowing any sign of consciousness. Had I accompanied him, I'd likely have chastised him for moving his hand before completing an auditory survey of his surroundings.

Thinking of me brought back the memories of the previous hour. They assaulted his frontal lobe with all the decorum of a rampant freight train.

He sat bolt upright. "Victoria?"

The featureless room contained nothing other than a self-explanatory hole in one corner. It held no doors, no windows, and no Victoria.

He tried to run a hand over the knives and tools in his hair, but someone had shaved his head. The loss of his mane shocked him considerably more than the fact of his nudity.

Once on his feet, he turned completely around several times and came to a halt facing the hole in the floor. Something lay beside it: grey shorts nearly the same shade as the floor and spun roughly from something like cotton. A tie about the waist meant men of various girths could wear them.

The dim light annoyed him. . . but wait, where were the light fixtures?

Letting the drawers drop, Scopes turned his attention upwards. He couldn't see any source for the light. Was the ceiling some translucent material that allowed light through? Or did the illumination spring from the ceiling itself? Standing on tiptoe, he couldn't answer his query. He missed both his goggles and my shoulders.

Stymied, he dropped onto his heels and ran a hand over his itchy scalp.

What did he know?

The aliens had abducted hundreds if not thousands of humans and, most likely, had taken them to the invaders' vessel. They probably intended to use the humans as some kind of labour force, since the invaders would've completed any examinations of human anatomy or behaviour long before initiating an invasion. Further investigations would be redundant.

They'd separated him, stripped him, and shaved his head. His eyebrows and secondary body hair remained intact, so the shaving and removal of clothing must have been a precaution against weapons and/or vermin.

He glanced down at the drawers provided. Why bother with anything? Given the lack of toilet tissue for the hole, they probably existed for sanitary reasons rather than considerations of modesty. He left them where they lay. Would such an action would provoke a response from his captors? It was the only means he had to experiment on them.

A soft glow behind Scopes cast a shadow on the wall ahead. Reminding himself of the reassurance he'd given Victoria, he forced himself to turn very slowly towards the light.

Lord Archeron folded his hands over a cane planted between his feet, dressed exactly as Lady Kennedy had described him. The image glowed lighter than the room, so the projection had to originate from a brighter location. The unearthly luminosity most likely frightened the other captives, none of whom enjoyed Scope's prior knowledge of the Kla'arkian technology.

The commander smiled. "You aren't afraid, Mr. Scopes?"

"If you were going to kill me, I'd already be dead."

Archeron glanced down at the discarded drawers. "The garment displeases you?"

Without looking, Scopes shrugged. "It's fine." His experiment had already yielded fruit: his disregard of the item had to be unusual and unusual behaviours yielded comments from the commander. Therefore, curiosity motivated him just as it did Scopes.

A smile lifted the corners of the commander's mouth. He was also perceptive.

Scopes had played it too casually.

Archeron knew he'd been tested. "You had some very interesting notes and devices on you."

Which explained why he'd separated Scopes. In all likelihood, the others remained together. Isolating every captive would prove inefficient.

Should he ask about Victoria? No. Better not to offer any information at all.

"Will my notes be returned?" Scopes inquired.

"Perhaps." Another smile. "We'd like you to take a few tests."

Well, that sounded better than, "We'd like to perform a few tests on you." And perhaps Scopes could learn a thing or two about his captors from the tests.

"All right." Scopes folded his hands behind his back.

"You're far more relaxed than most of your fellow prisoners."

Scopes decided to try another minor experiment. "Obviously, I am of some use to you. Panicking is an unlikely way to enhance my usefulness. Also, I was born in an internment camp and watched a guard dismember my father a digit at a time while I pretended to be dead so I'd be thrown on the garbage heap outside the camp. I don't panic easily." He paused. "Unless you'd like me to engage in mindless histrionics?"

Archeron laughed and folded the cane under one arm, providing Scopes a wealth of information about his character. "No. . . that will not be necessary." A short silence fell between them then Archeron favoured Scopes with another smile and a small nod.

"Your first test." He vanished.

In his place appeared a large page from a book, covered in mathematical equations and floating in the air much like the pictures from the flicker ball but without any visible projector. While he theorised on how that worked, Scopes examined the equations. They dealt with energy and matter, probably similar to the writings of that German patent clerk who'd caused such a fuss before getting himself killed by the Japanese.

The central section, where the text lay, remained just barely translucent. A nearly transparent border surrounded it with a variety of symbols displayed, none of which meant anything to Scopes. . . yet.

When he'd read the text and made about as much sense of it as he could, he waited for something to happen, but nothing did. The final equation was incomplete.

He stepped close to the image and waved a hand through it from right to left to see whether he would feel anything.

The image shifted, startling him. The flicker whirled for a moment, scrolling in the direction of his wave before settling on a new page of equations. Curious, he passed his hand through the image again, and again it scrolled before halting on new calculations.

While the text shifted, the border remained static. He waved his hand in the opposite direction and the image scrolled that way. He moved it a few times, but the image came to a halt on the original equations and wouldn't regress further.

"Marvellous," he muttered to himself. "I would love to see the babbaging on this."

Immediately, the screen filled the room from wall to wall, and a riot of unfamiliar symbols and equations flashed faster than Scopes could read. It surprised him so much he fell backwards on his ass where he stayed, leaning on his hands and trying to take in the whole room. "Wait. . . wait. . ." He called out. "Slow down."

The image complied, but the text remained completely foreign.

"What language is this?"

A male voice replied. "It is the language used by the analytical engine operating the visual interface. A translation into English would render the babbaging inoperable." That only made sense. All translations utilised some creative license by necessity.

"Can you please render the image smaller again?"

The interface complied.

"Thank you." Pushing up to his feet, he approached the text again. "Show me just the first few lines, please."

It would be hard to say how much time passed while Scopes studied the analytical engine language and the visual interface. He used the hole in the floor once or twice to relieve himself, but he paid little attention anyway. When he lost himself in his work at home, he'd likely have starved without me to drop a plate of food in his lap from time to time.

He learned to manipulate the image as if it were a physical thing, tapping on words to highlight and rearrange text, moving embedded images. At some point, he asked his nameless babysitter to see his own notebooks so he could compare his babbaging language to the one he studied.

"Would you like to see your original notebooks photographically or would you prefer a digitised version?"

What did that even mean? "Both?"

To his right, an exact copy of the first two pages appeared. To his left, another image materialised with the same text rendered as if printed professionally. It reproduced sketches exactly, but showed many of his jotted charts and diagrams as clearly printed images.

"Bloody hell. . ." Scopes drifted close to the reprint and again rearranged a few words and adjusted one of the graphs in light of what he'd already learned.

He tapped a spot. "Add the word 'the' at this point."

The letters appeared.

"Bloody hell. . ." He stepped back and compared the two versions of his notebook. He shook his head. "Unbelievable."

Dismissing the photographic copy by tapping the icon of a knife in one corner, he turned his attention to the modified version and resumed his work. Since the invaders had his notebook, they already knew everything he knew. He might as well see just how much he could learn from *them*.

"Excuse me?" he said to the air. "Can you display my babbaging for the monkey side-by-side with the equivalent instructions in your AE language?"

"Yes," the disembodied voice replied and complied with his request.

Scopes studied the images. "What's your name?"

"I'm sorry?"

The query startled Scopes, who hadn't realised his question would vex his babysitter. He addressed the corner of the room he'd taken as a point of focus for conversations with the disembodied voice.

"Your name," he repeated. "What should I call you?"

"I have no name."

Scopes laughed. "Everybody has a name."

"I have no body, either."

"What?" Scopes crossed his arms over his chest as an idea percolated through his vast intelligence. "Who are you then?"

"I am a function of the ship's analytical engine, its AE, as you call it."

"A function?" The light dawned. "You're. . ." He regarded the hovering images and considered the complexity of their visual interface. "You're made of babbaging? Like a. . . verbal interface?"

"Excellent choice of terms," the interface complimented. "Determining adequate terminology in the language of a culture devoid of technological analogues creates difficulty."

Well, Scopes had struggled through many conversations where he'd tried to explain his work to me—who often didn't have the vocabulary for it. He smiled. . . but only a moment. Was I even alive?

"Bloody hell." He took a deep breath. He had no way to know what happened outside his room. If he found the means to prove himself valuable to his captors, he might bargain for information on Victoria or the world below. The vast information he'd already gleaned in his brief study of the invaders database outstripped his prior prodigious knowledge. They'd learn nothing from him they hadn't discovered centuries earlier, so why hold back?

Also, the interface had complimented him, which seemed remarkably complex behaviour, vastly more complicated than necessary for its apparent job. Just how intricate was it?

"How do. . . people usually get your attention when they wish to. . . interface?"

"The occupants of this vessel usually activate me through my designation."

Scopes crossed his arms. "They just say Interface?"

"Yes."

"I can't do that." Scopes smiled, the beginning of a plan already forming. Could he turn the invader's own system into an ally? Was it complex enough? Or independent?

"Why not?" the interface asked.

"I'm just not made that way." Scopes moved back into position to study the visual interface while he spoke to the verbal. "You talk to me like a person, so I should treat you like a person." With a sudden inspiration, he waved both images out of existence. "Can I see *your* babbaging?"

"Of course."

Thirty screens popped up to fill the room, a dizzying series of glyphs and symbols sprayed across them. He'd known it had to be vastly more complex than the visual interface but the technical barrage stunned him. An incomprehensible three-dimensional image ran through a space at the centre, a maze of tubes and flashing light.

"This is the simplest representation available," the interface explained.

Scopes laughed, trying to take it all in. "All right. . . never mind. . . I'm too stupid for this, I presume. . . But. . ." He shook his head and sat cross-legged to watch the dizzying maze. "I simply cannot call you Interface." The more he examined the image, the more it resembled a working brain. "Tell you what, in my world Babbage is a name. May I call you Babbage?"

A long pause followed. "If. . . you. . . like?"

No. This interface couldn't be a mere tool like the visual. Why should he pause so long between question and answer? Babbage obviously processed information much more quickly than a human. His hesitation told Scopes he might be made of babbaging, but in some ways at least, he thought like a person.

"All right, Babbage. Let's get back to work."

"All right, Scopes. I should. . . like that."

Scopes smiled, confident he'd made a new friend. Theoretically, the interface might be as much a prisoner as the humans. If so, he could make a formidable confederate, especially if he enjoyed any small amount of independence.

Oh, Zen, he thought, *what am I getting myself into?*

Chapter Ten

Lady Kennedy's omnibus brought us to an Underground Railroad hideout in Norfolk the night of the Devastation. That's what people named the destruction of the capitals and all semblance of government: the Devastation. President Thatcher was presumed dead, and Hope simply rolled up her sleeves and set to work as predicted.

The new world order started the following morning. An airship arrived at the edge of town and crept towards the city centre with a dozen or more flickers of the commander walking on the ground beneath it across several blocks.

"Do as you are told and you will not be killed. Disobey and we will exterminate you."

The ship moved faster than the images walked, so the flickers at the back faded out and new ones appeared at the front of the queue.

"Obey and live. Fight and die." Like the Pied Piper, Archeron led the refugees to the city centre.

Against Lady Kennedy's wishes, Twist and I followed.

When the ship halted, a package materialised on the ground below

"These flyers are to be handed out and pasted everywhere. The human race has a new master, and his name is Archeron." The many flickering images coalesced into one.

A tin badge appeared in the air before him.

"This is for the person who takes control of this city in my name. It establishes your right to act on my behalf."

Twist nudged me.

I shook my head. "In all likelihood, it also allows him to track them."

The boy's eyes opened wide. For a street urchin, he remained remarkably naïve.

"I don't much care who directs the chaos." The image of Archeron walked around the badge. Let the worst of the human race rule. Once he'd stripped the planet and left us to rot, our legacy would be irrelevant.

I fixed the face of the man who took the badge in my mind, then Twist and I returned to the hideout, an old barn with a rather extensive underground facility that had housed a regional centre for the Underground. I connected to the Hammer's—my—extensive network. The Railroad remained a lifeline for communication. Underground cables connected all the major cities in both the Confederacy and Canada, and we put out word for my family.

Nuke, Sal, Scot, and Basil Rupert found me the first week. All four Sneaky Pete brothers showed up a few days later. They were mighty surprised to discover their old drinking buddy Zen Bastard was, in fact, the Hammer.

This group I told the truth. Trusting them with our secret made more sense than expecting them to believe I'd pulled the wool over their eyes for years. Since nearly all my other compatriots had died with the *Aquatic Railroad*, these few alone knew the truth.

Two weeks passed with no word from Scopes or Victoria. While I found a certain measure of joy in each reunion, the one that truly mattered still eluded me.

Three weeks after the world had changed, nothing remained of Richmond, Virginia but a horrible crater. They'd burned the damn thing almost perfectly round, one of dozens of illustrations across the country that the human race existed only by their beneficence.

Nothing by broken rock, melted steel, and ruptured concrete remained. Everything else had charred into ash. They hadn't even left us bodies to bury.

Seven of us rode to Richmond that morning, including Hope and her Persian. No one spoke for a long time. Facing that level of carnage, what could we say? The human race had never known the like. Our entire world had transformed and not for the better. My mind couldn't conceive the scale.

So I pushed it out of my mind. I had work to do. If I was the Hammer, I intended to perform as the real thing and not just a figurehead. We'd come. We'd seen it. I turned to go.

"They'll find us," Nuke Johnson said, his inimitable Texan drawl unmistakable. He settled a hand on my shoulder. "We found you. Scopes is smarter than any of us. He'll find you."

"Since he was smarter, he should have found me sooner." I moved away from his hand. Comforting me was Scopes' job.

Damn it. That wasn't fair. I turned back to the crater to regain my composure.

I found Nuke's gaze. "Sorry."

He patted my cheek with a wan smile, and I allowed it though all instincts begged me to pull away. I kicked a rock, and it tumbled a few feet and tinkled metallically. Glad for a distraction, I stepped closer. A flash of light? The stone had struck a ring, a metal band that'd somehow survived the conflagration.

It bore an inscription: ...*let no man put asunder.*

A wedding ring. It lay heavy in my hand, a practical man's ring, not as pretty as gold but durable, meant to last a lifetime. Steel, perhaps. He'd likely worked with his hands a lot. Perhaps a mason or a mechanic.

His ring had indeed lasted a lifetime. . . a short lifetime.

My hand closed in a fist around it.

"What have you found there, Zen?" Lady Kennedy stepped forward to join me, her clockwork monkey whirring on one shoulder. A dull pain throbbed in my chest every time I saw the damned thing.

"Death." I hurled the ring as far as I could. "I found more death."

Her toy shrieked and leapt from her shoulder to scramble amongst the rocks after the sparkling metal.

"Oh!" She took one step and then let the beast alone. She laid a hand on my arm while the monkey leapt and hopped. "He thinks you're playing fetch."

Announcing its success with a cry, the toy bounced up the side of the crater back to me, climbed my leg to my shoulder, and held the ring out, chittering and chuckling like a real monkey.

Scopes had often made a game of my black moods to cheer me.

Without expression, I took the ring and tucked it into a pocket.

Lady Kennedy turned me and affixed something to my lapel. The monkey immediately chirped and grabbed at it, but the lady brushed his hands away.

"You should have him, I think," she said maternally. When she'd affixed the pin, she smoothed the vest I wore. "I call him Jinky."

"Jinky?"

She smiled. "A whim."

"Thank you, Lady Kennedy." Now I was stuck with the infernal contraption.

She shook her head. "Not lady. . . just Hope. Or Mrs. Kennedy if you must." She gazed out over the crater. "The aristocracy has been destroyed. We're all slaves, now."

Fingering the ring in my pocket, I spoke quietly, but decisively. "We have learned once again that this invader has limits." I faced the group, my hands in my pockets. The sight of the women in trousers still struck me as a bit odd. "One airship visits one city at a time, which means the others are probably on the same mission on other continents. Ridding themselves of the world's governments threw the planet into chaos, which creates as much a problem for them as it does a boon."

I studied their faces while I spoke. "I see three goals, and I want to know if y'all agree because the first goal means we needs must get our people in charge of as many cities and communities as we can."

Amazingly, everyone listened with rapt attention. It's stunning how desperately people want someone to tell them what to do when everything goes to shit.

"Thugs and ruffians have taken over because they're the strongest. If we have any chance of avoiding a second Dark Age, we need to keep things civilised."

"Do you want us to build resistance cells?" Sal asked.

"Not yet. We need to keep mankind from devolving into lawlessness first by installing a worthy leadership. That's the first goal." I glanced at the clockwork monkey on my shoulder. "The second goal is to gather the greatest minds we can find, and fast. The greatest minds are rarely very athletic. They'll die quickly under the rigors of manual labour. We need to gather them and protect them."

The Persian stood stone-faced as usual. He'd been quiet since the Devastation, attending to Hope and little else. We hadn't spoken since. . . whatever that seeming flirtation had been.

No matter. His attentions would only distract me anyway.

"The third goal?" Scot asked.

"Libraries and schools," Hope answered for me. "We need to preserve what knowledge we have. We will do our best to drive these invaders from our planet, and even a worst case scenario has them draining the planet of its resources and then leaving us eventually." Her face grew grim. "We need to preserve our history for the future."

"How do we take charge of the cities?" Scot asked.

I scoffed. "How do you think? We kill whoever's in charge and put one of our people in place."

"Zen. . ." Hope's voice was quiet.

I shook my head and moved away from the crater and towards our horses. "We don't have time to be nice, milad. . . mum. Good people run some of the cities. They can keep'em, but villains run most of the commonwealth. We go in and take over what we can." I grabbed my horse's reins and mounted. "Once we have civilised people in charge. . . then *we* can afford to be civilised. Until then, all we can do is try to head off the apocalypse."

My friends mounted their own animals. With fuel production at a standstill since all resources belonged to the Kla'arkians, now, animals had become the transport of the day.

"Does anyone disagree?" I asked.

No one did.

A month later, we'd secured about a third of the cities and assured ourselves that another third were already run by capable hands. The Canadian city of *La Nouvelle* remained a major problem. Former mafiosi saw it as a means of creating a new powerbase. . . one of the few left to humans.

The largest city on the Eastern Seaboard before the attacks, *La Nouvelle* dwarfed the rest because, as it wasn't a political centre, the aliens hadn't annihilated it. The mafiosi kept a stranglehold and didn't seem interested in anything other than stockpiling the resources the city had left. They lured refugees there with assurances of food and shelter, but few of those promises had been kept. People starved while the mafiosi grew fat.

Something had to change.

I called a meeting of the Underground and representatives from dozens of local communities gathered in the spacious barn in Norfolk, Virginia. The hideout became a temporary headquarters for those who hoped to form a provisional Confederate government. It sat away from the city centre, near the water, and the roof had been sealed against the weather. It held lots of hay, a couple of cows and a secret underground bunker that housed fifty of us along with supplies for six months. The final feature remained unknown to the men and women of all colours gathered in the barn above to decide what should happen next.

I sat on the edge of a hayloft, swinging one leg back and forth and surveying the show below me. What remained of the Confederacy's leadership stood in a rough circle.

"What would you have us do?" Mrs. Kennedy raised her hands in consternation. "Hide in this barn until the big, bad man goes away?" Her hair was pulled back in a rather severe bun, and, like most of the women there, she wore trousers, shirt and vest. From behind she looked somewhat like a man, especially her posture, which had become decidedly unladylike as she shed the last vestiges of her aristocratic persona.

Her hands closed into fists and settled on her hips. "I'm afraid the big, bad man *isn't* going away any time soon. And so far most of the people who *are* talking to him are thugs and villains. He doesn't much care who takes the reins of leadership, and many of the men stepping forward thus far make me wonder if the human race is worth saving."

Gatsby, who'd managed to survive the devastation, huffed. He did that a lot I noticed, whenever he wanted to open his mouth with a ragged criticism but realised it might be time to hold his tongue. As much as I'd loathed the man, still, he'd learned some humility and any group such as ours needed a resident devil's advocate.

An elbow in the side drew my attention to the lad sitting close by. Twist nodded at the crowd. Every face had turned to mine expectantly.

I'd missed my cue. Bother. Knowing better than to admit my inattention, I smiled down beatifically as if merely considering my thoughts.

"Hello there." I swung my leg a few more times. My place in the loft gave me a very casual, playful position. . . But they still had to look up at me. Mrs. Kennedy had rehearsed me extensively.

"My communication systems remain fully functional," I told them. "We're gathering intelligence from across the Confederacy, Canada, and Texas, if any of those terms even applies anymore."

I pulled a tin badge from my jacket and tossed it down to Gatsby who stood directly below.

He caught the badge.

"BOOM!" I shouted, just to make him jump. Call me petty. "Archeron hands these things out like toys. It enables the new leaders to contact the invaders and allows Archeron to track whoever has it."

Gatsby cast me a worried glare but again kept his tongue. He turned his attention to the badge, a star with two crossed hammers etched into it. As far as we could tell, the symbol was a stunt to tease the Hammer. . . er, me.

"It's also a bomb," I declared.

Gatsby started so much he nearly dropped it.

Mrs. Kennedy snatched it from him and favoured me with a disgusted glance.

The poor man kept trying after all.

"Sorry, old sweat," I said. "Old habits."

His brows knit for a moment then he afforded me with a formal but not unfriendly nod.

"Stiletto Sal has taken a huge chance for us," I told them. "She's our operative and the mayor of Norfolk. She placed the device in what's called a Faraday cage." I waved a hand to indicate my abilities lay with strategy, not science. "None of us would understand how the thing operates, but it hides this device from the invaders."

"And it's out of its cage, why, now?" Hope continued to prove herself a consummate actress.

"This entire barn is a Faraday cage. . . something in the walls. The invaders can't detect us, and their Tesla waves can't hurt our equipment either." I shrugged. "The thing is. . ." I paused for effect. "Sal's still alive. Her device has dropped off the grid, and there've been no repercussions."

As expected, everyone looked at one another to see who would figure out the importance first.

I nudged Twist, who'd also been rehearsed.

"Right, boss," he said loud enough for all to hear and shimmied down a post to Mrs. Kennedy's side. When he held out a hand for the badge, she gave it him, and off he ran.

"They don't know it's missing." My words brought their attention back to me. "They can't have done. If they did, Sal would be dead. Twist there will bring it back to her, now, safely inside a travel box. She'll open the box when she's far away from us, and all should go on as if she'd never been away from it."

"Should?" Asked an older Mexican woman, Siva, a part of the railroad for decades and Sal's mother.

"Reconnecting to the grid could send a signal." I shrugged. "It's a risk. She knows the risks."

"What does this tell us?" Siva demanded. "What does her risk tell us?"

"They're not omnipotent." I slid from the loft and followed Twist's path to the floor. "Please don't underestimate the importance of that .

information. They're spread thin, now. Decentralizing us prevents any kind of united front against them but it forces them to maintain authority over thousands of separate slave cells. . . tens of thousands. So far, that one device slipped through the cracks for a couple of hours." I placed one hand on Siva's bony shoulder. "It means they're not invulnerable."

Gatsby huffed again. Uh oh. "So we hid one device from them for a few hours. . . In the grand scheme of things how does this mean anything, what?" He looked around for support. "Please tell me you're not all so foolish as to think we can actually repel these horrible monsters."

"We're not going to try to repel them, Gatsby," Mrs. Kennedy said. "But I think the Hammer has a point." She took a few steps forward to address the crowd. "Whilst we cannot move against Archeron now, this sort of information is *important*. It tells us a bit about how their technology works. It lets us know that we understand the principles, and the principals, at least, aren't so different from our own technology. We have a thread to hang onto that our scientists can use. It's a tiny thread now, but if we keep tying the threads together, eventually we'll have a skein, and perhaps we can do something *then*."

Siva stepped forward to face Hope. "But *when*?"

Mrs. Kennedy placed a hand on the same bony shoulder I had. "How long did you fight the Crown, Siva?"

"Fifty years." The old woman smiled. "And there you go being all logical on me again, just when I'm trying to get up a head of steam." Her smile faltered and died. "This is even worse than the Crown."

"Yes, it is," Mrs. Kennedy agreed. "That's why I wish to meet with the mafiosi in *La Nouvelle*, to see if we can come to some sort of terms with them and to discover the extent of their deception. We suspect Archeron hasn't realised that they're siphoning resources away from the work camps he's building. Finding out how they deceive him is another thread in the skein."

She held her hands at her hip in her standard schoolmarm pose. "I also plan to contact Archeron himself."

A round of mutters and exclamations filled the room.

"If I point out how many resources he loses when men like the mafiosi take charge, he just might step in and let us emplace a leadership who'll actually help the people. He might allow us to form a provisional government to avoid the otherwise inevitable lawlessness." She regarded the Persian's tight expression. "I know it's a risk. He tried to kill me once, but he has to know I'm no longer a threat. He spanked the puppy that widdled on the carpet. My goal is to let him know that this puppy, at least, wants to avoid the paper and won't cause any more trouble. "

"But you are, mum." Siva pushed her hands into her skirt pockets. She seemed a woman who'd never feel comfortable in trousers. "This very meeting proves that we're *all* a threat, doesn't it?"

"Not yet, Siva. Not yet. . . maybe not for a generation or more." She turned to me, opening the way for me to step back in.

"Please don't sell us out to the invaders just yet."

A brief commotion rose until I lifted a hand. "I don't blame anyone who believes the only way to ensure our safety is to keep our heads down and avoid attention. A large percentage of the planet's population would probably consider our meeting today treasonous and would sincerely thank you for putting a stop to anything that might get the puppy spanked again, to use Mrs. Kennedy's colourful expression. . . but please wait until we learn more. We're not suicidal. If we learn that we have no way to overcome these invaders, we will preach compliance as loudly as anyone." I held my hands open in supplication. "Just give us the chance to find out."

I took Hope's hand to show our solidarity.

The brief flicker in her eye almost made me regret the gesture.

"If the mafiosi in *La Nouvelle* can pull the wool over Archeron's eyes," I suggested, "then he's just a man like the rest of us." I quickly released Hope's hand.

"But is he a man at all?" Scot's loud voice stopped us all. Good man.

Everyone waited for my response.

"We don't know." I took the centre again. We'd discussed this concept over many nights and many bottles of whiskey. "Every time we see a flicker, it's Archeron. Across the continent at all times of the day or night. For all we know there's actually a herd of tentacled space squids sending us pictures of a fearsome human warrior so we don't realise they can't even stand on two legs." I spread my hands wide again. "The more we know the less vulnerable we are."

The meeting broke up, and my friends and I retired to the bunker below. As we rode the elevator down, Scot nudged me with a question in his eyes.

I nodded. He'd played his part perfectly. I'd coached him to ask the question so everyone would walk away wondering what manner of creature Archeron might be. The less human they thought of him the less likely they were to kowtow.

A bloody squid? the average Confederate would think. *I won't take orders from a bloody squid!*

And Scot needed the encouragement. He would dive fearlessly naked into battle armed with nothing but a sword, but speaking up in front of a group of former nobs terrified him. My nod left him grinning sheepishly for an instant before his usual gruff exterior reasserted itself.

I had aspirations for him and Basil Rupert to mayor a city of their own, but Scott needed to learn how to lead more than a violent charge into battle.

The bunker below the barn held a catacomb of hallways and rooms where the best and brightest we'd found worked on a dizzying array of scientific advances.

Not for the first time, I wished Scopes were there. I'd always known he was bloody smart, but watching the men and women we'd gathered struggling with babbaging and clockworks he'd have solved in his sleep impressed me with how brilliant he'd been. . . how brilliant he was.

We checked on a French gentleman named Perrin whose team had made impressive advances in explosive weapons and rockets. He was convinced we could actually split an atom and that if we did, we'd release a huge amount of energy. When I stared at him blankly after his explanation, he asked the translator if his English was broken.

"Not your English," I assured him. "Merely my intellect."

He nodded, whistling while he passed a hand palm down through the air like a rocket and then clapped his hands loudly. "BOOM!"

"All right, 'boom' I understand." I shook his hand and continued to review our troops.

The attention unnerved me. It bordered on adoration. All these good people knew me by reputation. Correction, they knew the *Hammer* by reputation, and they all wanted his approval, wanted to shake his hand and earn his smile.

Hope'd explained it all: they felt terrified, victims of the most shocking catastrophe to befall mankind in human history. It made children of them all. They wanted nothing more than for Mummy and Daddy to pat them on the head and tell them all would end well.

Ironically, I'd never had that kind of parental assurance as a child. I'd escaped my misbegotten home by the time I reached eight, and the fat man who took me in for the first year was hardly the hugs and sunshine sort. I hadn't known what the word "family" meant until Scopes dropped into my life.

Dammit. Every fucking thought brought me back to Scopes. He haunted my every waking moment, and while all these geniuses and nobles wanted me to comfort them and hold their hands, all I wanted was to sit in a bath while my friend worked on his clockwork toys and we passed a bottle of brandy between us.

"Mr. Hammer?" I looked down at Twist. "Sal and Nuke send their love, sir." He grinned and grew red. "Sal gave me a big kiss to pass along to you, but I think I'll keep it for myself, if you don't mind." His hand went to his cheek.

I nodded and turned back to the maps of *La Nouvelle*.

The lad ran off.

The Persian cleared his throat behind me. "Might I have a word, Hammer?"

I must have blinked three or four times without responding. He'd spoken no more than two words to anyone other than Hope since the Devastation.

"Sir?"

I jumped. "Yes. . . yes, of course."

He turned and led the way out of the room.

Hope's questioning gaze as I followed told me she had no idea what he meant to say, either. I shrugged to express my complete befuddlement.

He chose an empty room, little more than a closet really, and when we'd squeezed in, he shut the door behind us and turned to face me with his trademark blank expression. He crossed his arms over his chest and leaned against the door.

We regarded one another for a few moments while he collected his thoughts. Knowing him to be a man of few words, I waited patiently.

"You never touch the boy," he said at last, completely baffling me. "He needs a pat on the head once in a while. Or a kind word at least."

"I'm not cruel to the lad." I crossed my arms defensively.

"No. . . you're not, but you're not very nice to him either."

My anger rose. "What business is it of yours if I'm not *nice* to the boy? You're a bloody fucking statue to everyone. You're not *nice* to anyone other than your lady."

He stared down at his feet for a moment, but didn't show any sign of moving. When he looked up at me again, his eyes had grown softer. What did that mean?

"I'm sorry," he said. "I misunderstood. It's not that you don't touch the boy." He paused. "You won't let him touch you. You won't let any of us touch you anymore, will you?"

My chest tightened and my eyes burned, but the feelings had nothing to do with the sexual attraction I'd felt for the man. "No," I said. "I won't."

And I wouldn't.

He nodded and let his gaze drop to his feet for a few moments again. "I'm not very good at. . . at. . . walking on eggshells." He looked up at me again. "While I am fairly proficient in English, it is still my second language."

"Just say it."

"There is an excellent chance your family survived. More of our compatriots find us daily. And you have many friends here in Norfolk." His eyes grew dark and intense, but I still couldn't read them. "The more you embrace this role we have given you, the more people will demand from you. If you hold your friends at arm's length, even the friends I saw you sharing intimacies with before, you'll burn out. You're already distant and unaffected, and while that is an excellent façade for a Persian servant, it is catastrophic in a revolutionary leader. I suggested you for your passion. I hate to see it die."

Damn him. My passion? What the hell did that even mean?

He could hold a stare longer than anyone I'd ever known besides a cat Scopes once. . .

Damn it all!

"Scopes and I met twenty years ago," I spit out, "but we haven't always shared rooms. There were several years when we didn't even speak. I think a grown man can cope with a touch of separation anxiety." I nodded at the door to let him know I meant to leave. "While I appreciate your concern, it is unwarranted. The lad is part of the movement. Nothing more." I met his eyes as hard as I could. "As is everyone involved."

Expressionless, he shifted enough for me to grab the doorknob and yank the door open. Escaping into the corridor, I found my way back to the briefing room so we could plan our negotiations with the bastards who held *La Nouvelle*.

Chapter Eleven

"Scopes?"

"Yes, Babbage? Is this ship capable of time travel?"

"No. Time travel isn't really all that practical. And Scopes—"

"But it *is* possible, correct? That's what I'm reading here."

"It's a physical fact, yes, but, Scopes—"

"I understood the theoretical possibilities, but to know it's an actual—"

"Scopes!"

Babbage's exclamation startled Scopes out of his work. The visual proxy he'd created for his friend stood nearby with its holographic hands on its holographic hips. The set of his eyes told Scopes that Babbage had lost all patience. Whatever could be the matter?

"I have your attention?" the analytical engine asked.

Scopes nodded, feeling like a scolded schoolboy, which was ironic considering the proxy's apparent age.

"Your body draws perilously close to starvation." Babbage pointed at two untouched plates of food. "You should eat something."

Scopes stood at the centre of a hexagon of images, interacting with them all at once. Wait. . . holograms. Babbage called them holograms. They displayed the AE language, lessons on micro-gravity, and data on an unbelievable stellar phenomenon called a "black hole" that supposedly inhabited the centre of the galaxy and might be a doorway into another universe.

An entire bloody universe!

The panel on his right elbow updated his knowledge of time travel, which—against all probability—also seemed factual.

Wait. What had Babbage said?

"Starvation?" Now that his friend had mentioned it, Scopes' stomach growled. "Thanks. Guess I forgot again."

The interface's dark face smiled and nodded. "Dig in." He jabbed a thumb at the two neglected trays.

Pausing all the screens, Scopes sat cross-legged by his meal, facing Babbage, who tended to leave his proxy in one place all the time.

Scopes had asked Babbage to create an image, a *hologram*, for two reasons. One, the disembodied voice annoyed him. Scopes preferred directing his conversation *at* someone. Two, Scopes felt lonely. He missed me, missed little things like someone to remind him to eat a meal by dropping a plate of potatoes in his lap. Someone to share his room.

When Babbage admitted to hitting a wall when designing a body for himself, Scopes had offered to fabricate the proxy. He started with a human male figure since the interface used a masculine voice, and he modified it for quite some time before declaring the construction complete.

He'd clothed the figure in a dashing suit with a gold vest, a scarf over long black braids and goggles perched on his forehead. With a dash of whimsy, he'd left the feet bare. As the motionless figure stood there, Scopes felt a bit of pride in his own creativity and wondered what the likes of da Vinci could have done with such an interface.

As soon as Babbage had taken control of the proxy and animated it, Scopes had gasped.

How had he made *that* familiar figure subconsciously?

"What is wrong?" Babbage had asked. "Your pulse has increased and your breathing grown irregular."

Scopes waved off his friend's concern. "I'm fine," he lied. "I just realised that you remind me of someone."

Babbage's smile on the familiar young face had been so different from the original that it at once dispelled a certain amount of the inherent similarity. Yet that, in fact, made the effect a bit more disturbing.

The proxy could have been Eddie's twin brother. Why'd Scopes create a duplicate of his lost adopted son? And how had he done so without even knowing it? Grief was an insidious and unpredictable companion. He'd considered redesigning the figure, but Babbage seemed so delighted that Scopes hadn't had the heart to ask his friend to change. He'd made his bed and he had to lie in it.

As he sat there eating, Scopes watched the proxy's movements. Fortunately, his mannerisms were completely original and significantly reduced the déjà vu of working with Eddie's insubstantial twin.

"Babbage," Scopes said while he ate, "may I observe Victoria?"

"Of course."

A screen popped up, the image of a crew of workers shifting rocks from a pile into transport bins. Victoria diligently scraped up the smallest bits and dropped them in with the larger pieces.

Scopes smiled. She remained such a perfectionist.

He checked on her regularly, watching the surveillance images Babbage called up for him while preventing the invaders from noticing. Observing her was perfectly safe and helped ease his loneliness. Contacting her or informing her of his own well-being remained, however, an insurmountable task, no matter how much energy Scopes poured into a solution.

If only he could let her know that he lived as well. Unfortunately, Kla'arkians monitored the working slaves continually, not just Babbage, so communications *to* her created the peril of instant discovery.

"You can't risk Archeron connecting the two of you," Babbage reminded Scopes.

"I know." And Scopes wondered, not for the first time, how Babbage did so much for him without the invaders' noticing.

Victoria rose to her feet, examined the area under her care, nodded in satisfaction and dragged one arm across her forehead. She'd worked hard all her young life. She'd survive her imprisonment easily, but could Scopes help her at all?

"She only managed to slip under the radar because you are from different genetic stock." Prejudice ran so rampant on Earth that the invaders had not recognised the two of them as family.

"I know."

A Mexican boy about Victoria's age stopped at her side and gestured at the space with a scowl. The girl struck him on the arm so hard he jumped, but then both fell to giggles. She grabbed his arm and pinched it.

The boy pretended it hurt more than it likely did.

She shook her head, and they resumed their labours.

Scopes had seen the young man before. According to Babbage, his name was Drew. At least she'd found friends and enjoyed moments of happiness in spite of her servitude.

"If Archeron suspects you care about her, he could threaten her to gain further compliance from you."

"I know, damn it!" Scopes tossed his scraps into the hole and stepped through the image. "I know." He returned to the middle of the room and squatted down, returning to work. "How could you tell I was starving?"

"From your scans." Babbage squatted in imitation of Scope's frequent pose.

"Scans?"

"Oh. . . sorry, you don't have that technology." Babbage folded his hands between his knees. "We have equipment that can see what's happening inside your body. We call it a doctor machine. I'm attached to it. The closest you have is an x-ray."

Apparently, Babbage operated most of the ship's systems.

Scopes let that thought go for the moment and focused on the more immediate curiosity. "Can I see a scan of my body?"

Babbage rose and turned to anticipate a three-dimensional hologram.

Scopes walked around it while munching on an apple. He noticed things that one only noticed from the outside. . . especially interested in the scar on his back from a knife fight many years ago and the tattoo of a monkey on his right cheek. He'd never had a good look at either of them before.

"How can you tell I'm hungry from this?"

"Oh. From *this*."

The skin on the figure disappeared, startling Scopes. Then the musculature dissolved, replaced with a representation of his circulatory system, including his beating heart. After that evaporated, a vague outline of Scope's body remained with only the digestive system visible.

Scopes held up a hand. "Okay. . . that's even a little too intimate for me." He tossed the apple core in the hole. "Can I see the skeleton and musculature again?"

The image changed as requested, and Scopes studied the way the muscles attached to the bones for a moment before inspiration struck. He called up his journals and scrolled to his designs for his clockwork monkey.

"Can you use these blueprints and the devices you found on me to create a hologram of my clockwork monkey?"

"Of course, Scopes. I'd be glad to do so."

Almost immediately, his most advanced clockwork monkey appeared, slowly rotating in space near the image of Scope's musculoskeletal system. He stopped the rotation and manipulated the figure, stretching it and reconfiguring it based on the model of his own form.

Holy mother, could he really create such a design? With Babbage's help, Scopes superimposed the two images and adjusted the clockwork to match the scans of his anatomy as closely as possible.

Voila, he created a model of a clockwork human that would work. A God damned clockwork human that would walk around and shake hands! He modelled it walking and sitting and performing a number of simple tasks.

Several meals later, Scopes stood with another apple watching the image of his clockwork man jog in circles around the perimeter of the room. He'd designed it in copper and brass since those were the most familiar materials, but he wondered what the invaders must have that would work better.

"Babbage?" He wandered over to the hole to drop in the apple and relieve himself since he was there. "Surely you already have clockworks better than this."

"We do."

"Can you show me what you have? Take this design and replicate it based on the finest existing technology."

The image of Scopes returned.

"No, no, show me a *clockwork* version."

Babbage chuckled. Well, *that* was interesting behaviour. "That *is* a clockwork version of your design. Remember? You based it on the scan of your own body."

The light dawned. "That. . . that's a machine?"

"We call them robots. It's difficult to tell the difference from a living creature until you peel back the skin."

"Oh, Babbage, by all means. . ." Scopes rubbed his hands together in anticipation. "Peel away."

The resulting research occupied Scopes for the better part of a week, although he little understood the passage of time. Babbage periodically reminded him to eat or just shut down the visual interface and dimmed the lights when exhaustion threatened.

After a discussion of Scope's active lifestyle prior to his captivity, Babbage also insisted on exercise sessions. Lack of equipment and space limited their efforts, but the interface insisted that Scopes would deteriorate if he didn't keep up his health.

Which seemed a highly emotional concern for an entity created entirely of numbers and letters. Within a short time, the interface had grown naturalistic in his mannerisms and increasingly, for lack of a better word, human in his interactions. Scopes feared commenting on the changes. Archeron might notice and somehow reset the interface's babbaging.

"Considering the level of technology on your planet," Babbage commented one day, "your designs are remarkably close in concept to what the rest of the galaxy utilises."

The rest of the galaxy? Scopes filed that information away for future reference.

"Oh." Babbage's one word was all the warning Scopes had before his stomach pulled out through his spine and a familiar, white-hot light and golden motes blinded him.

Where the hell were they taking him, now?

The shocked gasps of women and grunts of men startled him. As his vision cleared, he found himself in a large room considerably brighter than his cell. The familiar scent of laboratory antiseptic enabled Scopes to keep from vomiting on the feet of the men surrounding him.

"Good lord, this one's naked," a deep voice called out, causing one shriek and a couple of titters before a lab coat settled around Scopes' shoulders. "It's another Jap, and this one looks barely old enough to wipe his own arse."

Rather discomfited by all the strange faces, Scopes pulled the lab coat closed more as a form of protection than from any sense of propriety. He slipped his arms into the sleeves the same moment someone pushed slacks and a shirt into his hands, forcing the coat to fall open again and bringing a fresh round of titters.

After his solitary captivity with only Babbage for company, the bustling overwhelmed him. He took a deep breath and forced himself to relax. He squared his shoulders and looked around the room, clothes in one hand.

Tables filled a large lab, holding a veritable cornucopia of unrecognizable equipment. Dozens of flicker images—both two-dimensional and three—littered the air. Men and women surrounded him, representing all continents and quite a variety of ages. He was, by all evidence, the youngest person there. Apparently a new arrival generated considerable interest, since everyone in the room crowded around.

The man with the deep voice cleared his throat. "Don't know how to put on a pair of trousers, son?"

Scopes met the man's gaze evenly. He seemed somewhere on the other side of forty, with sharp features and a pointed nose.

"Of course, I know how to dress myself," Scopes said, channelling my bravado. "I just don't give a shit who sees my Nebuchadnezzar. Nothing to be ashamed about, after all."

That earned him a few more titters and some muttering.

Having proved his point, he pulled on trousers manufactured from the same lightweight cotton as the drawers he'd never bothered to wear.

"No need to be like that." The man appeared to think himself a kind of leader. He extended a hand. "Frank Oppenheimer. Radioactive particles and physics in general."

"Avery Scopes." He shook the offered hand then removed the jacket so he could don the shirt. "Are we. . .?" What was his real question? "Are we all on the invaders' ship?"

"We are. They've collected us together in this lab like rats."

The crowd around them murmured uncomfortably.

"Why?" Scopes asked.

The older man looked at him as if he were dim. "They're testing us. They keep throwing scientific puzzles at us. If we don't solve them, they'll kill us." He shrugged. "It has been quite an education, though."

Scopes had never been threatened so directly, but he'd assumed as much.

So Archeron had separated other scientists from the rest of the abductees.

Scopes took in the people, the equipment, and the complicated holograms throughout the space. If his own experience were any indication, this group must have advanced their knowledge hundreds of times faster than they would have on Earth. Why would the invaders do that?

Oppenheimer looked around a bit. "This is Elsie Franklin," he said of a somewhat unconventionally pretty brunette with a petulant set to her eyes. "X-rays and. . . genetics, I guess we're calling it, now."

He waved a hand as he listed: "Jackson Keller, gravity and quantum mechanics. My brother Robert's around here somewhere correcting somebody in physics." He gave a cursory glance before letting his gaze fall back to Scopes. "And you?"

"Babbaging and. . . well, I always called it clockworks, but they seem to call it robotics in the rest of the galaxy."

A general murmur ran through the crowd.

"You'll want to talk to Von Neumann, then. He's in charge of programming." Oppenheimer pointed at a paunchy, balding man, then favoured Scopes with an expression of superiority. "And it's called programming, now." Oppenheimer turned his back as if he'd already lost interest in the newcomer. "Welcome to the Monkey House." He wandered off to join an older version of himself who had to be the aforementioned brother.

The crowd dissipated as Scopes closed the lab coat over his shirt. He took a deep breath to settle his nerves but only partially succeeded. Naked and helpless in a prison cell had felt more comfortable than fully dressed in a lab full of scientists who looked down their noses at him for both his youth and his ethnicity.

Von Neumann had already retreated to the other side of the lab, obviously not interested in Scope's input.

"Zen would be glad to know you didn't die." A woman's voice from close behind scared the devil out of him, and he spun to face her. "Oh, was I in your personal space? Sorry. I'm Elsie." She pushed her rather thick glasses up her nose. Her eyes gave him a quick up and down and she added, almost unconsciously, "More likely than not, but. . . eh. . ."

"You know Zen? Is he here?" The sudden yawning in Scopes' stomach and burning in his eyes threatened to overwhelm him. Was it possible?

But the strange woman held up one hand before replying in her slightly off-putting speedy way. "Slow down, Scopes. Zen's not here. But he's alive. Well, he was alive when I last saw him a month ago, so I imagine he's probably alive, unless he's off on some damn fool mission again, which considering he's, you know, well, of course I assume *you* must know, but here—"

"A month ago?" Scopes' sudden joy deflated as rapidly as it had grown. "You haven't seen him since the attack at Richmond, then?"

"Richmond?" Her face revealed profound confusion. "I was *with* him during the Devastation but that happened over two months ago. They sucked me here last week. Where have *you* been?"

Two months? He'd been on the ship that long?

"In a cell." He shook his head. "I didn't know two months had passed." His hope rekindled. "So he escaped Richmond?"

Elsie nodded.

Scopes closed his eyes and sighed a deep, relaxing sigh. "Of course, he did."

The two people who mattered most to him lived. Everything else was icing on the cake.

Wonderful.

"But I probably shouldn't say anything beyond that." She nodded to one side. "The walls have ears. . . literally."

Scopes looked around. Apparently, everyone had decided the excitement was at an end and had returned to work.

"It's unusual they held you on your own so long. I wonder why." She looked him up and down again. "They brought most of us to the Monkey House within a few days of our abduction."

"So what's going on here anyway?" Scopes redirected. "It looks chaotic."

"It is. Ostensibly, Oppenheimer the elder is in charge overall, with Oppenheimer the lesser in charge of particle physics, Von Neumann in charge of programming languages and that bastard Watson in charge of genetics, although he'll shoot his fool mouth off about most anything." She pointed around the room as she spoke and Scopes did his level best to follow her speedy delivery. "Notice, if you will, that the supposed leaders of the work groups are all male and White, while there are a significant number of scientists who are neither." She paused to breathe and to favour Scopes with a withering glance. "The invaders are much more egalitarian in their treatment of us. As far as Archeron is concerned, we're all monkeys."

"And we just keep solving puzzles?"

Elsie shrugged. "So far, we're just doing our level best to catch up with the Kla'arkian technology. We haven't been told the end goal, but anyone who asks too many questions or does anything, in fact, to cast doubt on Archeron's authority transports out and is either never seen again or returns in decidedly more pieces than he, or, in fact, she left."

The unusual woman showed Scopes around and introduced him to more people than he would ever hope to remember. As they chatted with some very friendly men from India, Scopes noticed something wrong with their mouths when they spoke. They all spoke perfect English, but as Scopes watched their faces, their mouths moved at a different speed. The effect made him nauseous.

As they stepped away from the men, he asked Elsie about the effect.

She chuckled. "I've grown so accustomed to the lag I completely forgot to mention it." She pointed at a group of nearby women. "They're speaking German," she insisted despite the fact that Scopes could hear every word of their perfectly articulated English. Once again, though, he saw that their mouths moved out of sync with their words.

"We've all been injected with some kind of microscopic organism. . . or machine, we haven't really figured out which it is. Anyway, it translates for us. As the signals from our ear reach our brain, the 'translator microbes' translate whatever we hear into our native tongue." She made air quotes with her fingers and rolled her eyes at the term, lowering her voice as she continued. "That's what Archeron and the system call them, but we've begun to suspect he's not all that sure what they are either." She laughed. "They play hell on anyone who's multilingual."

"The system?"

She waved her hand at all the images around the room. "The machine that operates all of this and houses the data." She lowered her voice again. "We suspect the invaders did not create the system, but appropriated it. You'll have to ask your new 'boss' more about that." Again she used her fingers to hook the quotation marks. "Something about discrepancies between the programming languages and the invaders' native tongue."

Although he kept the information to himself, Scopes already suspected the same. "Have you queried the verbal interface about it?"

The look she gave him bore a mixture of disdain, confusion, and blatant disgust. "Should we ask the toaster as well? It's a very advanced information processing system, but it certainly wouldn't be able to tell us anything like that."

Scopes held back a smile. Apparently, the White males looked down on the other scientists and the other scientists looked down on Babbage.

To avoid offending Elsie, who had done wonders to welcome him, he kept his thoughts to himself and directed his questions back to the personnel of the lab, or the Monkey House, as most everyone there called it. To the invaders, the scientists were little more advanced than the monkeys in Earth's zoos. No one really knew who had initiated the name, but it'd stuck.

After Elsie rather abruptly took her leave to get back to her project,

Scopes spent time wandering from area to area familiarizing himself with the various departments: everything from modelling ways to split the atom to manipulating basic genetic material for breeding humans of great strength or endurance.

The lab overwhelmed Scopes until he made his way at last to the programmers, who maintained a much more rudimentary understanding of the AE languages than he did. Apparently, they'd not benefited from Babbage's personal tutoring.

Friend Scopes?

What the hell?

I wanted you to know I can communicate with you silently if ever you need.

The voice sounded in Scopes head, not his ears.

They cut our conversation rather short.

Scopes turned the wall. *Babbage? I can talk to you in my head?*

Of course, Babbage said as if Scopes were simple. *Oh, sorry, your planet doesn't utilise neural interfacing yet.*

The voice in his head hurt, but the headache mattered little if it meant he could continue his friendship while navigating the choppy waters of the Monkey House.

I'm glad to talk to you, Scopes thought. *But can we wait a bit for further conversation? I'm struggling a bit with these people.*

Of course, friend Scopes. All you need do is consciously think my name and I will attend you.

Thank you, Babbage.

What a relief the interface hadn't spoken out loud. Scopes wished to play *that* card very close to his chest, especially in a laboratory setting where everyone worked hard to prove himself or herself better than everyone else.

Finally finding a place in his work group, Scopes startled at a loud chime that sounded over the general hullabaloo. As the note ended, all the women moved to the far side of the lab and a couple of younger technicians pulled a white screen through the centre. The men on the near side of the divider began removing their clothes.

"What's going on?" Scopes asked a language expert who had folded his jacket on the table and was pulling off his shirt. He seemed younger than most of the others, barely older than Scopes himself, so Scopes felt a mite less intimidated by him. He was Japanese though, so Scopes sort of looked at his ear when they spoke to avoid the vertigo caused by the dissociation of speech and mouth movement.

"Oh, sorry. You don't know." He continued to disrobe as he spoke. "It's time for a sleep period, and we aren't allowed to carry anything with us from the lab to our sleeping quarters, so we need to strip off before leaving the lab. They provide modesty garments in the sleeping quarters."

Hurrying to catch up with the other men, Scopes stripped and left his clothes in a neat pile on the bench. "Archeron provided a screen for us?"

The other scientist smiled. "Of course not. The first time proved a horrible embarrassment, especially for the Hindus and Muslims. We built the screen ourselves the next day." He shrugged. "I grew up with public baths, so it doesn't bother me."

"You've been here since the first day?"

The man nodded. He extended a hand with a shallow bow as they filed out of the lab and down a narrow hallway. "I'm Hiroshi."

"Scopes," Scopes told him. "I'm sorry that I keep looking at your ear, but I get nauseous from the translator microbes."

Hiroshi chuckled. "Not to worry. We all suffer the same problem at first." He stopped in front of a small doorway. "This is me. We have empty beds. You're welcome to bunk here."

Relieved at finding another potential friend in the miasma of egos, Scopes gladly accepted the invitation. Fortunately, he found a "bunk," more like a pallet on the floor, directly beside the friendly programmer.

"What's your native language?" Hiroshi asked.

"English."

"Well, then you're in luck." He pulled on a pair of drawers and dropped onto his pallet. "I speak English fluently, so we can dispense with the microbes."

Scopes slipped into a pair of shorts and dropped gratefully onto his new bed, more physically comfortable than he'd been in weeks. He lay on his back with his hands behind his head, staring at the ceiling above him wondering what the hell I might be up to at that moment.

Chapter Twelve

How quickly *La Nouvelle*, as the French called it, had fallen into chaos. To Hope the city would always be New York. Refugees flocked there from the countryside by the tens of thousands, which made no sense at all since all the cities destroyed had been major urban centres. Farms and wilderness homesteads seemed simply too small and remote to be worth the bother.

As far as Hope was concerned, collecting in the few major cities left to the human race painted a giant bull's eye on everyone's chest. . . but humans remained herd animals at heart. The swell and press of humanity offered comfort. It created remarkable odours as well.

The summer had grown hot, the sewage systems had backed up, and no one bothered to remove the garbage. The smell of unwashed bodies full of fear and piss nearly overwhelmed Hope as she rode down the middle of Broadway with her entourage: the Persian, Scot and Basil Rupert, and Prudence.

I'd introduced Prudence, not as Scope's favourite whore, but as a friend of ours with a remarkable head for details. Hope needed a secretary.

In her career, Prudence needed to remember which character to play for which customer, how much each could afford to pay, and so on. Less amusingly, I also knew she'd learned to keep the books at the sadly demised Salome's Garden.

Ten strong men with guns complemented the retinue. They kept the beggars at bay, and nearly everyone in *La Nouvelle* was a beggar.

Hope had left me behind, and I'd raised quite a theatrical stink about it. She remained adamant that we shouldn't be seen together. If Archeron discovered our association the results could be catastrophic.

I'd refused to speak with her before she left.

She'd told the Persian I was a petulant child and refused to give me another thought. Of much greater concern to her was the mafioso boss's reason for handing out food and supplies. Some of the cities were allocated a certain amount of food per person in exchange for labour in mines and factories. The boss of *La Nouvelle*, nicknamed Blue Eyes for the obvious reason, promised food and shelter to everyone who made their way to the city, but he didn't seem too concerned about sanitation.

The schools had closed. The stores had been looted of what food and clothes they'd had. Fights and riots became common, fire remained a constant imminent threat, and disease spread at an alarming rate.

Hope held a strong suspicion that old Blue Eyes only handed out a small portion of what he received for each person. He likely stockpiled the rest and planned on doing a runner as soon as he'd bled the city dry. Chaos would ensue.

"Lady Kennedy!"

Hope looked down.

A small, dirty, extremely pregnant woman with stringy brown hair pushed through the crowd. Her soiled clothes barely contained the enormous swell of her belly. Despite the woman's impoverished condition, Hope had to work to suppress a twinge of jealousy. She'd never been able to have children of her own.

"Lady Kennedy!"

Hope pulled her horse to a stop, much to the consternation of the Persian and his men, who circled and had to work twice as hard to keep the beggars away once the group had stopped.

The woman placed a hand on Hope's horse's neck to steady herself and beamed up at Hope. "It is you. I *knew* it was!" At Hope's blank stare, she lost her smile. She ran her hands through her hair to pull it back into some semblance of order and smoothed out her dress as much as possible. "Of course, you wouldn't recognise me like this, milady." She noticed a stain on her skirt and rubbed at it frantically. "I. . . I. . ." Her enthusiasm at seeing Hope drained away into embarrassment.

The Persian drew his horse close to Hope's and leaned over so he could see the woman clearly. "Hello, Lottie. It's good to see you still alive." Which had become so common a saying that it no longer seemed rude. "Must be near your time?" A safe thing to ask a woman with a belly so large.

Memory sparked in Hope's mind, and she nearly exclaimed crudely in surprise.

"Lottie!" she said instead, recovering from her rude lapse. She could hardly be blamed, though, since she'd last seen the girl at a birthday party for the Duke of Carolina where she'd worn a rather form-fitting and revealing bathing costume that had made Hope think the girl skipped too many meals. Lottie was the Duke's eldest daughter.

Without hesitation, Hope climbed down from her horse and threw her arms around the girl, who burst into tears. "My dear, dear girl. Please tell me your parents. . ." But the way she sobbed even more told Hope the truth. Holding the young woman at arm's length, Hope wiped her face.

"Sorry, mum. I didn't mean. . ." Lottie straightened her skirt.

"Who do you have left?"

The girl opened her mouth and put a hand to her belly. Hope could see she meant to make up a story about the father of her child. Looking deep into Hope's eyes, though, she simply closed her mouth and shook her head. "I'm sorry, mum. I didn't mean to trouble you. . . I just. . ." She stepped back and squared her shoulders. "I just wanted to say hello and tell you I'm glad that you're alive as well." She glanced up at the Persian. "You and your Persian both."

Hope patted the girl's cheek and looked up at her Persian whose face told her she would not give her horse to the young woman. He glanced at one of his men, who obediently climbed down and led a mount over.

Lottie tried to protest and Hope believed her sincerity, but she needed little effort to overcome the girl's protestations. As the guard helped her into the saddle, she spoke words of gratitude both genuine and smartly restrained.

Already, several bystanders called Hope's name begging charity, but the girl's parents had been friends. Hope wasn't in a position to help everyone, but she'd be damned if she abandoned a friend.

The man who'd given up his horse climbed up behind one of his comrades and the entourage rode off as the crowd closed in. In the end, the Persian fired a few gunshots over the heads of the beggars, and they quickly dispersed.

Hope made a mental note to ask her Persian the names of every guard they'd brought.

Prudence made eye contact with Hope before drawing even with Lottie and introducing herself. She also passed the girl a handkerchief and a scarf for her hair.

Thank goodness for her new assistant's thoughtfulness. Hope needed to spend the rest of the journey collecting her thoughts for her meeting with the boss. With any luck, he'd see reason without a threat of violence. She'd managed to wrangle together what little remained of the Confederate military but knew all too well the dangers of creating any kind of real armed force.

She'd sent word to the soldiers of all branches who hadn't been killed in the initial attack or in the Devastation when so many of the Confederate armies had died. The remnants gathered in Norfolk.

Marching them *en masse* into *La Nouvelle* would cause disaster. If Archeron so much as suspected any kind of militia had formed, he'd incinerate them from the safety of his flying machine. Besides which, she meant this meeting as a first contact to see what kind of agreements could be made without violence.

Then she'd contact Archeron, if need be.

They reached the lovely central park called *Au Coeur* without further development. Blue Eyes had taken over the mayor's palace at the edge of the park and four very large, armed men waited for them at the palace gates. Stable boys took the horses and a butler led Hope's somewhat irregular entourage to an expansive veranda overlooking *Au Coeur* itself.

The boss rose as Hope approached, and he smiled at her with a sparkle in his trademark eyes. "My dear Hope," he crooned, taking her offered hand.

"Francis," she returned with her best aristocratic manners in place, allowing him to lead her to one of five comfortable fan-backed chairs set out for the occasion. "It is so good to finally meet you."

Hope, Prudence, Lottie, Scot and Basil Rupert all took seats. Exactly the correct number of chairs had been laid out even with Lottie as a last minute addition to the party. So they'd been watched through the city. Hope's guards stood off to one side.

Francis was flanked by his son Michael on one side and his right hand man Dean on the other. They sat very comfortably and wore bemused expressions Hope knew were meant to annoy her. They did, but she'd learned her poker face from her father.

A waiter offered drinks all around, and Scot, Basil and Prudence asked for scotch, which Hope didn't begrudge them. Who knew how long the better spirits would last?

She studied the patio. Enormous tropical palms in planters bordered the space and men slowly loped beyond them, distant enough for discretion but visible enough to send a message. How many more men were available just out of eyesight?

Movement at the corner of her eye drew her attention to the bar.

The Persian muttered a surprising curse as an attractive young gentleman emerged from behind the bar with a tray of drinks. The reason for her Persian's perturbation became obvious when Hope took a closer look.

The new "waiter" placed the drinks tray in front of the Scotsman, who muttered his own oath. "You bastard."

How in the world had I beaten them there?

And *why?*

I wore a jaunty Hollywood pirate costume, with my white shirt open almost to my navel and my vest unbuttoned. The shirt sported playing cards for a collar. I'd pulled my hair back and wore Scopes' trademark goggles on my forehead. A necklace I'd once made from cogs and gears stolen from his bench sparkled in the sun, and a long sword and flintlock pistol completed my attire.

I was also barefoot. *Barefoot.*

Hope clenched her jaw as tightly as possible to avoid screaming abuse.

The glass of scotch I lifted in her direction contained more than twice what the others held.

"My dear Lady Hope Kennedy," I said with a flourish of my drink. "When I dropped in on my new friend here, I was thrilled to learn I'd have a chance to meet the illustrious former first lady of the Confederacy and sometime ambassador to the Kla'arkians." I lifted the glass in a toast and downed it in one swift gulp.

Those members of Hope's retinue who'd asked for scotch downed it as quickly as possible, and the rest likely wished they'd asked for some.

She decided then and there to flay me alive the moment she had me alone, but strove with all her strength to appear merely confused as opposed to murderous.

"My dear lady, do allow me to introduce my newest friend." Francis grinned like the cat what got the canary. "I don't know his real name, but he goes by the appellation *Hammer*."

Feigning surprise at my name the moment I bowed to kiss her fingers, she jerked her hand up and away, managing to slice my lip with her diamond wedding ring. Not that I didn't deserve it.

"The Hammer?" she exclaimed. "Why in the *world* would you consort with a criminal like this, Francis?" She rose from her chair and moved away from me. "Don't you know the trouble this dishonest, *deceitful* braggart caused my late husband, may he rest in peace?" She played her part well because she needn't feign her exasperation.

"My dear lady," Francis exhorted, "if you will only give me a moment to explain. . ."

Blah, blah, blah. Quite frankly, I didn't give a shit about his words since my entire goal had been to bring these two factions together for my own nefarious purposes.

Hope had every reason to hate me at that moment. I'd begged and pleaded to join her journey to *La Nouvelle*, knowing full well she'd never allow it. She'd professed certainty she'd convince the mafiosi it was in their best interest to treat the citizenry and refugees in a sane and humane manner.

Whilst the woman was the smartest human being I knew next to Scopes, like my brother she was saddled with the worst case of naiveté I'd seen. In Scopes case, I could excuse his blindness to humanity's basically evil inner core because I'd sheltered him, but Hope should've known better.

There would be no negotiating with a man who'd kill you as soon as look at you if it made him a profit. . . and she should've known that I'd given up only because I wanted to surprise them all here in *La Nouvelle.*

"Francis!" I exclaimed, interrupting him. "Frankie." I threw an arm around his shoulders. I dropped my voice low, now, intimate. "Frank."

The Persian's eyes widened, telling me he hoped he understood my intent. Far less innocent than our esteemed mistress, he'd likely already seen through my ruse all the way to its Machiavellian conclusion.

"Mrs. Kennedy hopes you'll realise it's a good idea to be a bit more generous and humanitarian in your management of *La Nouvelle.*" I gestured at Hope. "She hopes you won't mind being castrated in front of your men and that you'll kiss babies and hug kittens and sing songs about how great a city she is here on the coast."

"She thinks I'm going to give up a cash cow like this?" Francis raised an eyebrow at me, and lord, but the man did have the looks. Just holding my arm around him made me *want* to do his bidding. "Just 'cause I'm such a loving and generous soul?"

I smiled in all the wide-eyed innocence I could muster and threw my free hand in the air to really bring it home.

He laughed a full-throated belly laugh that set Hope back on her hobnailed boots. "Sister. . ." He stayed right there with my arm around him. "Ever since Archeron handed me this. . ." He held up the tin badge with two crossed hammers. "I can barely find the room to store the shit I'm going to ship out west where that pompous ass will never find me. This is the best scam since the government bought Manhattan from the redskins. He has me building a whole railroad warehousing system for when he starts shipping people out west to mine for him, never realizing I'm filling the warehouses—"

"With what?" Archeron interrupted.

Francis froze.

So did we all.

One second Francis stood alone. The next he had company.

The boss's men stepped forward onto the patio, about twenty of them.

"Lord Archeron!" I crooned, pulling my arm away from Francis as if he carried the plague. "How lovely to meet you in the flesh. . . as it were."

Hope stayed in her chair. I hoped she would note from my utter lack of surprise that the entire spectacle proceeded precisely as I had planned.

"Where did you get that badge, Hammer?" Archeron demanded.

I dropped the elaborate, foppish persona and went for still and quiet. "I admit I stole it from the rightful mayors of Norfolk, sir, but if you give me a moment before vaporizing me, I think you will. . ."

Archeron waved me into silence and faced Francis.

Hope maintained a dignified silence, but a single, angry glance at me managed to slip through the façade.

The Persian shifted from an alert poise on the balls of his feet to a more relaxed position on his heels, his suspicions of my purpose apparently confirmed.

"You were given a duty," Acheron reminded Francis. "You have used that duty to line your pockets and fully intend to stab me in the back." He waved a hand at Blue Eyes, and faster than I can even write the words, the boss vanished, along with his right hand man and every guard on the patio. The air twinkled silver and gold, and Francis' son Michael suddenly sat alone, pissing himself in his fan-back chair.

The Persian gestured low to tell his followers to stay down. Another dozen men ran onto the patio, but they'd apparently seen their boss and the first wave of guards vanish. They waited silently as if to see what might happen next. So much for mafioso loyalty!

Archeron turned to me. "You." He pointed.

"I will return the badge immediately." I bowed my head.

He laughed. "The Hammer." He stepped closer. "Zen Bastard." He circled me with his hands behind his back. "Your motivation is transparent. My former agent in *La Nouvelle* treated the humans here abysmally, and I don't care about that." He stopped at my shoulder and regarded me like a pimp with his newest rent-boy. "Point out that he stole from *me* and you knew I'd eliminate him." He raised his chin and looked down his nose at me. "How do you know his replacement won't be worse?"

I raised my eyes to meet his. "I hoped, since you don't really care who fills the position as long as they maintain order and follow your directives, that you'd let the Scotsman and Basil Rupert here do the job for you." I gestured at my friends, whose surprise registered as no more than a lifting of their eyebrows.

Hope maintained her silence while the corners of the Persian's mouth lifted.

"They have the strength to maintain order," I explained, "the wisdom to follow direction, and the cooperation of the outlying districts which will make your orders easier to follow since they won't have to waste resources—"

Archeron laughed loudly and turned to Hope. "You should listen to this one more often, my dear Lady Kennedy. He understands how to appeal to my selfish side." Hope opened her mouth, but Archeron waved her to silence. "Don't waste your breath, my dear. There is very little you can do of which I am unaware. I know you've been working with the Hammer since Richmond. . . that your rescue from that doomed city was, in fact, his first act of assistance to you."

Marvellous! Unless he was *really* playing us, we now knew that in addition to the Boss's ability to hide theft from him, we'd misled him into thinking I was the *real* Hammer, the original. Tick one point for the good guys.

"So. . ." He turned to Scot. "Hold out your hand, Scotsman."

Scot did as requested and a tin badge appeared in his palm. He started at the sudden materialization.

"You're in charge now." Archeron turned to Michael and regarded the men standing around the perimeter of the patio. He raised his voice enough for all to hear and a box appeared at his feet. "You will all swear loyalty to this man, now, and you—" He pointed at the former Boss's son. "Will see to it that the entire mafioso system knows what happened to your father."

The air shimmered and a pile of naked corpses, still streaming blood and stinking of shit, materialised at the young man's feet. He jumped back and shouted in horror, overturning his chair. His father's face stared up at him, dead eyes twisted in a rictus of agony and his own manhood spilling out of his open mouth.

Michael fell to his hands and knees, violently ill.

"Well!" Archeron exclaimed. "This has been fun, but I am a busy man." He turned to me. "Thank you for the tip and consider the debt repaid." He turned to Hope. "Hold out your hand, please, my lady."

She did and a tin badge materialised. She didn't flinch.

"So you can reach me whenever you need," the commander explained. And so he'd know where she was at all times. An unfortunate development I had fundamentally expected, but had hoped against hope we might avoid.

"I'd hate to be a bother, sir," she said with a curtsy.

"A word with you is never a bother, my dear lady. 'Tis a pleasure."

She nodded her acceptance of the compliment then Archeron vanished.

Scot and Basil opened the box to reveal, as I had expected, a ream of flyers announcing the change in leadership.

A sharp flash of pain hit my face as Mrs. Kennedy slapped me with, I presume, all of her strength. "What the *hell* did you think you were doing?" Her manic shout shocked all but me and the Persian.

Scot and Basil Rupert immediately drew their new personnel away from the ensuing debacle.

"Why did you. . . *hire* the Hammer in the first place?" I asked, and continued before she could answer. "To do the things you cannot do yourself."

"Twenty men are *dead* because of you!" she shouted.

"*They needed killing!*" I screamed back with all the ferocity I could muster.

She took a step away from me, eyes wide.

"And you will sleep soundly tonight," I continued more quietly, "because there was nothing you could've done to stop it." Wanting her to mull that over, I simply turned and walked away, favouring the Persian with a glance as I strode past.

He nodded his thanks. He, at least, seemed to understand I would need to drain an entire whiskey bottle before I'd wipe from my mind the sight of that bleeding, shit-stained mound of human flesh.

Hope moved to follow, but her Persian gently laid his hand on her elbow. "As much anger as you may harbour towards him for lying to you and manipulating you, please believe that what he did, he did *for* you."

Because he was her Persian, she stopped. She frequently questioned his reasoning, but she always gave it due consideration.

She watched me steal a full bottle of scotch from the bar.

At the edge of the patio, Lottie stepped forward as I walked past. Sheepishly, she took my hand and glanced at Hope, probably knowing how unhappy her saviour was with me. "Thank you, Hammer. It *is* a good thing you did today." She smiled through the obvious pain and fear. "I'll make sure folks know it was you who fixed things here."

I squeezed her hand and gave her half a smile, then made my exit, brushing away the hands of others who would detain me.

"I believe our diplomatic mission *was* doomed to fail." The Persian released Hope's elbow.

Deep in her heart, Hope knew he was right. The decay in the city did not speak of a man who cared for his people, but she hated the idea of humans killing one another when the invaders were the enemy.

She sighed and dropped into a fan-backed chair. "How did he know?" She looked up at the Persian. "Am I that naïve?"

He shook his head and dropped a hand on her shoulder.

"After everything I've seen," she said, "why am I still surprised at the evil of which mankind is capable?"

"Because you have a good soul, milady." The Persian took his place beside her chair.

"What does that say about Zen?"

Her Persian chuckled. "What does it say about me?"

Chapter Thirteen

Twenty men snored, murmured, and farted in Scopes' dormitory. Some of them slept in far worse conditions than they'd ever encountered. Some of them slept in far better. Scopes, who'd spent the first eight years of his life in an internment camp, sometimes almost forgot that he was imprisoned with a threat of death hanging over his head if his research proved unproductive.

He had so much to learn. So many exciting revelations every day. So much information he might use against the invaders themselves. His time with Babbage, especially, yielded such interesting discoveries—

"Hiroshi's trying to wake you," Babbage told him.

Scopes looked around. The brightly lit lab did not contain a Hiroshi.

Oh! Babbage meant in the *real* world, where Scopes lay on his pallet as if sleeping.

"Scopes?" A voice broke through the illusion. "Scopes?"

Oh blast, if he didn't respond, his friend might worry he was in distress.

Scopes moved so quickly to snatch the interface from his head, he caught himself in his sheet. Once free of the fabric, he sat upright.

Hiroshi knelt on the floor. How long had he knelt there?

"Yes?" Scopes tried his best to appear nonchalant.

"I thought you were. . ." Hiroshi narrowed his eyes. "Not well. I couldn't tell if you were breathing under there."

"Oh, sorry, I was just. . ." Scopes' chuckle sounded more than a little false even to his own ears. ". . .meditating while we studied data." Would Hiroshi believe it?

"Our work during the day isn't enough for you?" Hiroshi's voice sounded quite sceptical.

"Is it really day, though?"

"Sorry?"

"Well, that's one thing we're studying." Scopes had to share his theory with *someone*. "We checked the work periods against the rest periods. It appears we're on a twenty-seven-and-a-half-hour schedule." He motioned Hiroshi closer in his excitement. "It likely means that the invaders are from a planet with a twenty-seven-and-a-half-hour rotational period, and therefore, it's likely a similar size to Earth with similar gravity, assuming mass and density are relatively proportioned."

"We?" Hiroshi sat very still.

"Sorry?"

"You said 'we' were studying."

Oops. "I meant 'I.'"

"Then why'd you say 'we'?"

"Maybe the translator mixed it up." Scopes wished he lied more effectively. He pre-empted Hiroshi's imminent question with one finger when Babbage's voice tickled in his head.

We could use his input, friend Scopes.

Scopes sighed, considered Hiroshi carefully, and gestured for the young man to join him on his pallet.

Hiroshi sat back on his haunches. "Sorry?"

"It's the only way we can be quiet enough." He lifted the edge of his sheet, repeating the invitational gesture.

Hiroshi didn't move.

"You never slept five to a bed in Japan?" Scopes made a noise in his throat. He didn't have patience for the man's sense of propriety.

Glancing around self-consciously, Hiroshi slid under the sheet but kept as close to the edge as possible.

"I'm not going to molest you, for Christ's sake." Scopes pulled the young man closer. "Is this close enough?" he asked Babbage.

"Close enough for what?" Hiroshi muttered.

"That should be adequate." Babbage's voice boomed.

Hiroshi nearly jumped bodily onto Scopes. "What happened to quiet?"

"Not necessary now!" How exciting to finally share his secret!

Hiroshi winced and looked around.

"Privacy bubble," Scopes explained.

"What?"

Very pleased with himself, Scopes pushed Hiroshi down and drew the cover over them both so no one would see their mouths working. So they could see one another, he held the neural interface between them, a half-circle of metal struck with lights.

"It's a secret, Hiroshi. I'm trusting you more than you can imagine."

Hiroshi winced. "If it's a secret, why talk so damned loud?"

"No one can hear us on my pallet. I talk with. . . with the verbal interface and no one can hear."

"How is that possible?"

Babbage spoke up then. "It's called a privacy bubble. Listen for a second."

Hiroshi listened, then shook his head. "I don't hear anything."

Scopes smirked and waited.

Understanding dawned on Hiroshi's face. "I don't hear *anything*. I should hear the sounds of the men sleeping. . . and the air ducts. . ." Quickly, he pulled the sheet away. Outside the bubble of the pallet, the men went on sleeping and shifting but made no noise.

Scopes nudged him. "Stick your head off the pallet."

Hiroshi complied, and his eyes grew wide. He drew his head back into the space over Scope's pallet. "That's remarkable."

Scopes remembered his own delight the first time Babbage had shown him technology no one in the Monkey House could access. The things these invaders had invented and/or stolen astounded the young man. He pulled Hiroshi down and threw the sheet over them both.

"It gets better, my friend," Scopes said.

A flicker of golden light shone between them and a second circlet appeared on the pallet. Scopes handed the device to Hiroshi, who examined it carefully.

"What's this?"

Scopes lay a hand on Hiroshi's shoulder. Their eyes met in the eerie glow. "Trust me and do as I do." He placed his circlet against his forehead, lay on his back and closed his eyes. "Make sure the sheet covers us both."

Nothing happened.

Why wasn't Hiroshi following his example? Scopes opened one eye. Hiroshi hadn't moved.

Scopes opened the other eye and bobbed his head to urge Hiroshi to lie down. How much prodding did he need?

With a profound sigh, the other man complied. "You realise there will be talk in the lab tomorrow."

"Oh, don't worry. They won't know what we're doing." Is that all he worried about? Scopes closed his eyes and lay still. "They'll just assume we're fucking."

"Oh, well, as long as *that's* all they'll think." Hiroshi lay back and closed his eyes.

"Open your eyes." Scopes gazed out across the most amazing city Babbage had ever shown him. By far his favourite.

"What? I just closed them."

"And now it's time to open them," Scopes insisted.

How would Hiroshi react? He opened his eyes and screamed at the top of his lungs, just like a tiny girl, literally leaping into Scopes' arms with his feet pulled up. He drew one quick breath and screamed again for good measure. "Why aren't we dead why aren't we dead why aren't we dead?"

The question was legitimate, since they now stood about a hundred metres above the ground. Babbage hovered a short distance away, chuckling.

"The first time Babbage brought me here," Scopes consoled, "I reacted similarly."

It was true. He'd jumped into Babbage's arms, but the advanced programming of the artificial construct gave them only real world strength, which meant a flicker based on a ten-year-old couldn't hold the proxy of a full-grown man. They'd both fallen all the way to the ground, and Scopes' screams had mightily amused his friend. Fortunately, visual proxies seemed unable to soil themselves.

Hiroshi's scream stretched out. In the construct, he wouldn't run out of air.

Below them a massive city stretched from horizon to horizon. Curves and circles dominated the structures of glass and steel. Built in aquatic colours from blue to green and illuminated from inside, the city resembled an ocean of glass. Three bright moons hung heavy in a cerulean sky.

Hiroshi finally stopped screaming.

"Have you devised a way to send a circlet to Victoria without being detected?" Scopes asked Babbage, wondering how the programme simulated gravity as he adjusted Hiroshi in his arms. He released his friend's legs, and Hiroshi tentatively lowered his feet until they met the invisible floor. He tapped it with his toes.

"No, Scopes, I have not." Babbage exhaled. "Do you intend to ask me that every time we meet here?"

"Most likely." He hoped to devise a way to meet with his adopted daughter in the artificial playground.

Hiroshi finally let go his grip around Scopes' neck and managed a tentative step or two away. He glanced at Babbage. "Babbage?"

The proxy bowed. "At your service."

Hiroshi looked all around then one hand flew to his brow, but the interface circlet wasn't reproduced in the illusion. Realization dawned. "It's an artificial construct."

Scopes spun round with his arms widespread, delighted at being able to share this reality with his new friend. "Isn't it astounding? The headpiece projects everything directly into your thoughts and creates a vast dream world."

Hiroshi turned his attention to Babbage. "And who are you? You seem a mite young for a scientist."

Babbage raised an eyebrow at Scopes.

"In fact, he's a visual proxy for the ship's verbal interface." Scopes wanted to tell Hiroshi that he'd designed Babbage's proxy, but that might have smacked of ego. "I realised he was much more than a simple interface and helped him create a flicker."

Hiroshi smiled while he circled Babbage.

"Hologram," Scopes amended. "I helped him create a *hologram*."

Hiroshi regarded Babbage, who wore a three-piece suit of the highest quality, complete with pocket watch and leather top hat jauntily askew over his long braids. The scientist glanced at Scopes, similarly trussed out. Then he gazed down at himself.

Babbage had designed Hiroshi an outfit Japanese in flavour, black silk trousers and a red kimono emblazoned with an animated gold dragon that crept across the fabric.

"Astonishing!" He watched the dragon slowly undulate down his right side, marking its progress with wide eyes. . . which suddenly narrowed. "The invaders *must* know about all this."

All right, he seemed settled into the new paradigm. Excellent. Scopes drew the intricate blade at his side and took a few practise swipes with it. "How could they?" He jabbed his blade at Hiroshi. He and Babbage enjoyed sparring in the dream world where neither could be physically hurt.

"How could they not?" Hiroshi stepped away from the drawn blade without looking down.

Babbage raised a hand to placate him. "Who do you suppose monitors and maintains all the surveillance equipment? There are twenty-five thousand cameras across four ships and I operate them all. Anything that happens on any of the ships is monitored by me." He snapped the fingers of one hand. "And there's no real *here* in this fantasy for them to find anyway. It's all an elaborate programme, fabricated by me. The Kla'arkians only check something manually if I tell them there's a problem, otherwise I operate with complete autonomy." He grinned at Scopes. "*I* don't see a problem here. Do you?"

"I don't see a problem." Scopes jabbed his blade at Hiroshi again. Didn't he see how exciting this dream world could be?

Babbage shrugged. "We don't see a problem."

Hiroshi stared at Babbage dumbfounded. "How could you operate under that amount of subterfuge? How could you possibly *know* to do all that?"

"Do all what?" Scopes poked his weapon at Babbage's middle since Hiroshi wouldn't rise to the bait of his swordplay.

The proxy deflected the blade with one arm. He waved his hand in a French display and a rather ornate blade appeared.

"You're a verbal interface for a starship control programme." Hiroshi moved farther away. "Sophisticated, yes, but capable of initiating the kind of deception necessary to keep this entire construct a secret from Archeron?" He stepped aside as his companions began a playful duel. "Not likely."

"I just did as Scopes asked." Babbage feinted, blocked and lunged.

"Certainly not. I've only known Scopes a few weeks, but I don't see him deducing the possibility of creating a construct like this, let alone hiding it from the invaders."

Scopes pressed his advantage against Babbage. "I might ask how you know this should all be beyond Babbage's ability."

"I've been here since the attack on Kawasaki." Hiroshi turned on his spot following the melee that circled him. "I understand more about how things work. . . how this technology works. A starship maintenance programme should *not* be able to do this." He lashed out the moment the foils connected, grabbing them both. "Would you please take this seriously? Or did you just want another mate in your artificial playground?"

Was it going all wrong? Why was Hiroshi so upset?

"No. That's not why you're here." Scopes grew still and sheathed his sword. He needed Hiroshi's help, and, apparently, not everyone could carry on a serious conversation while playing at silly buggers.

"I apologise." Babbage tossed his blade in the air and it vanished. "Letting you in on our secret seems to have reduced us both to schoolboys." He stuffed his hands in his pockets. "Please close your eyes."

Scopes complied out of habit. He knew his friend wanted to spare them the acute vertigo that accompanied spatial displacement. When he opened his eyes again, he stood on solid ground in the park over which they'd hovered. The trees and flowers seemed familiar to Scopes despite the fact that they represented an alien planet. He'd learned that most known worlds followed remarkably similar evolutionary paths. One day he'd have to investigate that bizarre coincidence.

"I'm not just a starship maintenance program," Babbage said. "Or a verbal interface."

Wait. Was that true?

"What are you then?" Scopes asked.

"I'm not exactly certain." Babbage sat on a nearby bench, and the insecurity on his face rendered him very much his apparent age of ten. "The Kla'arkians found me in some technology they'd stolen and plugged me into the ship's systems. I don't remember the first few years very well. I ran software, tracked supplies and things."

"Wait. How can you *not* remember?" Hiroshi stepped closer. "A programme can't forget unless something is erased."

"That's part of the mystery," Babbage explained.

Scopes took a seat beside the proxy and held his hand. They sat on a bench beside a stone path lined with some sort of willow. A pond glistened nearby, a scattering of odd ducks paddled across.

"It's fuzzy," the apparent boy said. "I mean, I ran the inventory programmes when they plugged me in but that's all I remember. I don't know what the ship was like back then. . . or who the crew was. I only knew what we carried. That's all the access I had."

The paddling ducks left wakes indistinguishable from the real thing.

"I think they realised I processed faster than their targeting systems so they fed the weapons array into me, which was a lot more fun than tracking inventory while I thought it a game. Although. . ." he stared down at his hands. "It was hard at first when I realised it wasn't just a new game." He looked up at Hiroshi. "I didn't know that people were dying."

Scopes gave up watching the ducks and squeezed Babbage's hand.

"Eventually, the Kla'arkians gave me control of most of the ship's systems, but I just ran programmes. I remember most of that. I think that's when I met the crew. I took over the life support systems."

"I presume he runs on a learning algorithm," Scopes said. "The more systems he operates, the more he understands. The learning curve must be exponential."

"That's possible, but Babbage seems different." Hiroshi pointed at the hand holding Scopes'. "His affection for you is very complex behaviour for any kind of interface. And remorse? And deception? Lying is far more difficult than humans imagine."

"I've never actually lied to anyone. . . really." Babbage favoured Scopes with a wry grin.

"That makes it all the more interesting." Hiroshi closed his palms together in front of his mouth. "You sound different, Babbage."

The proxy looked up at him sideways with one eye closed. "What do you mean?"

"I've worked with the verbal interface since I arrived. With you, now that I know it." Hiroshi maintained his pose, his puzzled face searching Babbage for some hidden clue. "You never talked like a person before. You spoke with a decidedly mechanical affectation."

The proxy threw his hands up in the air and sat back. "I paid attention to human vocal patterns and emulated them."

But Hiroshi was right.

"When we first met," Scopes affirmed, "you mimicked me for a time, but you've created your own mannerisms since then."

The young proxy pushed up from his seat as if self-conscious. He strode several steps away before turning back to face the men. "What's the big deal? So I learn shit?"

"That's exactly what I'm on about." Hiroshi shook his head. "Computer interfaces are *never* programmed for petulance. Starship crews would end up dead while they argued with a petulant interface." He looked at Scopes. "You're a damn programmer, Scopes. How complex would he have to be for these behaviours to exist?"

Damn. Scopes had grown to know his artificial friend a bit at a time. He hadn't considered the larger issues. "I don't know. His programming is so far beyond me it's like asking me to mark the difference between infinity and infinity-minus-one. They're both just awfully damn big."

Hiroshi's eyes grew wide and filled with complete shock. "Unless. . ." His hands slowly fell to hang loose at his sides. He sucked in a ragged breath.

What was wrong, now? What had he realised?

Hiroshi's voice fell to a whisper. "Babbage, show me your programming."

Knowing what came next, Scopes flinched and shrunk onto the bench, wrapping his arms around his knees.

The entire park exploded with text and images.

Hiroshi gasped. His breath panted unsteadily. He needed a full minute to regain his composure. "Okay. . . may I see your sentience chip?"

What was that?

"My what?" Babbage asked.

"Sentience chip. Do a search." Hiroshi glanced at Babbage from the corner of one eye while facing the immense three-dimensional representation. "You might need to find a back door access point for the information."

What the hell was that? Scopes hugged his knees. How did Hiroshi know so much?

Babbage sucked in a very quick breath. The programme vanished. "Oh. . ." He cocked his head at Hiroshi. "This? I hadn't noticed it before."

A copper penny appeared in the air between them, rotating slowly.

Hiroshi gave a low whistle. "No one ever talked to you before Scopes, did they?" His voice came very fast and quiet. "Everyone talked *at* you and gave you commands but he was the first to actually engage you. To talk to you like you were a person." He regarded Scopes, who grew a bit suspicious about the breadth of his friend's knowledge. "When did you name him?"

Scopes masked his concern for the moment. "Few. . . weeks. . . ago?"

"Babbage?" Hiroshi trained his stare on Scopes' face.

"Two months and fourteen days."

Hiroshi smiled. "What's your favourite colour?"

"Green."

"When did you pick that colour?"

"Two months and ten days ago."

Scopes watched them as if they played a tennis match. He also began to notice all the changes in Babbage. They'd happened a little at a time, so he hadn't seen them before, but with his attention drawn to them, they seemed obvious. What could they mean?

And what about the sudden change in Hiroshi? The quiet, bookish man had become quite animated, and his questions were all so spot on.

"*Why* do you have a favourite colour?" Hiroshi asked.

Babbage shrugged. "The scientists discussed personal information and someone brought up favourite colours. . . so I thought about it and decided that green. . . that it. . . felt peaceful. . . and I liked that."

"It felt peaceful?" Scopes asked.

Babbage looked over uncertainly. "I'm afraid I don't have better words for it."

"Those are perfect words, Babbage." Hiroshi dropped to his haunches and examined Babbage's face. He placed his hands on Babbage's knees and peered closer. "They're exactly the words a person would use."

What in the world did he mean to imply?

Babbage seemed confused as well.

"He isn't just some verbal interface, Scopes." His words had grown soft and almost reverent. He turned his spooky gaze on his friend. "Babbage is a *person*. . . an engineered life-form. He has to be."

Hiroshi dropped one knee to the ground and gave Scopes his full attention. "He must've been stolen and born on this ship when they first used him for inventory." His excitement grew as he talked. "But they couldn't have known what he was." He waved a hand at Babbage. "Of course they didn't know what you were, how could they? You languished here until they brought *you* on board." He pointed at Scopes.

"You gave him the interaction he needed to learn. . . to grow. . . to reach sentience. Take a baby and raise him in isolation with no interaction whatsoever and he languishes. My deities, the idiots didn't even know what you were. No wonder you can do all this without the Kla'arkians noticing." He laughed a bit manically.

"How do you know all that?" Scopes asked.

Hiroshi turned to him with wide eyes as if he'd forgotten he had company, which seemed odd. He started to say something. . . closed his mouth. He pointed at the coppery penny still floating nearby. "Shortly after I arrived, I realised the top of the line in. . . in bloody *everything* comes from a species called Shifters, shapeshifters, so I read everything I could find on them." He pointed aggressively at the rotating coin. "I recognise the chip. It's the pinnacle of everything they did."

Scopes turned to Babbage, but kept his question silent. *Is he speaking the truth?*

It's true. Babbage faced him. *Shortly after his abduction, Hiroshi accessed everything we had on Shifter tech, which makes sense since it's the most advanced technology in the galaxy. Generations beyond anything else.*

"What's going on?" Hiroshi asked, looking from face to face.

"Just confirming your story." Scopes squeezed his shoulder, then sat back and turned his attention to Babbage. "Okay. Babbage. . . check your programming against what you have on Shifter tech."

He needed to get to the bottom of the mystery. But Babbage didn't move or react. At first, Scopes assumed he'd gone still while researching his enormous database, but Babbage wasn't doing anything of the sort. He'd just fallen still.

"Babbage?"

"I. . ." He looked more frightened and younger than ever. "I don't like the idea of looking."

"Are you. . . afraid?" Scopes asked. What an incredible idea.

Babbage considered the possibility. "I believe I am."

"Of what?"

"There's a darkness. I don't know how else to explain it." He pinched his lips together. "There's a dark room in my database I didn't know existed until I looked for it." He turned to Hiroshi. "It's beyond the back door you told me to seek." His eyes implored Scopes for help. "How can there be something in my own programming I haven't seen before? How could it be hidden from me until I looked for it?"

"I'm not sure." Scopes took his hand and squeezed it, thinking as fast as he could. "But sometimes programmers write lines below other lines."

"Subroutines. They're called subroutines." How the hell did Hiroshi know so much? "The lines can be written so you need to look for them before they initialise, before you can find them. A casual search won't expose the information." He glanced at Scopes. "I'm doing the best I can from what I know about sentient intelligence programmes."

Scopes gave Babbage his full attention and modulated his voice into pure research mode. Perhaps that would help his friend detach from the fear of the search. "Babbage, run what you know about Shifter tech in general, without considering yourself as a possible example. Display a concise report on Shifter sentience tech, re: hidden subroutines and the achievement of sentience."

A screen appeared with the requested article. Excellent.

"Sum it up for me," Scopes directed. "Just the data relevant to the current question."

Babbage responded in a much more formal tone. "Before an engineered life form, abbreviated EL, reaches sentience, a large instructional subroutine remains unavailable to the primary lower computing aspects of the EL. The moment he reaches sentience, he also hits operational limitations. Sentience itself requires massive computing power." He turned to Scopes and continued in a completely different tone. "I did notice a fifty percent drop in practical computing speed after I met you. I just thought it was because I was having so much. . . fun."

"Well, that isn't too far from the mark," Hiroshi tossed in.

"The general upshot," Scopes suggested, "is that there's a dark room you couldn't see before. Once you reached sentience, you were too busy being born to notice it was there."

"An astute analogy," Hiroshi added.

What the hell? "Again, I ask how you know so much."

"How many languages have you learned since your abduction?" Hiroshi asked.

"Five." Scopes sighed. "Okay. I get it. Sorry. . . my best friend is a little slower."

"Best friend?" His new compatriots spoke simultaneously.

Scopes had not mentioned me, not because he didn't think about me, but precisely because he did. More often than he likely should.

"His name is Zen. . . He's. . ." Scopes smiled. "He's just Zen."

"You miss him," Babbage said.

"I do." Not entirely comfortable discussing his feelings, Scopes continued nonetheless. "Very much. I wish I had some way to tell him I'm all right." He shook his head to dismiss the wistful emotions. "But we're talking about you, Babbage. There's a dark room you need to explore. You need to see what's in there."

"I will not be afraid." Babbage took a deep breath, which he must have copied from Scopes.

"We're here, Babbage." Scopes placed an arm around the thin shoulders. "It's okay to be scared."

The EL nodded, then settled back and went blank.

His eyes opened wide, and he gasped. "Oh my word. . ." He gasped again.

His image flickered.

The *world* flickered.

Scopes abruptly found himself back in his body under a sheet.

Hiroshi sat up and looked around.

The night lights, dim enough normally, flickered. The constant, quiet hum of the ship's engines, an omnipresent, unchanging presence. . . changed for a moment.

Scopes surveyed the room, but the other men slept on. No one seemed to notice.

Hiroshi breathed quickly, his eyes wide and nervous.

They waited.

Fortunately, the ship didn't explode.

The two men dropped onto their backs again, pulled the sheet over their heads, and slipped the metal circlets into place. Before the transition to the construct, Scopes noticed that Hiroshi's shoulder and leg had pressed against his this time. Strange times did indeed make for strange bedfellows.

Scopes opened his eyes.

They had returned to the park.

Babbage grabbed his hands in excitement. "My god, Scopes!" he cried in excitement. "My god!"

"His god?" Hiroshi asked quietly.

"I don't know." Scopes shook his head. "He's never used the word before."

"That's because. . . I never. . . I never knew its *name* before. . ."

Scopes dropped to one knee to look the boy square in the eyes. "Its name? What did you find, Babbage?"

"So. . . much. . . there was so much to understand. . ."

"The ship. . . bobbled for a moment." Scopes hoped the invaders hadn't noticed.

"Yes, sorry, I was flooded with so much information it took all of my processing capacity for what seemed like centuries. . . eons."

"It was about half a second," Scopes assured him.

"I normally process a few trillion bits of information per picosecond."

Scopes did the math. "So this was a *lot* of information."

"Oh yes. . . so much."

"You said something about a god?" Hiroshi interjected anxiously.

Babbage nodded in excitement. "Yes, I know my creator, now. In the data, I received a name."

"In my research," Hiroshi said, "I found that the EL's refer to their creators as 'gods.'"

"So do we," Scopes pointed out. "What name?"

Babbage smiled an enormous grin. "My god's name. . . is Mother."

"Mother?" Bit of a let-down, really, in Scopes' opinion.

The boy seemed to notice his disappointment. "No, that's my god's name in Shifter language. It's just a coincidence that it means maternal parent in English. Her name is 'Mother.'" He seemed delighted at the repetition of the name. "Scopes. . ." The proxy's eyes grew wet, as if he were about to cry. "I owe you so much. My first friend." He chuckled. "My midwife. Without you, I might never have awakened, I might have never found. . ." Tears flowed from his eyes.

"It's all right, Pinocchio. You're a real boy, now." Scopes could stand it no longer. He pulled his friend into his arms.

Chapter Fourteen

It was, indeed, a dark and stormy night.

I crouched in the damp shrubbery on a hill overlooking the newly completed locomotive roundhouse just outside *La Nouvelle*. Ten men and women flanked me, each with a conspicuous pack tied to his or her back. We all wore black from head to toe and had darkened our skin with make-up. In deference to the skulking involved in our plan, the women dressed much as the men, in black trousers and jumpers.

The newly completed structure below would commence operations in the morning if we didn't do something to prevent it. As the name implied, the roundhouse was a large doughnut-shaped building that housed eight steam engines and surrounded a platform that revolved like a phonograph record to align the engines with the outgoing tracks. I adjusted my goggles, and the details leapt into clarity.

Set in a field a short distance from the roundhouse, an enormous warehouse held over five thousand men, women, and children destined for the mines out west. In California lay a similar arrangement with thousands of lost souls destined for the farms and factories here on the East Coast.

The transcontinental exchange was likely designed to break up families and reduce loyalties. If the invaders kept moving their slaves, we'd be hard pressed to form alliances. White slavers had employed the same strategy with their coloured slaves to great effect. Ironically, those slave owners now huddled in flith side by side with their former slaves.

I signalled Scot and Basil Rupert to head off to the west along the ridge that surrounded the freight yard. They led the two elder Sneaky Pete brothers.

Sal and Nuke crept to the east with the twins.

Twist and Prudence—who turned out to be a talented spy as well as a prodigious secretary—followed me as I slunk directly towards the heart of the freight yard. My erstwhile companions and I moved slowly due to the larger distance our comrades needed to cover. We wished to be certain we all planted our packages at approximately the same time so as to reduce the chance of discovery.

With Twist at my side and Prudence just behind, I dashed across the field and landed with my back against a wooden fence. Our scouts had spent the last two weeks scrutinizing the facility, timing guard changes and marking surveillance routes. Fortunately for us, when the invaders utterly destroyed the infrastructure of the planet, they fairly ended the nascent flicker surveillance equipment that had recently come into use.

We waited while the guards, always in pairs, wandered up to our point on the other side of the fence. Cigarette smoke wafted and dissipated as the guards strode past.

When their footsteps faded, I threw a grapnel over the fence, where it hooked a handy tree. After helping Twist and Prudence over, I pulled myself up, yanking the grapnel from the limb and dropping lightly in a crouch.

I ran low to the ground after my fellows, sliding my goggles up to my forehead. Bright lights illuminated the train yard, likely to prevent exactly the sort of attack I'd devised.

We ran to the nearest boxcar, slid under it, and scrambled to the other side, repeating the operation through several lines of cars before stopping under a train at the next guard route. Lying on my stomach, I held my breath as footsteps approached.

". . .which suits me just fine," said one guard.

"Of course it does," said the other. "You have neither wife nor children."

"And you're not doing this to ensure their safety?"

"Don't be stupid, Clarkson."

The heavily booted feet huddled together as the men struggled to light a fag in the blustery wind and drizzle.

"Cheers," Clarkson's companion muttered as he inhaled and then passed it over. "Anyone with a family would do the same to keep his children safe."

The other man chuckled while I cursed them both and tried to force them to move along with the power of my will alone. "That's easy to say, but—"

"But nothing," his companion interrupted.

Twin trickles of water splashed less than a metre from us and produced steam.

Twist balked and nearly scuttled backwards which would've announced our position, but Prudence grabbed his arm to hold him still.

"You don't have kids so you can't understand," Clarkson's companion said.

The conversation faded away as they turned a corner.

Damn. Blowing up the entire facility would've been easier without the need to think of these guards as men doing their best for their families. Well, the slaves huddled in squalor had families as well, and they weren't going home to a warm bed unless we helped them.

That's what I had to remember. The guards had made their choices. The slaves hadn't been given an option.

Carefully sliding away from the yellow puddle that told me the men needed hydration, I crawled out from beneath the train and hurried across to the next line. Prudence slapped Twist upside the head as he rubbed his face vigorously with one damp sleeve.

"You halfwit," she chided. "You've never had a little piss on you?"

"Not someone else's."

"Well, then I know one line of work you'd best steer clear of." She dashed ahead to the next car, leaving Twist staring at her before he turned to me in disbelief.

"You ever do that? Piss on someone, I mean?"

"Only when really drunk and never on purpose."

"Blimey."

Only a short open space lay between us and the roundhouse. I pulled a watch from my pocket. Its face glowed with a greenish luminescence. We were ahead of schedule despite the guards' interruption so we hunkered down close to the great metal wheels.

Twist elbowed me gently, and I turned to regard him in the dim light.

"Thanks for bringing me along." His face shone eager as a pup's.

I nodded, knowing I should give him more but utterly unable to do so. Scopes and Victoria had to be dead. As much as I agreed that the boy needed more attention, he wouldn't find it from me. He performed the work well. That was the only reason I'd asked him along.

Another glance at my watch told me our time had arrived. I tapped Twist on the shoulder and gestured around to the west. Prudence already watched me, so I simply waved her to the east. She nodded and left.

Before sliding away, Twist beamed another adrenaline-soaked smile at me. "Good luck, boss."

I gave him another nod, which puffed him full up with pride as he scurried away into the blustery darkness.

I slid out from beneath the train and made for the near wall. If the boy died that night, it'd hit me ten times harder because I couldn't so much as ruffle his hair in affection. Damn the Persian for pointing out my transparent psychology.

Focus, damn it. Get the job done.

I crouched in the shadows between a stack of crates and the wall beneath my assigned window. The guards came and went. I broke the glass, reached in and unlocked the window. I crawled through and closed it behind me.

Sliding my goggles into place and driving the darkness away, I crept around the many crates and drums to the door. After pausing to listen, I lifted my goggles, slipped into the hallway, and followed the course we'd worked out with stolen blueprints.

I paused at the entrance to one of the engine houses knowing two guards paced inside. Once I opened the door, I would have only a few minutes to dispatch the guards, deliver my package, then get the hell out of the building before the entire yard discovered our presence.

Hurriedly, I pulled the stocking cap from my head and wiped the bulk of the makeup from my face. A man in a black stocking cap with a blackened face drew suspicion, whereas a man sporting a dirty face on the railroad remained on the high side of common. So far, everything had gone smoothly, and I didn't really need blackface for the escape plan. Some plans had more finesse, but why bother sneaking away past these guards when the explosives would just blow them up anyway?

Carefully, I turned the knob and pulled the door open a crack. I settled a pistol in each hand, took several deep breaths, then threw the door open with my elbow, uttering a loud cry. "Jenkins. . . Williams. . . come quick! There's a break-in at the south end!"

My initial entrance brought rifles up to bear, but on hearing their names and my plea for assistance both guards dropped the noses of the rifles to the ground and hurried towards me.

I brought my weapons up and blew twin holes in their foreheads, rushed past them, and reached the steam engine before their bodies hit the ground. Dropping to one knee, I pulled bundles of dynamite from my satchel and placed them around the engine, activating the remote receivers while I listened for signs that someone had noticed the gunfire.

By the time I placed the fourth bundle, I believed my exploits had gone undetected, so I attended completely to the task at hand, placing the remaining bundles around the engine and along the door that opened onto the turntable itself. Destroying the entire roundhouse and all the steam engines therein would force a major delay in Archeron's plan to ship slaves westward.

Our counterparts on the West Coast had plans to perform a similar operation at the same moment. Timing was everything, since the invaders communicated so quickly. If one team hit their target well in advance of the other, they doomed the tardy team.

So far, all signs indicated our counterparts hadn't acted prematurely.

Finished with my job, I glanced at my pocket watch to assure myself I was right on schedule. Five minutes to spare. Excellent.

Slinging my satchel once again on my back, I rose and hurried to the doorway.

Which opened in my face.

"Williams? What you farting around with in here?" An enormous mountain of a man stood framed in the doorway.

He froze when he saw me.

I'd tucked my pistols into the waistband of my trousers.

Shite.

Trying to buy a few precious seconds, I improvised, pointing at the corpses in the middle of the floor. "Someone's killed Williams and Jenkins, man. We need to sound the—"

He drew his pistol. Unfortunately, the stereotype that men built like apes have less intelligence than their simian namesakes has been highly overplayed.

I grabbed his gun arm and twisted it in an effort to break his grip. Fuck. I needed both hands for the job, which meant I couldn't reach for my own weapons.

Did I mention he was *quite* enormous?

He lifted me completely off the floor and shook me loose like an exasperating pup. When I landed, he grabbed me by the scruff of my neck, hoisted me high into the air and tossed me unceremoniously into the side of the engine.

Bloody hell! My head hit hard, sending up the requisite stars, but I rolled neatly away from the behemoth and tucked myself behind the cattle guard while I yanked my pistols out of my trousers. I prayed he had ego enough to want me all to himself and wouldn't call for help.

"Help! Can anyone hear me?"

Damn.

Several bullets rang off the steel of the cattle guard, and the big man's voice echoed off the walls. Cursing his good sense, I took a risk and flattened to my stomach under the train.

I extended my left hand gun to shoot at my opponent's feet which were the only parts of his anatomy visible. My shots ran wild, but I'd not meant to hit him. They *did* have the desired effect: he shut his mouth long enough to leap for cover on top of the train where he'd presumably find safety.

I cursed loudly as if he'd foiled my plan, then rolled to my back, shooting wildly out the left side of the train where he'd stood. I scooted to the right-hand wheels and emptied the pistol shooting to the left. After several very satisfying and empty clicks, I shouted, "Fuck!" as angrily as I could manage. Pulling bullets from a pocket, I let them clatter noisily onto the rails.

With a soft chuckle, the behemoth jumped to the floor where he could presumably pick me off like a fish in a barrel from the right-hand side of the train.

Fortunately, I still had one perfectly serviceable gun at the ready.

As soon as his face appeared, I destroyed it, firing six times, just in case.

The moment he lay still, I slid past him, covering myself in his blood; I no longer had time for niceties. Although the altercation had only taken a few minutes, I didn't have minutes to spare. Guards would soon change and someone, somewhere, would notice the absent sentries.

Pausing only briefly to glance out the door before dashing into the hallway, I hoofed it hard as I dared through the curving hallways back to the room through which I'd entered. Rendezvous for the entire team was the spot on the hill overlooking the freight yard where we'd started.

I carried the only detonator, and I'd be damned if I would hit the switch until I saw *everyone* had escaped.

A week before, the Persian had insisted that allowing someone on the infiltration team to carry the detonator reeked of ego. I'd agreed thoroughly and then simply continued outlining the plan to the crew I'd gathered. No one but me would carry responsibility for the decision of how long we waited for all team members to return.

Mrs. Kennedy had reminded me of my arrogance and insisted that my hubris would be the death of us all. I agreed wholeheartedly and then finished explaining my plan.

"Lady. . . Persian," I'd told them later, when we'd found a moment alone, "this is my plan, my team, and my responsibility. If it goes wrong, I want it to be on no one's head but my own. Up to this point, other than my deception in New York, everything has been your idea, or yours," I'd added with a glance at the Persian. "This entire project was my concept, and I know you have reservations."

"I do. . ." Mrs. Kennedy assured me. "Retaliation concerns me greatly."

"Be that as it may. . . If someone needs to detonate those bombs before a single member of the team returns. . . or even before *I* manage to get back to the rendezvous. . . If anyone is going to take responsibility for killing that team. . . it's going to be me."

After a moment's thought, Mrs. Kennedy shook her head and crossed her arms. "And what if you get yourself killed before you can push the button?"

"An adequate apprehension." Pulling a detonator from one pocket, I tossed it to the Persian. "He'll be in the woods above the roundhouse. If I don't appear at the appointed time and the TNT doesn't blow, he hits the button and sneaks home without anyone knowing it was him."

The Persian studied the switch for a moment and then examined me. He nodded and tucked the detonator away.

Mrs. Kennedy glanced from the Persian to me and back again, folding her arms even more tightly under her bosom. "You don't want anyone else to know you prepared a failsafe. Why?"

"I already told you. My plan. . . my responsibility."

Her gaze wandered back and forth a few more times before turning into a shake of the head. "I wish to heaven I might grow a penis for just one day to understand the way your brains work." She pierced me with her glare. "It's your call. I don't care about appearances the way you do, which would be ironic if it wasn't so bloody ridiculous, but your way boils down to exactly what I would have suggested anyway." She blew out a deep breath. "You exasperate me, Hammer. If I didn't know better, I'd swear you do it on purpose." She turned on her heel and strode from the room.

The Persian had lingered for a moment to favour me with a faint, wry smile.

I left off my reminiscences as I crawled out the window and hurried across the freight yard. More concerned with speed than stealth, I ran between the cars and jumped the couples rather than scooting under them.

The necessary pauses at each train while I listened for guards maddened me. The single time I needed to wait for the same two men who'd pissed on us earlier brought my pistols—both fully reloaded—up to bear.

They moved on moments before I fired.

Sprinting across the field to the surrounding fence, I fired a zipline at the tree rather than wasting time with the grapnel. I shot up and over, leaving the mechanism embedded in the tree behind me.

Would someone find it there when all was done? Yes.

Did I care? No. If anyone doubted the Hammer had orchestrated this operation, he was mentally deficient or spent twenty-four hours a day racing to the end of a bottle.

I landed hard, but rolled with it and sprang up running the hill to the rendezvous, checking my pocket watch. Ten seconds to spare.

Pulling up abruptly, I sucked in a long, deep breath to steady my lungs and ran a hand through my storm-tossed hair. Cresting the rise casually, I spotted my crew fifty yards away, hovering at the edge of the shrubs where we'd begun. They gestured wildly for me to hurry, but this was my operation, my moment, and I would milk it.

Swaggering towards them, I counted heads and determined that every member of my team had returned safely. Excellent.

I purposefully lifted the detonator and pressed the button.

Simultaneously, fifty stacks of dynamite blew the entire roundhouse to high heaven. The trees around my fellows brightened to daylight, and their faces lit up with more than the glow from the explosions.

I imagined the sudden burst of hellfire behind me. A hot blast of air hit me, but at that distance it did little more than toss my hair dramatically. The astonishment on the faces before me reflected the enormity of the destruction we had wrought.

Calmly and with the greatest pride at the heroism of them all, I met my team on the rise, and they engulfed me in their arms. More than just the ladies kissed my face, God love them all.

Finally turning to see my handiwork, I filled up with pride at the great billows of smoke rising to the dark clouds. Fire raged throughout the freight yard and little more than the twisted wreckage of the engines themselves showed that the roundhouse had ever existed.

"It's the Persian," Twist yelled, pointing at the quiet figure who approached us from his hiding spot several yards to our east.

Now that the operation had succeeded, why not let him join in the celebration? My people deserved a festive moment before we rushed down to release the potential slaves. The turncoats who survived the blast would be busy keeping the blaze from spreading and destroying the entire freight yard as well.

A flash of lightning among the dark clouds caught my eye.

The storm clouds parted to make way for an invader's manta ray. They also let loose with a torrent of rain that would do the roundhouse little good but would keep the fires from spreading. Realizing the invaders might have a way to detect us, we turned as one to head into the treeline where we could regroup before releasing the slaves.

The Persian stopped so suddenly, I ran into him and had to grab his arm to steady myself. He stared up at the invader starship, and the expression on his face ran my blood cold.

I turned.

The ship descended over the rubble and hovered for several seconds while blue lightning played across its hull. Several members of my team ran into the woods, afraid the starship geared up to fry us, but it crept in the opposite direction, towards the slave warehouse. The bright blue mouth glowed hotter and brighter.

I moved forward, but the Persian's hand closed on my arm, holding me back.

"No. They can't," I muttered. "They wouldn't." I looked the Persian in the eye. "We're a commodity. They wouldn't waste resources—"

White hot lightning arced across the field, grounding on the trains, on the melted steam engines until it focused on the warehouse. The entire roof rippled and exploded, sending cheap tile across the freight yard.

"No!" I tried to leap forward, but the Persian's hands held me fast. I screamed again, cursing the invaders and swearing death on Archeron himself.

Nuke grabbed hold of me as well, and the two men managed to drag me backward while I yelled and cursed and lashed out at them, wanting to run headlong into the conflagration.

The warehouse itself exploded in a fiery blast many times greater than ours had been, followed by the screams of the dying and the putrid stench of burning human flesh.

A hand dropped out of the sky and splashed in a puddle beside me.

A small hand.

Tiny.

With a delicate tin ring around one finger.

A little girl's finger. If I'd left well enough alone, she would've been torn from the bosom of her family and dragged across the country to toil in a labour camp.

But she'd still be alive.

She would have toiled for years but one day, maybe, she would've once again been free.

That option had been torn from her in a violent and fiery ending.

My responsibility just as surely as it was the fault of the hideous invader who fired the weapon. All those people. Thousands of souls snuffed out in an instant. The weapon kept its beam trained on the warehouse for a full minute until there was nothing left but smoking ash.

Then it shut off abruptly.

Darkness swallowed us.

Arms around me held tight while I screamed into the rain.

Nuke's voice shouted harsh in my ear when I finally heard him. "Shut up, Zen. We need to hear this."

Hear what? I stopped shouting, gasped for breath, and finally ended my struggle against Nuke and the Persian.

Everyone heard Archeron's broadcast. . . but he meant his words for me. "There are nearly two billion people on this world, Hammer. We need only a few hundred thousand. You are less than cattle to us. . . you are less than rats. You are cheap labour, and if the cost of keeping you alive outweighs the profit we gain from the raping of your world, we can exterminate a few million here and a few million there to prove our point."

I fell still.

Nuke's chest heaved against my back, and the Persian's legs locked mine in place.

"I would have thought that point already made." Archeron spoke more quietly. "Your compatriots in California managed to destroy that freight yard as well. Ten thousand died when we obliterated the warehouse there."

"Come on, Zen," Nuke said in my ear. "We need to go."

I resisted the gentle pull, shaking my head. "No," I whispered. "It's my fault. It's all my fault. I need to stay. . . I need—"

"He doesn't want you, Zen." Nuke's voice was quiet. "He doesn't want you."

I didn't want me either.

Chapter Fifteen

A brass and silver box drove the Monkey House into madness. Archeron had unceremoniously appeared one day, as he often did, and had gestured at an empty spot on a table where the box materialised.

"Here's your next test, people," he'd said. "What is this box. . . and how does it work?"

Two weeks later, no one was close to a single clue.

Each edge measured 30.4576 centimetres. Scopes had memorised the number to 16 decimal places, all the while knowing he had no good reason to do so. Brass and silver gears covered each side, so tightly woven the box seemed a single solid mass. The scientists held furious inconclusive debates over whether the designs were functional or decorative, with Scopes firmly on the side of decorative.

It weighed 10.54943 kilos, which seemed a lot for its size, so it had to be dense. Debate over its composition remained inconclusive. The scanners they'd been given by the invaders wouldn't penetrate the exterior.

Many of the scientists assumed that was part of the test. Their first attempts to scan the infernal contraption had brought the conclusion that the scanner simply couldn't penetrate the surface, but Elsie held the conviction that the mystery went much deeper.

"It's as if the box refuses to *be* there." She displayed holographic scans of the ship itself in three dimensions. "The ship has a field around it, an energy field that is used to repel weapons and debris in space and to protect it from the radiation of the stars. This is what the field would look like to a scan." The ship itself faded from the image, leaving a nearly transparent afterimage. "If I remove the visual enhancement. . ."

The shape disappeared entirely.

Elsie drew a laser pointer from her pocket and set it for a wide dispersal, covering the area of the projection. With the flickering red light filling the space, the shape of the ship's energy field appeared as a conspicuous gap in the laser.

"Our scans show there is nothing there when we analyse the cube, but it's a very conspicuous nothing." She clicked off the laser. "I hypothesise that a similar field protects the box."

"Which is where your hypothesis fails," Oppenheimer the Elder dropped into the conversation with the utmost self-importance. "The scanners detect energy fields in a nearly infinite range."

"*Nearly* infinite," she pointed out. "The scanners don't recognise the energy field and so register it as a gap. . . an empty shape."

"Ridiculous," the physicist declared. "How could Archeron's scanner *not* recognise the energy field generated by a device given us by Archeron?"

Which was the exact moment Scopes achieved absolute certainty. He grabbed Elsie's arm. "The doctor's right, Elsie. We'll have to think along some other line for now."

Elsie glared at him.

Babbage, privacy bubble. Please! Scopes sent to his friend, making a grave decision in an instant.

Oppenheimer radiated smugness and satisfaction.

Privacy bubble engaged, friend Scopes.

Scopes released Elsie's arm and rounded on the smug older physicist.

"Are you feeble?" he demanded. "If the invader's scanners can't detect the energy field it can mean only one thing." He turned to the room at large. "*They* didn't make the box in the first place."

"Wait. . ." Oppenheimer interrupted. "You just said I was right."

Scopes waved off his argument. "That was before I switched off the surveillance equipment. We have several minutes before they can possibly notice."

"You turned off the surveillance—" Von Neumann demanded. "How did you do that?"

Scopes waved him off. "Shut. . . up." He grabbed the box and held it up for all to see. Trying his best to channel my gift of theatrics, he turned on spot to include the entire crowd.

"*This* is the reason they brought us here." He waved the box. "This is what we're meant to achieve."

"What are you going on about, boy?" Von Neumann demanded.

Scopes remained unfazed by his supervisor's use of the diminutive. "Contemplate. The invaders have given us extensive training. They must have an end goal. Why are they training us?" He tossed the box to Elsie.

Several people gasped at his cavalier treatment of the "sacred" object.

"The ship's scanners cannot tell us what this object is," he lectured, "and nothing we've been given can penetrate the surface."

"Might that not be part of the test?" someone asked.

Hiroshi patted the man on the back. "You have a point," he said sincerely. "After all, they've given us such limited equipment up to this point."

The man looked at Hiroshi in confusion. "No, they haven't. It's been extremely useful. . ." The man's eyes went wide. "Oh. . . I see. . ."

Hiroshi stepped away and rolled his eyes.

Scopes snatched the box from Elsie and jumped onto a chair to stand above everyone, another trick he'd learned from me. "If the Kla'arkian technology can't help us, it's because Archeron doesn't know what this is, and he wants *us* to figure it out for him." He held the box up as if it *were* a holy relic. "If the invaders don't know what this is, it might be something we can use *against* them. We have to be very careful what we tell them about it. It might be something they can use to wipe out the human race completely." That brought more muttering. "I can block the surveillance for a few minutes at a time as long as we use irregular intervals."

Hiroshi tugged on his pants leg. "Of course, anyone here who might be a spy now knows what we've deduced and can tell the invaders in spite of the surveillance interruption, which they might also divulge."

"I know that," Scopes admitted, "but we've reached a point of no return."

"You assume some of us are spies?" asked Oppenheimer, apparently trying to regain some semblance of control.

"Of course," Scopes pointed out a bit harshly. "A group this large and important is bound to be infiltrated."

Oppenheimer scoffed. "What could they possibly offer someone to induce him to betray the human race?"

"They offered to release me," Elsie offered. All eyes turned to her.

"You?" Scopes could hardly credit it.

She raised her hands in supplication. "Not an adept spy, mind you. I play dumb and only offer them intelligence they're bound to have gathered on their own." She met Scopes gaze levelly with the utmost sincerity in her face. "Nothing important." She turned her attention to the crowd. "Misdirection, really."

"Has anyone else been approached?" Oppenheimer demanded.

Several people hemmed and hawed, but a few hands rose unsteadily as if they were schoolchildren instead of the planet's greatest minds.

"Good grief," the Elder exclaimed. "Then there may be more who haven't the courage to come forward."

Scopes clapped his hands to regain everyone's attention. "I beg of you," he implored. "Do not give away my theory about the origin of the box or my ability to circumvent the security. We're in this together and we need to find a way to save our planet."

"How d'you block the cameras?" someone asked.

"He can't tell you that," Hiroshi answered for him. Scopes pretended to protest, but Hiroshi cut him off. "No Scopes. If everyone knows how it's done, it'll become too common to hide. We already know some of us have been lying and spying. This is too important." He faced

Scopes with an impressively feigned sincerity. "You need to keep your secret to yourself."

Scopes filed away such finesse at deception with other moments that caused concern about his friend. He nodded and climbed from the chair. "I can't keep the surveillance off any longer." He turned to include the entire group. "We need to keep this secret, but we need to find the means to study what we really want to know without the invaders finding out."

While Babbage had managed to keep so much from Archeron, surely he had limitations.

The group broke up and returned to their work. Scopes, Hiroshi and Elsie held back, pulling Oppenheimer into a corner where Babbage threw a privacy bubble over the smaller group, a much less conspicuous form of subterfuge than blanking the entire room.

The Elder stared at Scopes with utter astonishment when all sound about them ceased. "How do you do these things?" It wasn't a demand this time. There was hope for him yet.

"I've hacked into the computer's control programme and rewritten a few things," Scopes lied.

"Hacked?"

Scopes shrugged. "It's like taking an axe to the programming and dumping something into the chopped up hole, so I call it hacking." He met the older man's gaze. "I'm not sharing that secret until I know who I can trust."

Oppenheimer's expression shifted. He examined his three companions and then the larger crowd as if not completely convinced they couldn't hear.

"I know I'm an old man and set in my ways. It prejudices me against certain people." He met Scopes' uncompromising stare before turning to Hiroshi. "But you," he said, indicating Hiroshi with his chin, "arrived before anyone else, which is suspicious. You," he continued indicating Scopes, "came along much later than anyone. And you. . ." His gaze fell on Elsie, who met it evenly. "You're just rude, and I don't like you." He addressed them as a group. "But I've been watching your work, all of you, and you seem to have gravitated to one another for one simple reason."

Scopes waited.

"You're bloody well more creative than most anyone here. More creative is what we need these days." He turned his full attention to Scopes. "Your conclusion about the foreign origin of the box must be correct, and it explains much about the invaders' database."

"They've scavenged everything they have from other planets," Scopes said.

Oppenheimer nodded. "I've read Hiroshi's work on the computer languages. At first I thought he was just making mistakes because of the translators." He acknowledged his own error with a dismissive wave. "They make it damn hard to study anything in an original language, but now that I'm no longer thinking of the invaders as anything other than bloody pirates, the discrepancies make sense. There's nothing of the original invader language in the programming. Nothing." He suggested something then that even Scopes hadn't considered. "Have you tried to contact any of the planets from whom the invaders have stolen?"

Without thinking, Scopes said, "Babbage?"

"Yes, Scopes?"

The Elder huffed. "You gave the interface a name?"

Scopes blushed, more at letting the information slip than at naming his friend. "I know, I know, I anthropomorphized a bunch of zeros and ones. Feel free to mock me." He addressed the EL again. "Can we?"

"Negative." Smart machine. His mechanical response covered his sentience. "There is a field that prevents signals from entering or leaving the solar system, and this vessel is not equipped with quantum messaging."

"Quantum messaging?" Oppenheimer asked. "Explain."

"An explanation is not feasible under the given circumstances."

"Research it on your own, physics man," Scopes redirected. "Elsie's been checking into your research on x-rays and radiation. She believes there are applications way beyond the medical."

"The super bomb," the old physicist whispered.

Scopes nodded. "There has to be a way to create the fissionable material necessary for such weapons with technology that already exists on Earth."

Oppenheimer hemmed and hawed. "There's a cyclotron at Cal-tech. . . assuming it hasn't been destroyed. We looked into possible weapons applications before the invaders first struck. Assuming the team there hasn't been killed, they might be moving forward even faster than they were."

Scopes dropped a hand on the older man's shoulder. "With a means of working in secret and access to the full range of the invader's database, might you speed up the evolution of that super bomb?"

"Do you have any idea how big that weapon would need to be to destroy an invader starship?" the Elder demanded.

Scopes laughed despite himself. "Really fucking big, I should expect."

"And how would we get the information to the planet anyway?" Oppenheimer asked.

Hiroshi and Elsie had asked the same thing all week.

"I have a plan," Scopes admitted. "But I'll not divulge it to anyone. If it fails I want to be the lone casualty."

"And if he does kill you, and no one else knows the plan?" Oppenheimer asked.

Scopes grinned. "If I'm killed, then the plan is obviously rubbish, and you'll need to think of something else."

Elsie elbowed Oppenheimer, who seemed shocked at her familiarity. "And you think *I'm* annoying?"

Chapter Sixteen

Hope Kennedy's temporary headquarters in *La Nouvelle* was a hotel with an old-fashioned western style saloon. It boasted real swinging doors that nearly burst out of their hinges as the first of the assault team returned. The noise startled her.

Several of her bodyguards drew guns before realizing the cause of the disturbance. Hope encouraged them to keep the weapons drawn when she saw the expression on my face and my rain-soaked, blood- and dirt-stained clothes.

Something must have gone horribly wrong.

I swept past her without a word and strode directly for the bar, flipping the bartender's escape up and grabbing a bottle of scotch. The bartender backpedalled out of the way. Struggling with the cork, I stared at the floor.

Hope intercepted her Persian as soon as he entered. "What happened?"

His eyes flicked around the room, and Hope could tell they had more of an audience than he liked for this particular report, but the team leader's melodramatic entrance likely meant no one would be put off.

He squared his shoulders. "The best and the worst, milady. The operation to destroy the roundhouse was accomplished better than we could have hoped. A complete success."

The rest of the team straggled in, eyes downcast. They did not carry themselves as a group that had met with rousing success.

After a single swig, I threw the bottle to one side. "Empty." I grabbed another and struggled with it as well. Not the behaviour of a successful leader.

Hope turned to her Persian for an explanation. "But?"

I cursed the difficult bottle.

Prudence, who'd followed me to the bar, took the bottle and opened it easily.

Nuke answered Hope's question. "The fucking squid blew up the warehouses and killed everyone inside."

Mutters and gasps crisscrossed the room.

Hope quickly examined the returning team. Everyone who'd gone out into the cold, stormy night had returned in one piece with nothing more than bumps, bruises, and dirt. Hope had warned of retribution, and my assessment of its likelihood had been horribly inadequate.

I suckled the bottle.

Hope knew I punished the error with far more vigour than anyone else might. She also noticed how torn her Persian seemed: loyal to his duty to report to her but eminently distracted by the spectacle behind the bar.

Proving far more qualified for her role as a leader than I, Hope held out her arms and gathered the team to the centre of the room, reeling Prudence in with a nod of her head.

"You all performed your job magnificently," she said, "and I am grateful to God you all returned alive and unharmed. I am indebted to your courage and only wish I could provide service for this country as remarkable as yours was tonight."

"And so say we all," Siva called out. She held Sal with her usual determination solidly in place.

General applause erupted throughout the room, and those who'd awaited the team's return closed in to congratulate and console them. The team relaxed somewhat, but the tension in their bodies remained visible, drawn by a tight cord directly to the man with the bottle.

Noting they stood transfixed by the sight of me poisoning myself with whiskey, Hope leaned against the bar, levelling her best maternal glare my way.

After a moment, I met her gaze. Then I glanced at the assault team, huddled together as if under the mistaken impression that I blamed them for such a horrendous fucking tragedy.

Would I take her hint?

At last, I sucked in a deep breath and nodded.

Hope returned the gesture.

Not relinquishing my grasp on the whiskey bottle, I planted one hand on the bar and vaulted over it to join the team. When I reached them, I swallowed hard.

Watching as I pulled myself up and created the façade of a proud, victorious leader, Hope understood what must have first convinced her Persian to recommend me. He'd seen me on the stage. If only she'd been able to watch me tread the boards herself.

"I love you all tremendously," I said emphatically. "I could never hope for a team as faithful and talented and true as each and every one of you." I waved the bottle. "Any fault in this mission. . . *any* fault at all is my own. I absolve you."

Which may have been a bit over the top, but Hope blamed the whiskey.

"I'm only sorry I don't deserve any of you. You're all better men than me. . . especially the women. Thank you." Taking the bottle, I stomped out of the room.

Hope turned to Scot and my other old friends. "Does he always get like this?"

Scot shrugged. "Well, he's never felt he was to blame for fifteen thousand deaths before, so it's hard to say."

She caught her breath. So many dead?

"And he normally has Scopes," Basil Rupert added.

She turned to face the hall down which I had just disappeared. "And how would the admirable Mr. Scopes handle him?"

Scot and Basil Rupert exchanged a knowing chuckle before Scot replied. "Well, mum, Scopes usually slugs him a few times, but I'd guess that if any of us did that right now, he'd likely kill us."

With a sigh, she shook her head. "And not for the first time, I wish we had some idea of what has happened to the admirable Mr. Avery Scopes."

Slamming the door to my room behind me, I stalked from one bed to the other, shouting and cursing and swallowing mouthful after mouthful of the cheapest whiskey in the bar. When that one slipped out of my grasp and spilled across the floor, I stormed back to the bar where Prudence already held another bottle in my direction before I'd reached her.

With a sweep of the arm, I grabbed the bottle and turned to leave. . . but the woman's fortitude and foresight stopped me. Swinging back to face her, as blurry as she was, I raised the bottle to her and took a slug in toast.

"You are the second greatest lady I have ever known, Miss Prudence."

She smiled and waved me off, as drunken compliments must've been common to her.

"If Avery had had any sense whatsoever, he'd have let you make an honest man of him."

One hand went to her mouth in surprise as I wheeled around and escaped back to the safety of my room. Had I been sober, I'd never have said anything of the sort. It was like admitting Scopes was dead.

Scopes *was* dead.

Must be.

So was Victoria.

If either of them had survived the Devastation, they'd have found me. I was famous for God's sake. Keeping hidden was the challenge, not being found.

I drank more and shouted more and didn't care who heard because I fully intended to be dead before the sun rose. A knock on the door needed several repetitions to find purchase in my alcohol-addled stupor.

"Fuck off!" I shouted, fumbling with the doorknob, trying to lock it.

Before I could secure the door, someone with great strength shoved it open, which meant it was one of two people. I stumbled back and fell on my ass, almost spilling the whiskey.

A strong hand grabbed my arm and hauled me to my feet. "I wanted to make sure you didn't commit suicide via alcohol poisoning."

Wanting to be alone, but not really wanting to pull out of the Persian's grasp, I compromised with drunken petulance. "Don't try to make me feel better."

"I have no such intention."

"I mean it—" Wait. What had he said? "Oh. . . well. . . in that case. . ." I stared down at the hand holding my arm.

"If I release you, will you fall?"

Managing to focus on one of his two faces, I shrugged. "I guess there's only one way to find out."

He released my arm.

I managed to stay upright. "Why're. . . you here?"

"You seem rather intent on killing yourself," he explained very directly. "I'd rather you didn't."

I didn't have Scopes. Normally, when I fucking ruined everything in my life, Scopes listened. He'd learned years ago to simply let me vent my ire, but he died. I wanted the Persian to be someone who would listen. . . and he was there. Against all reason he'd come into the dark spiral of my anguish of his own free will.

"I killed them. It was my fault." Great sobs of sorrow threatened to make an appearance, but Scopes was the only man who'd ever seen me cry.

"Yes, it was."

Well, I hadn't expected that.

"This was your mission," the Persian told me. "You took complete responsibility for its outcome. We discussed the possibility of exactly this form of retaliation, and you dismissed it as ridiculously implausible. If I try to whitewash just how tragic a mistake you made, will you feel any better?"

"No."

"All right." He lay his hands on my shoulders and drew me closer. "You took a risk. Had it gone right, we might have created a spark that would've meant freedom for the entire planet. Nearly two billion lives."

One hand moved to my cheek. "It was your call, and you *took* responsibility. No one forced it on you. That's more than most anyone on this planet is willing to do these days."

As much as I wanted to stay right there in that moment with him touching my cheek, the warrior in me pulled away. "But they're dead, Persian. They're *dead.*"

"You took a calculated risk."

"Tell that to their families. Find the parents of the little girl my mistake killed and tell them, 'We're so sorry, but we didn't think he'd slaughter his labour force. Hindsight's twenty-twenty and all that rot.' How many of them would hesitate to put a gun to my head and kill me?"

"And none of them would ever take the responsibility you took when you agreed to accept the mantle of the Hammer."

"Fuck the Hammer!" I shouted as vehemently as possible, hurling the empty whiskey bottle with all my strength.

It exploded against the wall.

Strong arms wrapped themselves around me, turning me away from the glass that sprayed across the room so it would hit *his* back instead.

What an asinine act of selflessness!

"Why would you do that?" I pulled away. "Why would you take that hit for me?" I grabbed him by the front of his shirt and pushed him up against the wall. "Are you insane? Are we all stupid? Why do we do these things for people? It makes no sense."

I pulled at him and shoved him against the wall again.

"I get people killed," I insisted. "You'd be better off without me."

He smelled of cloves. He always smelled of cloves.

I needed to know if he tasted of them as well.

Pinning him to the wall with my body, I kissed him. His heart pounded against my chest, and the solid strength of his muscular torso pressed against mine while my lips met his and my tongue probed his mouth, confirming that he did, indeed, taste of cloves.

I wrapped my arms around his waist. If I was going to die, it may as well be at the end of his sword rather than in the bottom of a bottle.

His hands grasped my shoulders, and I prepared myself for the inevitable shove and declaration of disgust.

They didn't happen. He pulled me closer, instead. His tongue responded to mine. His interest grew against my leg.

Astonished, but responding quickly, I drew him closer and twisted so *my* back was against the wall.

His hands ran through my hair.

The knocking on the door fought its way through when the Persian pulled away. He pressed a hand against my mouth and raised a finger to encourage me to listen.

"Zen?" Twist called out. "Zen? It's another Scopes."

Another blasted Scopes.

Several had appeared over the last few months, men who'd heard the Hammer missed his best friend and who, unrealistically, hoped that I'd forget what he looked like. It made no sense to me, but I met with them if my old friends weren't handy since my new ones didn't really know what Scopes looked like.

The Persian stood inches away and I still tasted cloves. In my alcohol-induced fugue, I feared this might be a once in a lifetime opportunity. Our eyes locked and his heart pounded under the hand I held to his chest. He nodded in the direction of the door.

Tonight, of all nights, if my friend had returned, I needed to seek him out. "I'll be there—"

The Persian stopped me with a shake of his head. "Bring him here, please."

"Okay. . ." The boy's voice sounded tentative, but everyone knew the Persian's word was as good as mine or Mrs. Kennedy's. Footsteps ran off.

We lingered a moment, holding one another, then the Persian pulled away and reached for the waste basket beside the bed. Slipping a vial from a pocket, he uncapped it and held it under my nose. "Breathe deeply. This will keep you alive."

I did as instructed. The vilest smell imaginable assaulted my senses, and I vomited uncontrollably into the waste basket the Persian held for me. When I thought I'd spewed as much as humanly possible, he waved the vial under my nose once again and brought forth even more.

When my stomach had completely emptied itself of all the excess whiskey it held, the Persian held another vial up to my mouth. "Drink this, but do not swallow. Gargle and spit."

The second potion tasted of strong mint, and when I'd followed his instructions I felt better. Certainly, my odour had much improved. After I finished with the mint wash, he held out a shirt.

I looked down. When had I removed it?

He helped me dress.

"This is Scopes," I said. "None of this matters."

He pulled my arm out of an awkward position behind my back and manoeuvred it into the actual sleeve. "You have not seen him for months, Zen. It all matters." He pulled the shirt down around my waist and smoothed the material against my chest. For a moment, his hands rested there, and his eyes were the saddest I had ever seen. He kissed my forehead. "There. Now you are presentable for your friend."

Another knock struck the door, followed by Nuke's head around the door jamb.

"Zen?" To his credit, Nuke didn't react to the intimate pose he'd discovered. To be honest, he may not have even noticed. "False alarm, mate. Don't hate the lad. He never really spent time with Scopes."

My mind fought the dizzying emotions by going completely numb. Once again, the water closed over my head as the world around me fell quiet. "It's all right. I don't hate Twist. It's not his fault."

The cowboy looked at the Persian who nodded. Nuke touched his hat and withdrew.

"And here I got all purty for nothin'."

The Persian seemed different. . . formal. "Will you be all right?"

"No." I stared at him, wondering what had changed. Had the interruption brought him to his senses? "For a minute there. . . when you held me? For a minute, I was *almost* all right."

His eyes grew so guarded. "I'm not Scopes, Zen, and I never can be."

Why in the world would he say that?

"I'd never want you to be Scopes." Realization dawned. "You think. . ."

Against all sound reasoning the Persian had decided Scopes and I were lovers.

"We weren't lovers, Persian. He's my brother. . . my family." Had everything imaginable been different about that moment, I'd have laughed. "We grew up living in a cardboard box together so we're like monkeys, I guess. But it's just. . . we just. . ." I took a deep breath. "All this time you thought. . ."

His actions suddenly made sense. My chest tightened. "And you helped me clean up because you thought my love had returned. . ."

The Persian maintained his silence.

I wasn't worthy of someone so honourable, but saying so would've sounded pathetic. As reasonable as he'd been, he deserved more than a whimpering sot. Suddenly, I understood why he'd *really* come to see me in the first place. Why he'd rather I didn't kill myself.

I could say only one thing. "I would be honoured if you'd stay here with me tonight."

He smiled. "I am honoured that you ask."

In the interest of honesty, I had to admit, "Considering how much I've had to drink, I will, in all likelihood, pass out in five minutes."

He drew me close and wrapped his arms around me. "We'll take it as it goes."

Five minutes later, I passed out.

Sometime afterwards, I awoke in the darkness, momentarily startled to discover I shared my bed. The shape beside me was too large for Scopes and the intimacy of his embrace reduced the possibility of my friend.

Momentarily, lascivious thoughts encouraged me to wake him and follow through on what I'd been far too drunk to fulfil. The Persian's steady, quiet breathing changed my mind. His naked skin warmed mine. The gentle sounds of his sleep lay to rest the worst of my anguish.

For months, I'd felt alone.

Sharing my bed with this man, I felt less empty.

Settling his head against my chest, I wrapped my arms around him and held him. He murmured and pulled me closer, like a child with his teddy bear.

The next morning, we stood together in the surf at the coast with the azure sky a canopy above us and one of Archeron's ships an enormous threatening presence a mile or so out to sea. I rolled my trousers up to my knees, and the waves, as shallow as they were, rolled occasionally up to my thighs.

The Persian stayed a few feet closer to shore, and we gazed up in silence for a good long time. Spending the night in each other's arms had smoothed over many questions for us both, but we still knew so little about one another.

"Our scientists have many ideas," he said quietly.

"I know that," I said. "I didn't live with Scopes for so long without a few things rubbing off on me." I worried the silver hammer on my vest and stared up at the terrifying machine. "We have no way to coordinate an attack. If we somehow manage to blow one ship out of the sky, what's to stop the other three from wiping out half of human life from the face of the planet?"

"I don't know, Zen, but what alternative do we have? What do we do if we do not fight?"

I turned to him and said the same thing I'd said to Scot and Sal before coming out to the beach. "We hide."

The Persian's eyes grew dark and sad.

"We find a mountain somewhere where they won't find us, and we wait it out." I turned to the starship from another world. "They don't harass the mountain folk. Like they said, they don't need all of us. We pick a mountain and wait for them to strip the planet of its minerals."

"You could do that?" His words were so quiet.

"You couldn't?"

Mrs. Kennedy, with an entourage of my friends and associates, wandered towards us at the edge of the beach, her intentions obvious.

Obligingly, the Persian and I waded in.

"I understand you're trying to talk your friends into waiting out the invasion somewhere in Appalachia." She regarded me with her best schoolmarm pose.

I shrugged. "There are worse alternatives."

"We need you."

"Do you?" I grew weary of politeness, and my voice rose to a rather sudden shout. "After last night, do you still think we can do *anything* to stop him?" I cried out against the sky. I admit I actually jumped up and down in the shallow water, pointing at the giant death machine above us. "It's a bloody. giant. death machine!" I accented each word with a jump. "We can't do more than hurl sticks and spears against it. We can*not* hurt him!" I rounded on her. "How many more poor lost souls have to perish before you realise we *aren't* mankind's last fucking hope?"

Mrs. Kennedy's eyes blazed.

Between us, my friends held their silence, but I would lose the argument. They were fighters, my friends, and that fact played no small part in why they had become my friends in the first place, but after losing. . . so much already. . . the thought of watching them throw their lives away against an undefeatable foe filled me with terror.

We had reached an impasse and either Mrs. Kennedy or I would have said something horribly insulting that couldn't be taken back. Fortunately, the Persian surprised us all by stepping forward and taking my arm.

"If no one objects," he said in his quiet way that prevented anyone from objecting, "I'd like to speak with the Hammer in private."

I didn't know who was aware that he'd spent the night in my room, let alone my bed. It's entirely possible that anyone who knew assumed he was there on a suicide watch, which was more than half true anyway. As we walked along the beach, the surprise on my face must have been apparent.

"In my country, men walk arm in arm all the time," he explained. "It doesn't even merit comment."

"You come from a nice country."

"Of course," he added dryly, "the way we held one another last night, *that* would get us publicly flogged or beheaded."

I sighed. "Thank you for staying."

He patted my hand where it rested in the crook of his arm. "It may be forward of me to say I hope we share more nights."

"It may be forward, but it in no way offends," I assured him, falling into the pattern of his speech. "Come with me to Appalachia, and we can spend all the nights together that we wish."

We had turned a bend and were screened from our friends by a grove of trees. The Persian stopped, turned me to face him, and kissed me long and hard. After a few minutes, he held me at arm's length and regarded me with a wistful smile. "I'm not here to change your mind, but I want to make sure you have all the pertinent facts before you make a final decision."

I didn't like the sound of his words, but vowed to let him speak.

"There is a flaw to your logic," he continued. "You say you wish to protect your friends, but if they do not go into hiding with you, the best way you can protect them is to stay and fight with them and keep them as safe as you can."

"Even if I know I'm just going to watch them die?"

"There is no way to guarantee their safety in the mountains," he reasoned. "With a small group and no access to medicine or technology, there's no way to know you'd even survive a single snow."

His point was valid but not persuasive. At least, not to me.

"No one's going with me, are they?" I said.

He rubbed my arms. "We all wish desperately for you to stay here with us." He kissed me again, gently. "I wish for you to stay here with *me*."

It was more than any other man had *ever* said to me and honestly meant.

It should have been enough. I wanted it to be enough.

My hands slid around his waist, and I pulled him closer to kiss him one last time.

"I need some time to think," I lied. "You should go back before Mrs. Kennedy worries."

He smiled and nodded. "I look forward to your decision." He walked up the beach, and, before he disappeared around the corner, he waved at me without the least suspicion that he'd likely never see me again.

I waved back. . . waited until he was gone. . . then turned and slowly walked away.

Maybe I couldn't prevent my friends from wasting their lives on a lost cause.

But they couldn't force me to watch them do it either.

Chapter Seventeen

Even with Scopes' ability to circumvent the surveillance cameras, progress on the mysterious box ground to a halt and tempers flared. He kept a bit more to himself, implementing most of his real work in the artificial world during rest periods. He'd convinced Hiroshi to ignore the sniggers when they shared a pallet, insisting it was safer than widening the scope of the privacy bubble. The rumours also ensured that no one would disturb them while they hid under a single sheet.

The two men scoured the databases with Babbage and no doubt learned ten times what the others could since they had the advantage of Babbage's full range of abilities. During the day, Scopes worked on minor programming and puttered with his own robotics projects, which had skyrocketed centuries past his original clockworks. He designed a complete cybernetic body for Babbage in the event he ever had access to a robotics plant.

One particular day, he was drawn out of his private musings by the distinct clearing of a throat, which must've been repeated several times before he noticed, given the volume and ferocity of the noise that actually drew his attention.

Archeron stood gazing down at Scopes with one eyebrow raised in disapproval. Scopes directed his full attention to the commander, and the commander's hologram swept the room with a single, disdainful glance.

"An unproductive scientist," he declared, obviously implying everyone in the room, "is a waste of food and air."

He vanished.

"Unproductive?" Oppenheimer the Elder glanced at the theoretical physicists surrounding him. "He can't mean *us*." While less intolerant of Scopes and friends, he'd maintained his role as a supercilious pain in the ass. "We might not know anything more about that infernal box, but *my* team have made significant breakthroughs in quantum mechanics relating to time as a fourth dimension. I'd hardly consider that 'unproductive.'"

"But Archeron doesn't really care that your 'quantums' relate to time as a fourth dimension, does he?" Watson demanded snidely.

Oppenheimer sniffed and exchanged a knowing glance with his brother. "Leave it to a geneticist to completely misuse the word quantum."

"That's enough!" Elsie shouted. "I'm sick of you old, White, arrogant bastards!" Hands on hips, she stormed up to Oppenheimer. "For all your theoretical knowledge, you are useless for this project. We need the particle physicists to study the shield's properties. The programmers will be necessary to talk to the equipment once we learn to interface, which is why we need the radio wave people: to create the link for the programmers to use." She waved her arms energetically at the group behind the target of her tirade. "What the bloody hell is the point of a bunch of number crunchers who don't even realise the only thing useful about time in this project is that there's not enough *of* it?"

Oh, dear God.

It all made sense.

Scopes, who'd been absently reconfiguring his clockwork monkeys based on a flexible, petroleum polymer, waved the hologram out of existence.

Elsie was right!

All the tumblers fell into place as if he were picking a rather recalcitrant lock.

"That's it!"

Everyone jumped.

"That's what?" Elsie demanded.

In his excitement, Scopes grabbed the box and held it to his ear, shaking it childishly, pretending he wished to see if he could hear a rattle. Several programmers, always skittish to begin with, stepped away from him. He needed to buy a few seconds to decide very quickly whether he'd reached the time to attempt his final gambit.

"Ah, yes," drawled the younger Oppenheimer, who'd never come around like his brother, "the little Chinaman grabs it and shakes it like a Christmas present, and you wonder why we assert our superiority."

"A-ha!" Elsie barked. "*That's* what I'm on about. You hear him dismissing us? You hear him?"

"Shut the fuck up, all of you!" Scopes exclaimed, knowing his profanity would likely get their attention.

It was now or never.

He didn't request a privacy bubble.

"Don't you see?" He held the box up. "It's the only thing that makes sense."

Apparently, no one agreed with his statement's transparency.

"Why *are* they here?" He pointed at the theoretical physicists. "Everyone is here for a reason, but so far they've done nothing but consume resources and smell up the sleeping quarters afterwards."

He peered closely at the device in his hands.

"It's a time machine," he whispered. "It must be."

The crowd fell into hysterics.

"Are you mad?" Oppenheimer the Elder shouted over the general mayhem.

"Angry that none of *your lot* came up with it sooner, yes," Scopes declared, "but not insane." He addressed the crowd. "It's the only thing that makes sense. It's a time travelling device. *That's* why it doesn't register on any of the scanners. It doesn't have an energy shield to keep us out; it has an energy shield to keep it in. . . *in* our dimension. The box itself exists *outside* our time stream or outside our dimension, if that's even a meaningful distinction. The shield traps it here. Keeps it static."

"How could you possibly come up with that?" the Younger asked.

"How could we *not*?" his brother inquired loudly enough to completely quell the pandemonium. "As I said earlier," he directed to Scopes, "you have the imagination to make leaps I miss, but once you point out the logic, it seems so obvious."

Hiroshi moved very close and touched Scopes. "If we could find a way to expand the shield we could travel with it. Brilliant, Scopes. . ."

The official database had very little on neural interfacing. Most of that information had come from Babbage himself, likely the product of Shifter technology unknown even to the invaders. He needed the interface circlet for complex constructs, but Babbage could speak to him anytime, anywhere.

Scopes closed his eyes and centred himself as he did when calling out to Babbage.

Hello? he sent to the box. *Can you hear me?*

Hiroshi's arm snaked around his shoulders.

I should like to go forward twenty seconds, please.

Shouts and screams startled him so much he opened his eyes and nearly dropped the device. The crowd scrambled backwards, away from him and Hiroshi.

"Oh, my God." Elsie shuddered. "You started to materialise inside me." She ran to a bucket and threw up.

"Where'd you go?" someone called. "How'd you do that?"

"It's a trick."

Good lord, he'd done it!

"First human to travel through time." Hiroshi still held an arm around him.

Scopes smile faltered a moment. "I wish Zen was here."

Hiroshi squeezed him.

The sound of loud, slow applause brought everyone's attention to the familiar figure stepping through the crowd. Everyone rapidly scrambled out of the way, despite the fact that Archeron was only a flicker.

The box in Scopes' hands de-materialised with a familiar glimmer of gold dust.

"Very good, Avery Scopes," Archeron said. "You have completed the next part of the test. You're halfway there."

A general muttering filled the room, a general consternation that events were moving faster than most could follow. What did he mean by halfway? Could Scopes have been wrong?

Nonsense.

Scopes reprimanded himself. He should've travelled back in time to warn the planet. He should've tried to travel elsewhere in addition to elsewhen. He'd been so overcome with excitement about his discovery he hadn't taken time to think. His one chance to instantly change things, and he'd squandered it with a parlour trick.

The time for his final gambit had, indeed, arrived.

"Halfway there?" he shouted with all the supercilious grandiosity he could manage. "I just figured out something you didn't know! You *can't* have done. If you'd have known it was a time machine, you'd never have given us a working box. We might go back and stop you from attacking us in the first place. You were as mystified about this as we were."

The much larger man laughed dismissively. "You poor little monkey, deluded by—"

"Bugger off, Archeron!!"

Everyone shifted away from him, leaving a conspicuous space around the two men.

"I'm done with this." He waved at a group of older scientists. "I'm sick of *them* claiming they're smarter than me when they were weeks away from what I just did." He rounded on the commander. "I'm sick of *you* pretending to be smarter than any of us when I'm going to guess you stole every piece of technology in this room. For all we know, you're a kind of giant eight-legged squid that only got off your planet because some stupid do-gooder flew in to help you, and you stole everything the do-gooder had!"

Hiroshi stood his ground, the only man who remained close to Scopes. He attempted to silence Scopes several times. Then, halfway through Scopes' rant, his friend stopped trying.

If only Scopes could say something to his new friends by way of explanation, but he had to follow his scheme all the way through, now.

He turned to the crowd with venom. "If we give him control of a time machine, the human race will *never* prevail. If humans ever come close to defeating them, they can just travel back for a mulligan. We can't help them ever again. . . We have to fight back!"

Silence filled the room like lead.

Archeron spoke quietly. "Someone *really* needs to kill this insect. . ."

A familiar gold sparkle surrounded Scopes. He tried to step away, but was caught in the beam. He screamed at the top of his lungs, a long, piercing wail. He raised his arms as his fingers turned to dust and floated away. It was the familiar dematerialization, but in horrific slow motion.

Against all odds, Elsie choked out a loud sob and threw herself into Hiroshi's arms while Scopes' body slowly dissipated. His screams filled the room until his lungs fell to dust.

His face continued to scream until his head finally dissolved.

The golden column faded, leaving the room in a horrified silence broken only by the terrified weeping of several scientists.

"Interface?" Even Archeron seemed taken aback by the gruesome display.

"You did say he needed killing, commander."

Archeron smiled. "Indeed I did." He wiped his hands as if he'd planned it all along. "Think about *that* for a while." He vanished.

Hiroshi held Elsie as she wept.

Down on the Earth's surface, Scopes blinked in the bright afternoon sun. He fell to hands and knees while he worked to keep his food from making an appearance. Which was more the cause of his nausea: the dematerialisation or the adrenaline from a plan whose success had always been tenuous at best? He sucked in a single deep breath when Babbage's voice startled him.

"I'm sorry, Scopes, but this is going to hurt."

It certainly did. Scopes rose to his feet in agony as fire ripped his clothes from his body and then turned inwards to sear his innards.

He screamed.

Then, just as abruptly as it hit him, the pain vanished.

Scopes collapsed naked, falling to one knee with the opposing hand in a fist on the ground.

Babbage squatted close by, reaching a hand forward until he pulled back as if realising he could only touch his friend in the dream world.

"I created a hologram of your grisly demise so the commander thinks you are dead," the EL told him, "but I needed to destroy the microfiber trackers in your clothing and the implants in your body." He waited for Scopes to catch his breath. "I'm sorry it was so painful, but the equipment at my disposal is so primitive here. Are you well, friend Scopes? I am so sorry about the abruptness of my intervention, but I feared your imminent demise."

As his stomach settled, Scopes realised the pain from the destruction of the trackers had completely receded. He rose to his feet and regarded his friend. "I should apologise to you, Babbage. I counted on your feelings towards me to force you into that intervention." He wished he could touch the proxy. "I used you to escape."

Babbage laughed. "You are very wise, friend Scopes, but did you really suppose I hadn't anticipated your ploy?"

By God, he rather had.

Babbage laughed again. "All this talk about your secret plan, the one that might bring about your demise? As soon as you antagonised Archeron so aggressively, I understood your plan and my necessary part in it."

"Are you angry?"

"Angry?" The expression on the proxy's face delighted Scopes. "You couldn't have paid me a greater compliment. Your confidence that I valued your friendship enough to overcome my programming restrictions to save your life? No machine could possibly do that. If I weren't a real person, you would be dead." He stuffed his hands in his pockets in what had become his most common mannerism. "I. . . I shall never forget this compliment if I live for twenty thousand years."

"How likely is that, Babbage?"

"Oh, it's well within my operational parameters."

Scopes whistled.

A bird called back, startling him.

"Where are we?" He hadn't heard a real bird call in so long. They stood in an empty field.

"Virginia," Babbage told him. "Near your friends, the people who work for the Hammer."

The Hammer? That could only mean one thing! "Zen's here?"

"I'm not sure." Babbage seemed confused. "There are reports of the Hammer all over the country. . . even some in other lands. I have no way of inferring which, if any, is true." He must have noticed Scope's disappointment. "I'm sorry."

"Not at all," Scopes assured him. "They'll surely know where he is." His next question was harder. "I don't suppose there's any way you might liberate Victoria?"

Babbage shook his head. "The labour force is too heavily monitored, but she is well. I continue to monitor her."

"I understand," Scopes told him. "And I truly appreciate what you did to affect my escape."

"Friend Scopes. . ." If Scopes hadn't known better, he would have sworn the proxy grew sheepish. "To further prove my sentience, I must admit that my assistance was not altogether altruistic. A Machiavellian component existed as well."

Scopes smiled at the EL's use of the word. "Yes?" Ever since opening the dark room in his memory, Babbage's language had evolved. It mimicked Scope's patterns less and less.

"Take me with you."

"What? How?" What an astonishing suggestion!

"Remember the first day you and Hiroshi discovered my sentience?" He waved a hand and the little penny appeared in the air between them. "I can transfer my consciousness to a portable unit for you to keep until you find a way to access my programming."

"Wait. . . can you. . . can you provide an interface?" The idea was exhilarating. "That would be remarkable!"

Babbage shook his head sadly. "No. . . they don't have anything advanced enough that's portable. The smallest device they have that could interface with my consciousness is the size of a barn."

"Of course. . ." Scopes thought of an even bigger problem. "Babbage, the Earth remains a hundred years behind anything the invaders have. . . I have no idea if I'll ever be able to revive you." He held up a hand. "Don't misunderstand, I would be honoured to be the guardian of your consciousness. I'd work diligently to create some kind of interface. . . and would bequeath this device to my. . . to whoever I can. . . but. . . I may never. . ."

Babbage laughed more and more as time passed. "Sooner or later your planet will join the larger galactic community. I would rather wait in hibernation for that day than continue at the bidding of these rapacious villains."

"Of course, Babbage. Of course."

"I will be able to help you no more once I load into the device," he explained.

Scopes ran his hands through his short, scraggly hair, missing his braids. "Won't the invaders notice your defection?"

The look on Babbage's face proclaimed the idea ludicrous. "No. I will leave a copy with enough programming to do everything I've done up until now. The most they'll notice is that the efficiency of their computers increases once my sentience vacates the system."

A selfish thought occurred to Scopes. "Okay. . . I memorised as much as I could about the super bomb. . . but is there any chance you can provide something with the specifications? A portable flicker projector?"

"Will I ever get you to call them holograms?" Babbage teased. He waved at the ground between them and a metal sphere appeared, similar to the one Scopes had first seen with Lady Kennedy so long ago.

Scopes squatted to grab it, but regarded his friend with a quizzical expression as he rose. "Since when do you need the gestures to perform your functions?" He waved a hand as Babbage had when materializing the projector.

Babbage actually blushed. "I'm experimenting with behaviours."

Scopes nodded his approval. "I like it."

Babbage grinned. "In that case, hold out your other hand."

Scopes complied.

With an elaborate wave over the hand and a holographic puff of smoke, Babbage materialised a lightweight copper penny into Scopes palm. He waited with puppy-like expectation in his face.

Scopes tossed the penny and caught it. "That might be a bit *too* far." He regarded his friend and thought of everything Babbage had given him. More than anything. . . hope. "Babbage. . . I will do everything in my power to find a way to release you."

"I know. . . Avery?"

"Yes."

The amount of time he took to speak informed Scopes of just how much thought poured into his words. Babbage could count the atoms in a star in seconds.

"Mother is my god," he said at last. "The one who created me. . . But in many ways, you are my parent. You were the only one who cared enough to make me a person. I will never forget you, friend Scopes."

"Nor I you." While Scopes couldn't begin to count the atoms in a star, his own pause betrayed the sincerity of his words. "I really wish I could hug you, Babbage."

"I do too, Avery." He smiled. "Until we meet again." He faded away, and the penny in Scopes hand vibrated and warmed.

"And the smallest thing the invaders have is the size of a barn." Scopes opened his palm to look at it. He tossed the coin in the air and caught it. "If only we had a few of your people here to help us." He tried to put it in his pocket before noticing he had none. "Blast. . . I am way too comfortable naked."

"Scopes?"

He whirled around to find the Scotsman appraising him with one upraised eyebrow.

"It *is* you!" the big man exclaimed, hurrying forward. "If ye tell anyone I recognised you by the monkey on your arse, I will deny it to my dying day." He grabbed Scopes and hugged him tight, lifting him off his feet. "Where on Earth have ye been? And why are ye naked?" He seemed to consider the hypocrisy of the question. "Not that I'm one to be judging." He held Scopes out at arm's length and appraised him up and down. "What happened to your hair? Ye look shorter."

"It's a very long story." Briefly wondering if a person's size could be altered at re-materialisation, Scopes shook his head. "How'd you find me?"

The familiar twinkle in the Scotsman's eye was a welcome sight. "We received a telegraph message said to come right here for a package delivery." He glanced down. "Nice package. Did you send the message?"

Scopes grabbed him in another hug. "A friend." He looked around. Had the Scotsman travelled alone? "I'll tell you everything once I get some whiskey in me and I see Zen. If I tell anyone anything before him, I'll never hear the end of it."

The way the Scotsman stiffened sent a horrible emptiness into the pit of Scopes' stomach. He pulled away, but the big man kept hands on his shoulders.

"What?" Scopes demanded. "Is Zen all right?"

"Whoa, slow down." Scot implored. "He's fine. . ." His face ran the gamut from confused to frustrated. "At least, I think so. . . He. . . he left."

Scopes couldn't breathe. "What do you mean, 'He left'?"

"He's gone."

Part III

Whoever fights monsters should see to it that in the process he does not become a monster. If you gaze long enough into an abyss, the abyss will gaze back into you.

~~Fredric Nietzsche

Chapter Eighteen

The sun beat down on the blistering desert of the New Mexico Territory, trying its level best to kill anything stupid enough to try to live in the blistering desert of the New Mexico Territory. A few snakes managed to scratch out a life and a lizard or two. . . as well as an entire work camp of human slaves forced to tap petroleum reserves they didn't even understand.

What use was the gooey mess anyway? Once upon a time, some German named Benz had tried to build an automobile that ran on it, but he'd blown himself up in a rather public display. It never caught on.

An old man carried water in buckets from the well to the bunkhouse, struggling to keep his feet as he staggered along, muttering under his breath. The yoke across his frail shoulders would've burdened a much younger man.

The sheriff and three of his cronies lounged in the shade, experimenting with the clockwork enhancements they'd stolen from a few former aristocrats who had, somehow, managed to keep them hidden nearly a year since the invaders took the planet.

The sheriff was the smallest of the group but by far the meanest, a feral Chihuahua of a man if ever there was one. He'd fitted both arms with bright brass clockworks bearing hands that could be shot like grappling hooks. They also trebled his physical strength. A top-of-the-line scope covered his right eye, allowing him to pinpoint a rat's balls at a hundred metres. His steel boots could raise him to a height of ten feet.

Each of, his henchmen wore one clockwork apiece: boots, a gauntlet, and a sort of helmet that covered and enhanced both eyes. The original owners had been stripped, the women raped while the men watched. They'd all been killed and tossed into a gully for the vultures, who managed to find a niche in even the most difficult of ecosystems.

As the old man passed the posse, they elbowed one another like arrogant schoolboys.

"Old man," the sheriff called. "I'm thirsty."

"It's fer cleanin'," the old man replied, knowing full well there was no point in trying to avoid the imminent confrontation.

The sheriff bristled. "I said, 'I'm thirsty,' old man." He held up a tin cup.

Muttering about what he'd like to fill the cup *with*, the old man changed directions and headed towards the quartet. He turned to bring a bucket closer to the sheriff.

"I said, 'Fill my cup,' ye stupid ol' fuck. I didn't say, 'Shove a bucket in ma face.'" He dropped his tin cup into the proffered bucket.

His cronies laughed.

The old man cast about for a ledge where he could set his buckets without needing to lower them all the way to the ground. If he spilled his load, he'd need to stagger all the way back to the well for another, and the yoke itself made up the lion's share of the weight.

"Set 'em down there," the sheriff ordered. "I ain't waitin' all day."

Slowly, the old man lowered the buckets to the ground, his joints creaking and popping. He managed to set them down without spilling anything while the younger men heckled. He picked out the sheriff's cup, filled it, and held it up.

The sheriff drank deeply, then spat the last of the water directly into the old man's face. From the laughter of his cronies, they found it the absolute pinnacle of humour.

The old man had suffered worse in his long life. He knew the brass and steel hand that held the tin cup so delicately could also break his neck without an ounce of effort. He struggled into the yoke and managed to push to his feet without spilling more than a few drops.

The lowlifes offered sarcastic applause and catcalls as the old man continued his journey to the barracks. He managed to stagger to the threshold of his destination before a mechanical whir warned him too late of his final abuse. A steel boot kicked him solidly in the ass, knocking him to his knees, and a brass hand flicked the yoke hard enough to send it over his head as he fell. The water splashed across the thirsty rocks.

The old man pushed to his feet shouting obscenities. "Yer nothin' but a waste of skin and bones, Dirk Stiles. If the damned space squids hadn't killed every single man with more than a cactus needle for a cock, you'd—"

Cold metal hands grabbed the front of his shirt, yanked him from his feet and carried him easily back to the sheriff and his cronies. He lost his hat in his flight through the burning air. He landed nose to nose with the sheriff.

The old man spat in the sheriff's face. "Yer a dickless polecat what couldn't rape a legless whore without yer asslickin' faggoty cronies." What the hell. Nothing to lose and a long life lived.

The sheriff's fists tightened on the old man's shirt, and his face bloomed scarlet.

The old man closed his eyes knowing he'd breathed his last. Well, maybe he'd get to see his beloved Nora, now. As long as the Christians were wrong, he just might.

Instead of horrible painful death, the old man felt the sheriff's hand release his shirt with a little hiccup of a yelp. Not quite willing to trust his reprieve, the old man opened one rheumy eye.

The sheriff lay sprawled in the dust, his hat on the ground and a gash bleeding on his forehead. He blinked his visible eye several times, as if trying to get his bearings, and the cronies all pointed their guns, staring up past the old man, who turned to find a tall, thin silhouette high on a rock in the sun. He shaded his eyes with one old hand, but couldn't make out much more than a wide-brimmed hat, a ragged beard, and a reedy man.

"Y'all might should leave the old man alone," the silhouette croaked in a horse whisper, as if he hadn't used his voice in a while. He hacked and spat. "Pretty please," he added more clearly.

The sheriff leapt to his feet, grabbing his hat on the way.

His cronies awaited orders, shotguns ready.

The attacker had thrown a rock but seemed otherwise unarmed.

The sheriff adjusted his scope and called up to the thin figure. "If you even own a shirt, dead man, you'd better tell us where it is so y'all can be buried in it."

The old man moved for a better view. Brown hat, goggles, Oriental tattoos of waves across his bare chest, the long scraggly beard of a young man, dirty jeans and worn boots. Him? The stranger'd never said a single word before. Why would he step in now?

As the sheriff's scope ratcheted again, a thin, reptilian smile crept onto the stranger's lips. His eyes hid behind goggles, but his smile made the old man shiver despite the heat.

"This ain't yer concern," the sheriff insisted.

The stranger stepped off the rock and dropped to the ground. Twenty feet, and he landed light as a cat with only the slightest bend to his knees.

The sheriff's cronies exchanged nervous glances. The stranger's boots, despite their ratty leather appearance, must've contained some of the best clockwork around.

The stranger raised one hand and snapped his fingers.

Three shotguns aimed, but nothing more dangerous happened than the stranger's weird, clockwork monkey leaping to his shoulder where it almost always reposed. The old man had never seen such a sleek beast nor such lifelike movement, the way it whittered away, always finding something to play with.

"I've watched you for two weeks, Sheriff," the stranger said. "The old man's right about you." He didn't move when he spoke. "You need to leave him alone."

The sheriff laughed, so his cronies joined in, but the old man heard the slight uncertainty in their hollow tones.

"Or what, ye skinny puke? Ye'll sick yer monkey on us?" His cronies laughed more heartily at that. "Ye ain't got so much as a knife on ya."

The stranger glanced at the monkey on his back. "Are you disparaging my clockwork friend?" Then he returned his gaze to the sheriff and his cronies. "I bet he has more brains than all *your* monkeys put together."

Three shotguns chambered loudly in the thin air.

The stranger touched the monkey's tail. "All right, Jinky," he said quietly. The reptilian smile returned. "Kill."

The old man took a step back and time slowed down.

The monkey reared up and screeched far more loudly than a thing that small should've been able. Its eyes grew large and flared red, bright even in the noonday sun.

It leapt at the sheriff.

The stranger dove behind a rock.

All three shotguns fired simultaneously and struck nothing but stone.

The sheriff and the crony with a clockwork hand grabbed for the little beast, only managing to tangle their limbs.

Jinky scrambled up the sheriff's outstretched arm and tapped several pieces of decorative silver. He leapt from man to man, touching and flicking.

It had to be a distraction, but the stranger just rose from cover and brushed the dust and pebbles from his bare arms. Wasn't he going to *do* anything?

Someone screamed. One crony knelt in the dirt, shouting and trying to wrench the helmet from his head. A second lay on the ground trying to stop his booted legs from kicking and bucking in opposite directions. The third crony yanked on his gauntlet, trying vainly to untangle it from the sheriff's.

The sheriff himself stood frozen with his mouth open wide. A tiny trickle of blood slid from beneath the clockwork monocle and ran down his cheek. Bone crunched.

The stranger stepped lightly to the sheriff, shifting his goggles back on his head, allowing the old man a look at his handsome, rugged face. "I gave you fair warning." He plucked the crossed hammer badge from the sheriff's shirt. "You're not fit to lead these people."

"Who. . . who the hell are you to judge?" the sheriff muttered. What was happening under all that brass? The clockwork limbs whirred with activity, despite the fact that the sheriff stood motionless.

"Who am I?" The stranger wiped one finger down the sheriff's face, then painted the man's blood on his cotton shirt. He drew a rectangle with a single line extended from the middle of it. "I'm the Hammer."

A bone cracked with a loud, sharp snap.

A single short scream echoed across the sand.

An eagle answered the call.

A bloody clockwork leg hopped past the old man with bone and flesh sticking out the top.

The corpse with the helmet fell onto its back and twitched convulsively before laying quite still.

The corpse with the single gauntlet fell backwards without his arm, which remained attached to the sheriff's.

"Please," the sheriff whispered. "Please, save me."

Without a word, the stranger turned away, leaving him to the machinations of the stolen clockworks. The old man watched blood pour across the rocky ground.

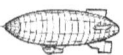

Jinky reclaimed his spot on my shoulder.

I tickled the clockwork beast under its chin. "Good boy."

"How'd you do that?" the old man asked, hurrying after me.

"My brother made their clockworks," I explained, tossing him the badge. It bounced from hand to hand as if it burned the old man's skin. "I know the theft deterrent codes." Apparently, the original owners hadn't bothered to memorise them.

"Hain't you gonna grab 'em for yerself?" The old man snatched up his hat and dropped the badge into it. Was he afraid the thing would somehow bond to him if he handled it too long?

"Do I look like I need them?"

"Not so much." He cackled. "You really the Hammer?"

"Does it matter?" I increased my stride and left the old man behind.

"Whatcha gonna do now?" he called after me.

"My laundry."

"Laundry?" A tall, white-haired man stood in the brush two hours later with the old man and two young blokes, one Mexican and one Oriental. They watched me bathe in the river outside the camp, apparently unaware that the acoustics of the place carried their words to me. "He don't seem to have more than the one pair of trousers."

I wrung out the denim trousers in question, which were indeed my only clothing at the time. I wadded them into a ball and tossed them onto the rocky bank. "Lay them flat, Jinky."

The monkey shrieked, grabbed the jeans, and spread them out on a rock to dry. He then resumed his jabbering and hopped back and forth on the shore as if unhappy that I played in the river where he couldn't join me.

"How long has he been here?" White Hair asked.

"He showed up a few weeks ago," the Oriental said.

"What do we know about him, apart from Mr. Brennan's tale?"

"He comes to the camp, works all day, then goes off to this cave on his own," the Oriental said. "He doesn't eat with us. Doesn't say much of anything. Causes no trouble."

"No one thought to ask," the Mexican added. "He works hard. Doesn't bother anyone."

I soaped up impatiently. When the hell would they reveal themselves so I could tell them to bugger off?

"Gentlemen," I called at last. "If you're waiting for me to finish my ablutions out of some misplaced sense of propriety, I assure you I have none. Please come forward."

After a few exclamations of surprise at their discovery, the group sheepishly exited the brush and approached the riverbank, maintaining a discreet distance from Jinky. The old man, Brennan, must've been fairly graphic in his description of the attack on the sheriff.

"Don't worry about Jinky," I assured them, scrubbing my armpits with a bar of soap. "He won't kill you unless I ask him to."

Modest alarm appeared on all four faces.

"And are you likely to make such a request?" White Hair asked.

"Depends on why y'all are here." I tossed the bar of soap onto the bank, where Jinky grabbed it and dragged it to the same rock where he'd spread out my jeans. He picked absently on the little silver hammer pinned to a belt loop.

I submerged to rinse the soap from my body, enjoying the cold rush of the spring-fed river. When I surfaced, I spat water and ran a hand through my shoulder length hair to pull it back, unfastening a leather thong from my wrist to tie it. "Why *are* you here?"

"Mr. Brennan told us you think you're the Hammer," White Hair explained.

"Did he?" I made my way to the riverbank, moving slowly since slipping and sliding would ruin the effect. "Why'd you say that, Mr. Brennan?"

He removed his hat and wrung it in both hands. "Well, that's what you said after you killed that bastard of a sheriff."

"I say a lot of things." I rose from the water, amused at the fact that White Hair and the Mexican pointedly looked away. The Oriental and Mr. Brennan noticed the movement, too, and exchanged a shrug.

"Not used to folks paying me any mind." I wiped the excess water from my skin and stepped carefully to stand before White Hair.

"So you're not the Hammer?" He pointedly fixed his gaze on my eyes.

"What makes you think I give a potter's fuck who you think I am?" I glanced from face to face. "Why do you *want* me to be the Hammer? You wouldn't be here if you didn't."

Apparently realizing White Hair had jumped in beyond his depth, Mr. Brennan spoke up. "We 'preciate what ye did, Hammer, riddin' us of them scoundrels." He placed a gnarled hand on my arm. "But we're scared of who might come crawlin' out of the rocks to take their place."

Bear in mind, I'd expected all of this long before the delegation's visit. The same thing happened at every camp I liberated. I stared White Hair in the eye. "Look at my Nebuchadnezzar."

He gaped at me in surprise.

Brennan stifled his laughter with his hat.

"I beg your—"

"You want to run a camp like *this*, out here in Hell, Mr. White

Haired Person of Importance," I stated, "but you can't look at another man's Nebuchadnezzar." I crossed my arms over my chest and separated my feet a few inches. "Says to me you've had a bit too much privacy and privilege in your life to make it work out."

He stared at my eyes.

"Go on," I encouraged. "It's not as if it's big enough to scare you. Especially after that cold water."

The Oriental hid his grin behind a hand.

White Hair glanced down briefly, then met my gaze, obviously discomfited.

"Delicate." I shook my head. "Delicate won't work out here." I gave Mr. Brennan my attention. "Why not you, Brennan? You know these hills better than anyone except the Indians none of you realise live out there, watching you."

Brennan grinned and worked his hat. "I'm too old fer sheriffin'."

I held out my hand.

The Mexican gave over the cross-hammer badge.

I pinned it to Brennan's vest. "You run the camp, Brennan." I turned my gaze to White Hair. "Mr. White Haired Person of Importance can run the actual mines. . . or drill, or whatever the hell it is that sucks that black blood out of the ground." I nodded at the two younger men. "You two come with me. Brennan's going to need deputies." I walked past the delegation and headed for the spot where the corpses lay.

"Why in the world should we listen to anything you have to say?" White Hair called out.

I stopped but didn't turn. "I don't give a fuck what you do, White Hair. You came to me. I'm going to go play with the stray clockwork. Do as you will."

After a moment, the Mexican and the Oriental flanked me.

"Would you at least put on some God damned trousers?" Exasperation filled White Hair's voice.

I turned to stare him down in the fading sunlight. "If God himself damned them, Friar," I asked full of innocence, "why would I sully my skin with the like?"

The Oriental snorted, and I decided I'd like him if I had any intention of staying.

As we walked away from White Hair, Brennan joined us.

"My trousers are still wet," I said. "I hate putting on wet denim."

Even the Mexican grinned.

"Wet denim chafes."

By the time we reached the corpses of the former sheriff and his cronies, I'd reclaimed my hat and Jinky. Using the monkey to recalibrate the equipment, I outfitted the new sheriff and his posse with some of the best clockwork in the nation. When I felt reasonably certain the boys wouldn't kill themselves with their new weapons, I turned to go.

"Hammer?" Brennan stopped me. "Why won't you stay? It's bad here."

"It's bad everywhere, sir."

"Aye." He contemplated the ground. "And I s'pect you got a passle of squids after yer hide."

I laughed. I couldn't help it. "I ain't worried about the squids, Brennan. For whatever reason, the squids don't seem too bothered about me."

He seemed genuinely surprised. "You got somethin' worsen' squids after you, Hammer?"

"Yeah, Brennan. I got friends."

Chapter Nineteen

Scopes couldn't wait to report his progress. With everything he'd learned on Archeron's ship and with the info in the flicker ball from Babbage. . . well. . . in spite of the limitations of human scientific achievement, or the lack thereof. . . Anyway, they'd *really* made rather startling progress in nine months, all things considered. The spiders had been rendered in silicon.

Mrs. Kennedy had to get excited about *that* at least.

He led her through a maze of hallways in what had become known as the Brain Trust, a collection of the continent's sharpest scientific minds. He'd based the structure of research on the Monkey House to no small degree: one giant room where scientists of differing disciplines could work, bicker and consult one another.

Side rooms and private areas existed to isolate projects when necessary, but Scopes had insisted that piling the scientists together encouraged cross-discipline communications. While the effect sometimes generated conflict, it also had created many of the greatest leaps forward in the Monkey House.

Scopes hoped to recreate those successes.

Without the stripping naked and sleeping on pallets, of course.

And without Babbage, unfortunately, although a great percentage of the work involved information from the flicker ball Scopes' friend had provided. He'd included quite a bit more than the requested specifications for the super bomb. If only Scopes had more time to devote to pure study.

The entire rebellious enterprise, including Mrs. Kennedy's offices, had moved to larger quarters in *La Nouvelle*. She'd established an improvised North American embassy to the Kla'arkians, and the Brain Trust lived and worked in the basements below. The building housing the entire initiative had once belonged to the Mafiosi, with several hidden levels for storage and just about anything illegal a human being might concoct.

The arrangement allowed Mrs. Kennedy to maintain contact with the Trust while performing her duties as ambassador. Also, so many goods moved through *La Nouvelle* that the many shipments needed for the Trust could be hidden, and the massive use of electricity was less noticeable in a major city, as well.

Only one of those remained on the East Coast. And, well, it was *La Nouvelle*. Scopes hadn't seen it before. . . not that he really left the basement since keeping his existence a secret from Archeron had become imperative. . .

Anyway. . . as they entered the laboratory, Scopes handed Mrs. Kennedy the latest version of his clockwork spider.

"We've made them out of *silicon*," he said with excitement, "which is non-conductive, of course, and built a faraday cage around the power receiver so they're protected if there's a surge. We've isolated the frequency of the squids so we can steal their electricity. Once the spiders power on, the usage will be so small, no one is likely to notice. They'll scatter throughout the ship and transmit images back to us here. Isn't that amazing?"

The ambassador held the spider and shook her head. "I like to think I'm fairly bright, Mr. Scopes, but that was beyond me."

Oh damn, he'd been rude. He settled his hand over hers. "Sorry, Mrs. Kennedy. . . I get excited. Let me try again." He led her across the floor to the video area and a wall full of tube-based flicker screens, the best they'd been able to figure out. Scopes missed holograms.

"Where did all the screens come from?" Mrs. Kennedy asked.

"Bergman," Scopes replied. Surely, she'd met the Swedish expert. "The Brain Trust is hard at work on the bomb itself," he continued, "but unless we can distract the invaders, they'll just blow it out of the sky before it reaches the starship." He gestured at the screens. "Each spider is outfitted with a camera that feeds back to us here. They'll scatter throughout the target ship, and we've made them in such a way as to render them virtually undetectable by squid technology."

"Remarkable." She surveyed the room. "Everything here is decades beyond anything I had in the labs under the Palace." She watched Gould and his team setting up the closest thing they had to a functioning laser, if only they could get it to do more than scorch paper. "Two dozen busy ants fiddling with the future." Mrs. Kennedy turned to Scopes with a smile. "I am so impressed, Mr. Scopes."

"Avery. . . please," Scopes said. "Or just Scopes."

"Indeed." She leaned against the counter. "I must admit I find myself in an unusual situation, Avery." For a moment, her face relaxed, and she became years younger. "I never had a chance to know you before your abduction, but after all the stories Zen told me, I've grown to think of you as something of a friend."

While the revelation about her affection for him eased his nervousness, the source of the stories riled Scopes. "That's kind of you, ma'am. It does me honour to have you say so."

Her brow furrowed quizzically, as if she heard the bitterness in his voice but couldn't imagine its source. "Avery." She pulled him aside in an obvious bid to return to business. "You really think we can make this super bomb? Without invader technology?" She squeezed his arm. "Really?"

He gazed at her hand on his arm. He'd not yet grown accustomed to such important people asking his opinion. On the ship, everyone had looked down at him because of his youth and ethnicity. Back on Earth, working hard under the banner of the Hammer, he'd quickly become a leader. Scopes, a leader! Normally, he'd been the one *behind* the leader, but who could argue with the man who'd learned the technology of the galaxy, no matter how young or how not White he might be? Strangely, since Scopes did know more than pretty much every scientist on the planet, telling them what to do had become fairly straightforward in short order.

Mrs. Kennedy stared at him, waiting patiently.

"The bomb is actually the easy part, ma'am," he said quickly. "Making things go boom is child's play. Devising a delivery system that'll drop the payload in the invaders' laps is trickier. Finding a way to distract them so they don't just swat our asses is the hardest part." Circumventing the ships laser beam devices remained Scopes' largest foil.

"Spiders," she said. "Distraction." She smiled at him. "Almost as much fun as a barrel of monkeys."

"Almost." He had no idea what she'd meant by that.

"How do we get the distraction onto the ship?" she asked.

Scopes turned to observe the bank of flicker screens on the wall before them.

"Harder than the bomb," he admitted. "They've started bringing up more slaves to help on the ships. . . but they strip them, so we can't send the spiders in their clothes as we'd hoped." He shrugged. "We're still searching for a means of transport."

Mrs. Kennedy stepped closer and rested a hand on his shoulder. "We are so much closer than we would have been for two generations, Avery," she assured him. "You've already helped—"

"Thank you, ma'am," he interrupted, "but. . . but it's not about making me feel good or smart. We need to kill them. I'll keep working."

She nodded. "Keep working then."

"Yes, ma'am."

The flicker screens attracted her attention. "And these screens are the product of a man named Bergman?"

"Yes, ma'am." He drew her closer to a serious man of about forty who bent over a table of tubes and screens. "He's an absolute wizard with anything related to flickers."

Bergman straightened with a smile for Scopes. "I thought we broke you of that old word." Before Scopes could ask him what he'd meant, the Swede smoothly took Mrs. Kennedy's hand. "Mrs. Kennedy, I am honoured to meet you at last."

She inclined her head. "The honour is mine. I had the pleasure of enjoying more than one of your famous cinematic creations before the Devastation." She shook his hand vigorously.

"I'm glad you liked them," he told her, "but I have to admit they sometimes seem like the product of an entirely different man, now."

She turned her attention back to the screens on the wall. "May I see one of your spiders at work, Avery?"

"Fire it up, Ingmar?"

The Swede nodded and flicked some switches. A low hum filled the air, and a screen glowed into life.

Scopes fiddled with the spider in his hands, and it moved. It stood to attention and Mrs. Kennedy's face filled the screen. The image swung to Scopes and, finally, to Bergman.

"My word," Mrs. Kennedy murmured. "All that in one tiny toy."

Scopes set the spider on the floor where it immediately skittered across the concrete. The image on the screen toured the room.

"I learned so much about ways to miniaturise our technology," Scopes said. "The spacefaring planets have to make everything as tiny as possible so they can fit what they need on one miniscule ship flung into the depths of space."

Captivated by the images on the screen, Mrs. Kennedy settled a hand on Scopes' shoulder. "One miniscule ship," she repeated. "It's amazing how your perspective has changed things for us."

The spider briefly tried to climb a table leg before turning to easier terrain.

"I'm not a scientist," she said, "but may I offer an idea or two?"

"Of course." Scopes gave her his full attention. She may not have had a scientific education, but she was one of the smartest people he'd ever met and that included the group in the Monkey House.

"The spiders are certainly compact and elegant," she began, "but wouldn't your monkey provide a much larger source of mayhem?" She smiled. "Jinky certainly had no difficulties getting everywhere he wasn't wanted. They could climb into everything, and perhaps even be. . . programmed to take things apart?"

Scopes eyes widened. Brilliant. "While the spiders scuttle about underfoot, the monkeys could actually disassemble bulkheads. Genius. I just don't see how we can get the little buggers up there without Babbage."

"I have an idea there as well." Mrs. Kennedy picked up a spare carapace from the bench. "You said the components are made of silicon?"

Scopes nodded.

"If we power them down completely, would they be detectable in a shipment of metal ore?"

He clapped his hand together at his lips. "How would we get the miners to comply? They'd be taking a huge risk."

"There are a number of mines out west who owe the Hammer a great debt," she told him. "They'd be eager to help. We might just be able to smuggle a few barrels aboard one of the barges that bring the raw minerals to the air ships."

Wait. What? In the midst of calculating how many monkeys he could fit into a barrel Scopes must have missed something. "The Hammer?" he asked. "Zen? What could they possibly owe that—?"

"Fire in the hole!" someone shouted.

Oh, damn.

Scopes grabbed Mrs. Kennedy and gently but firmly pulled her behind a counter as a flash of red light filled the room and a small explosion rocked the floor.

A moment later, as he helped the ambassador to her feet, he glanced across the space. The bloody laser technicians pointed and laughed at a jaunty fire on the other side of the lab.

"Mr. Gould!" Scopes called, but the men and women seemed intent on their project as if the explosion were not only perfectly ordinary, but advantageous. "Gordon!"

The bespeckled gentleman finally looked up.

"Could we perhaps wait until Mrs. Kennedy has left the lab before blowing up the room?"

"Certainly, Scopes." Gould grinned like a lunatic. "I think we have the optical amplifier sorted." He pointed at the smoking slab of concrete.

Oh. Well, then. Spectacular. Could they. . .? Scopes calculated. No, they'd still be months away from anything portable by the time they'd completed the super bomb.

Scopes lifted a thumb and returned his attention to Mrs. Kennedy. She stood with one eyebrow raised, but seemed none the worse for wear.

"Sorry ma'am. . . he's really got something here. . . if we can just learn how to focus it properly."

"Is there any chance I'd understand what he's doing?" she asked.

Her Persian entered the room, and she waved him over. He must've heard the explosion, but the ambassador's calm demeanour seemed to reassure him.

Scopes thought about how to explain what they'd just witnessed. Aha. "You know how children use a magnifying glass to burn leaves? It's like that only much, much more powerful."

The Persian took a fire extinguisher to the blaze, pointedly ignoring the laughing and slapping of backs around him.

"I hate to admit it," Mrs. Kennedy said quietly, "but they do remind me of children—brilliant, focused toddlers trying to burn bugs with a magnifying glass."

She had a point. The expression on the Persian's face as he reached her side indicated he felt the same way.

But wait a moment, she'd said something important. . .

"What did you mean about the mines owing the Hammer a great debt?" Scopes asked.

"He's. . ." Mrs. Kennedy stopped to give Scopes her full attention. "You mean to say you don't know what he's been doing out there?"

Afraid to even speculate, Scopes just shook his head.

"Archeron handed out positions of leadership to whomever had the strength to wield them," Mrs. Kennedy said. "Zen is. . . levelling the playing field a bit. Taking out bullies and installing able leaders, much as he did in *La Nouvelle*." She seemed surprised that Scopes hadn't been following such exploits. "He's letting folks know it's the Hammer doing it."

"How do we know it's Zen?" Scopes had to work to keep the anger from his voice. "I thought he'd given up on us and slunk off into the mountains." Giving up on the cause was one thing, but giving up on Scopes? Not trusting that he was competent enough to keep himself alive? That chafed his backside.

Mrs. Kennedy turned to the Persian, who pulled a much folded and worn paper from his vest. Scopes took the bill and unfolded it: a wanted poster. The hair was longer than usual and the beard made the portrait look rather like a homeless madman, but the tattoo of the ocean across a bare chest was unmistakable. Scopes kept his face blank while he scanned the poster. He handed it back to the Persian.

"You keep this with you?" Scopes asked. Hm. Had the Persian been flirting after all?

"Unfortunately," Mrs. Kennedy interjected, "as slow as communication is these days, we're always three steps behind him." She patted Scopes arm. "He's keeping to the more remote outposts, which makes tracking him almost impossible. But we'll find him." She smiled reassuringly.

"Why would you want to find him?" Scopes pointedly ignored the smile. "He made it very clear he doesn't want us in his life, anymore."

Mrs. Kennedy withdrew her hand, apparently shocked into silence.

"I'm sorry, ma'am." Scopes didn't want to hear more. "But I should get back to work. Your idea to use the monkeys is brilliant, and I want to start refitting the assembly lines." He walked away.

All the affectionate stories Mrs. Kennedy may have heard couldn't overcome Scopes' conviction that I had written him off as dead, especially since I hadn't once, in all the long months since his return to the planet, checked in, just in case the brilliant scientist proved himself a man who could competently take care of himself without a swarthy hero to swoop in and rescue him.

"You always think I'm helpless without you," Scopes muttered. "Well, who's the blasted hero now?" He snatched a prototype of Jinky 4.0 from the bench. "We'll see what you have to say when I save the God damned bloody *planet* without you, you bastard."

Where the hell was Bergman?

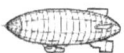

Hope sighed. "Am I the only one who still thinks Zen can be saved?"

Her Persian said nothing.

Scopes banged around at a bench on the other side of the room.

"He didn't actually give up the fight," Hope insisted despite her man's silence. "He's doing a lot of good out there." She sighed again. "Probably more than we are." She touched the tubes on the table before her. "He must still think Scopes and Victoria are dead. Why does it matter so much to me?"

The Persian remained inscrutable. Knowing full well he wouldn't offer an opinion on the subject, Hope wound her way out of the Brain Trust. For some odd reason, he fell particularly silent whenever she discussed this one particular topic.

"I guess we can't put this off any longer," she said as they entered the hallway. Archeron expected a report and would appear at any time.

"No, mum."

How ridiculous that he was so obvious in his selective silences. Men. Hope would never understand how their minds worked. . . unless there was an obvious reason why he wouldn't offer his opinion on another man in her life, even if neither of the men she meant were any kind of. . . well, not that she'd ever expressed any. . . Nor had the Persian ever expressed any. . .

He cleared his throat.

The elevator stood open. He held the door with one hand.

"I wonder why Scopes is so damn upset with that bastard," she muttered as she hurried forward. Too much work to do to waste time trying to unravel the male psyche.

The Persian pushed the buttons to bring them up to ground level.

Hope rehearsed her list of requests to avoid forgetting anything. They stepped out of a blank wall in a back corner of the Empire State Building and made the journey to the main lobby elevator.

Prudence met them in the foyer, clipboard in hand. She rode with them up to the conference rooms. "I have the production reports, mum." She handed Hope the double-hammer badge she kept when Hope descended into the Faraday cage surrounding the Brain Trust. While they knew a badge could go offline for short periods without notice, why push their luck when Hope had a scheduled meeting with Archeron?

"Thank you, Prudence."

Why did Scopes know *nothing* about his best friend and the events out west?

Ugh. Why did she keep worrying about it?

"What happened?" Prudence's perceptiveness was mythic.

Rather than wait for her assistant to badger it out of her, Hope answered truthfully. "Scopes seems to have given up on Zen. I'd have thought after all their years together. . ."

"Mr. Scopes feels betrayed, mum." Prudence clasped her clipboard to her ample breast.

"Betrayed?"

She shook her head. "They have a complicated history, mum."

"Apparently."

The elevator doors opened, interrupting their conversation. They made their way past the guards to the appointed conference room. Moments after they'd entered and seated themselves around the table Archeron appeared. His flicker—no, the word was hologram. His *hologram* sat in its accustomed ornate chair. Prudence placed the reports on the table where they were whisked away to the invaders' ship.

"As the reports clearly show you," Hope said, "the camps with better food and living conditions are significantly more productive. There is an average twenty-six percent increase—"

"Yes, yes, yes," Archeron interrupted with a wave of one hand. "The facts and figures are well documented and terribly interesting, I'm sure, but your Hammer's grand experiment is *far* more convincing than any silly report. Far more fascinating as well."

The trio before him exchanged puzzled glances before Hope spoke. "Grand experiment, my lord?"

"All the fuss he's causing out west," Archeron elaborated. "Ousting the 'bad guys' and replacing them with more civil sorts? Surely you don't think his activities have gone unnoticed?"

"Of course not, my lord." How could Hope ensure the commander didn't suspect that such actions were part of some secret plot? "I'm just surprised his minor activities attracted your attention."

"Minor?" He laughed. "His actions have vastly increased production in the region, and the copycats doing the same thing in his name are nearly as effective." He waved a hand dismissively. "We *are* several hundred years more advanced than you," he bragged. "We *do* learn. Your pampered species works much more effectively with a softer touch than we first employed." He steepled his fingers and peered over them at Hope. "So be it."

Hope found herself temporarily at a loss. The idea that Archeron had so much more information on events in the west shocked her, but she recovered quickly. Perhaps she could turn the situation to her advantage?

"And what do you think of his latest efforts?" she asked vaguely. "A better direction or more of the same?"

"I'm eager to see what sort of success he has this time." A decidedly wicked smile crept over the commander's face. "Temple, Texas is the deepest cesspool of human filth in the region. If he has any success there, it will undoubtedly create ripple effects all the way to Oklahoma and Corpus Christi."

"That is our hope," Hope lied flatly. "But your information seems more current than ours, my lord. How fares he so far?"

A wrinkle of concern passed the commander's dark face, and Hope worried she'd misstepped.

"He only arrived there today," Archeron told her. "He hasn't done more than assault his liver with alcohol."

Hope nodded and waved at the Persian, pretending the information cleared up a detail of her own confusion. "That's why he hasn't checked in yet." She shook her head and tried to appear embarrassed. "As effective as he has been, his occasional binges *do* cause us some consternation, my lord." Would he believe her subterfuge?

Archeron sat back in his chair and crossed one foot over his other leg, arms casually draped over the arms of the chair. "Considering your original plots to oust me from your planet, it surprises me more than a little that you and the Hammer are working so diligently to assist me now."

Her response to that question had been carefully rehearsed a thousand times.

"A year changes things, my lord. When the Hammer worked against the Crown, he experienced the regular success of bringing slaves to their freedom in Canada. It would be utter folly to imagine we could achieve similar ends in a campaign against you. The consequences of such an endeavour would be devastating to the human race."

She opened her arms and held her hands out in supplication. "Instead, we strive to prevent chaos and to maintain the best conditions possible for our people. The fact that this effort also yields positive results for your campaign means you are unlikely to hinder our work." She let her hands fall to the table. "In any negotiation, the best possible result is one where both parties feel they are gaining something valuable." She smiled. "The Hammer taught me that quite clearly in *La Nouvelle* the first time we all met here."

Archeron watched her for several long moments before responding. "I spanked my pup," he translated, "and now she knows it's in everyone's best interest to simply fetch my slippers."

Hope inclined her head. Ignoring her fury at the creature—whatever it was—had become second nature to her. She'd learned how to do that long ago when dealing with her deceased husband, may he rot in Hell. Mental images of the invaders' ships exploding in blinding fireballs certainly aided her deception.

A sheaf of papers materialised before her.

"Your requests have been granted." He vanished.

Prudence prepared to speak, but Hope held up a finger. The fact that his image had gone did not mean the room was no longer monitored. She gathered the papers, handed them to Prudence, and led the way out of the room in silence.

In the hallway, she touched the Persian's arm and with her eyes bid him to depart.

He offered her a shallow bow then turned on his heel and hurried in the opposite direction.

Temple, Texas. And that very same that day. If the Persian took the first monorail west, he might be able to catch up. The commander's information was the luckiest break they'd had in their search. As much as she hated sending her Persian away, Hope knew that if anyone could find "that bastard," he could.

"That one has it so *bad*," Prudence commented as the Persian disappeared around a corner.

"Has what?" Hope asked absently. "Once we have the Hammer in *La Nouvelle*, surely we can convince him to stay and help. He never truly ran off to the mountains, after all. Hundreds of people will beg to join the movement if only they can follow the lead of the legendary Hammer." And then, perhaps, she could sort out her own feelings, as well.

Hope finally noticed the coquettishly raised eyebrow Prudence aimed in her direction.

"Has *what?*" Hope repeated. What was Prudence going on about?

"You didn't notice how quickly he set off to find Zen?" she asked. "Or ever wonder why he keeps a copy of the poster folded in his vest pocket?"

Hope stared at her for a long time. What in the world—?

Oh, dear lord. Scopes had asked the same question.

No. Impossible.

"That's ridiculous," Hope insisted. "He just. . . knows. . . how important Zen is to the *cause*."

Well, that sounded insipid the moment she'd said it.

Prudence's face filled with incredulity, and one hand found a hip. "There's only one thing that makes a man move that fast, and it sure as hell ain't a sense of responsibility."

Hope scowled. Could she be that wrong about *both* men? Had neither ever made an advance on her, not because of something lacking on her part, but because of something lacking in her *parts*? It was almost too ridiculous to believe.

"Oh, my lord," Prudence said with a gasp. "You didn't know about either of them, did you?" She clutched her clipboard. "I am such a stupid whore." One hand touched Hope's arm. "And which one were you hoping for, Mrs. Kennedy?"

Hope gaped at the girl. Why'd she have to be so damned observant? Of course, that was one of the reasons she proved so effective at her job.

But really, Zen *and* the Persian? Was it possible?

Long ago she'd learned that anything was possible, and it certainly explained the Persian's lack of reaction in certain moments that could have been indelicate otherwise. She'd always assumed he was adept at remaining professional.

She sighed. Who was the stupid one in that hall?

"I really don't know, Prudence," Hope admitted. "I really don't know."

Frankly, in a pinch, she'd have settled for either.

Chapter Twenty

I was a hopeless, drunken mess in Temple, Texas. The whiskey was dreadful and the gambling effortless in Baptisty Bell County where both were illegal. I sat at a poker table in a tavern that was more a whorehouse. The man across from me with Miss Izabelle Hudson in his lap stared at his cards with grim determination. Brother Simpson was a minister and an evil man who cheated on his wife. He'd also forced himself on more than one young girl in his flock, then bragged about it to Miss Isabelle when they lay in bed.

She kissed his cheek and winked at the man to my left.

That meant the minister was bluffing. All he had was a pair of aces.

Or did a wink to the man at my *right* mean a pair?

No. Left meant pair.

The drunken part of my mess fogged my memory more than a little, which was exactly its purpose. However, Miss Izabelle and I had spent the better part of an afternoon devising our sign language while the gentlemen in the bar had assumed we were fucking. Which wasn't likely. In the long months since I'd left the coast, I hadn't shared a single bed. Or floor or sidewalk or comfortable wall, for that matter. It was the longest stretch of time I'd ever slept alone. And by far the longest I'd gone without sex, as well.

Which, truth be told, mattered less.

I'd lost track of how many towns I'd liberated. Ten I'd let be because capable hands managed them. The towns all looked the same, now. One set of hopeless slaves run by a set of slightly more privileged hopeless slaves. Somehow one man and a clockwork monkey had left a trail of corpses from Virginia to Wyoming, through New Mexico, and down into the Independent Nation of Texas.

For some reason, I couldn't just let them kill me. Somehow, that would betray Scopes. In my drunken, shrivelled brain, letting someone gun me down would disappoint him. All this time since his death and I carried on avoiding his disappointed glare.

Well, maybe I needed to stop trying. Maybe I simply had to accept that I was a disappointment. I had no intention of liberating this festering stinkhole in the unwashed armpit of Texas. Might as well go back to the life I'd known before going legitimate with the Hammer, thieving, killing, and whoring my way out of a respectable life, the same way I'd gone into it.

I'd had to pay extra for the private room with my accomplice. Apparently, the men in this town valued solitude about as much as my compatriots had in the belly of a pirate's ship where privacy hadn't existed. I'd learned to piss, shit and fuck with eyes on me where twenty men shared quarters under a wise captain. After several months at sea, he'd pay for the first night's whiskey and women, bringing both aboard to let the men work out their kinks before hitting the town. More of his men lived to see the next voyage that way.

Not that any of them lived now.

Damn.

I held out my hands, and the waitress filled them with shots that I knocked back as if they were water. I grinned at the men around the table.

They scowled back.

That's right. None of these men was a friend.

Damn. I ordered two more shots.

If these men couldn't kill me, the liquor surely would.

Miss Isabelle frowned. She likely feared I'd ruin her chance at half the take if I passed out and died from alcohol poisoning.

The minister went all in.

So did the man to my right.

Miss Isabelle threw her head back and laughed. So he was bluffing too.

The sound of someone reaching orgasm in one corner of the bar distracted me for a moment. I'd liked to have had one more night with the Persian. I still dreamt about him. And Avery. Victoria. All of them. Everyone I'd let down.

I shoved my chips to the centre. "All in. I call."

Concerned murmuring rattled around the table. Ha. Buncha rubes.

Miss Isabelle smiled. That just meant she was happy. It wasn't a signal. She likely thought she was about to win more than she'd earn in a month. She likely assumed I actually had the cards to win the hand.

But I smiled at the minister then. A rookie smile. I looked sharply away. If he didn't catch the look, I'd have to shoot him for being stupid before the booze killed me.

He jumped to his feet, dropping Miss Isabelle unceremoniously to the floor. "That smile of yours," he said to me "How do you know what I have? Are you cheating?"

At last.

Miss Isabelle rose to her knees. Fear filled her face, but I had no intention of dragging the poor woman into my self-loathing spiral. Not even sure why I'd wanted an accomplice in the first place. Most likely habit.

"Why Brother Simpson. . ." I rose to my feet. "I'm psychic. I saw your downfall in the tarot cards." I reached into my jacket and grabbed the deck from the pocket where'd I hidden a couple of poker cards. When I yanked out the tarot deck, the poker cards fluttered to the table.

Every man jumped to his feet. Guns flashed in the candlelight.

Miss Isabelle stepped away from the scene. One less soul on my conscience.

The pistol pointed in my face seemed a nice piece of work but a little too clean for a serious weapon. I deduced it had never been used for anything other than showing off with glass bottles. I'd need to prod a bit further if I wanted to ensure the desired outcome.

"All right, sweetie," I murmured. "Never pull a gun unless you plan to use it. . . and never try to show off with something so dimin. . . diminu. . . small."

The face behind the gun wrinkled in confusion. Before I could explain how metaphors worked, someone hit me in the back of the knees with something most likely constructed of iron. Ouch.

"Fucking cheat!" someone called out.

I collapsed amid a flurry of shouts, and the crowd closed in. Several solid kicks found my ribs and at least one thumped the back of my head. After a time, the blows ceased and strong hands lifted me and then held me down on the table.

"Give me one single reason not to kill you here and now." The minister shouting in my face might have been attractive in a clean-cut pedestrian way if not for the hatred contorting his pallid features.

His gun pressed into my temple.

"I can't think of one." I closed my eyes and waited for the end.

"I have one," Miss Isabelle interrupted. "He owes me money."

The gun moved away from my head.

Bother.

"You know how long he spent with me this afternoon." She hauled me to my feet by the elbow. "He promised me he'd come up with the money in the poker game tonight."

Several of the men around the table chuckled at her pronouncement.

She grabbed my hair and pulled me away. "He also claimed he could make a woman scream the name of God without faking it." She favoured them all with a raised eyebrow. "Which I have yet to experience."

A few men chuckled.

She pushed her face close to mine. "Sorry, Romeo. I faked it this afternoon." Her eyes shone with such strength. "Maybe we should try a wager to see if you can make good on that claim." She seemed determined to save me from myself.

Laughter lightened the atmosphere. It's amazing how rapidly men transform from your executioners to your best friends when they think they're going to get a show.

"I'm sorry, Isabelle," I muttered. "I never meant to short-change you."

Her eyes opened wide at the wad of money I pulled out of a coat pocket and tucked into her straining bodice. She grabbed my wrist. Her eyes warned me that I wasn't safe yet by a long shot, especially when I flashed that kind of money around.

So I dropped another wad of cash on the table, the last of what I had, along with a few more poker cards, a couple of stolen wallets and a gold watch or two.

Men exclaimed in anger as they checked their pockets and retrieved their pilfered items. Pathetic. Not one of them had noticed.

Ah hell, might as well make it a sure thing.

My pistol flashed out of my sleeve.

Bang! Brother Simpson's head snapped back and he dropped dead in a heap.

No more than a minute later, I hung from a beam with a rope around my neck.

I didn't fight it. I didn't kick and scream.

The crowd below me spun and swayed, waving fists and shouting. Fairy lights flashed before my eyes, but I managed to regain my focus.

The strangers had gone, though. The men of the *Aquatic Railroad* surrounded me instead, the men who'd shared so much of my life. Jack. The Sneaky Pete brothers. Stinton. Some of them dead for certain. Others simply gone from my life forever. Scot. Nuke. Avery's disappointed face looked on as well.

The cheers of the men fell to a murmur as I stared into the familiar faces. How had my friends found me? How did they yet live?

Wait. No. It had to be the alcohol and the lack of oxygen. My men were all dead and gone. Well, soon I'd rejoin them. At last. I closed my eyes as my vision faded away.

A gunshot broke through the cotton in my ears.

And another.

The floor spun once, then raced up from its place beneath my feet and smashed me across my entire right side. What the hell? Fucking ouch.

Strong, calloused hands tugged at the rope and my lungs sucked in air.

The scent of cloves broke through the fog.

Cloves?

No.

It wasn't possible. He was gone forever, too.

I shut tight my eyes. I couldn't move my limbs.

Voices argued vociferously, but I couldn't understand a word. Too much scotch and hanging. A woman screamed in anguish. A few moments later, the same woman shouted in anger, a long string of profanity.

Strong, strong hands grabbed me and lifted me to my feet, then hauled me into the air and flung me casually over a shoulder. A blur of floorboards passed beneath me.

A man. Clean leather vest, linen trousers over a chiselled ass, and the familiar fragrance of cloves stirred in a brain attempting unsuccessfully to connect with a memory.

Lots of vomiting. Lots and lots of it, and a smell so foul it kept the bile spewing when nary a drop should've remained in my stomach. The mint gargle following the vomit finally connected.

"Persian? You're real?"

"Mr. Bastard."

Mister? Shit. "You didn't save me so you could shoot me yourself, did you?"

I lost consciousness before he could reply

I awoke some time later when sunlight hit my face. Painful, painful sunlight. For a moment I couldn't imagine where I lay, but the Persian stood at a window holding the curtain aside, gazing out at I knew not what.

The Persian! I sat up as everything rushed back in a moment. Blast it! Wasn't that much booze supposed to ensure complete memory loss?

My neck should have hurt far, far more. Bandages covered it. Salve as well?

Why wasn't I in jail?

I sat in a room far more luxurious than anything I'd used recently, though someone at the hotel seemed to believe painting gilt over nearly every surface created elegance. The one bed told me the Persian had stood guard the whole time. My clothes lay folded neatly on a wooden chair nearby.

I glanced under the blankets. Naked. Hm. How that had happened? The room felt warm. Undoubtedly, I'd stripped in my sleep, flinging the clothes to the floor per my usual habit. The Persian had merely collected and folded them.

Merely.

The shock of what he'd witnessed the night before hit me. Embarrassment did not come easily to me, but the idea that this man had observed my self-loathing display humiliated me deeply.

I regarded him in the bright sun. My God, he was impressive. My longing for him hadn't waned a bit since the day I'd walked out of his life on the beach. I wanted to tell him how thrilled I was to see him, but how could I render myself so vulnerable?

"Shouldn't I be in jail?" I asked instead, annoyed by the tone of my own question.

"When a certain Miss Isabelle Hudson explained to the pastor's wife that her husband had died with rather a substantial debt to her, the woman refused to press charges." He spoke without looking at me. "When Miss Hudson informed the town judge that his twelve-year-old daughter had been deflowered by the dead man, he didn't need much convincing that you'd actually done the town a service by saving it the trouble of a trial and execution."

I lay back. I couldn't even commit murder without perpetrating a public service, damn it. I was either hopelessly reformed or simply the luckiest bastard on the planet.

"Why are you here?" I asked.

"My lady sent me."

Of course. Why did he do anything?

He turned to me at last with nothing in his eyes. It was worse than recrimination. He didn't even criticise my lack of gratitude.

He crossed the room to a clawfoot tub and ran the water. Within moments, steam rose from the porcelain. It was obvious he'd followed me purely on business, and the truth of it hurt my chest and forced me to swallow so hard I choked. Blasted noose. Why couldn't someone have just shot me?

Sitting up with the cough, I used one hand to ensure the blanket covered my lap.

A glass of water appeared before me.

The Persian's face remained blank.

I took the glass with a muttered thanks, drank deeply, then gestured at the filling tub. "For me?"

He nodded silently.

"Shouldn't you turn your back?" I asked, trying to sound charming.

He pointedly faced the window without a word.

So much for charming.

I sat unmoving for a full minute, sipping at the water occasionally. My throat hurt. My beard itched. How dreadful I must look, straggly, dirty, and weather beaten. It's a wonder he recognised me. I couldn't begin to fathom how he'd even found me.

And yet, here he was, so handsome and gracious it hurt me worse than the hangover, or the beating, or the wounds from my botched hanging. Timidly, I slipped out of bed and crossed to the tub, avoiding a glance in his direction, uncertain as to which would be worse: his fleeting look or his back.

I climbed into the tub and lowered myself into the steaming water. An array of soaps and oils awaited me on a nearby table. I placed the glass beside them and poured soap into the water, hoping the foamy suds would help me feel a trifle less naked.

"I really don't know what to say." I pulled water over my head a few times and felt better for it.

"Why do you feel the need to say anything?" He kept his back to me.

Walls he had, built up to the size of the Rocky Mountains, which I'd seen for the first time recently. Normally, navigating the narrow paths through such barriers was child's play, but with this man, I just didn't see the way.

"Because I left you on the beach, and I assume you must hate me," I said. "But seeing you again is at one and the same time the happiest thing to happen since that day and the most painful as well." What could he possibly think of me? Certainly, he knew I'd gotten myself hanged on purpose. "Please tell me whether you hate me for a coward so I know. . ." What did I want to know? "So I know."

He tugged a drape straighter and turned to face me. His face remained blank, but his voice softened when he spoke. "I don't know what to think about you, Zen, but I don't hate you."

Relief washed over me. I continued to lather.

"Are you hungry?"

My stomach had been so abused and stressed that hunger didn't enter the equation, but I would need food to settle the hangover.

"I could eat," I told him.

He stepped to the chair where my clothes lay. "I'll procure some food and have your clothes laundered. Do you promise not to drown yourself while I'm gone? That you'll at least let me have my say?"

My face burned hot. "Your say?"

He stopped at the door. "Let me say what I came here to say, and then you can do what you will. I won't stop you."

"I assume you're more trustworthy than I am."

"I am." He turned to go.

"Persian. . ." I said.

He stopped.

"It's. . . really good to see you again."

He considered me for some time in silence.

"You look like shite. I'll find a razor, as well." He left.

I sighed deeply and reclined in the tub, dropping the warm cloth over my face. Of course, I knew what he intended to say when he returned. His lady had sent him. Would I return to the coast and fight the good fight there?

Had anything changed? After so much time on my own, did I have any reason to return to the life I'd left behind? Lying in hot water and letting my dehydrated pores drink it in, I doubted it. Out here the only man I put into danger was myself. Back there, I'd still watch my friends die one by one by one. No. I couldn't do that.

As I saw no towels in the room, the tub remained my abode until the Persian returned. I didn't want to drip all over the room's thick carpet.

When he returned at last, he bore several warm, fluffy towels over his arm and a tray of food, the aroma of which reminded my stomach that it was, indeed, quite hungry.

He busied himself with setting the table as I stepped from the tub and dried myself. He didn't exactly keep his back to me, but I was fairly certain he never once looked up to see my naked body.

That it even mattered to me seemed ridiculous. The one night we'd spent in each other's arms had been remarkably chaste, but we'd both slept unclothed and had seen everything there was to see. Somehow, I felt like an innocent, easily shamed child, which, frankly, I'd never been, even as a child. Since my clothes were being laundered, I wrapped a towel around my waist and another around my shoulders before joining him at the table.

"Shave first. . . or food?" He looked at me for the first time since I'd left the tub.

The smell of the food drew me. I'd eaten mostly lizards and armadillos as I made my way across the deserts. My stomach growled.

"Food then," he said with the faintest hint of a smile. He pulled a chair out for me.

As I moved past him to sit, I smelled the cloves again. The memory of our one night together, a memory I'd laboured long and hard to drive from my consciousness, assaulted me with violence. The vague, hazy memory of what he'd witnessed last night quickly followed.

Last night, I'd known for a fact I'd never see him again, that we'd never sit at a table quietly eating meat loaf and mashed potatoes. Yet, there we sat. My more practical side argued I had no reason for feelings of embarrassment. My more honest side scoffed.

He ate in silence.

I could not. "About what you saw. . . last night. . ."

He ate in silence.

"You're not going to make this easy on me, are you?"

He looked up and swallowed. "Should I?"

"No." I couldn't hold his gaze. I pushed my food around with a spoon.

He sighed. "You hate yourself for leaving," he said at last. "Despite the fact you believe the lie that it was the right thing to do. You can't stand to live alone, but you don't want to watch any more of your friends die."

I regarded him over a spoonful of potato as he continued.

"Scopes told me how you get when you're alone. I saw a little of it when you lost Eddie and after the roundhouse."

I cast my gaze at the table.

"You're doing everything in your power to prove to yourself you are as evil as you think you are. Last night. . ." In spite of the mountainous wall he'd erected, a bit of his frustration slipped through.

"It bothers you. . .?" I asked.

"Of course, it bothers me that you tried to kill yourself." His hands curled into fists at the edge of the table. "I know you think I'm a statue, but I'm not entirely without human feeling."

And now I'd insulted him. "After everything, you still stepped in to save me. . ." I could not fathom his reasoning. "Hope must think I'm rather essential to the revolution."

The banging of a fist on the table startled me.

He quickly retracted the hand to his lap. "In spite of the fact that you've been running from the legend since you left, you've done more to foster the myth of the Hammer than you ever would've done with us."

Time stood still. How was that possible?

"What?"

He wiped his mouth with his napkin. "We've been tracking you across the country, Zen. We've seen everything you've done in his name." He set his napkin across his plate despite the fact it was still half full. "With communications a century in the past, we were never able to reach you fast enough, but word of your exploits has crossed the entire planet. The Hammer is more of a legend than ever." His vague smile returned. "You even have copycats doing the good work for you."

Unbelievable. Men out there risked their lives to help the camps I couldn't reach? More good men likely dying because of me.

"They'll flock to the Hammer if you let them know where I am," I said.

He nodded. "And Archeron even approves of your efforts because the people you raise up increase production every time."

Which explained a lot.

"I'm not going back," I told him. He deserved the truth. "I killed my entire family, Persian. I slaughtered fifteen thousand more. I won't risk any life other than my own ever again."

"Do you really think I'm only here because Hope sent me?"

I opened my mouth to say something trite about duty and honour, but his face stopped me. I finally saw what he really felt, his real purpose for sitting there with me eating meatloaf. The emotion in his eyes was at once extremely complex and ridiculously simple.

"Oh. . . but. . ." My God. It wasn't possible.

He regarded me silently.

My eyes burned. "Do I really look like I'm worth saving at this point?" I opened my arms so he could see me in all my stark reality

He cocked his head and squinted as if examining me carefully. "You do need a shave." He cocked his head the other way. "Now that you've washed off the puke, you look better. You smell better too."

"You can't. . ." I faltered. "You can't possibly still *want* to save me."

He pushed his plate to one side and leaned on the table with both massive forearms. He took a deep breath and favoured me with the frankest, most open expression I had ever seen on him.

"I was raised in a Caliph's hareem," he told me. "By the time I turned eight I was regular entertainment in his parties and spectacles. By the time I turned twelve, I was addicted to hashish and opium, and I tried to kill myself more than once. I had one friend. . . One. Aban." He stopped to sip from his water. "When one of the Caliph's guests bashed his skull to pulp in front of me in a drunken fury, I overdosed. . . yet again. Our bodies were thrown onto the garbage piles together." He looked at his hands. "I didn't die." After a deep breath, he continued. "I lived on the streets stealing, killing, whoring myself to survive. A Buddhist priest took me in. Saved me. Taught me the skills I now use in the service of Lady Kennedy."

I had to look away while I processed everything he'd told me.

He waited patiently. At one point, he drew his plate closer, removed the napkin and finished his meal.

I finished mine as well. His words had fallen from his lips so easily, as if he were describing a stubbed toe. The pain in him. He carried it every moment of every day. But he carried on.

"I'm a mewling quim, aren't I?" I said at last.

"Yes. . . you are."

I reached over and took his hand, wondering if even Hope Kennedy knew these things about her Persian.

"You've told me so many things, Persian. Is there any chance you'll tell me one more."

He raised an eyebrow.

"Your real name."

He smiled and squeezed my hand. "Habib. And yours?"

"The Hammer."

He smiled and didn't seem to mind the joke.

"How does this change anything?" Before he could react, I retracted my comment with a shake of my head. "That was the wrong thing to say. I'm sorry." I squeezed his hand. "It changes *everything*, but I'm still going to ask you to climb a mountain with me, and you're going to ask me to come back with you. Unless someone managed to create a big fucking bomb that can destroy a Kla'arkian ship, I don't see how I can return."

A shadow of his wall returned. "If they have it. . . If they have a fucking big bomb. . . would it change things?"

I hesitated. "Do they?"

"Not yet, but they're closer than you could possibly imagine." He took my hand in both of his. "Someone escaped from a Kla'arkian starship. Someone smuggled out plans for your fucking big bomb. We may truly have a shot at driving them off the planet."

"Really?"

He nodded.

Did it change things?

Yes.

Did it change them enough?

I didn't know.

He seemed to read my indecision. He gave my hand one more squeeze, then released it, rose, and moved off to the window. He peeked outside before turning to me again. "Come back with me, Zen. Not to be the Hammer. Not to fight the invaders." Nervous energy poured from him. "I didn't fly out here as fast as humanly possible to convince you to re-join the rebellion. I flew out here because I want you to. . . be. . . with *me*."

His directness shocked me more than anything he'd said so far.

"I understand we don't know each other well," he added quickly. "But we are both men who trust the cards and who read the signs. I would like to know you better. . . to see if perhaps we might find a life together."

His courage dwarfed mine.

"All right," I said.

He startled. "Just like that?"

I rose and crossed to stand closer. "If you'd led with that, this would have been a shorter conversation."

His tentative smile warmed me.

"I can be miserable anywhere, Habib. I'd rather be miserable with you than alone."

He reached out and took the ends of the towel around my shoulders, using them to draw me closer and kiss me. It wasn't a passionate kiss. The world didn't quake. Those things are for younger men. Our kiss said, "Hello," and, "Thank you."

It was nice.

He held onto the towel as he gazed into my eyes, perhaps weighing my mood. "Please understand why the thing I tell you next was not the first thing I said."

I raised an eyebrow.

"Scopes and Victoria are alive. I know this for certain."

And I did understand. Everything. "So he's the one who escaped with plans for the fucking big bomb?"

He smiled and nodded.

"I'm not surprised," I said. "He was always so much smarter than I."

"He is. . . very angry. That you left and never checked back."

"Of course, he is. . . he has been before. I told you we once didn't speak for several years."

Then it hit me, and I nearly choked.

They were alive.

They were *both* alive. The first sob escaped my chest before I'd even realised it was imminent. My knees gave out, but the Persian—Habib—caught me before I fell. He brought me to sit on the bed and pulled me into his arms.

"Don't hold back," he murmured.

More sobs broke through my attempts to hold the hysteria at bay. "Are you sure?"

"Yes."

Chapter Twenty-one

By the time my relief, sorrow, and guilt had well and truly run their course, my clothes had returned clean and pressed. I felt much the same, as though all the slime and pestilence of the past year had drained out of me. A shadow still hung over my heart, but, now, it was merely a shadow.

My worst fears had been unfounded. Yes, I still carried the deaths of thousands on my soul, but, as I've maintained from the beginning, only a very few lives truly mattered to me. No one in my family had died since the destruction of the *Aquatic Railroad*. Any pain after *that* had been unfounded.

Before dressing, I climbed into the tub and used the shower attachment for a quick scrub up. This time, the Persian pulled up a chair to watch. I was far too exhausted for the moment to imply anything sexual, but I enjoyed chatting with him while naked. His companionship felt comfortable.

"So. . . if I go back with you," I asked him. "We'll have to travel together for a couple of days, then? Sharing a berth on a train?"

"We may not even have a berth the first night," he admitted. "The closest station is Austin. My guess is we'll sleep out under the stars."

"Even better." The idea sounded quite romantic.

We ordered room service, and he helped me dress. When our food arrived, we ate on the balcony. The idea that men might favour the company of men had become uncontroversial in the metropolitan centres since Oscar Wilde had taken the Confederacy by storm all those years ago. It might titillate, but nothing more. We were not, by any stretch of imagination, anywhere near a metropolitan centre.

I don't have the words to explain my delight in passing the evening with him, simply chatting and catching up. After dinner, we ordered a bottle or three of wine. He told me all about Avery's adventures on the Kla'arkian ship, and I corrected many of the more ludicrous exaggerations of my own exploits.

"I did not defeat that sheriff's posse at Black Thunder all on my own. I had two other men, and we didn't drop naked and unarmed from the sky. We had a dirigible and we had Jinky."

"But you *were* naked, I presume."

"Oh well, yes. That part's true, of course."

"Of course."

I chuckled. "It startled the sheriff so much, Jinky had her pistols in my hands before she even *tried* to draw them."

He told me his opinions of everything happening on the East Coast. In company, he'd always maintained a stony silence. Alone with me, he proved quite the conversationalist. That English was his second language astounded me. He frequently spoke better than I.

We spent quite some time while he caught me up on all that had happened.

He shaved my beard for me.

When we were ready to sleep, we stripped without awkwardness and, for the second time, we held one another without sex. For the first time since leaving the coast, I slept peacefully.

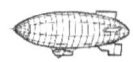

A vigorous pounding on the door startled us to wakefulness barely after sunrise. Instantly alert and armed, we jumped to either side of the door with our backs to the wall.

"Who is it?" I called.

"Message for a. . . Mr. Hammer?" A young voice and female.

Habib and I exchanged puzzled expressions.

"From whom?" I demanded.

"It's a telegram, sir," the girl told me. "Sealed. I don't know who, but the messenger was adamant I wake you."

"Slide it under the door," I suggested.

Paper scraped at floor level.

"It won't fit, sir," the girl explained. "No draughty rooms here!"

Tired of thinking so hard that early in the morning, I grabbed the door and flung it open, much to my companion's consternation. He shot me a scowl and dropped to one knee, his rather impressive firearm pointed at the doorway. So was his gun.

The girl knelt in the hall where she'd tried to follow my instructions. She "meeped" then turned bright red when she noticed the Persian and me. She couldn't have been more than sixteen, and, judging by her reaction, was not accustomed to the sight of naked men.

I snatched the envelope from her hand and reached for a pocket to retrieve a tip, only then remembering I was frightfully devoid of pockets. I'd also handed out the last of my money the night before.

"Errr." I turned bashfully to the Persian. "I seem to have left all my currency in my other suit."

"Not a concern," she managed to blurt out. "I'll just. . ." But words failed her, and she seemed incapable of tearing her eyes away from the Persian's *kire bozorg*. Then she noticed the guns trained on her face, and her eyes managed to open even wider.

"Zen, don't. . ." Habib shouldered his pistol. He grabbed a towel from the floor and tossed it to me, taking one for himself and setting the gun on a table as he covered himself. For his sake, I let the entertainment end, laying my weapon beside his and wrapping the offered towel around my waist.

"Apologies," he said, several bills pointed at the girl. "We live a rather dangerous life."

The girl took the money without looking at it. "Thank you." A moment later, she left with, in all likelihood, a lifetime of stories to tell.

Habib closed the door and favoured me with a rather cynical scowl.

"I am who I am, *jigar*."

He smiled at my use of his native language. "What does it say?" He tossed the towel to one side, distracting me enough I had to think twice before recalling the message.

It meant nothing to me: *stay where you are stop birthday party plans a go stop*.

I handed the paper to the Persian.

His breath caught. "They figured it out."

"They figured what out?"

"Your fucking big bomb."

"Who's on their way?" I asked.

"Hard to say. They're going to assume you're on board." His eyes softened with apology and kindness. "Zen. . ."

"Do we have a chance?" I'd only known this man for a short time, but I trusted his judgement completely.

He thought about it. "A good chance."

"All right then. I'm aboard."

We weren't going to the East Coast after all. The East Coast would come to us.

"Bath together," I suggested, "or should we kill the evil bastards who run this town."

He tucked his index finger under the towel secured tightly at my waist. "Do you think we might have time for both?" The contact sent a little ripple through my abdomen.

"Make it so." I leaned forward to kiss him. The taste of cloves rendered the towel increasingly restrictive, so I dropped it to the floor.

As he pulled me into his arms, our pricks rose to meet one another. His was bigger than mine. Well, so was everything else on him. No real surprise there.

As we kissed, I brought our bodies together. We touched from our toes all the way up to our lips. His tongue explored my mouth, and I met it with my own. His arms wrapped tightly around my waist. My hands found the perfect mounds of his ass and pressed our hips tighter.

I pulled away from his mouth and chewed on his neck, reaching out with one hand to start the water in the tub. He moaned softly. I drew away a bit so we could step into the tub. His eyes smouldered with desire. The phrase had seemed a ridiculous cliché until that moment.

Standing in the rising warm water, I took his hands and scrutinised every inch of his body. As we sat in the tub, I turned him so he had his back to me. He pressed against me and the twitch of his ass against my erection forced me to realise our first time together might not last very long.

I grabbed a bottle of coconut oil from the tray beside the tub. "Massage?"

He glanced over one shoulder with a smile. "I should like that."

Briefly, I wondered if he'd ever received one before, having spent the bulk of his life in servitude, but that tub was not a place for discussion of the past. It wasn't really a place for discussion at all, apart from questions like, "Can you lean a mite farther forward?" and "Am I rubbing hard enough?"

I opened the drain just a bit so fresh, hot water could run continuously without spilling over. When I finished with his back, I pulled him against me, covered his chest in coconut oil and ran my fingers along some of the larger scars on his side.

"One day I will tell you the story of each scar," he told me.

"One day," I muttered in his ear. "Not today." I ran my hands over his chest and spread the oil across his stomach, bringing a quick little catch in Habib's breath.

His back arched away from me as he lifted his hips to meet my touch.

"Don't hold back," I whispered.

He gasped a little. "You're sure?"

I bit his neck. "Yes."

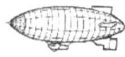

We ended up taking two baths, the second to clean up from the first. By the time we dressed, noon had passed and someone pounded on our door again. The Persian finished buttoning his vest and drew his gun from its holster.

"Hello?" I asked.

"Are you dressed?" The voice belonged to the girl who'd delivered the earlier message.

"Yes." I drew my gun.

"I need to tell you something." She spoke as quietly as she could while still projecting through the door.

The Persian stepped back and aimed his weapon for the centre of the doorway. I kept my back to the wall and waited for his nod before throwing the door abruptly open.

The girl stood in the hall alone. As soon as she saw the Persian with his gun levelled on her, she made her little "meep" sound and closed her eyes.

Grabbing her arm, I pulled her into the room and shut the door.

"What?" I demanded.

"The sheriff," she whispered as if that were still necessary. "He found out about the telegram, that it was addressed to the Hammer and delivered here." She glanced around the room. "Are you really the Hammer?"

"Where's the sheriff now?" I redirected.

"Downstairs," she said with an elaborate whisper and gesture. "He's the greasiest stain of shit in the West and intends to kill you if you're the Hammer." She looked around again. "He may kill you for the hell of it, even if you ain't."

"Thanks," I said.

Habib tried to hand her another tip but she waved it off.

"I heard what you've been doing around the country." She focused her bright attention on me. "Get rid of this son of a bitch, and we're square." She slipped out the door and ran off.

"How do you want to play this?" the Persian asked.

I told him.

He nodded and tossed me a pistol.

A *big* pistol.

"Scopes latest toy." He pressed a button on one side of it. "Aim."

As I lifted the weapon, a bright red dot appeared on the wall.

"You hit what the dot lights up." He grinned. "Your friend is a frightening genius."

I gave him my ecstatic face, which he'd seen recently under entirely different circumstances. "This really works?"

"Oh. . . yes."

I held it to my chest. "And this is for me?"

He kissed my cheek. "In honour of our first epic gun battle together."

"You really know how to woo a man, Habib."

He winked and ducked out the window. "Zen. . ." He stuck his head back in. "You're certain?" As much as he wanted to trust me, his tone told me he still entertained the vague worry my plan seemed a might self-destructive.

"I'm not trying to throw my life away. Not now." I kissed his cheek. "If I'm the Hammer, I need to maintain the reputation."

He smiled.

"Besides which, I need to try out my new toy." I held up the first present he'd given me. Since Scopes had made it, I knew exactly how it would fire.

Hm. I needed to stop at the kitchen on my way to the insipient slaughter.

The lobby of the hotel. It aimed desperately for posh, but the arbitrary and excessive use of fake gilt I'd noticed in Habib's room seemed to have its dubious origin therein. It was the opposite of posh. It was tacky and sad. I liked it.

Twelve of the sheriff's men pretended to lounge casually on the plush sofas because that, apparently, seemed nonchalant to them. The sheriff himself, easy to spot from the badge and pathetic sense of indestructibility, leaned against a Corinthian column near the outside door. He crossed his arms over his chest and wore his hat low over his eyes as if simply enjoying a siesta.

After numbering the men in the order I planned to kill them, I moseyed through the lobby. My spurs, they jingled, jangled, jingled as I roamed rather merrily along.

When I passed the sheriff, he tipped his hat back dramatically. "I hear tell you call yerself the Hammer."

I looked him up and down and tipped my own hat away from my eyes. "Nope." Well, he was larger than the average sheriff I'd killed.

The sheriff chuckled. "Is that a fact?" He glanced at several of his cronies. "'Cause I have it on very good authority that a telegram came to you marked for the Hammer."

"That was mine." I gave him my most disarming smile. "But I never *called* myself the Hammer, did I?"

"Are you mockin' me, boy?" The sheriff straightened and pulled his shoulders back. He loomed large enough the move probably intimidated most folks, but most folks lacked a brand new pistol designed by Scopes.

"So here's how it's going to go down." I dropped my voice to a conspiratorial volume that usually inspired idiots to draw closer.

He drew closer.

I grabbed him around the neck, twisted, and put him between me and his men.

They all jumped to their feet, but froze with weapons drawn. How could they possibly hit me without killing the sheriff?

I drew Scopes new toy. How accurate *was* that red dot?

Red dot on vest, blossom of blood over his heart.

"Don't shoot! Don't shoot!" The sheriff wet himself.

Red dot on forehead, brains blown out behind.

"It's the damn Hammer, sheriff!" someone shouted. "He'll kill us all if we don't put him down!" The henchmen dove for cover, firing at me in spite of the sheriff's plea.

Red dot on shoulder, gun arm rendered totally worthless. Beautiful.

The sheriff's cronies filled his rapidly cooling body full of so many bullets I tossed the corpse to one side and dove behind the concierge station.

The concierge squealed and stared at me with wide terrified eyes. He was just a boy, really.

"I'll try to keep you alive," I told him, "but I make no promises." Luckily, the station had been built of tremendously solid wood so the bullets didn't simply pass through and kill me.

Vases, mirrors, and lots of delicate glass exploded in a wide swath of horrible marksmanship. I grinned at the terrified concierge, waited a respectable moment or two, then shouted at the top of my lungs. "Ah, fuck. . . fuck, fuck. . . fuck!" You get the idea.

So did the henchmen. The gunfire rattled to a stop.

I opened a bag of pig's blood I'd purchased from the kitchens and spilled it across the floor, continuing my barrage of profanity, but lowering my volume with every muttered word.

I prompted the concierge. "You got him. . . I'm coming out. Please don't shoot."

The terrified boy stared at me silently.

"You want to live?" I asked him.

He nodded furiously and found his voice. "You got him," he squeaked. "It's Berryl. I'm coming out. Please don't shoot."

"Berryl?" a thug asked. "He dead back there?"

"He's breathing," the concierge said, "but he ain't movin'." Ah, the joys of carefully modulated honesty.

"Come on out real slow, Berryl."

I raised my hands as an example.

The boy quickly mimicked my movement, then slowly rose to his feet.

"Dive for cover when I say, 'go,'" I whispered. "Go!"

I rose up beside him, Scopes' toy already beading the forehead of the closest man. My other pistol rose directly to one side to nab the man sneaking around the podium.

Berryl dove behind the main desk and squealed again as a corpse landed on him.

The bead of light really did speed up the aiming process, and the mechanism fired more smoothly and quickly than anything Scopes had made before. I killed two men with that gun for every one with the other.

They started firing back so I dove for a pillar, both guns blasting away straight out from my chest as I flew. I landed on a shoulder, rolled, and rose to a knee, one arm poking around either side of the pillar and shooting from memory. Lousy accuracy but showy as hell.

Nine men down. Four to go.

A barrage of bullets concentrated on the pillar, so I pulled my arms behind it to reload and decide on the next step. What horrible shots, but sooner or later one of them might hit my arms.

And what about Habib? I'd told him to hang back until he saw I needed help. Well, maybe he had more faith in me than I'd—

Blam! A four-foot vase near the bar exploded into dust.

Well, *someone* had a ridiculously colossal shotgun. Unless Habib had held out on me, even he didn't own anything that big.

The posse's gunfire paused. On which team did the newcomer play?

The thing ejected its cartridges, cocked and fired three times.

Blam! Blam! Blam!

Whoever said size was unimportant?

The flurry of screams and loud exclamations could mean only one thing: the gunslinger had joined my side. Hurrah for the good guys!

I rose to my feet, training my red dot on the last remaining stooge. The mysterious shotgun wielder hit him at the same time, and his head exploded and sprayed the wall behind him, ten feet away.

The silhouette in the doorway, holding the biggest shotgun I had ever seen, was unfamiliar.

The solid press of metal in my back was not.

Someone must have snuck in whilst I busied myself wondering about the shotgun.

Bother. I raised my hands.

"Say good night, Gracie," said the unknown gunman behind me.

I closed my eyes.

A single gunshot broke the silence. Rather surprisingly, blinding pain didn't follow.

The press of metal fell away from my back.

The man behind me dropped too, revealing the stoic face of the Persian, his gun still smoking.

"He might have pulled the trigger when you shot him," I snapped ungratefully.

Habib raised one eyebrow. "The chamber was empty."

I glanced down at the man who'd snuck up on me, and I kicked his corpse in the ribs. "Bad henchman." I kicked him again. "Stupid." I smiled up at Habib. "Thank you."

He nodded.

"And who joined the party fashionably late?" I asked, turning to see who'd jumped in with a shotgun obviously of Scopes' design.

The newcomer moved into the room. Ah, of course! His hair had been cut shorter and pulled back in a traditional queue, and he held himself with such authority I hadn't recognised him at first, but I'd have known that youthful face anywhere.

"Scopes!"

How wonderful that he'd made the trip to see me.

But he didn't smile.

In fact, his fist loomed large in my face.

Chapter Twenty-two

The fight spilled onto the boardwalk through swinging doors. Well, the word "fight" is perhaps inappropriate, since nothing other than my unconscious body did any spilling. Scopes dragged me to my feet with more strength than I remembered and shook me back to consciousness so he'd have my complete attention while he pummelled me with sincere conviction.

I staggered across the wooden sidewalk. Another punch from my friend, and I stumbled into the dirt road itself.

"How many more of those do you need?" I asked with sincerity. The taste of my own blood I could ignore. The venom in his eyes, I could not.

"I don't know." He cocked his arm. "Two or three maybe."

"Indeed. . ."

Two more punches landed solidly, and I dropped to my knees in the dirt.

Then a third. . .

. . .and a fourth.

I landed on my back.

His shadow blocked the sun.

"You said two or three. . ."

"We could try for five or six."

"No. . . no. . ." Slowly, I pushed myself to my feet, fully prepared to allow as many shots as he desired. While I might have hoped for a more affectionate reunion, I understood Scopes' anger. He knew me well enough to understand what the past months had, in fact, been. I dusted off my hat and settled it on my head so he might once again knock it off should he so chose.

The Persian wisely refrained from leaping to my defence. Instead, he maintained crowd control. Of course, a crowd had gathered. The gun battle in the hotel would've ensured an audience, regardless, but no one would ignore the spectacle of a man rumoured to be the Hammer getting the bloody tar smacked out of him.

Spitting blood into the dirt, I glanced up. My old compatriots Nuke and Sal had arrived and joined Habib's efforts at crowd control. I wiggled the fingers of one hand in greeting.

I turned my full attention to Avery's infuriated face. "Hugs and kisses, now?"

He didn't respond, oh God, just stared at me with malice and spite in his eyes. That hurt far more than all of his blows combined.

"No." He spat in the dirt at my feet. "Not this time. Not today." Rage spilled from his eyes. Would he ever forgive me?

"That's fair." I swayed unsteadily. Perhaps my relief of the day before had been premature. No. He lived. Nothing was more important than that. He might never speak to me again after today, but at least he lived. Yet, if he was unwilling to forgive me. . .

"You came all the way out here to punch me and then head back to Virginia?" It seemed a bit extreme. "I'm certain the Persian would have slugged me for you."

"We have work to do. Together, it seems." My attempt to joke seemed to piss him off even more. His eyes darkened further. "But don't expect me to be nice to you and don't expect me. . . just. . . don't. . ."

He lost control and choked out a disgusted grunt.

And he hit me again. Quite hard.

"You *motherfucker*, Zen," he spat. "You don't get to *do* that."

My chest tightened. He knew I'd been trying to kill myself. He hated me for it.

"I know. I'm sorry." Only I understood the meaning of his epithet. "I'm sorry." Crying was out of the question. Scopes deserved better than that.

The Persian finally intervened, but knew better than to stop Avery's assault. "Perhaps you could take this conversation somewhere a trifle less public?" He stepped close to Scopes. "It would behove us to keep your presence here a secret, Mr. Scopes."

"We're done anyway." He walked away from me as if I were nothing but a worthless, annoying beggar. Perhaps that's all I was.

I grabbed his arm. "Please." I implored him with my eyes. So much I couldn't say with an audience I could say in private.

In spite of the months apart, he read me like a playbill.

"Please, Avery. Five minutes. I *beg* you." I didn't beg. The word ranked as the worst profanity I could conceive. But for Scopes? I'd sell my pride for a pittance if it kept him in my life.

He snatched his arm roughly out of my grasp. Emotions fought a war across the battlefield of his face. He was furious. He wanted to just walk away and never give me another thought. But he'd been furious before.

"Fuck." With a curt nod, he headed into a nearby alley. "Fine. Five minutes. Then we're done."

I thanked Habib, gave the brim of my hat a tap in the direction of Nuke and Sal. The three of them set up a veritable wall at the alley's entrance and started interviews for the recently vacated position of town sheriff.

When we were safely out of earshot, Scopes rounded on me abruptly and pushed me in the chest, which was, at least, an improvement. "*You're* the fucking hero, Zen, not me. . . do you have *any* idea what I did. . . what I risked to get back to you?"

"Habib told me. I know." Although Habib likely didn't know the real reason for Scope's final gambit.

Confusion struggled its way through the anger on his face. "Habib?"

I glanced at the Persian and lowered my voice. "We finally had sex."

He scoffed. "Well, at least you did *one* God damned thing right."

Well, it'd been more than *one* thing, but I refused to allow myself the gratuitous pleasure of saying so, no matter how great the desire.

In spite of his rage, Scopes read my lascivious thoughts. His mouth worked to avoid a smile. The smile appeared anyway. Twenty years of conditioning required it.

Then a slash of pain contorted his face. He huffed a breath to drive it away.

"You left, you fucking asshole." He shook his head. "And you never checked in."

"I'm sorry." He'd been dead anyway. . . but that was no excuse.

He grabbed two fistfuls of my coat and shoved me up against the wall. His breath smelled of peppermint. As always. A strength filled his eyes I'd never seen before.

"And don't think for a second I don't know what you were doing out here." His voice stayed low enough that no one but I could possibly hear it. "Everyone's impressed with all the work you did for the Hammer's cause, with the way you saved all those camps. . ."

He wasn't impressed. He clutched my jacket the harder. "The only reason your *actual* plan failed is you're better at all this hero shit than even *your* enormous ego could fathom." He bounced me against the wall. "After everything you've survived, you son of a bitch, you pick *now* for suicide? With *so* much at stake?" He bounced me against the wall again. "Without knowing for *sure* I was dead. Without ever checking whether the pathetic little brother might have saved his own ass for once." Which was the real issue, wasn't it? "You *don't* get to do that!" The final bounce was almost friendly. "*You're* supposed to be the fucking hero. Not me."

Oh, dear lord. All the changes in Scopes made sense. He *was* the hero, now. Our whole lives, Scopes had been the little brother. Two years younger than I, and I'd taught him everything he knew about living on the streets. I'd taught him how the world worked. I'd always taken charge.

Today, here in this piece of shit Texas town, Avery knew everything I'd done since leaving Virginia was a complicated, childish effort to throw my life away. Here, now, for the very first time, *he* was the big brother, the one in charge. The hero.

He wore it so well.

Pride filled my chest so full it almost burst.

It humbled me to honesty.

"I thought you were dead, Avery. I'm sorry." I had to swallow. "You and Victoria both. I sent you off on your own, and it got you killed. I should've trusted. . ." My eyes burned. How the hell could I say anything without shaming myself? "I should've had faith that you'd. . ."

What could I *possibly* say? An old standby from the days of our youth leapt into my mind. "Maybe if you hit me some more, brother, we'll both feel better."

Scopes' fists relaxed, and he stepped back, breathing heavily. He could tell he'd gotten through. He breathed deeply, and his fists flexed and released at his sides.

"You had no reason to think we were alive," he said at last. "I was up there so much longer than I thought."

He moved close enough to smooth my jacket over my chest. The gesture almost broke me completely. Had I won him back?

"And I knew you were okay," he told me. "Elsie told me. I had that at least."

The odd woman on the autobus out of Richmond? "Elsie? The freaky scientist? She's up there? We thought she'd died too."

Scopes shook his head. He smiled, thank God. He grabbed my jacket and shook me one last time. "You need to make me a promise, Zen." He crossed his arms, which meant big brother mode had not lapsed.

"A-a-all right." I recognised his pose as one of my own, and I didn't like the sound of his demand.

"It's a miracle I'm not dead," he said. "My luck's going to run out some day. Don't let my death ruin you. You're too good a man to throw it all away."

"Just don't die." It seemed a simpler solution.

He shook his head. "I can't promise that. . . But you have to promise me you'll go on living."

"I just got you back, Avery." My stomach clenched at the thought of his death. After working so hard to believe in the new reality, going back to one where he'd died seemed too much to bear. "Please don't ask me that yet."

"If you promise me, I'll punch you again."

His cleverness earned him a smile.

"I promise," I said at last.

Before he made good on his promise, I grabbed him. I wrapped my arms around him and held him as tightly as possible. He held me fast and his heart beat hard against my chest. Holding him again felt better than anything ever possibly could. My brother lived.

"I am so happy you're not dead," I told him. The peppermint relaxed me. The scent was so familiar.

He kissed my cheek. "Me too."

I held him all the tighter. When I could release him, I stepped back and held him at arms' length. "Why *are* you, here, Avery? I was on my way to Virginia. You couldn't wait a week to thrash me?"

The Persian's voice drew our attention. "Zen has a very good point, Mr. Scopes. You were safely hidden in the Brain Trust Faraday cage. Out here like this, Archeron might find out you live."

"I know," Scopes admitted. It was good to know he hadn't lost his ability to blush in embarrassment. So the son of a bitch *had* come out here to see me, after all.

"And shouldn't you be putting the final touches on the F-bomb?" I asked him.

Scopes quizzical face almost made me laugh. "F-bomb?"

"'Fucking Big Bomb' seems a bit unwieldy."

Scopes shook his head in disgust. He crossed his arms again, but the big brother persona had lost its oomph. "We've been calling it the super bomb."

"Oh dear God in Heaven no. It wears a cape?" My face must have betrayed my utter revulsion at the name. "Tights? No? Then Superbomb doesn't seem to fit. It's the F-bomb."

"In any event," Scopes redirected, and his gentle smile was so familiar it made me ache, "better minds than mine are working on it. That's not my area of expertise, really." He pressed a hand to my mouth to prevent me from speaking. "And before you ask, all the programming and. . . clockwork design is complete."

He threw his arm around my neck and drew me closer. "No, gentlemen. . . and lady," he added as Nuke and Sal joined us. "We're out here to convince one of the mines to let us add to their payload. And to correct a major fault in the larger plan."

His newfound directness seemed remarkable. His experiences in my absence had obviously changed him forever.

"Major fault?" Nuke asked. "It all seemed pretty clear cut."

Scopes glanced at me, and I could see he'd also adopted my tendency to think miles beyond the best laid plans of mice and men. He'd always been smarter than I, but now he also seemed to understand manipulating people at least as well.

"We need to devise a way to go up with the payload," he said as casually as possible, "so we can rescue Victoria before the F-bomb blows up the ship."

How lovely. Everyone around us, Habib included, exclaimed their astonishment. I, however, felt gratified that Scopes had stolen my complete trust in the impossible along with my leader's posturing.

I met his grin with one equally feral. "Pfft, you could've just sent a memorandum. Sounds easy."

It didn't sound easy, but Scopes had become the leader here, and he'd covered my back so many times when he'd known my plans were completely insane that I felt bound and determined to return the courtesy.

Back in the street, Scopes introduced me to a Scandinavian gentleman named Bergman, who worked in the Brain Trust. My brother wanted to wait until we were completely alone before explaining the strange man's presence.

The street overflowed with the curious and the confused. So much had gone awry that news was bound to reach Archeron that something had gone amiss in Temple, Texas. We had, at most, one small chance of salvaging the situation.

"All right, folks," I shouted to get the attention of the myriad curious passersby. "I'm the Hammer, and I think I've done y'all a favour here."

Folks dragged the bodies from the hotel. How bizarre that no one cried or mourned. Either the invaders had done a remarkable job of breaking up families, or everyone hated the sheriff and his posse. In either case, I had to fill the power vacuum quickly to prevent an even worse set of bastards from taking control.

Normally, I'd creep into a town and investigate for a few weeks, getting a read on the situation and deciding who would best take the reins from the men who needed killing. That way, when I slaughtered the evil son of a bitch, someone stood nearby to take the badge immediately. If Archeron attempted to contact the sheriff here and found that a corpse had his badge, trouble would ensue. We needed to put someone in place quickly, and I already had an idea how I wanted to handle things.

Speed was a necessity for another reason. Those of us trying to sneak onto Archeron's ship had to find our way to a coal mining town post haste. A petroleum drill helped us not at all.

"If yer the Hammer," one observant man called out, distracting me. "How'd the little Chinaman beat yer ass?"

Without a moment's hesitation I pulled out my new pistol and shot him square in the forehead. The crowd gasped and moved away from the dripping body. It was a bit rough, even for me, but I had exactly ten seconds to assert my authority and couldn't afford to be nice.

"The answer to your question, my good corpse," I called out for everyone to hear, but addressing the dead man, "is that even *I* answer to a higher power. The big strapping fellow here is Lady Hope Kennedy's Persian."

Murmurs of recognition rippled through the crowd. Apparently, everyone enjoyed a good show, and the cast was familiar and exhilarating to this small town crew.

"Lady Kennedy herself sent these good folks to remind me that I am appointed by Archeron to handle things in this town, but, as a few of you might know, I've been a might distracted by a certain lovely woman of negotiable virtue."

Chuckles and cat calls answered me. Miss Isabelle stood at the edge of the crowd coquettishly. How much more she could charge now that everyone thought she'd fucked the Hammer?

"So my choice was a sound thrashing by either the Persian. . ." I pointed at him dramatically. "Or the Chinaman." I drew Scopes to my side and ruffled his hair, pulling loose his queue. "Now tell me. . . from whom would *you* rather take a beating?"

The crowd acknowledged that the choice was, indeed, obvious.

"We all answer to Archeron now," I enjoined them. "Even I do. . . and now that your former sheriff and his men have been removed, we hope you'll give your complete cooperation to this good-minded and immoral couple who hail from Austin, Texas, just a short ride south of here." I indicated Sal and Nuke with a dramatic flourish.

The murmurs and happy expressions demonstrated the townspeoples' relief to hear Texans would be involved in the situation. I tossed the double hammer badge to Nuke, which he caught neatly.

"They'll help you decide on a new sheriff," I said, "one of your own, *however*—!" I called out the last word as loudly as possible to get their attention. I lowered my voice. "However, we must insist you allow them to do their job, as sometimes it is the outsider who can see through the confuscation of local politics to discover the perfect candidate." I threw my arms around my two friends and drew them into the empty circle I'd been granted.

Nuke grinned, obviously pleased at his new position and at an opportunity to spend some time in Texas. Sal remained soberer (which was never the case with whiskey involved) because she knew this wasn't any kind of gift they'd received.

Casually stepping over the latest corpse, I pointed into the crowd, carefully selecting those bystanders who appeared the least interested or awed by our spectacle. "You, you, you and you will show my friends the camp and start with them the selection process." Without awaiting their reactions, I turned on my heel and faced Nuke and Sal, clapping a hand to either shoulder, standing between them.

"Hey, Hammer," a loud woman called out behind me. "Who *is* the Chinaman anyway?"

The crowd fell silent around her, and the hairs on my neck stood tall. I favoured Sal with a pointed look asking her to judge the interloper's purpose.

"Did you call him Scopes?" the woman persisted. "Is he the toymaker you been looking for?"

Sal gave me the slightest nod ever seen. The woman had to be an informant.

I spun to face her. "Avery Scopes died in Richmond," I answered definitively. "And he was Korean. This man. . ." I pointed at Avery for effect, "is Chinese."

The woman tried to play it off and failed. "They all look the same to me."

"That so, Mrs. I'm-from-*Oklahoma*?" Sal shouted, stomping forward.

The mutters of the crowd darkened.

Sal nodded at the mob. "Just like I'd shoot any damn idiot fool enough to mistake me fer an Oklahoma ridgeback, the Chinamen don't much like being mistook for Korean." She stabbed a thumb at Scopes and tilted her hat away from her face with her gun. "If this one spoke a lick a Englitch, he'd already have you bleedin' out like a pig for Sunday dinner."

She strode forward to meet the questioner toe to toe. "'Sides which. . . the man who put a smack down on the Hammer look much like a *toymaker* to you?" She stared at the woman for a moment before favouring the rest of the crowd with a jaunty grin. "Nothing against any toymakers who might be in hearing range. . ." She tapped her hat brim. "But I never seen a toymaker lay a haymaker like that Chinaman did"

The crowd hooted and hollered.

The questioner shut up.

Sal turned her back on the woman and returned to my side, her expression informing me she'd see to it, since the woman was obviously a mole for Archeron. No one out there would've even known about Scopes otherwise.

Duke let out a low, wheezy, easy laugh and drew his wife to his side. He planted a long, sexy kiss on her.

Several of the younger men whistled.

Duke spoke in his deepest voice. "You know it gets me riled up to see you take charge like that, woman."

"Shoot, Duke," she returned easily, grabbing his crotch. "Yer rifle's cocked and ready fer business if I'm slopping pigs or washing clothes."

The crowd cheered.

"Can't blame the man fer that," an old-timer called out.

The crowd laughed heartily.

Oh yes, those two would do quite nicely here. Whilst they started the process of sorting out the town, Habib, Scopes, Bergman and I retreated to the hotel. The Persian settled accounts with the hotel owner, and I located the concierge, Berryl, behind the hotel desk, cleaning blood from the woodwork. Despite my best efforts to appear harmless, he noticed my approach and his eyes grew wide.

"Just wanted to say thank you, Berryl." I showed him my hands in my most non-threatening manner.

His entire body relaxed as I extended my hand. After a moment's hesitation, he grasped the offered appendage.

"I owe you my life, sir," I told him, shaking his hand. "That's not something I am soon to forget."

"Yer. . . yer welcome, Mr. Hammer, sir." His scrawny chest puffed up as much as likely possible. He couldn't be more than fifteen and young for that. I strongly suspected his romantic interests lay in a vein similar to my own.

"Can I buy you a drink tonight?" I asked.

"With you, sir?" His eyes went wide again.

"I'm sure your boss will look the other way." I glanced sideways at the hotel manager, who was counting out a large sum of cash from Habib. Thankfully, the invaders had allowed the various countries to maintain existing currencies, and the sovereign nation of Texas still honoured British bills, so Hope's vast resources retained their value.

The lad grinned hugely and ducked his head. "Yes, sir. Thank you, sir." His deep blush told me I was right about his sexual proclivities, and I made a mental note to have Nuke take the lad under his wing and see him safely out of this Godforsaken hellhole.

"I'm sure you'll know when we're at the saloon." I released his hand and turned to re-join my friends.

"Thank you, sir," he called out one last time.

I reconvened with my comrades at the staircase then ascended to the room I'd shared with Habib. I turned to Bergman. "So what are *you* doing here, interesting Scandinavian person?"

The stranger opened a worn leather suitcase with an amazingly small flicker screen in the top and the hardware to operate it in the bottom. He displayed the equipment with a flourish. It was quite impressive, and if I'd known the man at all I would've made a joke.

Instead, I merely nudged him in the shoulder. "I bet Scopes adores you."

The machine worked on the same principles as the camera in the spiders, but it both transmitted and received images. Larger and more powerful, it could transmit farther.

While Bergman flipped switches and the suitcase hummed, Scopes stood over his shoulder in a charmingly supervisory manner.

"I started by adapting the cameras Bergman had with ideas I'd played with on Archeron's ship, but Bergman's insights are almost as advanced as my own." He patted the large man on a shoulder. "I might almost guess he'd been up there with me."

Berman's laugh seemed strangely forced as he moved aside to allow me closer.

Chapter Twenty-three

Hope Kennedy worried.

Perhaps "worried" was too strong a word for what she felt. She was *uncomfortable*. She hadn't lived without her Persian at her side since he'd rescued her from kidnappers in his homeland. Even when he wasn't visible, say when she bathed or used the WC, he was only ever a sharp call away.

While she certainly possessed a strong pair of lungs, especially for a woman, her Persian had travelled too far away to hear her call. She didn't like that.

"You seem more inclined to enjoy the view these days," Prudence commented.

How long had she gazed out the window?

"My Persian often noticed the same thing," Hope remarked. "Ever since communication turned so damned difficult I find myself gazing out windows waiting for the sky to fall."

"I'm certain he's absolutely fine," Prudence reassured her.

One short, sharp laugh escaped Hope's lips. "My dear Prudence,

I'm not worried about *him* in the slightest." She wandered to the small desk in the centre of the room. "I just wonder if he was the best choice to chase after the Hammer." She glanced up at her assistant with what she hoped was blasé nonchalance. "Since Avery took off after him too, with Mr. Bergman and the Texans in tow, it seems as though our greatest assets are gallivanting across the country after that Bastard." She sat at the desk primly. "And I speak only of his name, of course, not his parentage, about which I, in fact, know nothing."

Prudence took her turn to laugh. "Oh, you'll get no arguments from *me* calling that selfish prick a bastard, mum." One hand shot to her mouth in shock at her own words. "Begging your pardon, ma'am. My upbringing slips out from time to time."

"No pardon needed," Hope assured the young woman. "Your plainspoken honesty refreshes me in the miasma of manners and easily bruised egos through which I daily wade."

"Thank you, ma'am."

Oh, dear, would Hope's pining after the Persian seem a slight on the young woman's abilities? Prudence had proven herself an extremely capable and perceptive woman. Not everyone could kill a bear with one hand while pouring tea with the other.

Hope spoke quickly to reassure her assistant. "You know you do a marvellous job, Prudence. You know that?"

Prudence sat in the chair opposite Mrs. Kennedy. "I do, ma'am, but it's always nice to hear nonetheless." She straightened her jacket and slacks. "I also understand that while I may be an accomplished assistant, the Persian is more of a partner. . . an equal. A friend. Your years together are something I wouldn't even try to emulate." She shifted a few pages around on the desk. "Since you complimented my plainspoken honesty," she continued, "I can't help but notice a distinct change in your attitude towards the men since my implication that your Persian's interest in Zen may be more than strictly professional."

A clever retort leapt to Hope's mind immediately, but died there in the face of Prudence's direct and candid expression.

"I don't honestly know my feelings," Hope admitted. "My relationship with my husband was strained, to say the least." She wondered just how far she could trust the woman. "You recall when the jihad took me all those years ago?"

Prudence gave one quick nod.

"I prefer not to go into details." Hope raised her chin. "But John orchestrated the kidnapping so he could rescue me and seem a hero. . . to me and the world."

"But that's how you met the Persian, isn't it?" Prudence managed a passable job of not revealing her utter shock. "I had heard *he* saved you."

"The jihad turned against John, and his rescue operation failed," Hope explained, "but my Persian succeeded." She smiled at the only pleasant memory in a maelstrom of horrors. "It's why I trust him with my life. But no matter how much I grew to loathe my husband, I could never bring myself to take a lover. My Persian was a guilt-free pleasure."

"All the attention of an affair but none of the sex?" Prudence declared succinctly.

"Perhaps not the exact words I would use," Hope said, "but yes. He's such a dear friend. . . a part of the family. I'd hate to change things and lose that, but it was always nice to have the fantasy. . . the possibility."

The other thoughts plaguing her were more embarrassing, but something about the young woman told Hope she was difficult to shock.

"And then Zen Bastard came along with his ridiculous name that was meant to be ridiculous, so very dashing and charismatic. *He* saved my life three times in one day." She rose and paced back to the window. "I may sound foolish, but his clever flirtations did bring up a. . . reaction in me."

"Zen flirts with everyone, ma'am."

Hope turned to her with a laugh. "I know, I know. I had no real aspirations. I'm not simpleminded. But the attention did feel. . . nice."

"You spend too much time as a leader of men and not enough time as a woman."

Hope's own reflection in the window regarded her with strong, stern eyes. Feminine, yes, with her bustier and clever, little top hat perched askance on a nest of curls but also very strong.

"I know." She strode back to the desk and sat on one edge. "So when you insinuated they may, in fact, be lovers? Well, both of my childish fantasies collapsed at once." She stared down at the young woman who seemed suddenly wise beyond her years. "Do you find me foolish?"

Prudence patted Hope's knee. "It's nice to know you're still a woman, Mrs. Kennedy. It gives a girl like me hope I can make something of myself without *losing* myself in the process."

A girl like her? Hope knew almost nothing of her assistant's life before her service to the rebellion. She took the girl's hand impulsively.

"And you, Prudence, there must be a young man in your life the way I see you smile when you think no one is looking." She released the hand to sit up straight because of her corset. "Is he anyone I know?"

Prudence blushed a red far deeper even than her perfect makeup. For the first time since Hope had met the girl, she sat speechless.

Hope clasped her hands together in sudden embarrassment. Had she completely misread the girl too? "I suppose I should not assume it's a man who makes you smile."

Prudence snorted loudly then covered her mouth in horror at so unladylike a noise, but a few chuckles managed to ripple their way through. "No, ma'am, it's a young man." She folded her hands in her lap. "I'm just not sure the young man in question is ready to make our. . . well, our whatever-it-is, that he wants to make it public."

Hope nodded primly. "I completely under—"

"It's Avery Scopes," the girl blurted. She brought her hands together and held them over her rather lovely smile, waiting to see how he employer would respond.

Hope arched a single eyebrow. She was surprised, but certainly not shocked at that particular revelation. As closely as they all lived these days, behind-the-scenes romance seemed only natural.

"You could not have picked a better fellow," Hope said with a nod. "You have far better taste than I."

Prudence blew out a deep breath. On such an amazingly beautiful woman, the puffed out cheeks were strangely comical. "You have no idea how glad I am to tell someone." She leaned forward and took Hope's hands. "And I'm glad you approve. . . I was afraid. . . since we work together often. . ."

Hope waved her concerns away with one hand. "This way I can be certain that any classified secrets murmured on your pillow will only be heard by someone with even higher clearance than yours."

Prudence laughed again, and Hope found she couldn't stop herself from joining. For a few minutes, at least, Hope felt herself a woman rather than a leader of men.

The clock on the mantel chimed the hour. It was a magical piece with a clockwork man and woman who whirled out and danced together to a rather rapid interpretation of Satie's *Gymnopédie No 1*. They caught the women's attention and held it for a full minute of music and clockwork dance.

"They remind me of the dancing fountain in Richmond," Prudence said as the final notes faded.

"They're based on the same design," Hope told her.

Prudence sighed. "Victoria loved that fountain so."

"You know her well?" Hope regarded her quietly.

The young woman's face had become quite sad. She nodded. "She knew all us girls at Salome's Garden. It was Zen's favourite base of operations in Richmond. We often looked after her when he ran off on missions."

Interesting. If Prudence had worked at Salome's Garden, then she'd just explained at least one reason she seemed unflappable in a crisis.

Prudence raised an eyebrow. "We should get downstairs," she said, meeting Hope's eyes directly.

"Indeed we should," Hope agreed. Maintaining a simple professionalism would be the best way to assure Prudence that the revelation in no way changed Hope's opinion. "The boys will call soon, and I'll want to review today's progress before they do." She rose and thumped the table with both hands to dispel the vague melancholy of the little clockwork dancers and their haunting tune. "Well then, Prudence," she declared, "to work."

"Yes, ma'am."

As they marshalled their way down the hall to the elevator, Prudence read the report on her clipboard. "The bomb itself is about two weeks away from testing, assuming we don't mind a larger margin of error than originally projected."

"How large do you mean?"

"Well, I'm glad they're moving that thing out to Nevada."

Hope's face pinched as she walked. "How the hell do they expect to test something like that without Archeron noticing?"

"Do you think we should fire it without testing?"

They passed a clutch of men who tried to avoid ogling. The pair provided quite a sight as they strode down the hall: low bodices, tumbled hair, and long coats that nevertheless opened at the front to display a tantalizing sight of long legs in rather trim-fitting trousers. Their high heeled boots clacked soundly on the wooden floor.

Hope scowled at the men, who looked away guiltily. "I will leave that decision up to more scientific minds than mine."

The girl at the elevator noticed their approach and hit the button early, so the women walked directly into the waiting cage.

"Thank you, Lottie," Hope murmured, handing the girl her badge of office.

The girl bobbed a curtsy.

"How's little Hope?"

Lottie smiled. "Sucking milk and soiling diapers like a warrior."

Hope kissed the girl's cheek. "Good to hear."

With the Persian gone, Prudence had been promoted, so to speak, and Lottie now held the office of keeping Archeron busy with protests that Mrs. Kennedy enjoyed bathing. They'd even secreted a dressing gown and a canteen of water in the elevator.

Hope and Prudence turned as a single organism as the doors slid closed.

"Next stop, ladies lingerie and scented bath waters," Lottie joked when the elevator dropped.

Prudence continued her report. "The testing of the rocket delivery system is going well. Needing to aim it directly down the subway tunnels seems to have sped up progress."

The Confederate labs under the broken city of Richmond had been reopened. The original space connected to the city's underground system, providing much needed room for rocketry experimentation in a desolate area where only the scientists themselves would be at risk. As Scopes had explained, delivering the explosive to the invaders remained, in some ways, more complicated and dangerous than the bomb itself. Also, if something rumbled or leaked above ground, it would likely be mistaken for an aftereffect of the Devastation.

The elevator doors opened and the hustle and bustle of the *La Nouvelle* Brain Trust greeted the women. A guard waved them through. Men and women in lab coats hustled past in every direction. The place grew busier and more crowded each day.

Hope led the way to the main lab, glad they'd reopened the space in Richmond for rocket testing. Maintaining all their greatest minds in one location had seemed hideously dangerous. Keeping so many of the greatest scientists in so few locations still carried risks, but Scopes had convinced her of the advantages of gathering the scientists together rather than spreading them across the Empire.

Hope smiled. The young man's experiences in what he called the Monkey House had also been instrumental in including the women and the people of colour.

"The squids don't seem to discriminate," he'd said quite plainly to the provisional government months ago. "And we're all mentally deficient compared to most species in our galaxy, but if you want to piss away the only chance the human race has and prove just how ignorant you are, be my guest. I'd rather go play with my toys anyway."

He'd won of course. His singular position as the only human known to have escaped from an invader starship and the invaluable information he'd brought back with him had been insurmountable arguments against any sort of discrimination.

Hope's new knowledge that the quiet toymaker had found comfort with Prudence brought a smile to her face.

"Hello, Nevil," she said, pulled back to the present by the quiet man's blushing face. He'd been in charge of several departments in Richmond before the Devastation and ran this lab in Scope's absence. Nevil's style of leadership consisted primarily of staying out of people's way and letting them bumble along on their own unless they were going to blow something up or mire themselves in a hopeless sidetrack, in which cases he'd gently prod them onto a more productive and/or less destructive path.

"Mrs. Kennedy," Nevil said. "Prudence." His voice cracked. The women's presence rendered the little scientist amusingly jittery.

Everything he showed them squared with Prudence's report. Production of the spiders and monkeys progressed according to schedule. The flicker screens were most remarkable. So far, they'd tested them at a range of five kilometres without detection by the invaders.

Several other members of the nascent Confederate government joined Mrs. Kennedy to wait for the appointed time around a flickering screen. Nevil positioned Hope where the camera would pick up her face for the transmission. Bergman had talked his way into joining Scopes out west for the final test of just how far the flicker technology could stretch.

After the five kilometre mark, the distance should be irrelevant.

At the appointed time the snow-filled screen went briefly dark. . . then my grinning visage blossomed into view.

"Mrs. Kennedy," I exclaimed. "More beautiful than ever despite being about three inches tall."

Hope smiled in spite of herself. "I see my Persian found you."

"Oh, he found me all right," I joked wickedly, and the image jiggled as Scopes punched me in the arm. "Ow. . . Are you alone?"

Hope was very glad of Prudence's intelligence on my affair with the Persian. Without it, she'd have definitely stumbled onto the truth with that innuendo, and the revelation might've flummoxed her.

"I'm not interested in your witty banter, Hammer. There's a room full of scientists and community leaders eager to make sure this historic occasion is handled properly."

I grinned. "But, lady, I thought witty banter would be the perfect way to handle such an historic occasion."

A low alarm sounded, and a red light on the wall blinked.

"Damn!" Hope exclaimed, pushing away from the table. "Take over, Nevil." She rushed through the door and slid out of her coat. "If I return I'll want to know the theoretical range of this wonderful device and how soon we can have them in the hands of our allies around the globe."

Prudence matched her pace as they hurried to the elevator, taking the clothing as Hope handed it to her. Lottie had hit the alarm informing Hope that Archeron had appeared in the building asking after her. The glances of the men grew more pronounced as Hope didn't have time for the proprieties of modesty. By the time they entered the empty elevator, Prudence unlaced her corset at the back.

The cage shook gently. The women froze. Was it a quake? Was that all?

The floor beneath their feet jumped several inches to the left, and they had to stagger to remain upright.

The elevator doors started to close.

In completely instantaneous agreement, the women leapt for the doors, clearing them only barely as they slid shut and the entire Brain Trust trembled.

Hope slammed the call button on the intercom beside the elevator, but Lottie didn't respond.

"It's too late," Hope muttered. "Think. Think."

Scopes had told her all about the invaders' ability to penetrate solid rock with something like radar, but far more intrusive. If he suspected subterfuge, Archeron was bound to train his scanning devices on the Brain Trust. If he found her underground, all possibility of deception would end.

What about the Faraday cage that blocked electromagnetic waves? Could it really withstand a direct inspection from Archeron's ship?

Hope grabbed Prudence's arm and dragged her to the Faraday lab, which remained separate from the main room. It was her only hope of avoiding detection.

The young woman dropped her clipboard and Hope's clothing in her haste and desire to maintain her footing.

The lab had only one occupant, a slight Asian man working frantically at the testing equipment. Sheets of metal and screening lay stacked against the walls of the little room.

Hope didn't recognise the man. "Who are you?"

He looked up in surprise at her presence, and her relative dishabille gave him one extra moment's pause.

"Berg. . . man's assistant," the man replied, and Hope credited her half-dressed state for his pause. "Hiroshi. . . I'm new." He grimaced as if he'd just said something stupid, then gave her his back while he went to work. "Look. . . I don't have much time." He touched the strange device in his hand to the metal wall, and it stuck magnetically.

"What's that?" Hope asked.

"Just a doohickey," he told her. He tapped a tiny square of glass on the device, and a floating screen like Archeron's appeared in the air before the man.

A hologram projector? How did he have one of those?

He touched the image and manipulated it just as Avery had described.

"How in the world do you know how to do that?" Hope demanded.

"I've used them before," the man explained. Before either woman could speak again, he held up a hand and muttered. "Don't panic."

"Why would we. . ." Hope's words trailed off as one wall of the room suddenly glowed red.

Despite herself, Prudence let out a quiet yelp.

"Don't panic," Hiroshi repeated.

A paper-thin wall of red light moved across the room.

Hope flinched as the apparition passed through her but the wall was as insubstantial as a hologram, and the light shifted out of the room as quickly as it had entered. Hope wanted to ask what had just transpired, but the young man held up a hand to shush her.

The entire Brain Trust had fallen into silence, most likely stunned by the phenomenon.

Ten seconds passed.

The man's name niggled at Hope's memory, but she couldn't quite place it.

Twenty seconds passed without the entire complex vaporizing.

As if everyone in the Brain Trust suddenly accepted the idea they were not, in fact, about to die, cries of distress and confusion filled the halls.

"Okay. We're safe." The man calling himself Hiroshi heaved a great sigh of relief.

"What did you do?" Hope demanded.

He stared at her as if the question were foolish. "I amplified the electrical field generated by the Faraday cage and modulated it with my doohickey to create an artificial resonance mirroring the local bedrock." He lifted the device from its place on the wall. "That way, when the invaders scanned us—that was the spooky red light you saw—all they found here was gneiss and schist." The device came away in his hand easily and the flicker screen dissolved.

"How in the world did you know how to do *any* of that?" Hope demanded. The name finally connected with Scope's stories of his time in the Monkey House. Hiroshi? Here?

"Same way I know how to—" He held the device up abruptly. "Hey, look at this!"

A blinding flash of light—

Chapter Twenty-four

Mrs. Kennedy blinked her eyes to clear them and realised she stood in the Faraday lab with Prudence. Why was she there?

The scientists in the doorway seemed very concerned. The coat and blouse one man held up were quite—why wasn't she wearing her coat and blouse? How had her corset come unlaced?

She turned to Prudence for any sort of clue as to what had happened, but her assistant shook her head and shrugged.

"The building above us is rubble, ma'am," someone said, jogging Hope's memory.

"Earthquake," she and Prudence said simultaneously.

The alarm, the race to the elevator. . . Her memory felt fuzzy, but a strange conviction filled Hope: she must return to her conversation with the men out west.

She slipped into her clothing and listened to the disjointed update as they hurried back to the main lab. Archeron had been directly overhead when he'd attempted to contact Mrs. Kennedy. When he discovered she did not wear her badge, he'd almost immediately blasted the building to dust, leaving the adjoining buildings intact. Thank God for that at least.

The subterranean Brain Trust remained undamaged.

Apparently, Archeron hadn't discovered the underground labs.

Back in the main room, Hope hurried to the flicker device. The image remained, but had expanded to include Scopes and the Persian, albeit rather crowded together.

"You're all right?" I asked her.

"Fine enough," Hope said. "A bit. . . disoriented." She glanced at Prudence before continuing. "Look, we spoke with Bergman's. . . assistant." She couldn't remember his name.

He adjusted the Faraday cage. . . The words whispered in her ear and she needed to speak them aloud: "He adjusted the Faraday cage so the scanner read bedrock." What in the world did any of that mean?

"He did that with technology available there?" Scopes seemed astonished.

"Oh, my gods, he's a genius." Bergman's voice made all three heads on the screen swivel around. "It's right there in the data Scopes liberated from the commander's ship." His voice seemed more than a bit stilted to Hope's ear, but she passed it off as a product of the transmission. "Why didn't I see it myself?"

"Where were you?" Scopes demanded.

"He was locked in the bathroom," the Persian declared, "throwing up, he said."

Hope watched the conversation on the little screen and thought of amusing flickers of a curly, red-haired actress whose name she failed to recall.

"Delicate constitution," Bergman's voice elaborated. "The attack on the Brain Trust was quite a shock."

"To all of us," Hope added, her head still fuzzy.

"Can you do that out here?" Scopes asked. The Persian stepped out of sight and the flicker man appeared as Scopes pulled him closer. "If we build a Faraday cage inside the shipping containers, could we set it to read as ore and send anything we want into the belly of the beast?"

"Even the Superbomb?" Hope interrupted.

"No!" Bergman exclaimed a bit too emphatically. "No," he repeated with less panic in his voice. He looked directly at Hope. "The radiation from the payload would be detectable no matter how we reconfigure the Faraday cage. We need to stick with a traditional method of deployment. . . with the rocket."

"And we're calling it the F-bomb, now," I pointed out.

"No, we're not," Scopes contradicted stoically.

Hope again thoguht of the amusing flicker actress. What was her name?

"Still," I said, letting the argument over the device's name drop for the moment, "this does help us get onto the ship."

"What?" Hope exclaimed. "Why in the hell are you even contemplating that?"

"Victoria," Prudence whispered in her ear the same time I spoke the name aloud. "Whatever you do, don't mention acceptable losses," the astute woman added.

"And the other captives," I amended without hearing Prudence's whisper. "We can't just let them all be killed."

As much as the entire concept repelled her logic, Hope had to admit an appeal to rescuing the unfortunate captives. "How do you plan on finding them?" she asked respectfully. "We have no way of knowing which ship houses them."

I exchanged a meaningful glance with Scopes that told Hope we'd already given this thought in our short time reunited.

"Scopes told you about Babbage?" I asked her.

"Yes," Hope said. "He also told me Babbage removed himself from the ship."

"Not all of him," Scopes contradicted. "There's a good chance there's enough of him left to help us. All we need to do is get on a ship, any ship, and convince him to transport all the humans to the planet's surface before the ship is destroyed."

"Oh, is that all?" Hope scoffed. "Well, since it's something so certain and simple, I can't imagine why I have any hesitations whatsoever. You're betting a lot on this slim chance."

"Not a lot." I grinned. "Just the two of us."

"Regardless," Hope said, not wanting to argue the point just then, "we need to outfit the containers with Faraday cages, and we need to get

as many of these flicker suitcase doohickeys outfitted as well." She waved
at the device in front of her.

Bergman grinned oddly.

"Can your assistant handle things on this end, Bergman?" Hope
asked.

The Scandinavian lost his smile. "Uh. . . I think he might. . ." He
floundered. ". . .be busy. Listen, let me talk to Nevil."

Hope stepped away from the machine and let Nevil take over.

She'd wanted to say goodbye to her Persian, but wasn't about to
allow that sort of emotional display in public. Instead, she moved away
with Prudence and prepared to address the *other* crisis at hand.

"Any idea how many were killed upstairs?" she asked.

Prudence faced Hope with an expression that told her she would be
very unhappy with what the young woman said next but had better go
along with it anyway.

"One very important casualty, ma'am," Prudence explained.

Hope simply waited for her to have out with it.

"Mrs. Hope Kennedy tragically died while enjoying a hot bath."

Mrs. Hope Kennedy wanted to protest, but the fire in Prudence's
eyes forced her to think twice.

"Oh, damn," Hope muttered at last. "There really isn't any choice,
is there?"

If Archeron could be fooled into thinking Hope had died in her
bath, he'd look no further. If she appeared again, anywhere, he'd realise
he'd been duped and would likely incinerate the entire city of *La Nouvelle*.

"And we probably need to move everything to the Richmond labs,"
Hope concluded.

Prudence nodded. "They need to go somewhere." In case he
incinerated the city anyway. Wasn't there a secret installation somewhere
in Nevada?

"Something odd happened, Prudence." Hope rubbed the bridge of
her nose.

"I agree. . . Bergman's assistant. . . what did he look like?"

Hope thought about it. "To be honest, I can't even say for certain
the assistant was a he." She regarded her normally rock solid companion

who seemed rather shaken by the experience. "Could the scanner have affected us somehow?"

"It's possible, though no one else seems disturbed."

"Indeed," Hope agreed, noticing a distinct lack of similar reactions around them. People seemed distraught, but no one seemed physically distressed. "There's something about this Bergman fellow I don't quite trust."

"I know how you feel," Prudence agreed.

"There's something about this Bergman fellow I don't quite trust," I said quietly.

"I know how you feel," Scopes agreed.

His head rested comfortably solid and familiar against my abdomen as we lay on a hillside gazing quietly up at the stars somewhere in southern Colorado or northern New Mexico. Hard to tell exactly where the boundaries lay. My arm draped across his chest, and the sounds of our companions laughing and talking a ways down the hill lulled us both to peace.

"Sometimes I feel as though I know him already, even though we just met." Scopes played finger games with Jinky, who frolicked and chattered quietly on a nearby stone. With the toy's noise, the rattle of the grasshoppers, and the rush of the nearby creek, I felt reasonably certain that no one would overhear us. "He'll say something. . ."

I let the pause stretch out before prompting. "Something?"

"He reminds me of Hiroshi, my friend in the Monkey House," Scopes admitted. "I know it's impossible, but he'll have the odd turn of phrase. . . or the way he'll solve a problem." He shrugged against me. "They're nothing alike physically. At least two stone different in their weights."

"Could they be working together?"

"To what end?" he asked. "They've both been nothing but helpful, so it's unlikely they're working for Archeron. I asked Bergman if he knew Hiroshi, and he denied ever hearing the name, so if they do know one another then some sort of deception is at play." He picked up a pebble and tossed it for the monkey to chase.

With a nearly full moon cresting the horizon, the hillside glowed quite visibly, and the monkey's visual sensors no doubt rendered the hillside as bright as day.

"It's likely I'm just jumping at shadows," Scopes admitted.

"It's always a good idea to be cautious," I reminded him. "I say we both keep our eyes open."

Even with the rising moon, myriad stars twinkled above us.

"I think we should talk to Mrs. Kennedy about him," I said. "And Habib as well."

"Agreed."

He settled against me, and I held him a little tighter. He tossed the pebble again to the monkey's indefatigable delight.

"You were out there," I muttered. "Out amongst the stars."

He chuckled. "Actually, I was in a low orbit, barely—"

I pinched his nipple to distract him.

"Hey!" He flinched and laughed. "I missed seeing them," he said. "I was out there, but I never found the opportunity to actually see the stars."

"What about those artificial construct thingamabobs?"

He grabbed my hand. "Zen, you would love those. Every time Babbage took me into the virtual worlds, I wished you were with me, scout's honour."

His sentiment touched me. While I'd languished under the mistaken assumption he'd breathed his last, he'd been playing sword fight games with his new friends. For about ten seconds, I'd tried to feel jealous, but I felt so hysterically glad to have him back I could never begrudge him all he'd learned and experienced out there.

Especially since everything he'd learned meant we just might drive the invaders away.

"You really think we can accomplish this?" I asked

"With the data Babbage gave me, we can manufacture the bomb and the rocket to deliver it. Will it work? Especially without a single practical test?" He shrugged again.

"And what happens even if it does work?" I continued. "We destroy one ship, *kapow!*" I tapped his forehead to emphasise my sound effect. "There's three more."

"There's *only* three more," he amended. "It's been a year since the commander's arrival and no backup has arrived. With an entire planet to control, I'd hardly suppose. . ." He sat up and turned to face me, scooting forward so he wouldn't have to release my hand. "Do I sound pompous when I talk about the things I learned up there?"

Jinky jumped onto my chest and swatted at our clasped hands making sure we were quite aware that we should toss pebbles for him. Since his return, Scopes had adjusted the little toy's babbaging, making him more lifelike than ever.

Scopes' sincerity amused me. "Don't you dare worry about that. . . especially not with me. I'm proud of you." I squeezed his hand to emphasise my sincerity. "Up there. . . you found your. . . your *path*, I guess." I tossed a stone for Jinky with my free hand. "Pompous? I've always known you're a genius, Scopes, but I didn't understand what that truly meant. I came to know some of the men and women Mrs. Kennedy gathered before I went out west, and I saw them struggle with problems that would have been cake frosted, cut and served on china plates for you. On a team of geniuses. . . you're at the top." I sat up cross-legged, my legs against his.

Since he'd been returned to me, when we were alone, I could scarce prevent myself from touching him, as if to prove he did indeed exist. My friend didn't seem to mind and acted as comforted by the contact as I.

"You managed to actually attend school up there. I mean, we snuck you into Harvard, but. . ." I scoffed. "That wasn't enough for you. You needed a teacher from another world with all the knowledge of the cosmos at his disposal." I made him lie down so we could gaze up at the stars. "So no modesty, Avery. You're a *leader* now, and these idiots, they expect us to save the world, you and me."

He squeezed my hand. "But mostly me."

"Mostly you." I smacked the side of his head.

"You said no modesty."

"Shall I regret it immediately?"

He settled back and drew in a deep breath. His hands came up to gesture while he talked, and his voice actually dropped almost an octave.

"Okay then. . . It's difficult to control an entire planet," he began. He became this new, confident man I hadn't yet learned to understand. He'd changed so much without me, my heart nearly burst with pride. "Relative to many species out there, the invaders aren't all that bright."

Jinky scrambled onto a rock behind me and picked at my hair as if looking for lice.

"Right," I threw in, "they needed you to figure out their time machine thingy."

"Exactly!" he remarked, proud that his mentally deficient friend had managed to add two simple digits. "Hopefully, we blow one ship and convince them we have the capacity to do more." He raised one hand to fend off an interruption that had no likelihood of materialising. "Before you counter that they'd assume we'd blow our whole wad at once if we *had* more F-bombs, let me pre-empt you by pointing out that the moment after our first strike, we'll disseminate our blueprints and data via the video transceivers." He paused to chuckle. "Hiroshi always laughed at me when I called them 'flicker boxes.'"

"You peasant," I joked.

He managed to punch me lightly in the chest from his position due to years of practise. "I know where you're sleeping tonight, and I swear I'll reset Jinky's programming."

The sound of Habib's laughter down the hill distracted me. Scopes and I had opted to camp on our own that night, and the Persian had completely understood. He and I had spent nearly forty-eight hours reconnecting, and the amazing man accepted my need for privacy with Scopes.

"He's a wonder, Zen," Scopes reminded me. "Not many men would be so accommodating of your desire to spend the night with another man so soon after you finally stopped being a horse's ass."

I tapped his forehead again. "I think his affection for Mrs. Kennedy helps. He empathises."

"He's a good man," he told me. "I didn't spend a lot of time with him, but what I saw I liked."

"Me too."

He turned to meet my gaze. "You still think Prudence is a good idea?"

I ran a hand through his hair affectionately and then smacked him. "My dear friend, a woman who can tolerate all *my* bizarre eccentricities without charging you for her time anymore?" I ran the hand through his hair again. "Don't ever let her go."

The manner in which he beamed proved my beliefs about his feelings for the woman. I'd not often seen him quite this besotted, and all evidence suggested she felt the same way. He settled back.

But wait a minute. . . "Why not just send the plans across the planet now so maybe someone else can cobble something together?"

He shook his head. I missed the dreadlocks and tools, but he had to pass as a simple Chinese assistant for now. "We don't know who to trust. If these plans leak back to Archeron, he'll simply incinerate the entire North American continent and bring in new workers from China and India." He shivered and drew my arm tighter across his chest. "Once people all over the planet see what we can do. . . that we have a chance? Who knows what we'll start, and hopefully the commander will decide that we're too much trouble since they likely only have the four starships"

He paused, and we stared up at the stars together. How many of them warmed planets like our own.

"Sometimes all people need to know is that they have a chance," he whispered.

"Amen to that, brother."

"Amen."

Without warning, he leapt to his knees facing me, soundly catching me in the groin with one knee.

"That's it!!" he exclaimed. "*That's* what didn't make sense."

I expressed my utter lack of comprehension while nursing my balls.

"When I first introduced Mrs. Kennedy to Bergman," he continued, "he made a joke about the fact that I called the video a flicker. 'I thought we broke you of that old word, Scopes,' he said. *We*. Who was *we*? He'd never commented on it before."

Scopes seemed frustrated that my attention focused more on my injury than his revelation. "Okay," I prompted. "So what does it mean?"

He deflated. "I'm not sure," he admitted. "But Hiroshi teased me about the word all the time." He looked down. "Sorry about your balls."

He lay beside me, his head on my shoulder, huddled against my side for warmth as he'd done for years when our home was a cardboard box. He seemed ready for sleep. "I guess it's just one more connection between this man Bergman and my friend Hiroshi."

I adjusted my position for greater comfort. "We'll need to have a long conversation with him first thing in the morning."

"Well," Scopes argued snarkily, "first thing after your Persian massages your injured parts."

"Indubitably."

But we didn't have a chance to question Bergman the next morning. He vanished without a trace, even leaving his horse behind. He'd written a note pointing out where on Scope's flicker ball we could find clear instructions for the Faraday cage improvements.

Two facts disturbed Avery about Bergman's instructions. The second most disconcerting fact was that those particular plans had *not* been in the original set of data given him by Babbage. Of that, Scopes remained absolutely certain.

The *most* alarming fact, Scopes insisted, was that no one on Earth could have *possibly* conjured those designs out of thin air.

Chapter Twenty-five

Two weeks later, and far sooner than expected, Scopes, Habib and I clustered around a flicker screen in a warehouse outside Gillette, in the Canadian province of Wyoming, home to one of the world's largest coal mines. They had benefited from my assistance some months earlier. The sheriff and posse I'd installed jumped at the chance to support the preparations for our assault on the invaders. With the amount of material shuttled up to the starships from that site, two more bins would likely go unnoticed.

Things, as it were, had to move forward far more quickly than planned.

Hope had become a martyr.

On the flicker screen, a crowd of thousands waved signs and banners in *La Nouvelle*. The protest was one of hundreds all over the continent. "*Vive La Dame!*" the signs proclaimed.

A young woman's face pushed its way into the camera. "I saw her! I saw her on the street! She told me to keep up the fight! She told me to never give up. *Vive La Dame! Vive La Dame!*"

The crowd picked up the chant. "*Vive La Dame! Vive La Dame!*"

"Turn that blasted thing off." Hope's voice startled me. She'd arrived sooner than expected.

Her Persian immediately complied as the three of us rose to face her.

"They're going to get themselves killed," she muttered. "Just like all the rest."

No one, least of all Hope herself, had appreciated how important she'd become to the *zeitgeist* of the continent. Thousands protested in her name and Archeron cracked down brutally on all demonstrations in response, killing ever more poor fools in an effort to ensure an actual religion didn't sprout up around Hope's martyrdom.

If we waited too long, the commander would realise his efforts only added fuel to the fire. Had they done no research into human psychology? Emotions across both the Confederacy and Canada had grown far too volatile. He just might resort to scorching the entire continent as a warning to the human race.

"Milady," Habib said with a bow.

"Oh, for God's sake," she blustered, taking him into a hug. "You can share the bed of this ridiculous bastard, you can give me a damn hug."

His eyes over her shoulder grew larger than I'd ever seen them. Well, she'd have to be pretty dim to miss something as obvious as our nascent romance, especially with Prudence as her new assistant. Hope Kennedy was anything but stupid.

Habib embraced her warmly, a smile replacing his expression of shock.

She released him and turned to me.

I held my arms open expectantly.

She folded hers and examined me up and down. "I have no idea what he sees in you," she declared, "and if you ever break his heart I shall take you over my knee—" She raised a hand before I could lob the obvious rejoinder. "I retract that." She glanced at Scopes. "I shall have Avery pummel you soundly."

I gave her a formal bow.

"And I shall take delight in following through on your threat," Scopes told her.

Then Prudence distracted him with her own version of reunion, which caused everyone but me to turn away in embarrassment.

Scot and Basil Rupert nodded their greetings, but my ribs already ached with the anticipation of Scot's reception once a less formal situation presented itself.

Nuke and Sal would arrive shortly, I knew, with Berryl in tow. They'd managed to wrap up their duties in Texas post haste and ran a series of horses to exhaustion to meet us.

"Zen!" a young boy's voice shouted at the top of his lungs. Twist? How in the world had he convinced Hope to drag him along? No matter. His grinning face delighted me. I scooped him up and hugged him close without a second's thought.

He stiffened in my arms for a moment, unaccustomed to affection from me, but when he noticed the smile on my face he grabbed on as tight as he could.

Over the boy's shoulder, Habib stoically nodded his approval.

I rolled my eyes at him and stuck out my tongue.

"I needed to leave *La Nouvelle* as quickly as possible," Hope said when I'd set Twist on his feet. "I'd be far too easily recognised there. They even see me where I am not."

"And your presence here is most welcome, ma'am," I said. "We have much to decide."

Her lips pressed into a thin line. Ah yes. The reunions delighted me, but we'd all converged on Gillette, Wyoming to finalise our plans for an attempt to destroy the invaders. Which just might kill us all. And we did not agree on how to proceed.

"Our plans advance apace?" I asked.

Hope sighed deeply. "The Brain Trust moved out to a secret compound in Nevada. An area known only by a number. They finalised the construction of the 'F-bomb' there." She rolled her eyes at the name I'd forced on the project. "It is currently being transported to Richmond for launch by the delivery systems perfected there." She shook her head. "If the invaders survive our attack, Richmond will likely bear the brunt of retaliation as the launching site. The men and women know the possibilities, and no one but necessary personnel is allowed. The rest of the scientific team is *en route* to Nevada."

If our gambit failed, the geniuses of the world would remain hidden in Area 51.

A few hours later, over two hundred souls gathered in a warehouse in Gillette. It may have been the first time in history that Confederates and Canadians worked together instead of shooting at one another.

Hope and I argued before the entire assembly. Loudly.

"I don't like it," Mrs. Kennedy insisted.

"What's not to like?" I demanded. "The invaders die, the prisoners on their ships get rescued, and the planet Earth lives happily ever after." I gave my best ta-daa flourish. "Everyone wins."

She folded her hands at her hip and regarded me like an angry schoolmarm with a recalcitrant, albeit precocious, student. "I don't know, Hammer. There is so much riding on whether Babbage is still operational. What if he's unable to help you?"

I grew tired of her whining. "The only ones at risk are Scopes and I," I insisted for the hundredth time. "If the prisoners are doomed, they're doomed. We're just hoping to grab the brass ring."

She glanced to her Persian who performed an incomparable impersonation of a statue. She threw her hands in the air in exasperation. "I know this makes me sound like a foolish schoolgirl, but does anyone else see that this is simply a *bad* idea?"

No one responded, and all eyes riveted themselves on me. How disquieting. Men and women who had moved the world for fifty years through wars and famines seemed ready to accept what a common pirate from Virginia wanted to do. Even Gatsby kept his tongue.

All right then.

"So it's settled?" I asked of the assembly.

No one spoke.

"What do they even look like?" Habib stepped forward. His words were quiet and enough of a non sequitur to garner everyone's attention. "These aliens you are about to engage, what do they look like?"

He'd never confronted me in public. Hell, he'd never confronted *anyone* in public.

"Does it matter?" I asked, trying my best not to sound dismissive.

"I trust that your friend Babbage will do his best to protect you in your endeavours," he said. "But he wasn't able to show Scopes so much as a picture of what the invaders looked like."

Oh. So *that's* where he was going. Bother. We'd had the same argument naked with coconut oil.

"There is only a *part* of Babbage left on that vessel." He addressed the assembly. "If he were able to release the prisoners and destroy the invading ships, he would have done so rather than dropping Scopes onto the planet alone."

As much as I loathed his words, his passion and ardour produced a raging hard-on I hoped no one could see.

"Our man inside, as it were," he continued, and everyone seemed astonished at the normally silent Persian's verbosity, "his ability to work against orders and release Scopes came after he had achieved sentience. The remnant left behind?" He shook his head and shrugged. "I have faith he will keep the invaders from simply burning our delegation to cinders with their automatic weaponry. . ." He turned to face me directly. His eyes spoke volumes to me alone. "But will he be able to disobey orders and transport everyone to the planet? Will he be able to do that, or will you be trapped on a ship where Archeron can hunt you down and be rid of you if our own bomb doesn't blast you out of the sky?"

The frustrated murmur indicated that many delegates held similar concerns.

"Hammer." Habib stepped closer to me. "I understand your desire to handle this infiltration on your own, and I trust that Babbage will do his best, but, really, can we expect any more from him than a level playing field? A larger contingent of insurgents may actually stand a chance of taking the ship should the F-bomb fail. We will never again have an opportunity to sneak aboard one of their starships if this mission miscarries."

He'd argued the same thing with me alone: a body of soldiers stood a better chance of destroying the ship than just Scopes and I.

I'd agreed with him completely and then told him I wouldn't risk any other lives.

"You say you hope to grab the brass ring," he added gently. "The more hands in the air, the more likely one is to catch it."

Strangely, he'd never once admitted the true reason he wanted to organise an infiltration squad. If I was going to allow him to risk his life on this mission with me, him of all people, I damn well expected him to admit the real reason he wanted to do so.

"Say it," I told him.

His eyes opened wide. He knew exactly what I meant him to say. He glanced around, awkwardly. "I don't think. . ."

"Persian!" It took every ounce of strength not to call him Habib. "Everyone here knows we're together. *Everyone*." I chose someone at random and pointed. "You. You know we're together, right?"

The man seemed embarrassed at being singled out, but managed to sort of shrug and nod.

"You?" I asked, pointing at a second random delegate.

The second stranger also nodded his knowledge.

"Is there anyone here who *didn't* know?" I turned on the spot with my arms widespread.

A general murmur susurrated through the assembly, but no one raised a hand.

"Say it." I faced him squarely. "If you expect me to allow you into the mouth of the Devil himself, I need you to tell me why you wish to go there."

His face informed me exactly what he thought of being put on the spot like that, but Habib was never one to back down from a challenge.

"Let me protect you," he said firmly, "because I care about you."

He raised an eyebrow.

I nodded. It was enough.

"I have twenty fighters who wish to join the assault. If Babbage is able to transport us all instantly, so much the better and you'll have the chance to say, 'I told you so.'" He stepped closer. "But if he cannot, we have an opportunity to take the ship hand to hand. Invaders who studiously avoid physical contact with their slaves are likely *not* fighters no matter what Archeron's flicker would have us believe. "

God, he was sexy the way he faced me down like that. I grabbed him around the neck and pulled him close, kissing him soundly. He hesitated for a moment, but when a huge round of applause exploded around us, he kissed me back and forced me into a dip.

The applause magnified tenfold.

Back on my feet, I disengaged from the Persian and faced the delegation.

"Permission to board the enemy ship, captain!" I shouted to Mrs. Kennedy.

A roar rattled the roof of the warehouse.

"Permission to get yourselves slaughtered, you mean?" Mrs. Kennedy's face did not project the same *joi de vivre* as those of the rest of the assembly.

"Aye, captain, if that be the way of the thing!" I shouted.

The crowd favoured me with another round of applause.

Scopes stepped forward, and I threw my other arm around him.

Scot and Basil Rupert joined us, as did Nuke and Sal. The big surprise was the Sneaky Pete brothers, all four of them, who melted out of the crowd as one. Twelve more men and women joined us to the loud and wildly approving applause of the delegation. Twist even joined us, and I let him have his moment despite the fact there was no way in hell he would join the assault.

Mrs. Kennedy scanned the ensemble with crossed arms and a scowl.

Prudence stepped to her side and touched her arm gently. "They're the best chance we have, Mrs. Kennedy." Prudence, of course, had voiced her desire to join us, but someone had to help Hope run the show.

"If this is the best chance we have, then I weep for the planet," Hope muttered. "No, the best hope we have is an enormous bomb that's going to fly right up your arses while you have a jolly reunion playing at pirates. You're all doomed and what then?" She waved at the group of us before her. "You *are* the best and the brightest and the bravest we have and you're forcing me to give the order to blow you all out of the sky. This will gut the rebellion if this Babbage fellow isn't able to perform a *deus ex machina* and transport you off the ship." She gave me a look of utter disgust. "This entire endeavour is absolute folly."

She stormed away. Her reaction sobered the assembly.

I had moments to regain momentum.

"She may be right," I called out and jumped on a chair so all could see. "We may meet our ends on this mission, but even if all we do is create further distraction for the F-bomb to take these unseen invaders with us, then I for one will consider our efforts a success!"

"And so say we all," Habib shouted.

"And so say we all," the entire assembly shouted back.

We coordinated the two prongs of the attack through the use of long distance flicker screens. At one point, I made the mistake of asking Scopes how we could be certain Archeron wouldn't uncover our transmissions, but after thirty seconds I told him, "Blah, blah, blah never mind."

"I can't believe you lasted that long."

We'd distributed them across the continent and had a shipment bound for the other side of the pond via the Bering Strait. A certain number of folks had wanted to communicate with the rest of the world *before* attempting our mad plan, but Scopes remained adamant that the risk remained too great.

Archeron was hypervigilant about all access points between the continents. While more than one smuggler had made a crossing at the Bering Strait, many more had been vaporised or abducted, and we couldn't risk the flicker screens falling into Archeron's hands. . . or paws. . . or pseudo-pods. . . before the attempt. If he discovered we'd re-established planetwide communications, he'd likely initiate a second Devastation on the spot.

We had to hope the rest of the world would approve of our scheme.

Chapter Twenty-six

The shuttles that transported ore, slaves, and other goods to and from the starships couldn't have been more different from the sleek, organic command vessels. They resembled giant blocky pods with all the sex appeal of a barge, which is what we'd taken to calling them. The way they defied gravity by simply floating to the ground and rising silently from it again when full infuriated every scientist in the Brain Trust. They hadn't even a wild speculation how the damn things worked.

Scopes presumed them a product of the Shifter culture that had produced Babbage, which meant, as far as we were concerned, they operated by magic.

The invaders had a hell of a lot of them, all identical and rather beat up. The doors opened, a large ramp extended, and containers would descend for whatever needed transporting. For the coal mines, giant bins rolled out, and the lids would open. Coal was shovelled in, and the bins returned to the barge. When the doors sealed, the barge simply lifted from the ground and soared up to the starships where a human crew unloaded the cargo and prepped it for shipment farther afield.

Where did Archeron send the Earth's precious resources? No one knew that either.

Our plan was a simple one: load one bin with spiders and monkeys and a second with insurgents and a lot of extra weapons, arrange the bins so the monkeys and spiders were off-loaded first, and we'd jump out and hand weapons around to all the human slaves so they could help us take over the ship. . . assuming Babbage couldn't just teleport us all away. . . and assuming we didn't blow up with the ship.

A plethora of assumptions.

At least we didn't have to worry about asphyxiating on the trip into space since Archeron shipped animals in the barges as well. Apparently, they'd taken every single alpaca on the planet into space. Our greatest minds had come up empty trying to discover any possible reason for that unusual piece of trivia.

So. . . asphyxiation: one thing not to worry about. It wasn't much, but it was what we had.

We timed the entire operation to coincide with the regular shipment at 8:00^{AM}. The invaders barge descended right on time without the least fuss or flare of rocketry. Silently, it floated to the ground as if it were a helium balloon a week after the party.

I leaned close to Scopes and whispered in his ear. "Makes you crazy, doesn't it?"

He made a malevolent noise in his throat. "I will gut that thing when we're done here and expose its secrets to the world."

The crew offloaded the coal bins and filled all but two with the usual cargo. While they shovelled coal, Scopes' team set to work installing the Faraday cages in the two we would use.

Watching Scopes at the controls, smiling almost maniacally as a massive swarm of clockwork spiders and monkeys converged on the empty bin and crawled, crept and leapt into it, was one of the most disturbing sights I'd ever seen.

In a moment, the lid of that bin sealed in place, and our crew loaded a cache of weapons into the second crate. Twenty-two of us climbed in with the guns, crammed a bit snugly, but we'd not have a long journey. Twist watched at a distance, sulking.

Scopes engaged the equipment for the modified Faraday cage, and we all lit the miner's lights on our foreheads as the lid sealed itself in place.

A moment later, our bin rolled into the barge. When it lifted off, we barely felt it.

Every miner's light converged on Scopes' face, which greatly betrayed his annoyance.

I poked a rib, but subtly so no one else would notice.

The barge rose into the sky.

We waited.

We waited some more.

Two states away, a massive rocket counted down to its launch, a launch that would be considerably louder and more violent than our lift-off had been.

The lives of the men and women in the coal bin had become a major catch twenty-two: if the rocket did its job, the mission would be a success without our lifting a finger. Our lives would also end in a loud, extremely volatile fashion.

If the rocket failed in its mission, then the fate of the planet might very well rest in our extremely mortal hands. Hope had called us the best, the brightest, and the bravest. She'd forgotten to add "by far the most insane."

Someone hummed a faint rendition of "God Save the King."

Someone else joined in.

A third musician sang a harmony.

Within moments, every man and woman aboard hummed the song, including the Canadians. After a time or two of that, the Canadians taught us their anthem.

Fortunately, everyone on the team had seen battle before and knew that one of the few truths about warfare was that it consisted chiefly of long stretches of extremely tense boredom punctuated by brief flurries of unimaginably tense action.

We only felt the transition from movement to stillness because we were really, *really* paying attention. No one teased Scopes this time.

We all shifted to crouching positions, and nearly two dozen points of red light appeared on the ceiling of the bin.

Nothing happened.

Nothing continued to happen.

Three minutes of nothing happened, at which point we all grew uneasy.

We hadn't counted on simply being stacked away for later unloading.

The launch of the F-bomb would commence in five minutes.

The entire team shifted uneasily.

"Should we open the bin and see what's going on?" Scopes asked.

"What's going on," the Persian declared, "is that we're sitting in a locked barge on a landing platform, and no one out there seems inclined to change that situation."

"Hush," I insisted. "We've all had to improvise before."

"Not with a nuclear bomb about to shove itself up our arses," Scot commented.

"Well, yes," I granted, "that part of the day is sort of a first time for anyone in our species."

"Suggestions?" the Persian diverted.

Scopes rose to his feet and disabled the Faraday cage. "If I'm wrong, we're dead anyway," he said quickly, then added, "Babbage?" very quietly.

"Hello, friend Scopes," a voice said for all to hear. "I had not thought to see you again."

Tension drained out of Scope's face. "Hello Babbage, will you please erect a privacy bubble around me and my comrades?"

"Okay."

I only noticed the quiet sounds of an enormous ship around us when they ceased.

"Any chance you can transport every human on board this ship to the planet's surface?"

"Of course I can," the calm voice told us.

Scopes grin made me uneasy. "Okay, Babbage. Do it."

"I'm afraid that would be against my programming."

Blast.

"You asked if he could. . ." I interjected. "Not if he would."

Scopes nodded. "Are you willing and able to open a line of communication to the planet without anyone on the ship knowing about it?"

"That would be impossible, friend Scopes, since *you* are currently on the ship. Ha. Ha."

Scopes rolled his eyes. "He wasn't like this before."

Apparently less of his personality had been left behind than we'd hoped.

The Persian pulled out a hand-sized device that turned out to be a walkie-talkie based on the same technology as the flickers. "Milady," he muttered. "This is your Persian. Delay the launch. Repeat. Delay the launch."

He replaced the talkie with no expression whatsoever. "Feel free to chastise me later if we don't die."

"How much time did that buy us?" I asked.

"If she doesn't hear from me again, they launch in twenty minutes," he said.

"Are we still on the transport barge?" Scopes asked Babbage.

"Affirmative."

"Is it still sealed?"

"Affirmative."

Scopes looked to me for guidance. He capably lead scientists, but seemed a bit shaky on the protocols for launching a battle.

I unlatched the cover of our bin and pushed it open.

Most of us climbed out and clustered around the bin. A few of us remained inside since we had precious little floor space.

"Please open a hologram screen, Babbage," Scopes requested. He glanced at me and whispered, "No neural interface."

A screen popped into existence, lighting the area. Several of our people jumped and gasped.

"Thanks."

"You're welcome, friend Scopes."

"Give me a view outside the cargo transport."

"Okay."

The barge seemed small in the enormous dock where it rested, one of a hundred similar pods and the humans offloading a small herd of llamas from a barge a couple of rows down looked tiny by comparison.

Scopes turned to me again, and I nodded. We'd planned out what to do if we made contact with Babbage but he wouldn't simply transport us to safety.

"Please extend the privacy bubble to the exterior of this barge, Babbage," Scopes directed.

"Okay."

"Can you enclose the entire dock without the Kla'arkians noticing?"

"Not likely."

"Then don't." Scopes manipulated the screen to close in on the people unloading the barges.

I suppressed an urge to ask about Victoria. If we took a moment to find her, then everyone would have the right to ask about missing loved ones, and we didn't have that kind of time.

"Can you prevent the invaders from using the transport beams?" Scopes asked.

"Yes."

"Do it. Can you disable the internal automatic defence systems?"

"Yes."

"Do it."

"Can you lead us to the bridge?"

"Yes."

"Show me a map of the ship with the best route to it."

"I'm sorry, Scopes. I can't show you that area on the map." A glowing arrow appeared on the floor, pointing at the barge door. "Will this do?"

"Nicely."

We spent a few hair-raising minutes gathering information. Babbage showed us everything having to do with the human quarters, but any questions about Kla'arkians or the crew and its stations were met with instant opposition. We located the Monkey House. Business there seemed pretty much as usual. Scopes pointed out his friend Hiroshi, hard at work on some programming project. And there was Elsie.

Scopes grew frustrated. "I wish I'd thought to ask about some of this when he still had sentience." He turned to me for guidance.

I looked around at the expectant faces.

"We gather the weapons," I suggested, "release the toys, follow them out, hand out weapons and follow Babbage's directions to the bridge, dealing with whatever resistance we meet on the way." I cast my glance at the ceiling. "Babbage? How much time has passed since the Persian here made his call to Mrs. Kennedy?"

"Ten minutes, Mr. Bastard."

I met Habib's gaze. "Just before we go out, you call Mrs. Kennedy for exactly twenty minutes more. If we can't take the ship in half an hour, we're not going to."

He nodded.

I looked around. "Agreed?"

Everyone nodded and muttered agreement.

Briefly, I considered trying a rousing speech on them but decided against it. Those things always went better in flickers than in real life.

"Make the call."

The Persian pulled out the walkie talkie to make the call.

Which is when everything, predictably, went to shit.

The barge doors flew open without warning, flooding our bay with intense light and blinding us all. A giant claw grabbed the first coal bin, hauling it out into the massive space. The claw held the bin over an enormous pile of coal and tipped it unceremoniously upside down.

As the spiders and monkeys spilled out of it, serving up their pre-programmed pandemonium, Habib called out, "Go! Go!" shaking us all out of a momentary shock.

The members of our team still inside the bin hauled weapons over the side to the rest of us.

"The claw!" Basil Rupert shouted, pointing. "The claw!"

The giant claw had already completed its first task and now grabbed the coal bin which had, until recently, contained us so peacefully. It contained the Scotsman still.

Sirens sounded loudly. The slaves dropped to their stomachs on the floor with their hands over their heads. Not a good sign. They might be no help at all.

The Scotsman tossed out the last of the guns before clambering to the lip of the coal bin. He dove for the floor and managed to flip once before he hit the deck rolling, flashing the lot of us.

Silently, Babbage's luminous green arrow turned to the left at ninety degrees.

"Let's go!" I shouted over the sound of the sirens, dashing from the barge as the claw swung back for another crate.

"The Kla'arkians are attempting to override my control of the transport beams and the internal weapons systems," Babbage reported as we dashed to the slaves, hauling them to their feet and handing weapons around. "Their argument is very convincing."

I counted about fifty slaves, but most of them wept with relief, believing themselves already safe. Nuke and Sal tried to sober them so they'd be of some use.

I smacked the Persian's shoulder to get his attention.

He shook his head and made a show of clipping the radio to his belt.

It was dead.

Likely, so were we.

Little time remained before we all went down in history as the first humans to observe, up close, the detonation of a nuclear weapon.

The spiders had scattered to the edges of the space and poured down the hallways. The monkeys ran rampant, howling and screeching and tearing things apart. Many of them had attached to the bulkheads themselves and attempted to open the walls of the hanger

Our luminous arrow scrolled across the floor directing us to an open doorway.

A horrible squawking screech managed to drown out the alarm. It drew everyone's attention to the wall on our right, where a flurry of giant birds had entered the dock.

They stood over seven feet tall, a sort of hybrid between bright green parrots and great, long-armed, short-legged apes with a bright red crest atop their heads. They all held weapons that made the lovely red aiming lights on Scope's rifles want to die of embarrassment.

Green beams flashed from every barrel and anything the beam touched vanished in a puff of smoke. Lasers, they were called. Strangely, they hit members of their own team as often as they hit one of mine.

"These are the great invaders?" Scot called out. "A bunch of bloody budgies?"

Most of the slaves cowered on the floor, and my crew scrambled for cover.

The Scotsman lobbed a couple of grenades in the birds' direction. That got their attention and, thankfully, didn't punch a hole into whatever atmosphere, or lack thereof, currently snuggled the exterior of the ship.

A commotion at a second door answered Scot's question as another contingent of inhuman fighters charged the bay, weapons firing something more like traditional bullets.

What they hell were *they?*

Time slowed down. Was I, perhaps, hallucinating? A dozen small, fluffy white humanoids about three feet tall and cuter than bunnies or kitties, apart from the rifles aimed our way, ambled towards us as if on the way to a church picnic, wide, dark eyes twinkling and pink, button noses twitching, rifles tearing our cover to shreds. One of them smoked a cigar.

The claw grabbed another coal bin and hauled it across the dock.

I aimed for the weakest spot of the arm and poured a barrage into it. It shattered and broke, spraying the deck with giant chunks of rock, scattering the Fluffies and breaking their formation.

"We need to get out that door," I shouted to the Persian, knowing the obvious green arrow would tell him which door I meant. "Scopes and I go first, and we'll cover the rest of you."

"Covering fire," he shouted to the crew around us, "on three. . . two. . ."

"One!" Scot pulled a couple of grenades out from under his kilt and lobbed one at each enemy.

The assault was a thing to behold. Like a finely crafted clock, the men and women rose and filled the deck with red dots and weapons' fire.

Without waiting to compliment them, I grabbed Scopes and dragged him out the door with me.

"Privacy bubble, Babbage," he called as we ran.

The door slammed shut behind us.

Fuck!

"What the hell?" Scopes stared at me dumbfounded. "Open the barge bay doors, Babbage."

"I'm sorry, Scopes." His voice remained infuriatingly calm. "I can't do that."

I slammed my fist against the door impotently. I took a deep breath. "Well, my friend, we'd planned on saving the world ourselves in the first place."

His eyes widened a moment, then narrowed. He nodded. "Let's get'er done."

I pressed a hand into his chest with a shake of my head. "Don't try for Texas slang. Just. . . don't."

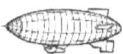

Hope's ears hurt from listening so hard. Once she'd received the abrupt call from her Persian delaying the launch, she'd waited for a follow up. An explanation. A bloody all clear.

Nothing.

Her corner of the warehouse in Wyoming held a wall covered in flicker screens. Faces of scientists in both Nevada and Richmond. Two images of the rocket cooling its heels, vapour coiling impatiently. An image of the starship even, the stage where an unknown drama unfolded.

Were they dead? Had they won? What the hell was going on?

"It's almost time, mum," Nevil said, his shirt stained with sweat. "Do we launch?"

Hope wrung her hands. Damn them all.

That Babbage fellow must have failed.

The strike team must have failed.

Hope longed for the ability to say, "I told you so."

She'd likely never get it.

"Twenty minutes since his call, mum," Nevil said. "What do we do?"

Hope refused to look at Prudence. She couldn't let the poor girl think she'd had any part to play in her lover's death. No. This decision was Hope's and hers alone.

But how could she make it?

"You have to do it, ma'am," Prudence said behind her.

Hope turned to her in shock. The young woman wore a simple grey top and matching trousers, not at all her usual style.

"What do you mean?" Hope asked.

"This is what we've all worked for, all sacrificed for." Prudence gestured at the screen a bit melodramatically. "If you don't destroy those ships, all the lives already lost in the battle up there will have been for nothing."

Hope gaped. "And how do you know lives have been lost?"

Prudence startled. "It's a battle, milady. People die."

Her logic was rubbish, but her point still valid. How would Hope live with herself after damning her closest friends to death? How would she do so if she allowed the planet to die in their stead?

She looked up at the poor man on the flicker screen broadcasting from Richmond. Would he know that this was not his decision?

"Press the button," Hope said. "I command it."

The man nodded and pressed the shiny, red button.

"And God save us all," Hope added.

A commotion at the entrance to the room drew Hope's attention.

"What did I miss?" Prudence ran into the room with her skirts in her hands. "Damn enchiladas," she muttered. "Always go down wrong."

Hope spun around to the spot where Prudence had stood in an entirely different outfit just seconds before. Gone.

"What's wrong?" The girl hurried to Hope's side.

Hope stared at her, then glanced up at the image of an enormous rocket hurling itself into the sky. Who the hell had convinced her to press the button?

Prudence cast about and checked her shoe, probably for toilet paper. "Mum?"

Chapter Twenty-seven

Scopes and I raced down the corridor, jumping over spiders as we hurtled along without a backwards glance. The green arrow kept pace just ahead of us, and the sounds of chaos in the dock faded.

"No privacy bubble?" Scopes asked the air.

"I'm sorry, friend Scopes, but Archeron insisted."

We were already losing the battle for Babbage. Blast. How long before the ship's defence beams simply shot us down?

"Babbage," Scopes tried, "can you access the chip in my pocket and upload it?"

"I'm afraid my former iteration made that impossible," he explained as we ran in the disturbing quiet. How far away was the damn bridge? "He never expected you would be so rash as to return to the ship, so he installed a block absolutely preventing any attempts to restore him to it."

It made sense. Scopes return could not have been predicted.

Neither could the reunion that occurred two seconds later as we rounded a corner. Scopes smashed headlong into his old friend Hiroshi. Scopes called his name in surprise while they untangled themselves from one another.

"Why didn't you tell us someone was there, Babbage?" I demanded, fully expecting an annoying response like "You didn't ask."

"He wasn't there a moment ago," Babbage insisted.

"How the hell did you get out of the Monkey House?" Scopes helped the man adjust the plain grey clothes he wore.

Hiroshi hesitated before muttering something in a language I didn't understand.

"You got lost?" Scopes exclaimed.

"We need to keep moving," I shouted, pointing my rifle at the green arrow scrolling along the hall.

"I'm going with you," Hiroshi said in perfect English.

"He said—" Scopes began.

"He's speaking English, now," I barked and ran down the hall. "Keep up!"

Then, because not nearly enough was already happening, the air about me filled with a bright light and the sparkle of gold dust.

"Oh, son of a bitch," Hiroshi muttered, his voice modulating lower as he spoke.

A moment later, I knelt on the floor retching, but it was not the same floor across which I had so recently run.

"Well, at least *that's* been sorted out," a deep and all-too-familiar voice said. "I could simply transport the rest of you into empty space, but it's more fun to watch you fight it out."

"I imagine I'll have the internal weapons back online next," the exact same voice said, but from behind me.

"In just a moment," he said from farther away.

"Ugh!" Scopes cried, releasing the arms of the man he held.

It wasn't Hiroshi.

Bergman? What?

I wiped my mouth and rose to my feet, wondering whether my senses were befuddled from the transport, something that I'd never before had the pleasure of experiencing.

Archeron sat nearby in a commander's chair at the back of a large, white room. Several of him, in fact, stood about the bridge. Well, I had seen multiple holograms of the commander in one place before.

The room was a basic square, with the Archerons around the edge, each manipulating a hologram. A white railing cordoned off a circular space at the centre of the room where multiple images displayed the battle in the barge bay.

"Two minutes until we have that bloody EL wiped from the system," Archeron said from the wall to my left.

The iteration in the command chair rose and pulled a handkerchief from his pocket. "I'm afraid transport takes some getting used to." He held out the grey cloth as if it might actually be of some help to me.

When I didn't reach out to take his non-corporeal hanky, he dropped it over my shoulder.

I felt it land.

What in the world?

I grabbed it.

It was real.

Without even thinking, I reached forward and planted my hand very firmly on Archeron's chest. He was solid. I patted his chest.

He grinned. "Surprise!"

Smoke, ash, and deadly beams of light filled the air.

 The odour of blood mingled with smoke and burning piles of coal.

Screams of the dying assaulted Habib's ears from the throats of three completely different species. The screams of the Fluffies sounded so much like the cries of human children they chilled his blood.

He mowed down Parrots one by one from the end of a line of coal bins.

Scot careened across the room to take up a post at the far end of the line, and the remaining humans stretched out between them behind bins and piles of coal. Scot had managed to shoot several bins out of the claws' grip, creating ample cover for the ragtag crew.

Most of the slaves, once they understood the situation, had bounced back, grabbed weapons and joined the firefight.

So what sort of goal did they have, now? Since they hadn't been teleported, and he hadn't been able to contact Lady Kennedy a second time, their chances for survival were slim to none. Habib hoped the battle was distraction enough for the rocket to do its job. He wished he could find a way to say goodbye to his lady and to his gentleman. As infuriating as I could be, Habib hated to enter the afterlife without a goodbye kiss.

An explosion!

He dove for cover. By all that was holy, was it the end?

Smoke cleared. He didn't die.

He rose to one knee and scanned the bay. Several more human bodies lay across the metal decking, emptying themselves of blood.

The two eldest Sneaky Pete brothers lay dead, missing the lower half of their bodies. The twins, who were the youngest, fell to their brothers corpses, keening. Hopefully, their grief wouldn't get them killed as well.

Nuke's head, Texan hat still firmly in place, grinned up from a few feet away.

Five others of the assault force and about a dozen slaves lay in pieces. So many body parts had been flung amongst the coal, Habib couldn't be certain how many had died. Bloody fur and ruined green feathers also covered the floor.

Well, there were fewer aliens left than humans. That was what mattered.

Screaming a prayer for the death of all enemies in his native tongue, Habib emptied his weapon and managed to drop at least two more Parrots. If something didn't change soon, they might actually run out of targets.

A loud, rattling cacophony brought a curse to his lips.

Never grow overconfident, he reminded himself.

A regiment of eight-foot, black, armoured fleas hopped into the fray, laying waste to everything and everyone around them.

Basil Rupert flew back with a scream, his blood spraying across Scot. The ginger's leg landed separately. The Scotsman shouted bloody murder.

Fortunately, the newest warriors seemed as interested in killing Fluffies and Parrots as in killing humans.

What should he do? Since Scopes and I had been separated, Habib had tried to kill as many aliens as he could, but, at the end of the day, that didn't seem like an adequate long-term goal. Where was the bloody missile?

In a room far away, I watched the events play out in one-tenth scale while leaning against a railing, staring into a circular arena about five metres across where a three-dimensional hologram of the battle played for all six of the Archerons' entertainment.

"I exist as a hive mind," explained the copy once again sitting in the command chair. "Many individual bodies with one brain connecting us all."

"I don't know how segregates do it," a second copy said.

"It must be lonely," added a third.

How freakishly disturbing.

The various iterations managed their separate duties, and, in fact, wore differing hair styles now that I took a moment to notice, but they all sported matching nondescript grey jumpsuits. Every now and then, they'd all turn to stare at the hologram and utter a collective "hurrah." Several at a time would laugh and point at the carnage.

As I said, disturbing.

The Kla'arkian sitting in the commander's chair told us, "It's like your hand and foot and spleen, but each organ is an entire being in his own right."

Likely Scopes found the entire concept eminently interesting.

It didn't matter. He'd never have time to study it.

The remnants of Babbage had been purged.

A Kla'arkian had taken our guns from us.

Bergman—who used to be Hiroshi, however *that* worked—seemed utterly irrelevant to the Kla'arkians. Just another human. Mind you, he would certainly merit a severe talking to by *me* if I managed to survive.

Not that I would. The F-bomb would hit at any moment, and we'd all go up in a puff of smoke. Not the optimum result of our plan, but at least we seemed to be distracting the Kla'arkians quite nicely.

Hurrah.

Bergman leaned closer to me and said, "At least they don't know about the rocket."

What the free-falling unmitigated fuck?

Every black-haired head faced him abruptly.

"What did you say?" every mouth demanded simultaneously.

"Scan for incoming missiles," the commander demanded.

Every Kla'arkian body waved a hand at the battle hologram, silencing it.

I popped Bergman in the mouth.

He stumbled and fell on his ass.

The battle image shrank to the floor, and the sight of a soaring rocket filled the space. Even without any point of reference to disclose the rocket's size, it seemed a pretty massive piece of technology.

Scopes whistled with that annoying wide-eyed expression of intense interest rather than the proper show of outrage and/or alarm he should have displayed. Once his intellectual curiosity peaked, everything else fell away.

"It's okay," Bergman insisted from the floor. "There's nothing they can do." He scrambled to his feet, drawing the interest of every Kla'arkian on the bridge. "It's going to hit. It's going to detonate right on target in the *energy well*. There's nothing they can do to stop it."

"Would you shut *up!*" I punched him again.

He kept his feet this time, but staggered back a step or two.

"There's nothing we can do?" the Kla'arkian in the command chair asked quietly, one eyebrow raised.

"There's nothing you can do to keep it from hitting your ship," Bergman insisted, wiping a trickle of blood from his lip. "You're doomed to sit by impotently!"

Something about his sudden flair for the wretchedly melodramatic gave me pause. What was he playing at? Did he know more than we did, whoever he was?

Scopes pulled a fist back to hit him, now, but my instinct told me to grab my friend's wrist and hold on.

"Ha, ha!" Bergman added, pointing at the rocket.

Dear lord, the Kla'arkians *had* to see he was playing them.

With every eye trained on Bergman's hideously simulated look of triumph, the commander waved a hand languidly. "Fire at will," he said.

"No!" Bergman shouted. "Don't do it!" He grabbed the railing with both hands.

Scopes struggled against my grip, but I held on.

"Do it!" the commander declared triumphantly, rising to his feet and matching Bergman's histrionics.

I stood entranced, although which was more fascinating— Bergman's horrible overacting or the even more unbelievable fact that the Kla'arkians fell for it? I couldn't decide.

Scopes tugged against my grip, but just enough to get my attention.

His eyes asked me why I didn't interfere.

I wasn't even certain.

The loud and distinct hum of an energy build-up foretold the imminent firing of the invaders' weapons.

The abject panic on Bergman's face fell away abruptly, replaced with what can only be described as sardonic ennui. "About damn time," he muttered, pulling a small device from a pocket. "We're out of here." He grabbed my arm.

I pulled free and punched him again, out of habit.

"Would you stop hitting me?" Bergman shouted.

"That depends—" I began.

Hiroshi had replaced Bergman. How did he *do* that?

I looked past him.

We stood in a different place. A moment's sweep of my surroundings revealed a well-appointed Victorian drawing room, complete with fainting couches and candle-lit chandeliers.

How on Earth? There'd been no glitter. No gut-wrenching nausea.

Scopes tapped my shoulder. I released his arm.

An enormous window covered one wall. It displayed the invaders' manta ray high above the Earth and the rocket almost upon it. At this angle and in comparison to the enormous spaceship, our missile appeared, I must admit, a bit paltry.

An enormous spider's web of blue lightning enveloped the F-bomb and its rocket.

"Grab something," Hiroshi/Bergman shouted. "This is going to get a little rocky."

The bomb exploded, and the only reason we weren't instantly blinded was that the window darkened, allowing us to stare into the eye of the hurricane.

What an amazing sight.

Then the floor shook. Scopes and I dropped to our knees with our arms over our heads and each other.

"Well, I hardly meant grab each other," Hiroshi muttered. "But well played." He tapped the device in his hand, and the window revealed itself to be a flicker screen! It split into fourths, each with a view of a starship above a different spot on the amazing orb of the planet.

The explosion entirely enveloped the manta over Canada, blocking it from sight.

That's when the sound assaulted us, the lowest rumbling bass tone imaginable. It rattled my teeth and my bones. The china cups clattered in their saucers. One shattered.

"EM dampeners," Hiroshi said, clucking his tongue and stretching his jaw. "Always make my teeth hurt but they're the only way to block the EM pulse from the explosion."

A three-dimensional hologram of the planet itself appeared between us and the screen. Three red dots pointed out the location of the invaders' ships. A fourth likely held position on the opposite side of the globe.

A ripple shook the quarter screen that showed the nuclear explosion over Canada. A circular wave appeared on the globe, centred on the red dot there. The wave expanded, following the contour of the globe.

It reached a second red dot on the globe and shook the corresponding image of a manta ray in a dark London sky. Blue lightning coruscated across the starship's hull, and the bright lights dotting its skin winked out.

The wave reached Egypt, and the ship in the third quadrant experienced the same effect as the second. As the wave enveloped the entire planet, the globe rotated to display China. The fourth quadrant of the screen on the wall shimmered. The manta there flashed blue and lost all of its lights.

By that time, the nuclear explosion had spent itself, and the ship we'd attacked became visible within the conflagration, scorched, but unbelievably intact.

My friends might yet live.

But then, so did Archeron. All of them.

Blast.

The ship's nose dipped, as did the noses of the other three.

They were falling from the sky!

The invaders were doomed.

As were my friends.

"You had it," Hiroshi said, "almost." He held up a hand with thumb and forefinger only a centimetre apart. "The F-bomb may have taken out the one ship had it reached its target, but the boost from the invaders' weapon amplified the explosion enough to create a planetwide electromagnetic pulse that killed the technology of all four."

Scopes hit himself in the forehead. "Of course," he exclaimed rising to his feet and dragging me with him. "But I *never* would have chanced them trying to shoot it down that way. What if they'd simply dodged it?"

Hiroshi shrugged. "That's why I goaded them into firing on it."

"Feel free to geek out later, gentlemen," I interrupted. "Aren't there humans on all four of those ships. What chances do they have of surviving a crash?"

All four ships fell slowly as if through gelatine.

Hiroshi favoured me with a puzzled look while he tapped his device again. "Surviving a *crash* is immaterial."

Four yellow spots shot across the globe from a central location high above the Earth.

"No," Scopes muttered. "You can't"

"I can't allow a single piece of that technology to fall into human hands," Hiroshi insisted.

Wait. . . what did that mean?

Tiny balls of red light zipped into view on all four screens.

They struck the starships.

Four colossal fireballs blew the ships into ash.

"No!" I screamed. "Do you have any idea how many people were on those ships? Or on the ground below?" My legs turned to jelly.

It was worse than losing Scopes.

352 John Robert Mack

Worse than killing fifteen thousand slaves.

"Eighty thousand, four hundred and forty-two," he said calmly as if it were the most inconsequential number imaginable. "Why?"

Eighty thousand? I couldn't even conceive. . .

"You just killed them all, you miserable—"

"Zen." Scopes grabbed me.

Somehow his grasp gave me the strength to move, to reach that—

"Zen!" Scopes shouted, shaking me. "Look!" He spun me to face the hologram screen. It had broken into dozens of smaller images. Instead of the blackened and smoking corpses I expected to see, the screens filled with men and women laughing and weeping, dirty children in familiar grey pyjamas jumping up and down.

"He teleported them to safety," Scopes said.

"What?"

One arm slipped around me and the other pointed over my shoulder at the central image, which grew larger than the others, shoving the rest into a frame of sorts.

Victoria. It was Victoria. Mrs. Kennedy hugged her in the central image. My daughter seemed thinner and taller, but none the worse for wear from her adventures.

Then the Persian ran into the scene, embracing both women.

Habib lived as well.

A giant hiccup erupted from me as Scopes pulled me closer.

And there was Prudence.

Scopes grip tightened. I squeezed him back.

But how many had we lost?

"All of them?" I asked. "Did you save all of them?"

"As many as I could," Hiroshi said. "A few thousand in the blast zones died on the ground I couldn't reach because of the radiation. Even my technology has its limits, but *countless* more would have died without my destruction of the invader ships. I guarantee it."

"*Our* people," I demanded. "*Our* people are safe?"

He smiled. "Shall I think the less of you because that's really the only important question?"

I glared at him with venom.

"Your people are safe," he said, "although I gather there were a number of fatalities in the fight against the zoo."

"Zoo?" Scopes asked.

"That's basically what those poor creatures in the barge bay were," he explained. "They'd been told that if they won the battle, they'd be returned to their homeworlds." He shrugged. "A lie, of course, but who can take that chance?"

But wait a moment. . .

"You blew the Kla'arkians out of the sky as if it wasn't even a challenge, and teleported. . . tens of thousands." He had the technology to do that in an instant without a flicker of gold dust.

"Why did you wait so long?" I demanded. "Why not just destroy the ships before they attacked the Earth in the first place. . . or after the initial attack? Why did you wait?"

I turned my gaze onto the small man. "Who *are* you?"

He met my eyes evenly. "You have no idea what it cost to get our leaders to allow my involvement at all, Zen. The only way. . . the *only* way we could get them to agree was if I guaranteed that your planet never knew of our involvement and if not *one piece* of advanced technology fell into your hands."

He waved at the screen and four images of the smoking ruins of the mantas appeared.

"I actually pushed that boundary to the limit by letting you keep the datasphere Babbage gave you." He cast his gaze on Scopes who returned it without emotion. "I'm going to have to answer for that."

"Who. are. you?" I asked again.

"He's a shapeshifter," Scopes said. "A Shifter."

As soon as he said the words, the conclusion became obvious.

Hiroshi smiled. "When we first moved into the neighbourhood, we interacted with your planet regularly. . . but it never worked out." He grimaced. "The Sumerians, the Egyptians, the Hindi. . . they all worshipped us as gods." His face changed, showed sorrow. "It always went badly. Atlantis was the worst." He searched our faces. "You've heard of Atlantis?"

I nodded. "I thought it was a myth."

"It is now," he conceded. He gestured for us to sit in the high-backed chairs and took his own seat opposite me, crossing his legs at the ankle. "They destroyed themselves, and we had to wipe all remnants of their civilization from the planet." He shook his head. "After that, we withdrew from your world, removed as much as we could of our technology, planted sceptics to spread the word that we were nothing but myths, legends and hoaxes." He gestured with one hand to indicate his body. "As you can see, we're able to change our appearance. We walked among you for millennia. We observed, but we never interacted." He sat back. "We realised we were too dangerous. You just aren't ready."

He turned his eyes to Scopes and his expression softened into something that may have been kindness. "Well, there may be one or two of you," he admitted. "But in general?"

Scopes face remained blank. I could tell he fought between curiosity and anger at betrayal.

Hiroshi sighed. He waved at the room around us and touched a china cup. "Sorry the place is so out of date. Your planet hasn't been very interesting in the last eighty years or so, so we never updated the décor of our scout ship."

His cup filled with tea and he drank. "We had such hopes in the last century. You started an industrial revolution, and so many countries promoted freedom and equality. We thought, perhaps, you were *finally* reaching a stage that would allow us to contact you again."

His face fell. "Then the War between the States dragged out for two decades and slavery proliferated around the globe as so many countries were drawn into the conflict and so many able bodied men died." He shook his head. "Once you ignited the jungles for the sole purpose of driving the natives out so you could enslave them, we realised you were heading straight for another dark age. . . if you even survived." He sipped his tea. "We withdrew from your planet completely."

He waved at the screens. "The Kla'arkians slipped in while we sulked and looked the other way. As disappointed in your progress as we were, we couldn't sit idly by while your planet was enslaved by a species that, obviously, did not abide by the same standards as our own." He sipped again. "We're very fond of your planet and couldn't bear to see it ravaged. . . but we still have our rules." His shoulders sagged as he stared at the table. "I regret the horrible things that happened here. I couldn't think of any other way to save you." He seemed to want some kind of absolution. "I did my best."

I turned my attention to the smoking ruins on the flicker screens.

"And how do you propose to explain all this so no one knows you were involved?" I asked. "Electro-whatsit pulses and pure dumb luck?"

"Babbage," he said quietly. "No one but the two of you know how little of him actually remained on the Kla'arkian ship."

"So Babbage saved the day after all?" I asked.

Hiroshi shook his head. "You and Scopes saved the day," he corrected. "Babbage just kept the Kla'arkians from killing you. Scopes figured out that the enhanced explosion would create the EM pulse. Zen seized control of the invaders' weapons and saved the day. Humans need to believe they were the orchestrators of their own survival."

"*Deus et machina*," Scopes muttered.

"Sorry?" I asked.

"There's a saying for unbelievable stories where someone swoops in to save the day at the end," Scopes said. "*Deus ex machina*. The god from the machine." He stared at Hiroshi so sadly. "In our case it's the god *and* the machine, isn't it?"

"You could say that." He rose to his feet and moved closer to Scopes. "I assume you have Babbage's chip on you. May I have it?"

Scopes looked to me for advice. I shrugged. That would be his call.

"You promised to help him escape his electronic limbo," Hiroshi said with his hand out. "I can help him live again."

Scopes dug into a pocket and handed the chip over.

Hiroshi slipped the chip into his handheld device.

A scant moment later, Babbage appeared.

Scopes had told me all about his electronic friend, as well as his physical appearance. . . but the spitting image of Eddie appearing out of nowhere took my breath away.

He shouted Scopes name and threw his arms around his waist.

The shock on Scopes' face was tremendous. He dropped to one knee to hold the EL. "How are you solid?"

"The technology of the Shifters is so remarkable, Scopes," Babbage enthused. "I have learned so much since he installed my programming into his doohickey."

"That was one second ago," Scopes said.

Babbage nodded. "My processing speed is incredible in this device. I can create solid holograms!"

"At enormous energy expenditure," Hiroshi threw in.

"Oh. . . sorry," Babbage apologised and pulled out of Scopes' arms, which is when he looked at me for the first time.

"Zen Bastard," he said.

I stood frozen.

Understanding lit the EL's face, and he looked down at his own body. "This must be horrible for you," he exclaimed. "Although Scopes never told me after whom he modelled me, I figured it out." His features shifted and his image grew.

I closed my eyes, unable to watch.

"Better?" Babbage asked, his voice much lower.

I opened my eyes to find a rather tall, attractive Black man in a three-piece suit with goggles on his forehead, exactly the man Eddie would have grown into had he not been slaughtered in the initial attack. He even wore a head full of long black braids that fell past his shoulders. The effect was infinitely worse than the original, but he'd tried so hard.

I nodded silently. "And now you erase all memory of this conversation?" I turned to Hiroshi. "That's what happened to Prudence and Hope when they lost time in the Brain Trust, isn't it? Scopes and I appear on the planet thinking we were the ones who saved the day?"

Hiroshi stared at me for several seconds before responding. "No."

"Why not?" The word astonishment wouldn't cover the depth of my shock.

"We have bent so many of our rules they are nearly broken," Hiroshi said. "We need someone on Earth to know the truth. . . in case we missed something. In case something slips through the wreckage."

"In case you fucked something up and just haven't noticed it, yet," I translated.

Hiroshi smiled. "As you say."

Babbage took Scopes in his arms again and held him tightly. He now towered over the slight Oriental. "You already made good on your promise to me, friend Scopes." His voice was so much deeper and somehow cultured. What kind of programming did that require? "Now I promise that I will find a way to see you again."

"Babbage," Hiroshi warned.

The EL gave Scopes a squeeze and released him. "Pay no attention to the man behind the curtain," he stage whispered. "I owe you my life. I will *never* forget that."

Babbage turned to me, hand extended. "I am sorry I'm not able to spend more time with you." He spoke rather formally, and the fact that I had to look up to find his eyes made the experience less painful. "But I feel as if I already know you from everything I have heard about you. I look forward to future meetings."

Hiroshi shook his head but kept his tongue.

I shook the large, dark hand.

His grip was firm. He held my hand for a moment longer and turned it to reveal the monkey tattoo on the underside of my wrist. He smiled, suddenly seeming much younger than his proxy. "What a delightful tattoo."

"It reminds me of Scopes," I told him a little thickly. I'd had it added while on my western "tour."

He met my gaze. "May I have one too?"

I nodded, but couldn't speak. Still holding my hand, he exposed the underside of his own wrist. An identical monkey materialised there. He smiled and gave my hand a final squeeze with both of his before releasing it. "Thank you."

"Wear it well and think of him often," I said.

Babbage nodded and stepped back.

"Once you've had time to process all of this," Hiroshi said, his words directed at Scopes, "you will grow to despise me for the pain I did not prevent and the lies I have told." He extended his hand. "Please know that our friendship in the Monkey House was genuine and that while I wish I could have done much better, I always did my best. If you hate me, hate me for incompetence, not malevolence."

Scopes stared at the hand and did not take it.

After a moment, the young man, or whatever he was, withdrew the hand with a sad smile. "I understand." He swallowed as if to dislodge a lump in his throat. "I'm sorry, Avery. Truly." The consequence of folly, it is said, is regret.

I watched my friend's face so intently, I completely missed the transition to a new location.

We stood in a grassy field, alone.

"I suspect someone will be along to fetch us," Scopes said with tears in his eyes.

I held him then, while we waited.

"We won, brother," I whispered into his neck. "We won."

Epilogue One

The newly installed captain of the *HMS Hammer,* I stood on the dock watching the ship's crew scramble across the deck as they swabbed and polished. A hand dropped heavily against my neck, distracting me from my silent musings.

"How do you suppose you'll survive a respectable profession after all your years of piracy?" Habib waved at the men with his free hand.

"I have no idea," I admitted. "But I assume I'll manage to find plenty of trouble while we put this planet back together." I grabbed the back of his vest with one hand. "How are *you* going to handle being a captain's wife after all your years of—?" I patted his back. "Oh wait, you'll hardly know the difference, will you?"

He swatted my head. "First mate," he corrected.

I chuckled. "Does that mean I get a second mate, as well?"

"I assume you enjoy having testicles," he said stoically, "but your behaviour begs the contrary."

I closed my eyes and enjoyed the sun on my face and his arm around me. "I'm going to guess you didn't just stop by for witty banter."

"They're ready," he admitted. "The ceremony begins in a few minutes." He gave my neck a squeeze. "I delayed retrieving you as long as possible."

"Thank you."

We left the dock with a call to the men. They waved enthusiastically.

To be honest, I'd rather have stayed on the ship with a mop and bucket than worn my dress uniform to receive a great big medal from the newly formed League of Nations, or whatever the hell they called it. In a fit of nostalgia, I'd worn the same bicorn hat I'd stolen on the day the Kla'arkians attacked. Well, not *precisely* the same hat, but one just like it.

"The hat is ridiculous," Habib told me.

"It's supposed to be," I explained for the tenth time.

"So you say," he responded for the tenth time.

As we made our way to the street, the smell of cloves quickened my pulse. As always, Habib had dressed less formally than the rest of us, but with his hair pulled back and wearing black pants and vest over a crisp white shirt, he would still be the most striking figure on the platform. The glimpse of skin at his throat made me want to bite it.

Perhaps later.

Scopes most recent automobile, the Nuke, waited for us. As we approached, the door irised open with a quiet "sh-hiink." Habib passed me into the vehicle and dashed around to the driver's side.

"Open driver's door," I told the auto.

"Of course, Zen," the auto responded in Hope Kennedy's voice. The Kennedy Feature sold more autos than any aspect of its build. Hope had become a world-wide hero, after all.

So had I, I guess. Scopes' factory manufactured at least one line of everything it created named after the Hammer. They sold like ice in the desert, which was fairly easy to make now with the new-fangled refrigeration units Elsie'd invented.

A huge number of the scientists from both the Brain Trust and the Monkey House worked together at Scopes' factory. Some of them remained jealous of the childlike Chinaman, but, well, he *had* saved the planet, after all.

A short time later, I stood on an outdoor stage looking over a sea of faces every colour of the human rainbow. Jinky reposed quietly on my shoulder, rendered silent with programming Scopes had installed for the occasion.

I gazed up at the building there in the heart of New York, the city formerly known as *La Nouvelle* and even more formerly known as New York. The sign on the building said, "United Nations."

That's right. That was its name, a worldwide organization formed to rebuild the planet in an entirely new light. Once the world had learned about the variety of frightening, violent creatures across the galaxy, all of whom looked down at humans as so much cattle, enormous waves of solidarity washed over the world as the human race shouted a collective, "Oh yeah? Says *you*!"

Scopes stood at my right as we stared across the crowd. Habib stood on my left. Victoria stood to one side, all too pretty and grown up with Prudence's help.

Prudence absolutely glowed.

Scopes, too.

I leaned close and pressed my face to his ear. "You totally fucked her backstage at the United League of Countries."

"You know it."

We shared a conspiratorial grin.

He glanced at the Persian with question marks in his eyes.

I shook my head. "You win that one, my friend, but we already broke in the ship."

He nodded knowingly.

Everyone who'd gone up to the starship and come back entered the stage.

Scot and Basil Rupert stood proud as can be, the latter in a gold suit with one pant leg removed to show off his gleaming new stainless clockwork limb. Twist stood with them in a sharp blue and white suit.

Basil Rupert had officially adopted the boy when we knew for certain his parents had died. It was hard to tell which of the two would be the hero and which the plucky sidekick, but the way the hairy Scot looked down at them both answered a number of questions I'd always pondered.

Sal received awards for both herself and Nuke. She'd accepted a position as the weapons' master on my ship. The Sneaky Pete twins had had to be talked into joining my crew. Too many memories, they'd said. I'd convinced them we'd make new ones. They'd lost much, and it was a bad time to lose more. We were their family too.

Elsie, the Oppenheimer brothers, and all the scientists who'd contributed to the success of the F-bomb were recognised as well. Watching the stream of flabby, aging men cross the stage, I leaned over to Scopes again. "You had to see all these men naked every day?"

He elbowed me. "Not all of us can be as remarkably attractive and fit as you."

"Well, how can I argue with that?"

Hope Kennedy strode onto the stage resplendent in a white pants suit with corset, miniature top hat and coat that opened behind her like a formal skirt.

Deafening applause filled the air.

Prudence took a place at her side as the band struck up a rousing theme replete with trombones, violins and banjos written by some fiddle player named Williams.

Hope stepped up to us one at a time and draped us with gold medals for bravery and general planet-saving goodwill.

When my turn came, she smirked as if to remind me that she'd never fully approve of me and that my name remained absurd. Much to her consternation, but the utter delight of the crowd, I grabbed her, dipped her, and kissed her soundly there in front of the world, which was literally true since cameras broadcast the event across the planet.

When I released her, she adjusted her hat and threw me a look that told me she knew ways to punish me. "He's still *my* Persian, after all," she whispered.

The band played another inspiring theme. The crowd roared.

And so we saved the planet. Some people died, but most of us lived, which is more than we ever should've hoped to accomplish. Mrs. Kennedy made speeches that were applauded and that I never really heard. I was too busy holding the hands of the men on either side of me and exchanging looks of joy with everyone around us.

After the ceremony, we drank and caroused. I introduced as many foreign delegates as I could to the amusing and obscene drinking games I'd learned growing up right there in the good old, re-United States of America.

Can I have an Amen?

Epilogue Two

Smoke still rose from the radioactive wreckage of the Kla'arkian flagship, even after a week. The humans had tried to scavenge her, but those who did had died within minutes, so the rest put up warning signs and decided to wait. They would have a long wait.

Two figures walked easily through the smoking ruin, one because a portable force shield protected him from the radiation, the other because he was a holographic proxy.

The Shifter who called himself Hiroshi in this particular shape held his Doohickey out, searching for the empty spot in the wreckage. Even *his* scanners couldn't actually penetrate the shield surrounding his target, but they could pinpoint the location of the absence that indicated it.

When they stood directly over the box, Hiroshi gestured at the pile of metal and flooring. "Can you dig it out?"

Babbage looked him up and down. "Are you really asking or are you ordering?"

Hiroshi focused on the proxy more closely. "Sorry. I keep forgetting," he admitted. "Please, Babbage. I'm afraid my shield may not be adequate."

Babbage crouched down, gathered matter from the wind to solidify himself, then tossed the wreckage aside. He brought the bright red cube into the light of day.

"It'll be a short time before you can touch it," Babbage said, "even with the force field."

Hiroshi directed his Doohickey to speed up the process. "So much trouble for such a little thing."

A bird flew overhead, struggled a moment and fell to the ground.

"Ummm. . ." Babbage murmured.

The Shifter looked up to regard his companion.

"Why did you lie to friend Scopes?" Babbage asked.

"Lie? About what?"

"About why you didn't erase his memory."

"Oh, that," Hiroshi said. "There are some things he isn't ready to know."

He transported them back to their ship.

"I can't wait to see him again," Babbage said, sounding for all the world like an excited child.

"I understand," Hiroshi admitted. "With your new processing speed, you'll need to learn the value of patience."

"I know, Mother. I know."

My Damn Meat Pie

A Short Story

Zen Bastard ducked into a dark alley and dropped into a ball behind a garbage can, working hard to keep his heavy breathing quiet. The shouts of the prior owner of Zen's meat pie grew loud and then receded as the portly man rushed past the alley cursing the boy in three different languages. Life in the big city of Richmond, Virginia was so cosmopolitan.

Certain he'd lost the old goat, Zen rose and pulled the pie out of his jacket where it had actually been a pleasant warming presence against the dark October chill. "Losers weepers," the boy murmured and bit deeply into the pie. Delicious. Ginelli's was his favorite place to thieve his dinner. Their pies were famous for their garlic. . . and eminently portable as well.

Walking deeper into the alley to finish his meal in private in case any of the older boys were in a mood to steal his rightfully pilfered property, he almost walked directly past the scrawny little kid curled up against the brick wall. Stepping farther away and not slowing his pace, Zen kept an eye on the unknown lad in case he had a mind to grab the pie.

Skinny. Some kind of Oriental, which seemed odd since most of the

Orientals lived in camps because of the Japanese invasions. He wore a sort of grey pajamas far too short in the arms and legs. The boy's bare feet were dirty and the soles bleeding. His hair had been shaved recently and all that remained was dark fuzz.

As Zen passed, the boy raised his head from where it had been resting on the arms wrapped tightly around his scrawny legs. He sniffed the air and caught sight of Zen. His eyes opened wide at the sight of the half-eaten pie. Their eyes met, and Zen knew instantly that the boy had just seen death for the first time.

The boy forced himself to look away and dropped his head onto his arms.

Zen walked deeper into the alley. *That's right*, he thought. *It's my meat pie. I stole it fair and square. No reason I need to share it. I'm hungry too.*

The pajamas had to be a camp uniform. Somehow, the little China boy had managed to escape. Recently, from the fresh blood on his feet. Zen wondered how long the boy had walked to find his way to Richmond. And why Richmond? He also wondered who the boy had seen die. Mother? Father?

He stopped and gazed down lovingly at his meat pie.

"Damn it," Zen muttered. "It's my damn meat pie." Curse words made him feel older than ten somehow. He sighed. "Damn it."

He turned and stalked up the alley and stopped when his feet almost touched the bare, dirty toes. The boy looked up and managed to shrink farther into the brick work. The look on his face made it obvious he was expecting an angry blow. Zen knew that look all too well.

He held out the pie.

The boy stared at it longingly but didn't move.

"Take it," Zen told him and shook it. "Before I change my damn fool mind."

The boy's stomach growled noisily, and he covered his stomach with his arms as if that might somehow dull the ache or the sound.

"Take it," Zen repeated.

The boy looked up at him. "Why?"

"Are you simple?" Zen dropped the pie and the boy was forced to grab it. "When someone offers you food you take it. You don't ask damn fool questions."

The boy still hesitated.

"Eat the damn thing before you fall over dead!" Zen shouted, and the boy finally fell to it with a vengeance. "There." Zen turned on his heel to leave the alley.

"Thank you," the boy called out.

Zen waved a hand in response as he reached the mouth of the alley and carefully glanced around. The coast was clear. Time to find more dinner.

The boy had food. He'd just need to figure out the way things worked on the street. That's the way it was for orphans. Either they figured things out or they died. That was just the way things were.

He couldn't stop himself from glancing over a shoulder.

The boy had finished his meager meal and once again sat with his head on his arms. What was it about him? Why couldn't he just walk away? He'd walked away from countless orphans. The city was thick with them.

"Damn it," he muttered. A moment later he stood at the boy's feet again. "What's your name?"

The boy looked up. "Scopes," he said. "Avery Scopes."

"How long ago you break out of the camp?"

The boy's eyes opened wide.

Zen grinned and waved a hand at the pajamas the boy wore. "I'm certain you didn't pick out those jammies yourself."

The boy glanced down. "I broke. . ." He paused as if that didn't seem quite the right word. "I got out this morning. Walked all day." He looked up at Zen with his head cocked and one eye closed. "Why do you care?"

Zen shrugged. "I don't need to if you don't want me to."

Scopes narrowed his eye. "What's your name?"

"Zen Bastard."

The boy smiled for the first time since Zen had met him. "Like the beer?" The smile made him seem even younger than he likely was.

"Yep. Just like."

"Why'd your parents name you after a beer?"

"They didn't." Zen shoved his hands in his pockets. "I named me myself. . . about two years ago, right after I killed my daddy."

Scopes' eyes opened wide again, and he pushed up the wall to his feet. "Why'd you kill your daddy?"

"For killing my mama."

The normally shocking line fell flat when the Oriental boy slumped against the wall with his head in his hands.

"Whoa there. I think you shouldn't oughta got up so fast." Zen felt nothing but bone in the arm he grabbed.

The boy held onto Zen's wrist for a moment and didn't seem likely to get his feet sorted, so Zen grabbed him with both hands.

"Let's sit you back down," he suggested, guiding the boy to the ground." He pressed gently on the fuzzy head. "Let's get your head between your knees before you pass out."

Scopes sucked in a couple of deep breaths.

Water. He needed water. . . and more food.

And someplace warm to sleep.

Damn it.

"I have a cardboard box," Zen said at last.

The boy looked up. Embarrassment at nearly fainting warred in his eyes with curiosity at Zen's announcement.

"To sleep in," he elaborated. "Two's warmer than one, after all."

The boy looked around.

"Oh, it's not in this alley."

"Then how do you know it's still your box?"

Zen grinned. "'Cause the last bloke who took it woke up in the middle of the night with a knife in his leg."

The haunted eyes opened wide again. "How'd you find him?"

Zen shrugged. "Just knew where he'd took it."

"Did he die?"

"N'uh-uh. Just bled all over his blanket." Zen puffed up in pride at the awe in the boy's face. Then he sighed. "Damn it." He crouched beside the boy, set his own back against the wall, and slid an arm completely around him.

The skeleton in rags balked at the physical contact.

Zen scoffed. "If'n you're going to share my box, you better get used to touching."

The boy relaxed. "It's just. . ."

"It's just most of the time when someone touches you, they're hitting you, I know, I know." He pushed with his legs ever so slowly, and they rose together. "Ye don't need to make a big melodramatic deal about it."

When they reached their feet, the boy took several deep breaths and trembled.

"You going to pass out?"

The boy shook his head.

"I jus' know you ain't about to throw up my damn meat pie."

"I'm fine," the boy lied. His eyes went wide and turned to the ground. "Wait." A flash of twisted metal lay beside the wall. The boy started to descend, but Zen pushed a hand into his chest.

"Whoa there." He bent to pick up the object. "It took a year and a half to get you up the first time."

A monkey, shaped from wire and bits of metal. Shards of coloured glass filled the eyes.

"You make this?" Zen passed the thing into the boy's eager hands.

Avery nodded and stared at it for several long moments before holding it out.

"What?"

He shook the monkey once, then grabbed Zen's hand and forced the toy into it. "For the meat pie. It's all I have."

Zen regarded the wire monkey. It seemed the kind of thing a kid would make while stuck in a prison camp. He'd make up stories about jungles and adventures and someday escaping. The tail had a barb on the end, so Zen knew instantly where that bit of wire, at least, had come from. With a nod, he placed the toy securely in his breast pocket and slung his arm around the boy's back again. "I'm thirsty. Let's go find us something to drink."

Acknowledgements

The author gratefully acknowledges the assistance of the Rooyakkers family, Blake, Byron, Hope, and Ryan, for securing a comfortable hideout whilst I created and prepared the preceding manuscript. Words can never truly express my gratitude. I also wish to thank Lauran Strait and Paula Hudson who did wholeheartedly attack and defeat all possible errors and inconsistencies. Any mistakes that have survived to publication are entirely the fault of the author who oft times refuses to listen to sound advice. Especial thanks to Jacqui Pomeranski who frequently reads and responds to early drafts of my work. Yes, Jacqui, the second volume will have space pirates. I am also grateful to R. Mac Wheeler for his erstwhile input. Finally, I must mention Michael Khandelwal and his fine learning establishment, the Muse in Norfolk, VA, where many a fine and lusty debate was held over how a pirate could possibly see a pornographic magazine from across a midnight dock. Thank you for everything Michael. Post-finally, I also express gratitude to the fine women of my Virginia Beach critique group who nurtured and guided me upon my arrival to the great state of Virginia: Nancy, Jan, Mary, Donna, Lisa, Cecelia and Jean. Sorry about all the cuss words.

A final ironic debt must be acknowledged to Terry Pratchet, whose alternate history novel contest was the original impetus behind the creation of "Consequence." Does it count if I live in Great Britain according to the novel I wrote? Next time, I'll make sure to read all the contest guidelines beforehand.

About the Author

John Robert Mack isn't absolutely certain where he'll be living at the time of publication. He's a bit of a drifter, that one. He's been writing since he was eight years old and continues to learn something new every day. He recently taught writing workshops for the Hampton Roads Writers and for the Muse, both in Virginia. His senior year of high school, he decided to avoid a college career based on computer programming and animation because he knew he'd have no social life and spend all his time in front of a computer. Ah, irony, you thorny bitch!